THE ZOMBIES OF TASMANIA

By M.C.ROONEY

The Van Diemen Chronicles

The Zombies of Tasmania
The Lightning Lords
The Violent Society
The Arrogant Horseman
The King of Control
Tales from the Collapse
The Distracted
The Cykam War

Hobart, Tasmania, Year 2044

Rain thumped against the windshield of Jon's new car as he travelled homeward on the old Southern Outlet Highway. It rained more and more in this day and age. Politicians still claimed the weather patterns remained the same, that climate change was an unproven science, or as a bygone politician in power once so eloquently said, "Was absolute crap". However, even the most docile of the population would have noticed that over the last decade, natural disasters had been dramatically on the increase.

Jon watched the Holonews on the dashboard of his car, but his eyes kept drifting upward to look at the flowing traffic ahead. The self-driven car was a ten-year-old technology designed to get you to and from your destination without rear ending other vehicles or breaking any of the road laws. You simply entered your destination manually into the car computer or by voice recognition, then sat back and relaxed. Jon, however, did not like the idea of not being in control of his own vehicle. So, after eight long years of watching and waiting to make sure this technology actually worked, noting it didn't lead to any increase in road fatalities—in fact it saw a significant reduction— procrastinating for the last two years and suffering being called an 'old fart' by his co-workers for not having one of these flash bang new cars, he finally gave in and purchased one. The cars did have all the normal old-fashioned driving accessories to be used in case of an emergency, but they were hidden in the spacious dashboard. You were encouraged not to use them, instead just to get in the car and put your seatbelt on.

But even now, two weeks after he purchased it, whilst the car navigated through the traffic, his foot would still reach for the clutch or brake, and both hands were held up as if to grab the wheel, making him look to passing vehicles or pedestrians as if he was pretending to be a tiger or having some sort of fit. If this continued, he thought, he may just give himself Repetitive Strain Injury.

Taking a deep, relaxing breath, he settled down to watch the Holonews. Flicking through the hundreds of channels that provided up-to-date, boring news in the areas of politics, vanity news in the world of today's sports heroes, movie stars and their hot new young girlfriend or boyfriend, and the manufactured news in the world of musical entertainment as the latest popstar was churned out of the Reality Show machine to produce a song of absolute drivel, become an instant millionaire, then never be heard of again. Jon was a rock 'n' roll fan and proud of it. It may have died decades ago, but he loved the raw passion of rock as opposed to the slick, polished sound of today's music; it had soul.

He stopped at the news reports of escalating violence between China and Japan; there were even reports of biological weapons being used, which was unusual. It was not unusual that these weapons were used in today's world, but unusual that it was being reported on, as ever since the financial collapse of the USA, all media outlets were slowly being bought out by other rich countries, namely China. Using the age-old adage of "So long as it does not affect me, it is not my problem," which usually meant denial, fear, or selfishness, he changed channels to see, standing in front of the Tasmanian Parliament, the local up-and-coming politician Carl Cooper, who was in the Opposition and touted as a future party leader, complaining about the current government's position on the economy. Tasmania had two main political parties, and for the most part, they had enjoyed a power-sharing arrangement for decades.

By power-sharing, Jon sarcastically meant that for four years, one party governed, then there was an election where the vote-weary public, outraged at the lack of any economical progress would oust the governing members; then, for the next four years, the other party governed and were eventually thrown out and replaced by the previous mob. A never-ending political cycle where neither side made any real difference in their efforts to improve the well-being of the constituents.

The poor economy was based on the facts that Tasmania had a small population, small industries, and the candidates for election were chosen by their party because they fell into line with that party's manifesto. This really meant they had no individual thought process whatsoever, providing no new ideas to the problems that faced society today. They just rehashed the ideas that had failed so miserably in the past. Damn, it always bothered him that the more poorly the government performed, the happier the Opposition looked. Cooper looked smugly satisfied. *Well,* he thought wryly, *at least by being poor, big business did not own some of our politicians.* A great man once said: "Government of the people, by the people, for the people." It sure didn't turn out that way.

Next on tonight's news, the presenter solemnly announced the tragedy of the privately funded space mission to Mars. Since the demise of NASA, any space program was funded by a group of eccentric billionaires who gathered finance through their own personal fortunes and the promise of exclusive Holonews rights to any footage of the mission and of that on Mars. The first successful trip had taken place in 2023 and had been followed up by missions every four years, but those were one-way missions with the intention of building colonies on Mars, with no intention of the space travelers ever returning. This all changed on the latest mission, where the astronauts intended to reach Mars, collect relevant samples, and return, just like the legendary Apollo Missions to the moon. However, on the descent through the Earth's atmosphere just a half-hour ago, the presenter announced that the returning module had burnt up, killing all on board and destroying any scientific data they had collected. Finally, he switched over to the new channel on the block, a channel privately owned by the new Christian Brotherhood of Tasmania, to see a handsome clean-cut young man in a suit named Peter Rainswood shouting in self-righteous anger.

Yes, this was the new religious channel colleagues at work had told him to avoid. Affordable only because religious orders still did not have to pay any taxes. They could lobby governments to change the laws using money from the faithful, but didn't pay taxes required by law, and nobody in parliament had the balls to question why.

Over the last hundred years, mainstream religion had been in steady decline in the Western World, which had led to the rise of fundamentalists like this guy, who would gather numbers of people who loved to point their fingers at everyone else in judgment and claim they were God's chosen whilst being unaware that they were actually the architects of the decline of religion because they were all hateful bastards who were batshit crazy. This man was raving about the rising of the dead and the time of judgment, of all things.

The car computer informed him that the fuel tank was nearly running on empty. He entered the pre-programmed Margate Service Station into the computer so it would make a pit stop on his way home. The computer was voice activated, but he found he had to repeat the destination a few times to be understood properly. Probably because he was not a morning person and tended to mumble a lot, and at the end of the day, he was tired and grumpy, so he mumbled even more. To avoid the hassle of it all, Jon thought it was far easier to enter a destination manually.

The car slowed down on the main road, indicated to turn right, entered the station, and navigated its way into the vacant service bowser. The bowser's arm mechanically joined with his car and then entered the precious petrol, without him having to leave his car.

Yes, petrol. In a world where huge technological breakthroughs were being made every day, his car was run on a fuel system that was now over one hundred fifty years old.

He could understand the need for oil from a money point of view; it was expensive, and therefore, the government made a lot of taxes from it to fund roads, education, the health system, etc. However, it was a crazy catch-22 situation, where fuel helped run the world's economy, keeping people in jobs, housed and fed, but was destroying the environment at the same time. It was a ticking time bomb, just waiting to explode. Also, nobody with an open mind could deny that wars had been fought purely over oil supplies, and thousands of innocent lives on both sides had been lost. Some world leaders had a lot to answer for.

There had been a battle between the Oil and Coal industry and the Free Energy industry for over a century now. Nick Fields, a young eighteen-year-old who worked at Jon's office, was a mad conspiracy theorists. He told him all about the alternative energies that had been suppressed by governments over the years, in order to protect their countries economy. The fact that Free Energy was just that, free, would always mean the politicians would do everything in their power to stifle their growth. Society was built on money, it was just a plain and horrible fact.

Nick had told him the story of a crazy inventor called Nikola Tesla, who wanted to give the world free energy. Jon found him fascinating. He seemed to have been written out of the history books for some unknown reason, even though he was the main inventor of most of the 20th Century electrical technology. Nick, as he had a tendency to do, would elaborate on the most obscure and dubious of Tesla's inventions, such as the Death Ray, which was linked to US President Ronald Reagan's Star Wars Project, The Earthquake Machine, The Weather Controller, and of course, Mind Control.

Tesla was quoted as saying that our entire biological system—the brain and the earth itself—work on the same frequencies. If we can control that resonate system electronically, we can directly control the entire mental system of humankind. After Tesla died in poverty in 1943, J. Edgar Hoover's FBI agents had taken all of his personal belongings and notes from his hotel room.

Slicing his money card through the car computer to transfer his 'hard-earned' to pay for the fuel, Jon programmed his car to take him home.

Sighing, Jon Dayton turned off the Holonews and looked at himself in the rear-view mirror. He was forty-four years old now, had dark hair that was greying a little, hazel eyes, and was one hundred and eighty-six centimetres tall and still physically fit. His parents had passed away, and his siblings had long since moved to mainland Australia, and he now realised that he had grown up to be a cynical, lonely, and miserable old man. He tried to be happy, he really did, but as the years went by, he became tired of this superficial world.

A world with nearly nine billion people, a reduced food supply, and failing environment all didn't add up to a rosy future. A society headed for the abyss, and nobody seemed to care. People seemed more caught up in who the rich and famous were dating, or the latest fashion, or what was happening in their favourite

soap opera, than what was happening in the real world.
Although, try as he might to think of some way out of the
world's problems, he couldn't provide an answer to any of this.
He might bang on about how inept the politicians were, but if he
was in their shoes, he probably would have been just as useless.
This just made him sadder. Perhaps he should give up and join
the 'sheeple', as Nick liked to call the general population. They
seemed happy.

The car finally arrived at his home, turned into his driveway, and
stopped in a slow and smooth pace. He had made it home safe
and sound, he thought wryly; perhaps tomorrow he could relax a
little more on the way back to work. He meandered up to his
house and placed his face against the retinal scanner, which then
allowed him to enter. His home was an average three-bedroom
house with no particular features to make it stand out. He did
like to take care of the garden, so the outside of the house
looked quite respectable, but the inside was very sparse and
bland. He just found no motivation to improve or change
anything that was inside. Two of the bedrooms were empty and
had been for the entire twelve years he had lived here. I guess it
could be said he was a typical bachelor. He never had any kids,
not because he didn't want to, but because he never met the
right woman to marry and have a family. He had such a tragic
record of choosing the wrong woman that, sometimes, he
thought the universe intended him to become a psychiatrist.
There was the loveliest girl at work named Sarah. He had been a
distant admirer for years now. But she was thirty-one years of
age, way too young and good for him, he thought glumly.

Settling on his average-looking couch, he quickly ate some nuked
lasagna from the microwave and guzzled down a beer from the
fridge before watching the Thursday Night AFL Football game
between Hawthorn and Darwin.

He never bothered to listen to any more of the news that night
and never looked outside the curtains of his windows to view
the strange yellow comets that could be seen in the night sky by
everybody in Australia, perhaps even the world. Comets that
could be seen by the naked eye, but strangely couldn't be
captured by any camera or video. He would hear about it

tomorrow, though; he would hear about it quite a lot.

The elevator opened, and Jon walked onto the eleventh-floor office, where he had spent the last fifteen years working for the government. He was halfway to his desk when he noticed a large number of people standing at the windows. Funny, he thought, there must have been an accident in the street below; strange that he hadn't noticed it on the way in. Walking farther in, he noticed that they appeared to be looking up in the sky rather than down. Nick Fields, the eighteen-year-old kid who was obsessed with Tesla, was among the group. He was skinny, with spiky dark hair, glasses, and kind of nerdy looking but was a good lad, nonetheless. He had moved down from Launceston in the northern part of the state on a short-term work exchange program. It was his first time away from his parents, so Jon hoped he had spent his time in Hobart being drunk and getting laid, but had the feeling that it was more likely that he spent his time on the computer at night, speaking to his worldwide friends about the last government conspiracy. Nick turned around and noticed him, then gave a big laugh.

"Bloody hell, Jon, did you see the comets?"

"The what?"

Nick gave Jon an astonished look. "The comets. You know, the ones that have been in the sky for the last twelve hours?" Jon must have had a blank look on his face because Nick then said, "Jesus Christ, Jon, you must be the only person in the world who hasn't seen them."

Abashed, Jon mentioned that he had fallen asleep in his car this morning and had a habit of walking with his head down from the car park to work, or anywhere, for that matter. Moving up to the window, he couldn't see anything unusual in the sky at first, but then, yes, if you looked really closely, you could see yellow streaks of light moving across the horizon.

"Was it easier to see at night?"

"Yep. Clear as day," Nick replied with a grin.

"What does the Holonews say on the matter?" If anyone was to know what was going on, it would be Nick. Even if he tended to go for the extreme versions of conspiracy land, sometimes what he came up with made a lot of sense … sometimes.

"Well, that's the interesting part, Jon. The government hasn't said anything of any substance. Just that they are looking into the matter. But when the news cameramen film the comets, or whatever they are, nothing comes through on film. I've even tried it on my Holophone. It's like its unfilmable or something." Jon was about to ask him more on the matter when a loud grumble came across the room in the form of a giant, two hundred-centimetre-tall man.

"What are you dopey buggers doing gazing out the window? Sit your fat arses back down and do some fucking work. What is it, bush week or something?" This led to everyone automatically moving back to their work cells and picking up the phones to work, even though Ray wasn't a manager nor did he have any authority over anyone. And he wasn't even actually doing any work himself. Despite the colorful language, this was actually what his mate Ray Beasley would describe as friendly banter.

"And how are you, you stupid prick?" Ray said, wrapping his big arm around Jon's shoulder. Ray was an ex-AFL Footballer for the Southern Kangaroos, and like most Footballers, he could be a bit rough around the edges. He was a forty-year-old divorcee with three young boys, whom he had sole custody of. He had dyed blond hair, and like a lot of ex-athletes, had stacked a few extra pounds on since retirement, but underneath the added layers, he was still as strong as an Ox. He was also one of the best friends Jon had ever had.

"Yeah, I'm okay. Just been chastised by young Nick here about not knowing about the comets last night."

"Really? You hadn't noticed the lights at all? By Jesus, you are a hermit, aren't ya? Too busy dreaming about Sarah, no doubt," he said with a big grin.

"Shut up," Jon replied, his face flushing. "She's just a good friend, that's all," he said, quickly glancing around the room to make sure nobody had heard, and most importantly, that Sarah wasn't nearby.

"Yeah, sure, mate. Sure." Laughing, Ray moved over to his desk and picked up his headset to connect himself to the phone queue, which would receive calls from all outside organisations.

Back in the old days, people used to converse over the phone without seeing each other's faces. That gave both callers the advantage of not allowing the other person to see the emotions on your face. This all died with the new operating phones, which allowed both callers to be connected via computer with all relevant applications on the one screen, and also being able to see the other person's face. So if you had dumb people ringing up with dumb questions, you would have to maintain a friendly demeanor at all times. This helped most of the office employees to become very good poker players. All except for Ray, who, unfortunately, had been called into the manager's office a number of times over the years for abusing customers. It was quite funny to listen to, though, Jon thought with a smile.

With Ray gone, Jon turned to Nick. "Right, you can stop grinning and fill me in on what's happening."

"Well, I've been on the Internet talking to my buddies around the globe. They mentioned something about Chemtrails. But even I couldn't understand any of that; then they mentioned the Mars crash and—Oh, shit, here's Dave."

Jon looked up and saw Dave Lawson sauntering over to his work cell. Dave was twenty-five years of age, with short brown hair, was muscular, and had a humungous beard, which was the fashion of the day with young men, and also made him look about forty. Whilst Nick was way too much into conspiracies, Dave was sceptical of everything, and the two of them had some colossal arguments. Jon thought these two were exactly the right guys to talk to about this.

"Are you going to shave that thing off your face yet, Dave? It's looking very pubic."

"Ha! No way, Jon. I love it. Been a cool look ever since Ned Kelly." Turning to Nick, he said, "Well, has 'conspiracy boy' come up with any ridiculous ideas about what's going on in the sky?"

"I have, actually," Nick said primly. "You probably would as well, if you didn't have to spend the night brushing your beard a hundred times before bedtime." Nick paused. "In your nightgown."

Dave sighed. "You're kidding me, right?"

"Well, it was a good try," Jon said. "Just the delivery wasn't quite right." Looking up at Dave, he thought the mental image of the joke was actually quite funny.

"Anyway, you were talking about the Mars crash yesterday?"

"Yes, the returned spacecraft that burnt up in our atmosphere. The astronauts were bringing back samples that could have contained anything."

"And …?" Jon said, prompting Nick for more information.

"Well, that's it. The samples would have been locked safely away, no doubt. But when they burnt up in our atmosphere with the astronauts, the poor bastards, within the hour, we began to see those yellow lights. Coincidence, maybe, but a good chance of being true."

"But surely the atmosphere would have burned everything to a crisp?" Jon said.

"Maybe, but who knows what a mineral from another planet is like." Nick switched on the computer graphics on his desk. "I mean, look at this photo from the old NASA website. Photo number PIA 17083."

"Here it comes." Dave sighed again.

"This panoramic photo was taken by the Mars Curiosity Rover in 2013.

"He's going to mention the duck again," said Dave, exasperated.

"When you focus the photo in a certain area," Nick continued, "you can see what looks like a duck walking along the ground."

"For fuck sake!" Dave cried.

"And when you look up a bit farther, there is a very unusual large black rock that looks like it has some sort of legs."

"They're just rocks!!"

"And, Dave, when you swing to the top right, there's a man standing in front of a hut."

"They're just bloody rocks, for Christ's sake."

Jon looked at the photo as Nick and Dave started arguing. He had to admit it did look like a man in a spacesuit standing in front of a building. But a rock it had to be, as mankind hadn't reached Mars until another ten years had passed. Leaving Dave and Nick to their debate about the Face and Pyramids of Mars and the word Cairo being Arabic for Mars as he had heard so many times before, Jon walked over to Ray and found him stretched across his desk, pointing at the screen and growling to a perplexed customer, "There it is! Open your eyes, mate; that's where you need to change your password."

"Everyone seems to be arguing today," a feminine voice said from behind Jon.

He gave a start at the sound of her voice. Sarah always did have a way of sneaking up on him.

He turned to look at the lovely face that he spent most of his waking hours thinking about. She was a small, slim girl with long auburn hair, full lips, and green eyes, and he always felt rather protective towards her, amongst other feelings that he tried to suppress.

"It's been a strange day. What with all the odd stuff going on in the sky," Jon replied, trying to sound cool, and failing miserably.

"I know," she answered with a smile. "I noticed you interrogating Nick. Has he come up with any ideas as to what's going on?"

"Only the Mars crash, which sounds crazy, but could be the best bet we have at the moment." God, she was beautiful. He tried not to look at her because he would eventually end up gazing into her green eyes or he would stare at her lips, wondering what it would be like to kiss her.

"The government seems to think there is nothing we should worry about," she replied

"Anyone who believes all of what they read on the Internet is a fool," he replied, "but anyone who believes all of what the government has to say is a bigger one."

"My word, you sound almost as bad as Nick," she said, laughing.

"I'm sorry. I just don't trust the government, that's all," he said, feeling his face redden. "I mean the politicians, not us, the workers. I mean we're okay ..." *Jesus, just shut up, Jon!* he thought frantically

Laying a hand on his arm, she said, "Speaking of the government, I just came over to tell you that the minister from Canberra is coming in today, so we all need to put our name badges on and be on our best behavior." She glanced at Ray, who was still pointing at the password screen and mumbling the word 'idiot' under his breath.

"Oh, okay; thanks for the heads-up, Sarah," Jon replied sheepishly.

She then focused intently on his face, paused for a few moments, and after taking a deep breath, said, "I was wondering if you would like to have lunch with me today. As in, like, a date?"

Nick and Dave stopped arguing, Ray froze with his finger still touching the screen, and Jon mentally soiled himself, but just managed to say, "Sure, Sarah, that would be nice."

Sarah let out a deep breath. "Great. At 12.30 p.m., then? We could go across to the Café Salmonella." This was the joke name a lot of people called the takeaway shop across the road.

"Sure, Sarah, that would be nice," Jon said again, still absolutely gobsmacked.

"Okay, then, see you soon," said Sarah, smiling, as she walked back down to her end of the office.

Jon stood there, motionless, for a few more moments after she left. Sarah Butler had asked him out! *Am I dreaming? I have never been this lucky, ever. This is starting off as the best day of his life. It must be the comets,* he thought, trying not to laugh gleefully out loud. He glanced around at his friends and noticed they were all grinning at him.

"Get back to work," he said weakly and then walked over to his desk with the sound of their laughter ringing in his ears.

Hobart City Hospital

Brenda Harrison watched as her mother lay dying on the hospital bed. Her labored breath was becoming shallower as the minutes went by. The cancer had spread to most of her vital organs, and the doctor said it was only a short matter of time before they would lose her. Brenda didn't know how she would cope without her mum.

Celia Dyson was the matriarch of the family, always making sure her kids were well looked after. Even after they had all grown up and moved away, she was the one they would contact for comfort and advice. So when her mother had fallen ill, Brenda had made sure she got the best care that she could afford. But sometimes the Big C could not be stopped, and Celia's time was coming to an end.

Looking out at the corridor, she noticed a number of hospital staff members were running. There seemed to be some screaming coming from somewhere. Perhaps some mother-to-be was giving voice to the last stages of childbirth, she thought ruefully.

Doctors and nurses were underpaid in her mind.

Not just an everyday profession, where you went to work hoping purely that you earned enough to pay your bills, but a job where you actually cared about what you did and the people you looked after. They were a credit to themselves and society in general, in her eyes.

Hearing a rattled breath from her mother, she moved over to her bedside and saw that her mother was gone. A sob of grief escaped her as she gathered and held her mother's hand one last time. *What was she going to do without her?* she thought sadly. Leaning over the bed, she moved closer to kiss her mother goodbye. She paused suddenly when she felt a strong grip enclose her hand. Was this a bodily reaction of muscles when someone died? To her shock, her mother's eyes slowly opened. *She is still alive!* she thought joyfully. *What a fool I was to think she had passed.* Her mother then tried to speak, but all that came out was a low groan. Her eyes were focused on Brenda but showed no recognition. There was also something different about her face that she couldn't quite put her finger on. She was so stunned by all these events that she didn't even try to evade it as her mother quickly moved closer and bit deeply into her face. Screaming, she fell backwards to the floor in utter disbelief. What had just happened? Terror filled her as she huddled on the floor, shaking. After a few moments, she tried to get off the floor, but her limbs were not responding. She was vaguely aware of someone running into the room and being attacked by her mother, who was now standing. Her heart seemed to be bursting in her chest. The heat, the unbearable heat; it seemed to be burning her from her insides out. She couldn't even command her voice to scream now.

Within a minute, she fell into unconsciousness, a state from which she would never return. When her heart finally stopped, her body slowly stood up, and the empty shell that was Brenda Harrison began its intuitive search, the search for sustenance, the search for food. And the most ample supply of food in this town was just out the door, just down the street, a food supply of over 220,000 people, in the old town of Hobart.

The Brooker Highway, Northern Suburbs, Hobart

Steve hit the throttle as hard as he could as he ran the red traffic light on his new motorbike. Sharon, on the back, screamed in delight as they barely avoided being sideswiped from one of the cars coming through on the green light on this intersection.

"Bloody hell, Sharon, that was a close one, eh?" Steve shouted as he gunned it down the highway.

"You dickhead! You could have killed us, you idiot," Sharon replied, laughing.

The laughter soon stopped when they heard the familiar sound of the police siren in the distance.

"Shit," said Steve. "If we turn off at the intersection to the Tasman Bridge, we should be okay, I reckon."

"I don't know," said Sharon, suddenly worried. "Perhaps we should just pull over and let the cops book us?"

"No way. I just got me P Plates, Sharon; cops would take my license for sure," he replied. "Anyway, this is such a great day; we'll get away with it. I mean, look at those comets in the sky."

The comets in the sky were a wonder, but Steve should not have been looking at them when he turned off the highway travelling at over one hundred kilometres an hour, and just when a truck decided to pull out of the intersection in front of them.

Hitting the side of the truck, Steve was instantly killed when his neck was snapped. Sharon, protected a little by Steve's body, suffered a broken back as she was hurtled fifty metres farther down the road.

Turning her head of her ruined body, Sharon saw what was left of Steve alongside of the truck. His helmet was broken in half, and she could see the pulped mash of his head covered in blood.

The cops had now pulled up in their vehicle and surveyed the scene with dismay and were soon joined by the distraught truck driver.

It was then that Sharon thought she had gone from the nightmare of this accident, which she knew to be in a state of reality, to a complete state of insanity as Steve began to slowly stand up.

The two policemen and the truck driver stood in a state of disbelief as he slowly stumbled over to them. One of the policemen, waking from his shocked stupor, came forward and offered him a comforting arm, which Steve bit into deeply. Screaming in agony, the policeman fell halfway to the ground whilst the other policeman, in his terror, pulled out his revolver, and after shouting a few warnings, shot Steve three times in the chest. Despite these supposedly killer shots, he continued to stumble towards the armed policeman.

The policeman, despite his years of experience and training, was completely and understandably freaked out by this whole situation and dragged his convulsing partner into the car and took off at high speed. The truck driver, seeming to forget his remorse for causing the accident, quickly dived back into his truck and did the same in the other direction. Steve, having lost contact with three humans who could fill this aching hunger in his stomach, turned his attention to the only other human in the area.

Sharon was a seventeen-year-old trainee hairdresser in North Hobart. She loved her job and had recently found a wonderful boyfriend by the name of Steve. Although she had only been dating him for a few months, she thought that this relationship could really turn into something serious. Sharon was unable to move as he bit into her stomach, and the last memory she would ever have was of Steve holding up her intestines, with her own screams echoing in her ears.

Firthside, Kingston, South of Hobart

Trevor pounded his fist on the door. "Hey, any of you pricks up yet?" The house was a two-bedroom unit that had been clean and presentable once upon a time, but was now occupied by six drug addicts and had been reduced to an absolute pigsty.

Slowly, the door opened, and a spotty youth said in a soft voice, "Have you got it?"

"Of course I got it, you dumb shit. Did you think I came over just to look at your ugly mug?" Christ, these heroin addicts made him sick. If it wasn't for the steady flow of cash they provided, he wouldn't come within a barge pole's distance of them.

The kid paid the cash, and Trevor threw him the stuff, not wanting to have any contact with the spotty idiot's hand.

"Just be careful," he said. "It's pretty potent stuff. It comes straight from China." *Or somewhere in Asia. Or maybe from Melbourne*, he thought. He really didn't care where, so long as he got his money.

Strolling down the road, he stopped at the top of the overpass and looked down on the Southern Outlet. Lighting up a cigarette, he watched resentfully as cars travelled north and south on their way to their very important appointments in their very important lives. *I could have had a good job*, he lied to himself. Truth was, he had always been a lazy rat bag. His main concern was and would always be for himself, and he didn't care who he had to step on to get what he wanted.

After ten minutes of contemplating what he was going to do for the rest of the day—Maccas or KFC?—he noticed, to his left, a figure walking out of the druggies' unit. He was soon followed by five other people, all in different states of undress; the last he was sure was the spotty youth he had just given the drugs to. What the fuck were they doing? They were clearly off their chops from the way they were wandering around aimlessly. For fuck's sake, he thought, the neighbours were surely going to ring the cops now, and no doubt these cunts would drop his name right in it.

The first person out of the unit caught sight of him and started walking towards him. He was definitely off his nut; there didn't seem to be any emotion crossing the guy's face. About to give the guy a mouthful of abuse for walking outside drugged up, Trevor was stunned into silence as the guy reached out to grab him. Fighting him off, he was shocked by the fact that the freak appeared to be trying to bite him. Grappling with the unhinged guy, Trevor noticed from the corner of his eye that another of the drug-fueled idiots, this one wearing a leather jacket, was heading in his direction. Trevor had always had a bad temper, and in his anger, without thinking of the consequences, he picked up his attacker and threw him off the overpass onto the southbound highway. *Shit,* he thought as the body hit the ground and was crushed by an oncoming car.

What the fuck am I going to do now? Being a drug dealer was not going to sit well in front of the judge, even without adding a murder. Staring down at the crushed body below, he watched as it started to twitch and then slowly rose. *What the fuck did I give those guys?* he thought, amazed. Still staring, Trevor had forgotten about the guy with the leather jacket, and he gave a wail of pain as he bit into the back of his neck. Staggering away, he grabbed at his neck in a numb state of shock. What the fuck was going on? A simple drug deal had turned into a fucking nightmare. He started to run. He had to get away from this place as fast as he could, but glancing behind, he noticed that the guy with the leather jacket was chasing him. His expression was completely empty of emotion, which reminded Trevor of that old *Terminator* film. His heart seemed to be coming out of his chest, and a burning sensation was creeping all over his body. He distantly heard the sounds of car horns, cars smashing, and screams coming from the highway as he crashed face-first into the pavement.

The leather-jacketed attacker stopped as he watched the food writhe on the floor. He sniffed the air. The hunger that was focused on this body had now abated. He sniffed the air again and started moving in the direction of the highway. He was soon accompanied by the body of Trevor as they moved amongst the traffic jam of what was once a free-flowing highway.

Government Building, Hobart

"I'm sure, as you know," the minister announced, "we are in tough economic times."

"Like the last twenty years," Ray mumbled quietly by Jon's side.

"And if we all pull together …" the minister continued.

"You simple peasants can take a pay cut," mumbled Ray.

"—we can come out of this with a much brighter future," said the minister.

"You're unemployed, whilst I sit drinking pina coladas on a sunny Queensland beach with my $500,000 a year politician's pension," replied Ray.

Jon normally would have struggled not to laugh, but his eyes kept glancing across at Sarah, who was standing by the department manager. It was normal for the mornings at work to drag, but this morning was excruciatingly slow. What was lunch going to be like? What was he going to talk to her about? She saw him looking at her and gave him a small smile that settled his nerves a little.

Looking at the window, he wondered what the faint noise was that he could hear from outside.

"Can you hear that noise?" Jon asked Ray quietly.

"Yeah, I can hear a lot of shit coming out of the minister's mouth," Ray grumbled in reply. Fortunately, he still kept his baritone voice quiet.

The minister prattled on for another ten minutes about how exciting the future was, and how this was truly an exciting time for the department, and how everything was truly going to be so exciting from now on, when a loud explosion and screams were heard from outside.

Everybody rushed over to the window, and Jon heard a few gasps of shock, including an involuntary one from his own mouth.

The normally docile streets of Hobart, where people would casually walk around doing their business, was now in complete pandemonium, with buildings burning, cars jamming the streets, and people running in every direction.

No, Jon realised, they weren't running in every direction; some of the people seemed to be chased by other people.

Jon looked around for Sarah, and upon seeing her, he walked over. She looked terrified, which was probably what he looked like himself. Not caring what anybody thought, he placed his arm around her shoulder. "How is our brave minister handling this?" he asked quietly.

"He bolted at the first explosion," she replied a bit shakily, moving her body closer to his. "He probably thought this was all about him. Is it?" She looked up at him. "I couldn't see out the window properly due to the rush."

Jon looked around the floor and noticed that half the people had already left, and the rest were lining up at the elevator to leave, or gathering at the fire escape stairwell. No doubt they were heading straight to their loved ones and perceived safety. Jon could not blame them, but he didn't like the idea of rushing outside without knowing the full facts of what was going on. Guiding Sarah to the window, he called out, "Ray, Dave, Nick! Get your arses over here." He wasn't sure they were all still there, but he was relieved once they had all come over. "Okay," he said once they were all within hearing distance. "Before we go rushing out into the chaos, I want to know exactly what is going on." Taking a deep, calming breath, he gestured to the street outside. "Now, what do you see?"

"It's like a fucking war zone," Dave said.

"But if anyone was to invade Australia, I don't think they would start in Tasmania," replied Nick. "A terrorist act, perhaps?"

"Maybe, but the buildings on fire are from the other end of town. Why are the people in the street below running so randomly? They are even heading directly towards the fires," replied Dave.

"Okay, so we can rule out invasion and terrorism, then," Jon confirmed. "Now I want you to just look at the people. What are they running from?" Jon just wanted confirmation of what he thought he had seen before. Everyday people were running away from each other, but he couldn't understand why. Sarah was staring up at him with an enquiring look.

"Bloody hell, some woman just jumped on a man," Ray exclaimed, "and not in a good way."

"Fuck me, is she biting him?" said Dave, sounding shocked. Looking down, they all watched as a woman tore into a shell-shocked man who was fending her off from the ground. She was joined by another man and woman, who were now both kneeling over him. Jon noticed the man on the ground had stopped struggling but couldn't see what the three people were doing to him. They continued to watch for another minute until, finally, the three attackers stood up.

'Oh no," Ray whispered.

Dave and Nick stood there in horrified silence. Sarah began to shake so hard that Jon had to tighten his grip around her shoulder. *The blood*, he thought; *the blood was everywhere.* The three attackers had eaten the man alive and walked away with blood all over their faces and clothes. But the most insane thing was that the man who had been attacked was still alive and crawling away, only using his hands because his legs and torso were no longer connected to his body.

"I can't believe what I just saw," Dave finally said.

"Perhaps they are all just rocks," Nick replied.

Local High School, Kingston, South of Hobart

At one hundred twenty kilograms and just under two hundred centimetres tall, the imposing frame of seventeen-year-old Harry Beasley strode quickly down the main school corridor, carrying a 45-centimetre pipe wrench in his right hand and holding his fifteen-year-old brother, Jack, by the scruff of his collar in the other.

"Where is the little bugger?" he growled, sounding eerily like his father, Ray.

"I don't know, Harry," said Jack, looking smaller than his big brother at just one hundred eighty-seven centimetres tall and weighing in at just under one hundred kilograms.

"The teachers had us all lined up in grades outside, waiting for our parents to pick us up or the police to arrive. I didn't see Billy with the grade sevens. And then …" he trailed off, looking at the floor.

Then the dead arrived, Harry thought.

Half an hour ago, he had been at work, doing what he loved as a newly apprenticed mechanic. Next thing he knew, people were running and screaming, being chased by people from a living nightmare. He didn't know what was going on and didn't care. All he knew was that he had to look after his little brothers.

Family was family, and they were all that mattered. Dad had drummed that fact into his psyche ever since their mother had run out on them. He took a punt and ran to the school in the hope that Jack and Billy would stay where they were and was proved to be partially right.

"You sure he wasn't with the grade sevens?"

"I'm pretty sure, and I did look for him, Harry. He wouldn't have run off on his own. I'm sure he would have looked for me," he said, trying to gain his brother's approval.

"Well, if he wasn't with his classmates and teachers, then where the hell was he?" said Harry.

Harry and Jack suddenly looked at each other.

"Principal's office," they said together.

"Right, you lead;, you've been there more often than I have," said Harry, who started running.

"That's crap," replied Jack, running alongside his brother. "You know you made life hard for me, being your younger brother. I couldn't get away with anything. 'Beasley, did you do this? Beasley, did you do that? You're just as bad as your brother Harry' the teachers would all say."

"Well, did you do any of those things they accused you of?" Harry replied.

"That's not the point," Jack insisted.

They quickly came to the administration office, which appeared to be deserted. Lifting his pipe wrench, Harry stepped into the office and saw the severed head of Deputy Principal Miss Archer on top of the office desk.

"Heads up, Jack," he whispered.

"Not funny," replied Jack.

Walking slowly past what was left of Miss Archer, Jack noticed that her eyes were following him. "Harry, she's still alive!"

Harry looked back. "You're kidding?"

"No, Harry, her eyes are following me, and her mouth is moving."

Harry stepped back and looked into her eyes. Yes, the eyes were definitely aware of him. Very empty, but very aware. This information and what had happened this morning suddenly provided a clear answer in his mind, and just as he was about to tell Jack what he had realised, he heard a scream come from the principal's office.

"Yep, that's the little bastard," said Harry.

Lifting his size fourteen steel-capped workman's boot, Harry kicked down the door and saw his little brother, Billy, huddled in the corner. A small hunched-like figure was standing over him. On hearing the door burst open, the dead principal turned slowly around to reveal a dead face. A dead face covered in blood.

He had obviously just been enjoying the company of the lovely Miss Archer.

"Principal Dooger, we meet again," said Harry. No doubt there was a time when Principal Dooger would have recognised Harry and probably would have had him escorted off the school grounds, but that principal was now gone, and only an empty husk remained. *He wasn't really a bad old bloke anyway,* Harry thought as he raised his pipe wrench up and crashed it down on his skull. He followed this up with three more hits, just to make sure.

"Jesus, Harry. That was a bit overboard, wasn't it?" said Jack.

"No, Jack," replied Harry. "It's the brain. The dead can walk because their brains are still working. Look at old Dooger there." He gestured to the crushed head on the ground. "Think that old bugger is going to get up? Look at Miss Archer's head." Harry gestured again. "What's making her glare at us more than usual?"

Jack was about to agree when Billy flung himself into Harry's chest, sobbing.

"It's all right, mate; we got you, mate, we got you," said Harry, patting him on the back.

Billy was the youngest at twelve years of age, but he already had the look of his brothers, as they all had the look of their father. After a moment, with their father in mind, Harry said, "Billy, I want you to find a Holophone. There should be one lying around this office somewhere."

Wiping the tears from his eyes, Billy went in search for the office phone.

"Jack, I want you to seal the doors and close up the windows any way you know how. We need a few minutes to ring Dad, and I don't want to be disturbed by the walking corpses, okay?"

"Yes, Harry," said Jack.

They both soon returned, and Harry dialed up his father's number. The Holophone was a small disk-like object and was the brand new technology of the day. It didn't just allow you to talk to the person you were ringing but gave a live holographic projection of them as well. Anything that was within two metres of the callers could be seen too.

His father soon answered the phone, and he seemed to be in an office as per usual, but Harry couldn't see anybody around him. He normally answered the phone with, "Help me, Obi-Wan Kenobi, you're my only hope." which he seemed to find extremely funny. However, today, he had a deadly serious expression on his face.

"Harry, where are you, mate? Is that your brothers in the background?"

"Yes, Dad," Harry replied. "We've had some weird stuff happen in Kingston. I don't know how to say this but—"

"Dead people are coming to life?" Ray offered in a flat voice.

"Yes, how did you know? Is it happening in the city?"

"Yeah, mate; they're all over the place. They got us a bit boxed in at the moment." Noticing Harry's worried expression, he added, "Don't worry, Son. I'll get out of here somehow. Jon's coming up with a plan as we speak."

Looking at his other sons, he added, "You boys listen to your brother. Go home, lock the doors, shut the windows, and keep as quiet as you can, all right?"

"Yes, Dad," they replied in unison.

"Billy, you okay? You look like you have been crying."

"The principal tried to eat me, Dad," Billy replied, his voice still a little shaky.

Harry took over. "It's fine, Dad. As soon as the trouble started, I hightailed it up here and found them. Our house is only five blocks away. I think I can get them there safely."

"You saved your brothers, then," Ray said, his voice sounding a bit choked.

"It's nothing," said Harry.

"It's everything," his father replied, wiping at the corner of his eye. "You've made me very proud, boy."

Harry looked back at his father in silence and started to wipe at the corner of his eye as well.

Finally, Ray said, "Harry, the number to the gun safe is 342812. You take the guns out like I showed you, give one to Jack, and a small pistol for Billy, but don't take out the special gun, okay?"

"Yes, Dad," Harry replied.

"These are not toys, William Beasley. Do you hear me?"

"Yes, Dad," Billy replied.

"Jack, if Billy decides to act the fool, you have my permission to clock him one."

"Sure, Dad," Jack said, sounding a bit too eager.

"I wouldn't choose to put guns in your hands at such a young age, boys. But these are dark times. The darkest I've known," their father said whilst rubbing his forehead with both hands. Harry had never seen him look so stressed.

"Remember what I taught you at the firing range," Ray continued. "You know how to use these things. So if anyone dead or half-dead comes knocking on the door, you put a bullet in their head, you hear me?"

"I hear you, Dad," Harry replied. The bullet in the head comment reminded him. "Dad, I think I know the way to kill them, the dead ones that is," he said, looking over at the still-unmoved principal. "I mean *really* kill them."

Government Building, Hobart

Jon stood at the eleventh-floor window, looking down on the Hobart streets. It looked like the panic had stopped. Nobody was running anymore; the people were just walking around aimlessly in no particular direction, and without any particular purpose. This should have eased Jon's fear, except for the fact that all of those people on the streets had injuries ranging from small bite marks to missing limbs. A distant crash could be heard to the north, and Jon noticed most of the dead turn in that direction. *Well, that's very interesting,* he thought, as a partial plan formed in his mind.

Everybody had now left the floor except for Jon and his four companions. He wondered if any of his other workmates had actually made it to safety or whether they were now down on the streets, waiting for them. Waiting for some fresh meat, he thought morbidly. The building had mostly clear views of all the surrounding streets, so Jon had asked Sarah, Ray, and Dave to go to the north, south, and west side of the building to see if they could spot a quick exit for them. He had doubts they would be successful, though, as the undead were constantly on the move, and the abandoned cars were jamming the streets, making both a run for it or driving a vehicle out of Hobart virtually impossible. He asked Nick to get on the Internet with his global buddies and find any information he could about this epidemic and how far it had travelled.

Think, Jon, he told himself, *there must be a way out of this.* Watching the streets, he noted that all the shops and store doors had been left wide open in people's panic to leave the city.

A looter would have a field day in town today, he thought; all the food and supplies that you would need. His eyes drifted over to the abandoned Sports Store. All the supplies I need?

"Nick. Are you there, mate? I need to know if you can—"

Jon stopped in mid-sentence as the elevator announced its arrival. Who could be coming back up here?

He stood motionless as the minister walked out. Well, it looked like the minister, but half his face had been removed.

He can't know how to use the elevator, surely? Perhaps he stumbled into the empty elevator and accidentally knocked one of the floor buttons. God knows I've done that a few times, Jon thought.

Sarah and Dave came back to the area where Jon was standing.

'I thought I heard the elevator, Jon," Sarah said.

"Yes, you did, Sarah, and we have a visitor," replied Jon, nodding towards the dead minister, who was now focused on him.

Sarah gave a sharp intake of breath.

"Now this is going to sound stupid," Jon continued, "but I do have a plan on how to get us out of here. However, it does involve doing something crazy."

"It's been a crazy day," said Dave looking very pale.

"I need to know if these things are attracted to noise," he told them, pointing towards the minister. "So if we could all circle it at a safe distance and try to gain its attention one at a time …"

"Are you sure, Jon?" said Sarah.

"Fairly," he replied, smiling at her. "But we have to know, Sarah, and this is as good a chance as any," he finished, sounding more serious.

"But what if it doesn't work?" Sarah protested mildly.

"Then we each make a bolt for the elevator or the fire escape stairwells behind us," said Jon.

"Okay, let's do it then," Sarah agreed, sounding nervous but determined.

"Dave?" enquired Jon.

"Okay," said Dave, "but why do we need to know, Jon?"

"I'll tell you in a minute," Jon assured him.

The experiment involved Jon, Dave, and Sarah standing at the three farthest parts of the room and individually calling out loudly and stamping their feet to attract the dead minister. Each time the minister would be focused on its victim, he would become distracted by a new noise and turn towards the person making it.

Just then, Nick and Ray came back into the room.

"What the hell are you doing?" asked Nick.

"Is it election time?" said Ray.

"We've just been studying the dead, and we just found out that these bastards are attracted to noise," Jon replied. "It might help us with getting out of town."

"Is that so?" replied Ray. "Well, Professor Beasley has come up with an answer of his own." Lifting the nearby fire extinguisher, he walked over to the minister and proceeded to pound his skull into the floorboards. Setting the now-bloodied fire extinguisher down, he said, "Compliments of my boy Harry."

All the others stood in silence and watched to see if the minister's body would move.

"He's not getting up," said Jon.

"Nope," said Ray. "His brain is pulp, so the body does not respond."

Of course, thought Jon, thinking of all the injuries of the dead in the streets.

"So they only die if we destroy their brain? Holy crap, Nick, you're going to live forever," Dave said, laughing.

"Very funny, Dave," Nick replied. Revenge for the rock joke, no doubt, he thought.

"Ray, how are your boys?" Jon asked quietly.

"They're safe for now, Jon," Ray replied, "but this epidemic has spread all the way through Kingston, and maybe beyond."

"Shit," Dave said, walking away to call his girlfriend, Christine, who also lived in Kingston.

"That's what I came back to say, Jon," said Nick. "The Holonews is down all over the country. I couldn't contact half of my friends around the globe on the Internet, and the ones I did manage to talk to in the US, France, and China say the same thing has happened there. The dead are rising everywhere."

Sarah picked up her Holophone disk and moved a few metres away. Soon, a short-statured woman appeared on the Hologram feed. "Sarah. Thank God you're alive."

Jon thought it was Sarah's mum, Jane Butler. They certainly looked similar. She was an ex-Huon Valley Councilor who still had some important contacts by all accounts.

"Mum, has the virus spread to the Huon? We heard that Kingston is in a mess," said Sarah.

"Yes, dear, it's spread here, but maybe it's because we are a small community that we have managed to contain it somewhat and have set up a barricade at the Grove junction."

"Mum, do you know that by shutting down their brain, you can kill them?"

Jane nodded. "A few farmers started with shots to the chest, and then, when that didn't work, a few of the better shots started aiming for the head. Word has spread, don't you worry. They won't find the Huon folk easy meat."

Sarah gulped at that analogy.

"Where are you now?" her mother continued.

"I'm still stuck in the city, but Jon is coming up with a plan to get us out," said Sarah.

"Jon? Is that the man lurking in the corner there?"

"Yes, Mum," Sarah replied.

"The one you've been moping about for the last year?"

"Mum," moaned Sarah, turning a deep shade of red.

"Come over here, boy. I want a few words with you," she commanded.

Jon shuffled slowly over so Sarah's mum could get a proper appraisal. Jane Butler definitely looked like Sarah, albeit a bit older, but Jon thought Sarah must have taken after her father in the personality department because Jane Butler was sounding like a complete ball-buster. Sarah had been moping about him?

"Are you listening to me, boy?" Jane suddenly asked in a commanding tone.

"I'm sorry. What?" Jon stumbled in reply, realising Jane had said something.

She had been moping about him?

"I said, how are you going to get my daughter out of that hellhole?"

"With alarms, hunting knives, mountain bikes, grid iron gear, and a whole lot of luck," replied Jon.

"What? Is that man mad, Sarah?" Jane said in shock.

"No, Mum, he's not, and I trust him," Sarah replied, making Jon's heart warm.

"Well, Jon Dayton, listen to me, and listen well," said Jane Butler, who appeared to be looming out of the Hologram as if to strangle him. "I charge you with the protection of my daughter. And if you fail in protecting her, I will hunt you down. Do you hear me? I will find you, and you will wish the dead had caught you first. Do you understand?"

"Yes, Mrs Butler," Jon replied meekly.

"Well, that's settled, then." Turning to Sarah, Jane continued, "Head for Grove as soon as you can, and be careful, my girl. I love you, sweetheart," she said, her voice now completely different, sweet and loving.

"I love you too, Mum," Sarah said. Avoiding looking at Jon, she switched off the connection.

Turning around, Jon caught Ray grinning at him. "You better check to see if you still have two left," Ray said, chuckling.

"Indeed," Jon agreed.

"What was that about grid iron gear?" asked Nick.

"Well, firstly, I need to know if you can hack into the local security system for all the nearby stores and sound the alarms. Now don't act all innocent. I know you don't spend all your time just chatting with your mates on the Net," Jon said.

"I can do it," replied Nick, "especially with nobody around to try to track me down. Do you want the whole town or just a certain area?"

"Just the streets to the west, because when the undead start moving in that direction, we are heading over to the sports store to the east to gather some items."

Dave came back to the group and said his girlfriend was at home, terrified, but he had managed to calm her down, and she would wait for him to come for her.

"All right," said Jon. "Just before we start this journey, I need to confirm that we are headed for the Mt Nelson Steps, which should then lead us up to fire tracks, which should take us across Mt Nelson. Then, we go down to the old road alongside the southern outlet. It's the best way to avoid the most number of dead people from where we are now. Does anyone have any quicker ways of getting to Kingston?"

When nobody replied, Jon said to Nick, "I know you don't live down that way, but I'd like you to come with us."

"Sure, Jon, it's not like I have anywhere else to be," Nick replied, grinning.

"Okay, then, Nick," Jon said. "Crank those alarms up. Crank them loud. Very loud, Nick."

Rainswood Christian Spiritual Retreat, Mt Nelson, Hobart

Peter Rainswood lounged in the spa, sipping champagne whilst watching the latest movie from China on his theatre-sized TV screen. *A shame Hollywood collapsed,* he thought. The Chinese films are quite good, but watching the subtitles could be a bit of a drag. Perhaps he could ask one of the 'faithful' to join him in the spa. That new young blonde girl with the big tits would surely love to accompany him in her efforts for spiritual enlightenment. Dumb as a box of hammers she was, just the way he liked them. Perhaps he could 'enlighten' her brains out if he was lucky. Peter Rainswood was the 'face' of the new Christian

Brotherhood of Tasmania. He was young, handsome, and charming, but also selfish and vain. He could read from the auto-cue perfectly as he raged against the sins of mankind and was an ideal poster boy for fleecing the masses of their cash. Sure, his insane father, Paul Rainswood, was a dedicated Christian man who wrote the sermons and actually did believe in the drivel he preached, but Peter didn't believe in God at all. All he really believed in was making heaps of cash in the here and now and living in the most absolute comfort that money could buy.

With a big grin on his face, his thoughts kept drifting back to the new girl. *What was her name? Kathy, Kath, Kylie, Katrina, Kelly?* His smile suddenly melted on his face as his little sister, Mary, entered the room.

"Why are you still in the spa, moron?" she said. "Father asked for you fifteen minutes ago. He seems quite happy about something."

Mary was sixteen years of age, blonde and pretty, and the biggest pain in the butt that he had ever met. Peter detested her.

"Well, he can wait a little longer, cant he, you little whore?" Peter snapped.

Mary sighed. "Are you still using that Mary Magdalene joke on me? She wasn't a whore. There was never any mention in the bible of her being a whore. You would know that if you studied it for more than five minutes."

"Well, why does every movie keep depicting her as such?" Peter said sarcastically.

"Well, big brother," she replied with equal sarcasm, "believe it or not, the movies you watch on TV are sometimes not based on actual facts. And when you run a male-dominated religion, it's not a good idea to promote the fact that Jesus treated a woman with respect and equality."

"That's just your interpretation on things," said Peter.

"Well, isn't the bible mostly based on interpretation?" Mary replied.

"'If a priest's daughter defiles herself by becoming a prostitute, she disgraces her father; she must be burned in the fire,' Leviticus 21:9," Peter said in his self-righteous tone.

"I'm not a whore, and father isn't a priest. He got a certificate online, remember?" Mary replied.

"That is a secret, Mary. Don't say that out loud," growled Peter.

"Well, you might want to consider that burning someone alive is a tad cruel, perhaps?" replied Mary.

"Okay, then, shit for brains," he said, "try this one: 'Let your women keep silence in the churches: for it is not permitted unto them to speak; but they are commanded to be under obedience, as also sayeth the law. And if they will learn anything, let them ask their husbands at home, for it is a shame for women to speak in the church' I Corinthians 14:34-35"

"I'm not married, and we're not in church," said Mary.

God, I hate her, Peter thought.

"Now get your arse into gear and go see Father. I'm not joking. He's actually become animated about something. He is waiting for you outside the front of the church," Mary continued.

"All right, I'll be there in a minute." *Stupid bitch,* he thought, as she left the room.

Toweling himself down, he put on some fresh clothing and went in search of his father. The 'retreat', as they liked to call it, was a massive mansion built in the back hills on top of Mt Nelson, which overlooked Hobart. It could only be found by driving up a gravel track from an old road that runs alongside the Southern Outlet from Kingston to Hobart. *Or perhaps when some dopey greenie tree-hugging bushwalker got lost,* he thought.

Making his way outside, he found his father with all of his 'flock', praying loudly in front of the freshly built church, which was supposedly where all the deep and meaningful debates took place about the sanctity of the church and so forth.

Looking idly around to see whether the blonde girl was about, *Karen,* he thought finally, *that's what her name is.*

"My son, the time has come at last," his father said, laughing joyously.

There she is, Peter thought, catching a glimpse of the blonde girl. *Sweet Jesus in heaven, she has some ripe curves.*

"...the dead have risen," his father continued.

"What?" said Peter, coming back to the conversation at hand.

"The dead have risen," his father replied.

"What do you mean, the dead have risen?" *Has he finally gone mad? He had been heading that way for years.*

"It's all over the news, Peter. Or was until the TV networks collapsed."

"What do you mean the TV networks collapsed? How are we going to make money if the TV networks are down?" Peter exclaimed. He had to get a straight answer to know what was happening.

"Mary!" he shouted. "Where the hell are you?" She would know what was up. A stupid mole she might be, but she had some sense about her, unlike this old wrinkled prune in front of him. *God, am I going to be that ugly when I'm his age?*

Mary shouted across the gathering. "Yeah, what do you want?"

"Come over here!" replied Peter.

"What's the magic word?" said Mary.

Bitch. Bitch is the magic word.

"Please," Peter said instead, gritting his teeth.

Mary walked over in no apparent hurry. *Take your sweet time about it, you little shit,* Peter thought angrily.

"Now, what's going on?" Peter demanded. "Father keeps going on about the dead rising. Is this true?" *It couldn't be, could it?*

"It's true," said Mary.

"What the fuck? You're kidding, right?" Peter said, shocked.

"No. Father and I have been watching the news for the last hour or so. There seems to be great panic all over Australia, indeed most of the world. A virus of some sort has allowed dead bodies to rise and attack other people," said Mary.

"The vengeance of God it is, Mary," said their father.

"Of course, Father," Mary replied, rolling her eyes.

Peter stood in stunned silence, trying to take this all in. *Wait, she said what?*

"An hour? You knew a whole bloody hour and you didn't think to come and warn me?" he exclaimed.

"Mary told me you were in prayer. I didn't wish to disturb you," their father replied.

"I was in the spa!" Peter shouted.

"Oops, sorry about that," Mary said and grinned at him.

"Well, what the fuck are we going to do?" Peter's head was

bursting. He felt like screaming.

"We stay here and pray, my son. The time of judgment is at hand. The Lord is slaying all the wretched sinners, but we shall be protected under the sheltering hand of God," said Paul.

"Well, can't we make a break for it, run to safety somehow?" pleaded Peter, looking at the various cars in the garage. That Porsche would surely outrun any disaster.

"We have the safety of God's church, my son," his father insisted softly.

"The virus—sorry, Father, I mean the wrath of God—has spread from the city to Kingston. There is nowhere to go," Mary said, sounding serious for the first time today.

"So, settle yourself down, my son, and await the coming of God's son Jesus," their father said, laughing again.

"Sure, Dad," Peter agreed. "I just need to go grab my bible, and I will be back in a few minutes."

Turning back to the others, Paul Rainswood, pastor of the Christian Brotherhood of Tasmania, started singing a hymn in preparation.

Peter quickly ran off to his private apartment inside the complex. He would be back in five minutes, like he said, and he would bring his bible. There was safety in numbers after all, he thought. But just in case Jesus didn't show up, he would also bring his pistol that he kept hidden in the wardrobe.

Tasmanian Parliament House, Hobart

The Tasmanian Parliament building was constructed between 1832 and 1840 from golden honey-coloured sandstone that was quarried from nearby locations in Hobart. It really was a lovely building, with a touch of detail and craftsmanship that was so lacking in today's modern buildings. The surrounding area was known as Salamanca Place.

Salamanca Place consisted of rows of sandstone buildings, formerly warehouses that had long since been converted into restaurants, galleries, craft shops, and offices. It was named after the victory in 1812 of the Duke of Wellington in the Battle of Salamanca in the Spanish province of Salamanca

Today, Salamanca Place was having its own battle, a battle that already had been lost.

"Keep those bloody things out of here," Bruce Cunnington, who was the current opposition leader, shouted. His chins and guts were wobbling as he strode the parliament corridor, instructing the security guards to hold the front door.

"Carl!" he shouted. "You awake, boy? I need you to talk to the premier. Find out if he has contacted the prime minister yet!"

Carl Cooper just stood there in disbelief with a kitchen knife in his hand, which he thought might protect him. He looked at the bloodied mess of people groaning and banging their hands, even their heads, against the doors and windows of this old building and wondered what the hell had happened to his hometown.

How was this possible? He had walked into parliament this morning, confident that he had finally got the numbers to roll this fat fuck out of the leadership job so he could have a crack at being premier himself. He was young and fit. Surely the public would think he had more charisma than tubby lard Cunnington. And now it appeared the world had come to an end.

"Carl, I need you to—" were the last words Cunnington said as the security door crashed open and hordes of the dead piled into the government house. Cunnington screamed and fell as his enormous gut was ripped open. Carl still stood unmoved as security guards fired their weapons into the mass of frenzied freaks. He was vaguely aware that one of the security guards had thrown a new Shadwick manufactured hand grenade into the attacking mob.

Hand grenade, he thought, coming out of his daze. Those things were bloody powerful, so he threw himself to the floor as the building was shaken by an almighty roar, and he felt himself covered in a thick blanket of water.

He wasn't sure how long he lay on the floor. He was definitely knocked unconscious by the blast, but for how long, he couldn't say.

Groggily standing up, Carl was suddenly aware of all the groaning going on around him. *Maybe people were injured or coming back to consciousness like him*, he thought. Taking an unsteady glance around the room, he noticed that the people groaning were actually dead. One of them looked suspiciously like the security guard who had thrown the hand grenade to begin with. He froze as the dead kept walking straight past him. *Fucking hell,* he thought, *am I dead too? Why are they not attacking me?* Looking down at his clothes, he noticed that he was absolutely covered in blood and gore. It wasn't water that had covered me when the explosion happened; it was people's blood and gore. *They think I am one of them. Maybe it's because I smell just like them,* he thought deliriously. *C'mon, Cooper, you've been in tighter spots than this. So you're surrounded by a bunch of blood-sucking parasites; it's no different from a normal day in parliament.*

Staring down at the kitchen knife that was still in his hand, he noticed that there was a long, large rope lying on the floor. Coiling the rope up into a loop to fit his other hand, Carl Cooper formed a plan in his mind.

What was Cunnington saying? Get to the premier's office? I might do that right now, he thought determinedly.

Premier Pratt sat in his plush office with all the latest technology at his beck and call and could do absolutely nothing. All the power that he had possessed this morning had suddenly evaporated. He had been on the phone to all the authorities, trying to form some sort of defense plan to this catastrophe. But as the day had progressed, contact was lost with each and every one of them. Tasmania had no regular army to fight back. He was powerless.

He had tried to ring his wife all morning, but she would not answer the Holophone. He knew in his heart that she was dead. *Perhaps she was walking to him now, baying for his blood,* he thought. The prime minster and all his cabinet were bunkered down in Canberra somewhere. He knew that they had called out the army, and there were some serious battles going on. But how could you control a situation like this? How could society rebuild itself from this disaster? How could this chaos be stopped? It would take years to rebuild, maybe decades.

Australia was now vulnerable to any outside attack, but the prime minister had assured him that this was happening all over the globe. The world had gone to hell. *It all happened after we saw those bloody comets in the sky,* he thought, *perhaps they were somehow part of this?* He was then jolted from his thoughts by a knock on the office security door. He had heard plenty of groans and bumps from the dead people against the heavy security door in the last half-hour, but this sounded like a definite knocking. "Who is it?" he called out lamely.

"It's Carl Cooper, Premier. Can you let me in? There are a lot of unfriendly people out here."

Checking the outside security cam, he confirmed it was Cooper, albeit a Cooper who looked like he had been through an abattoir. How the bloody hell was that bastard alive? Of all the people he wanted to survive, he would be the last chosen. Despite what the public thought, parliament was filled with politicians who genuinely cared about the people they represented. But Carl Cooper was not included in that group; this man only loved power. It had been obvious from the day he was first elected that this smug prick was on a power trip to the top. He was surprised he had waited this long to try to usurp Cunnington's position.

"Yes, just hang on a minute." *I should just let the bastard rot out there,* he thought, whilst opening the door. But he was curious as to how Cooper had survived.

Opening the door, the premier was taken aback by the stink coming from Cooper. He was absolutely covered in blood and … was that someone's intestines?

"Quick, shut the door, Pratt, before those bastards get in," snapped Cooper.

It's Premier Pratt to you, Cooper, he thought angrily, closing the door quickly.

"How on earth did you survive?" the premier asked as he moved back to his desk and sat down.

"I'll tell you in a minute," Cooper replied. "I just want to know what's going on first."

Pratt looked over at Cooper, who appeared to be carrying a large kitchen knife and had a rope coiled around his left wrist. *Perhaps I don't want to know,* the premier thought.

"It's happening everywhere," the premier replied. "Armies are battling the dead. Communications are down across the country.

I think we are on our own, Cooper."

"What about the army reserve? Have they been called in?" Cooper said, circling the room.

Pratt looked at him in confusion. "Army reserve? You know, there are only twenty reserve soldiers stationed at the Anglesea Barracks. Anyway, I have called them already. A captain by the name of Joe Mason told me to 'fuck off' when I asked him to come and defend the parliament."

Joe Mason, Cooper pondered.

"So they have a good supply of weapons, then?" Cooper continued.

"Yes, I guess so," Pratt replied. "Why? Are you intending on going there?"

"Yes, we are both going," said Cooper.

Pratt was about to say that he could not run out on his duty as premier when he felt Cooper's knife enter his back. He tried to scream in pain, but the knife must have penetrated his lung, and all that came out was a gasping noise. He slumped forward as Cooper stabbed him two more times.

"I'm sorry, Premier, but I needed to know what was going on, and I need a constant supply of dead blood if I'm going to get out of here," Cooper said, whilst tying a hangman's noose around the premier's neck and hogtying his hands together. "Right, we are all set to go now. So just hurry up and die."

The premier soon complied and then stood up back up. Cooper, with a secured grip on the neck of the dead body, wiped the blood on Pratt's back over his face and clothes and pushed the groaning ex-premier towards the door. Out in the corridor and onto the streets, they began their unhindered slow walk forward toward the Anglesea Barracks, in search of the soldier named Joe Mason.

So this was the journey of the last Tasmanian Premier.

Hogtied, pushed, moaning, a dead heart, and constantly being stabbed in the back, it was a politician's life for sure.

Fortunately, this was not an event that was ever recorded in future history books.

Grove, approximately thirty-one kilometres south of Hobart

Three senior citizens of the Huon Valley stood near the barricade at the Grove Junction. You would think that Police Commissioner Ian McCulloch and Huon Mayor Jake Swain would be the leaders of the conversation, but both were leaning forward in an almost bowing motion to the diminutive figure that was the ex-Huon Valley councilor, Jane Butler.

"Are you sure these boys are good shots?" said Jane.

"Yes, Jane, and we have a constable here to make sure they behave," replied the police commissioner.

"Well, why do they have that music playing so loud? I mean, I enjoy AC/DC as much as the next person. But the volume is giving me a splitting headache."

"We have had reports that the dead are attracted to noise," said the local mayor. "Our barricade only runs along this street for so far, so the incoming dead could quite easily move around us. If we attract them here then we can take them out before they make any move on to further townships."

"Humph! I suppose that is good thinking," Jane replied. "Well done, Jake."

"Thank you, Jane," said the mayor, grinning like a schoolboy complimented by his favorite teacher.

"Ian, you have some men stationed outside the valley hospital and aged care homes?"

"Yes, we have, Jane. I've arranged shifts to make sure there are two men stationed there at all times."

"And do these men know what they have to do if a patient or an elderly person should die there?" Jane asked quietly.

"Yes, they do, Jane," he answered just as quietly.

Turning to the mayor, she said, "Now, Jake, how about the food situation? Do we have enough to see out the next few months?"

"The valley is bountiful in fresh food and farm animals, Jane," replied the mayor. "We export more food than we import; I'm sure we can see out more than a few months if need be. However, I doubt we shall be seeing fast food products for some time."

"Well, there's a blessing at least," replied Jane. "Well, take me to these men, then, Police Commissioner."

The police commissioner took her to the three men who would take first shift of shooting in the head any human being who appeared to be already dead.

"Jane, I'd like to introduce you to the Huon Valley's first line of defence," said the commissioner.

Three men who appeared to be of middle age came forward and introduced themselves.

"G'day, Councilor," the first one said. "My name is Crabman, and this is Robbo, and that one over there is the Grogan."

Dear God, it's the Three Stooges, thought Jane.

"Now, you know what to do, don't you?" she asked aloud.

"Yes, Councilor. Anybody who shows up here groaning and wants to take a bite out of my arse, I put a bullet in their dial."

Well, that about covers it, thought Jane. *We should be safe as houses from now on.*

"Well, just make sure they are dead before you shoot them. Some people do groan when they are in pain, you know," said Jane.

"Right you are, Councilor; will do. There will be no troubles in the Huon tonight. Mark my words," he said as he walked back to the barricade.

"Have we got enough ammunition, Commissioner?"

"Most farmers have enough to protect their livestock from predators," replied the commissioner, "but if half of Hobart descends on us, we won't be able to stop them."

Looking back up the highway that led to the city, she wondered where her daughter was now. *Hurry up, Sarah,* she thought. *I don't think I would want to live any more if you died.*

Mt Nelson Steps, Hobart

Sarah panted as she pushed her newly acquired Barrow Mountain Bike up the steps that led directly up the side of Mt Nelson. To the left, houses resided next to a road known as "the bends", which consisted of seven very sharp corners as the road wound its way up the mountain. Sarah noticed a few faces peering nervously through the windows of some of the houses as she walked up. It was nice to know a few people had survived, but Mt Nelson was so close to the city. How would they be able to survive being so close to the dead?

It wasn't exactly a hard climb up the hill, but after the rush of leaving the city, she found that as the adrenaline was leaving her body, she was starting to feel more and more tired.

"I think I ruptured my balls," said Ray grimacing.

"Well, I'm not sewing them up," Jon replied.

Sarah looked back at them and grinned. The sight of a two hundred-centimetre giant riding a small push bike, whilst wearing a grid iron uniform and complaining about how much his nuts hurt would have been pretty funny if not for the fact that they had to maneuver past hundreds of the groaning flesh-eating monsters.

"Are you going to ring your kids now, Ray?" she asked.

"No, I can't just yet, Sarah," he replied. "As you know, these Holophones are expensive and ..." He trailed off, embarrassed. *And you can't afford to use it for too long,* thought Sarah, *as your credit will run out and you don't have enough money to recharge it because you have three kids to support on only one wage.*

"Well, we'll make a quick call when we reach Kingston."

"Will do, Sarah," replied Ray. "I can't wait to see them again."

Sarah's heart went out to him. She had never met Ray's boys, but you could tell the way he talked about them over the years how much he loved them. Perhaps the mother running out on them when they were young made them closer.

Sarah took a moment to think of her own mum. She was in the same boat as Ray. If she kept calling her mother every five minutes like she wanted to, her credit would soon run out as well. Holophones were for the rich. People like her and her companions could only use them sparingly.

"Jon, can we take these uniforms off now? I think we are past the most danger," Nick asked.

"I'm sweating like a pig, Jon," Dave added.

Sighing, Jon took a long look around them. "Okay, but keep the knives close. If we're attacked by the dead, we have to grab them and stab them through the eyes. Remember, there are a lot of houses up here."

He's becoming a leader, she thought. *I don't think he has realised that the group always defers to him when a decision needs to be made.*

As she dropped her helmet to the ground, she became aware how quiet everything was. Hobart was a city of 220,000 people, which was small compared to the major cities of Australia, but you could always hear the hustle and bustle of a modern city. Now you could not hear anything, apart from the calls of a magpie and a nearby dog barking. She looked down on the city from where they stood and saw no movement, apart from the odd person walking aimlessly. *Hobart's dead,* she thought. It was such a nice old town. A bit isolated, and some people had taken to calling it Slowbart, but it was a peaceful place; the people were good by and large, and now it was gone.

"Sarah, are you all right?" Jon said quietly, noticing her sad face as he moved over to her side.

"Yes, I'm okay," she replied, "just a bit exhausted from the ride."

"You did well. I was having trouble keeping up with you."

"Oh. Watching me, were you?" she said, smiling.

"Yes," he replied quietly. "Yes, I was."

And just for a few moments, they stood there looking into each other's eyes.

"*Ahem*, excuse me, you two," said Ray, "but I think I just heard a dog yelp." He then trundled over to a nearby house.

"Bloody hell," Jon said. "I better go with him. If someone's hurt a dog, there is going to be World War declared on Mt Nelson. Nick, Dave, you watch after Sarah."

I'm not a porcelain doll! But she was inwardly pleased that he was so protective of her. *And what about that look he just gave her?* she thought, with a big grin on her face.

"Ray, wait up," Jon said, running after him. "You can't go wandering off on your own in search of a dog. You never know where the dead might show up."

"Sorry, mate. I just heard a dog yelp in pain. You know I can't stand the abuse of animals, especially dogs," replied Ray.

"Anyway, you looked to be gaining 'half a mongrel' yourself, looking at Sarah," he said, laughing.

"Bloody hell, I was not," Jon said, blushing.

Rounding the nearest house, they stopped as they saw that one of the dead had cornered a black-and-white sheepdog that looked to have been bitten. The poor dog looked terrified, and the dead man just looked terrifying.

Ray calmly picked up a nearby metal garden stake.

"Only the sickest of scum hurts a dog," he said loudly.

The creature turned slowly around to walk towards Ray, a low moaning sound emanating from its throat.

"Time to really die," Ray said as he drove the stake straight through its head and into the weatherboard house behind.

Bending down, Ray held out his hand to the dog.

"Come here, boy," he said in a kindly voice. "I won't hurt you."

"Ray, it's been bitten. You don't know what effect the virus has on a dog," Jon said.

"No. I think he's okay. The bitten humans were convulsing within a minute. This boy is just scared. Aren't you, mate?"

The dog slowly came forward, and Ray placed a soft hand on his head. Looking the dog in the eyes, he murmured soothing words, and then looked at the bite on his neck.

"Is it deep?" asked Jon.

"No, only looks superficial, I think," replied Ray.

"I wonder where its owner is."

"Probably has a stake through his head."

"Well, we better get going. I'm sure he'll be fine now," Jon said. He knew where this conversation was headed, but he hoped Ray would think with his head not his heart.

Ray just looked over at Jon.

"Oh, come on, mate," Jon said, pleading. "You know we have to keep quiet. I'm sure he'll be yapping all the way to Kingston."

Ray just kept looking at Jon.

"All right, we'll just let the dog decide. If it stays here, then it's on its own. Deal?"

"Deal," replied Ray.

They both said nothing as they walked back to the others. As far as Jon could tell, Ray didn't call the dog or look back.

"Did you find the dog?" asked Sarah.

"Yes," replied Jon quietly. "It's all good. But Ray wants to keep him."

"It could be risky if he's a dog that barks. But I must admit Ray is definitely good with animals," said Sarah.

"Well, we have decided to place this in the hands of fate," replied Jon.

"What do you mean?"

"If the dog follows us, then we keep him. If not, then he will have to look after himself." Jon felt cold at being so callous, but the safety of the group came first, especially Sarah.

They walked on for a few minutes, then Sarah said with a smile, "Fate has decided, Jon."

The dog had run after them and placed itself by Ray's heel. *It's a trained sheepdog,* Jon thought. *I bet you Ray knew that from the get-go.*

"Lady and gents," said Ray, "I would like to introduce my new dog to you all. For his name, he will simply be called Dog. If it's good enough name for Mad Max, then it's good enough for me."

"Billy will love that dog," said Sarah.

"He sure will," replied Ray with a big grin.

Fate had decided well, as he was a great dog for hearing the dead before any of the humans could. When he stopped with his ears perked up, he would give out a low growl, and the group would then move away from the direction in which he faced. Time and time again, they avoided numbers of dead, and Ray would look at Jon more and more smugly. Slowly, they made their way through old bushwalking tracks and fire trails and finally came to a clearance. Dog had now stopped and faced straight ahead. But strangely, he didn't growl. Moving to go away from where Dog was facing, Jon thought he heard a familiar sound.

"Wait up," said Jon. "I can hear a noise, but it doesn't sound like groaning."

"It can't be," said Dave.

"Fuck me," Ray grumbled.

"I'm having a high school flashback," Nick said, laughing.

Sarah looked at Jon. "Is that … is somebody singing a hymn?"

How long were these idiots going to sing? Peter Rainswood wondered. Father started singing hymns half an hour ago, but we aren't a famous male choir from Wales, for fuck's sake. Some people's voices were now so raw, they sounded like they were breaking wind, not singing the highest praises to God.

Under the guise of checking to see if he left his wallet in his car, which he was not questioned about, even though someone surely would wonder why you would need a wallet in Heaven, Peter had moved the most expensive 4WD that they owned into a position where he could make a quick getaway if need be. Strangely enough, Mary had brought out her push bike. What a dumb bitch, he thought. He was about to suggest to Father that they give up on the singing for a while, when all their voices suddenly stopped. This reminded him of an old Western movie, where the bad guy would enter the saloon, the music and talking would suddenly stop, and a gunfight was about to begin.

What are they looking at? he wondered, as he placed his hand in his jacket pocket to feel the comfort of his pistol. If it was a gunfight, then he was going to be ready to run away as fast as he could. He was a coward, but at least he was an honest coward, he thought, as the migraine was starting to build behind his eyes.

Looking down the pathway, he saw five people and a dog walking out of the bush land. And they all had mountain bikes? *Mary should get along well with them,* he thought sarcastically. There were four men and a female. Two of the men were tall and looked to be in their thirties or forties. One was a nerdy-looking kid who looked about twelve, and the other could have been twenty or fifty for all he knew, as he had one of those massive beards that some youths or grandfathers would wear.

The woman was a slender redhead who looked quite tasty. If the blonde proved unsuccessful, he would like to have a crack at her, but one of the men exhibited by his body language that she was taken. Or that he was protective at least.

Anyway, he was soon to learn that they hadn't come here for any salvation or protection at all.

"Welcome, brothers and sisters. I am the Reverend Rainswood.

Have you come to seek the shelter of Christ our Lord?" Father said.

"Um, no, mate, just passing through," said the biggest man.

Wait! Was that Ray Beasley the ex-footballer for the Kangaroos? Peter used to watch him play when he was a kid. Eight years in the AFL for the fledgling Tasmanian side, played only 104 games as he spent most of the time off field for suspensions.

Peter remembered when he broke the Collingwood Captain's jaw. 'It was an accident,' he was reported to say at the tribunal, while the footage showed he had five of the Collingwood player's teeth stuck in his elbow. Peter always enjoyed the footy, until Father found his calling and decided that sport was of the devil and not to be tolerated.

"I hope you don't mind us crossing your land?" said the second man, placing a protective hand on the girl's arm as he looked over at Peter. "We are running from the troubles in the city and are on our way to Kingston."

"Kingston is in great peril, my friend," his father replied. "God has descended in righteous fury to kill all the wretched sinners of the world."

"Yes, we saw the devastation in the city. People were killing and tearing each other apart. I can't say I would be proud to claim a God who caused that," the man replied. "But to each their own, I guess"

C'mon, Sarah," he said in the direction of the group and gestured to the woman next to him. "Goodbye," he said to Peter's father, nodding his head and walking onwards.

Peter knew his father never gave up so easily and was not surprised when he approached the big footballer.

"What about you, big man? Do you believe in God?"

"Which one?"

'Why, the one true God, of course."

"Well, there have been over a three thousand Gods worshipped throughout our history," he replied.

"The Real God," said Father insistently.

"There's over two hundred Gods worshipped today. I need some more information," said Ray.

"The Christian God," Father said, now exasperated.

"And which one of the forty-odd denominations would your God be, then?"

"The Christian Brotherhood of Tasmania," snapped his Father.

"Oh. *That* God! Yeah … no, sorry. I don't believe in *that* God, mate," said Ray as he walked away.

Well, Father, Peter thought, *you do ask for it sometimes.*

Peter felt at his forehead, as he had always suffered from splitting migraines, which usually led to violent outbursts. *Yes, here it comes,* he thought as he watched his father walk away to start singing, another hymn that was soon joined by sounds of burps and farts from the faithful. *It was going to be a long day,* Peter thought, as he unconsciously gripped the pistol tightly.

The dog began to follow his master, then turned around and growled back at the bush land.

Must have smelt a cat, Peter thought, as Ray Beasley gave a shrill whistle and the dog scampered after him.

Jon decided that they would only ride their bikes on the long, open stretches of the road, as they could see for greater distances. On winding roads and paths such as this gravel track, which they presumed was the driveway, they would just have to walk and rely on Dog to warn them of any trouble.

"You're getting subtle in your old age, Ray. Do you think the reverend will get it?" Jon said.

"No, mate," Ray replied. "Guys like that have the blinkers on; they believe what best suits their needs."

"Bloody expensive mansion," said Dave, turning his head around to look back at the house.

"Are they singing again?" Sarah said, looking back as well.

"Trying to, I think," said Nick.

"Did any of you notice the young man who was carrying a gun?" Jon asked.

"What?" exclaimed Sarah.

"Which one was that?" said Nick.

"Peter Rainswood," Jon answered.

"You mean the guy from the TV show who says what everyone else is doing wrong, then asks for your money?" said Dave, who strangely didn't seem surprised by the gun comment.

"That's the one," Jon agreed with a nod. "I was glad when we moved on so quickly."

"You were a bit rude to the older man," said Nick.

"Yeah, I was." Jon sighed. "I'm sorry, but I just don't like people claiming that mass murder was a divine event." He had his views on God today but kept it to himself. Plus, people might think he was a bit crazy if he voiced them.

Sarah was looking at him as if waiting for a further explanation.

"That's why the place was so plush," Dave said.

"They make lots of money, Dave. Bloodsuckers, the lot of them," Ray replied.

"Did you see that beautiful blonde girl?" Nick suddenly asked.

"Yeah, bloody oath, she was smoking hot," replied Dave.

"Did you see her, Jon?" Nick continued.

"No, can't say that I noticed, Nick," Jon lied, avoiding Sarah's sharp look.

"She had a mountain bike just like ours," Nick replied.

Jon, Dave, and Ray all shared a confused look. Which blonde girl was he talking about?

They continued on for a few more minutes, and then Sarah brought up the religion conversation again. "I'm sorry, but with all the death we have seen today, I have to ask. Does anyone here believe in God or the afterlife? Dave, you go first."

Dave turned to Sarah and shrugged his shoulders. "I was watching the sports news and saw a man who had won a football championship, thanking God for his help. Then I turned over the news and saw the massacre of over a hundred children in an African village. If he exists, then he has strange priorities."

Jon had to agree with that. He had seen a woman on the news recently, being interviewed about a natural disaster in her town. She thanked the grace of God for saving her life in a town where two hundred people were killed and ninety percent of the houses were destroyed. A God that decided to save a few when other families were heartbroken at the loss of their loved ones didn't sit right with him at all.

"What about you, Nick?" Sarah continued.

"Well," said Nick, fiddling with his glasses, "to continue on with what Dave said about the sportsman winning an event: Say, for argument's sake, God did intervene and helped that athlete win. Well, what about the other athletes? By helping one person win, God has helped the other person lose. There is a balance involved in all things, and to intervene in a human's future would be a never-ending game of cause and effect. So I don't think that God is involved in humanity's history at all. We all have free will," he finished.

"Well, we're all a bit philosophical today." Sarah laughed, then asked, "What about you, Ray?"

"Religion is for fucking idiots," said Ray.

"Okay, so much for the philosophy," replied Sarah. "Just so you know, I believe in God, but I can't prove it exists. And that's my point. Nobody can prove any of it, ever. So if you do have your beliefs, then good for you. I wish you well. But never for a moment consider your beliefs to be a fact, or that your beliefs should be forced upon another individual as such."

Jon looked at Sarah and smiled. Not only gorgeous but smart as well. One of the dumbest quotes he ever heard was, "You don't need evidence; you just need belief." Peter Rainswood had been the one who said it.

People didn't realise that the people who used that quote were saying it because they wanted you to follow their belief, and for you to forget about evidence. Blind obedience was another name for it. If ever there was a phrase to turn us back to the dark ages that was it.

"Now, Jon Dayton, it is your turn," said Sarah, smiling at him.

Bloody hell, he thought. This was all about getting him to open up on his feelings. He should have never said 'divine event'.

"Ah, it's nothing, really," Jon said.

"No way, mate, you got to open up," Ray protested.

"Hey, Ray, all you said was they were all fucking idiots," Jon replied.

"What do you mean? That was opening up for me." Ray grinned.

"C'mon, Jon," said Nick.

"Don't be a big blouse," Dave said and laughed.

Sighing, Jon said, "Well, it's all to do with what happened today.

The dead, did you see their eyes? It was like they were an empty shell. Something had left them. I know I can't prove it," he looked at Sarah, "but I don't think they were there anymore. I mean the real person that they were before they died."

Taking a big breath, he continued, "But that's not entirely what I mean by all of this. If a person survives death and goes on to another plane or dimension or whatever, it means that right now, your consciousness is part of your body, but also separate. It means that if we survive death, then the centre of our being right now is not our brain and body, but our thoughts and memories. Go to your local graveyard and dig up a two-hundred-year-old grave. That body is still there," he said, gesturing with his hands. "It was just a shell. I know I'm rambling, but if we are just thoughts in the physical world, then how far do we go back? Is time and space relevant? Is this part of us immortal? It could mean that when we die, we just go back home. Perhaps that is our reward for living in this crappy world and surviving all of what we have seen today." He sighed and almost felt like crying.

Nick and Dave just stood in thoughtful silence. Ray bent down to scratch Dog behind the ear. No doubt, he was embarrassed that his friend had come out with such hippy rubbish. But Sarah just came up to him and placed her hand on his cheek.

"A man of many layers," she murmured.

He was crying a little, he realised. He had always suffered from anxiety badly. *She must think I'm a stupid little boy,* he thought.

"It's just been a long day," he said, trying to regain control of the situation.

"I know," was all she said. But the compassion was in her eyes. It was only then that he noticed that the singing from the mansion was getting louder.

"Is it just me, or do the Rainswoods sound like they're now shouting, not singing?" he said.

"Perhaps the 'rapture' is about to happen," said Ray.

"It has a frantic sound to it," said Sarah.

It was then that they heard the gunshots and screams.

"Well," said Ray, "the Rainswood kid has either had a gutful of the shit singing or they have just come under attack by our dead friends."

"Either way, we are getting out of here now," said Jon, and then they heard the loud screech of a car.

"Get off the road," Dave shouted, as they all jumped into the surrounding bushes with their bikes and Ray with Dog under his arm as well.

Jon looked up in time to see a massive 4WD vehicle speed past them, just barely keeping on the driveway. It looked like Peter Rainswood driving.

Looking around for Sarah, he let out a sigh of relief that she was safe. A little disheveled, but fine nonetheless.

"I'm sorry, Sarah. I had no time to cover you," he said.

"I can look after myself, you know?" she said, but smiled to take the edge off it.

"I think that was Peter Rainswood," said Nick.

"Yeah, I think so too," replied Jon.

"That little prick, wait till I get my fucking hands on him. He could have killed my dog," Ray growled.

"He could have killed you too, you know," said Dave, laughing.

"Take more than a 4WD to kill me, young Dave."

"I know that, old mate, tough as nails you are," Dave said, smiling.

"Indeed," replied Ray. "Did I ever tell you about the time me and the Hawthorn's Full Forward Cossie Bollinger went toe-to-toe in the first game of the 2028 AFL season?"

"Yes, quite a few times," replied Dave. "Six weeks' suspension you got." Looking at Ray's arm, he continued, "And you can put your dog down on the ground now."

"Oh, yeah, sorry, little mate," Ray said, placing Dog on the floor. The dog just licked his hand in adoration.

Saved by Ray twice in one day, Jon thought, *but we still owe Dog a few more lives for his good hearing.*

"Is everybody's bike still in working order?" he asked.

"Yeah, I think so," said Nick, being young enough to know what he was looking for when giving all the bikes a once over.

It was then that Dog gave a sharp look behind them.

"If he starts growling, we head off fast," said Jon.

But Dog just kept looking, and soon they saw a young girl on a mountain bike similar to theirs, riding up behind them. She was standing upright as she rode, and Jon noticed that on the seat behind was the Reverend Paul Rainswood.

A blonde girl on a bike, Jon thought, looking back at Nick, who looked well pleased at the new arrival. Ray, Dave, and Sarah had all twigged to this thought too, and they all shared a smile.

"Your girlfriend's here, Nick," Dave teased with a soft chuckle.

"Please, shut up, Dave. I'm begging you," said Nick quietly.

"Okay, Nick. No worries," replied Dave with a grin.

The young girl slowed to a stop as she reached them.

"Great minds think alike," she said, looking at their bikes. "My name is Mary, and you of course have met my father." She indicated the devastated man behind her.

"Nice to meet you, Mary," said Jon. "I'm sorry I didn't introduce myself before; my name is Jon." Gesturing to his friends, he continued, "This is Sarah, that big lout there is Ray, the bearded oaf is Dave, and the guy hiding behind Dave is Nick."

"Pleased to meet you all," replied Mary.

She really was *cute*, Jon thought, as he looked back at the hidden figure of Nick.

"Nick, say hello to Mary," Ray prompted with a grin.

"Hello, Mary," said Nick, looking at his shoes.

"Are there any more survivors?' Jon asked quietly.

"No. I don't think so. Father and the faithful prayed, but to no avail. The dead just walked up and started ripping into us," she replied with a shiver. "We scattered in every direction, and I only just managed to get Father on the bike."

"That was very brave of you," said Nick, who was now looking up at her with admiration.

"Why, thank you, Nick," she replied, and Nick blushed with embarrassment.

"You did very well," Sarah said to Mary with compassion.

"God didn't show up then, mate?" Ray said to Reverend Paul with no compassion.

"No ... no ... no, he didn't," mumbled the reverend, "but God moves—"

"In mysterious ways," interjected Ray. "Yes, we have all heard that one before. Your son was moving in a mysterious way in his

4WD when he almost ran us over, too." Looming forward, he said, "He ran away and left you behind. He's a complete prick, do you know that?"

"Yes ... I ... he was a troublesome lad. Psychiatric problems as a child," Rainswood mumbled.

Jon thought Ray was being a bit harsh on the reverend, who had just seen all his 'flock' killed most likely, but Ray's father had had a dark episode as a child with the local Catholic priest. So from the day he learnt of this, Ray had little time for men of the cloth. Oddly, the reverend's daughter, Mary, seemed to be struggling not to laugh.

"We are heading to Kingston," said Jon. "We have a few family and friends there whom we need to find. It will be dangerous," Jon continued, "but you're most welcome to come with us, if you like?"

"Well ... umm ... we could go back ... home," the reverend started to say. Jon thought he was starting to look a bit deranged.

"Yes, that is very kind of you, and we will go with you," Mary interrupted, not looking at Jon, but instead, looking over at young Nick, who was now staring back.

That's very interesting, he thought, smiling inwardly, and then he involuntarily looked over at Sarah, who was looking back at him. Such lovely eyes Sarah had. Windows to the soul, he heard it said. She must have a beautiful soul, he mused. Sarah's cheeks looked flushed, and he figured his must be too.

Still looming over the reverend, Ray all but growled, "It's good that you didn't leave your child to torment and death."

"Well ... of course I wouldn't," said the reverend.

"Then you agree that a father shouldn't leave their child to torture and pain? That when you really love someone, you protect them no matter what?" said Ray.

"Well, of course I agree. What sort of father would do such a thing to their child?" replied the reverend, aghast.

"A cruel one! An evil one! Here endeth the lesson," said Ray as he walked away with his bike, closely followed by Dog.

Another subtle lesson maybe, Jon thought, but a lesson about some of the evil priests of today or the fundamentalist's idea of God and hell, he wasn't sure.

The reverend was looking at Ray with a bewildered expression as he walked away, but strangely, his daughter, Mary, was watching Ray with an almost affectionate smile.

Strange family, Jon thought.

In a few minutes, they reached the bottom of the gravel driveway, which joined on to the smoother old road that ran alongside the Southern Outlet. The road was mostly flat with a few hills, but on the open areas, where they had a good view in all directions, they rode their bikes quickly.

The closer to Kingston, the more anxious Dave and Ray seemed to look. Each seemed to be half-reaching to their Holophones in their pockets for most of the ride. They could hear the groans of the dead up on the highway, and there appeared to be smoke coming from some of the abandoned cars, but the old road provided a good protection for most of the journey. Finally, they came to a clearing that opened up a clear view of Kingston, also sadly, a clear view of the burning houses and lots of dead people, hundreds of dead people. Ray's Holophone then started to ring.

The Beasley Household, Kingston

"I'm bored," twelve-year-old Billy sulked, sitting in the lounge room of the family house.

"Just shut up," said Jack, "and stop mucking around with the pistol."

"I'm not, Jack; it's just so boring waiting for Dad," he replied.

"Well, do you want to go out and play with the dead men again?" Jack shot back. "Remember what Dad said, 'these are not toys', and also remember he gave me permission to smack you one if you misbehave, you little snot rag."

"Be quiet, both of you," said Harry, looking through a slit in the closed curtains of their house. "Do you want to draw their attention to us again?"

The run back home had gone relatively smoothly as he had only had to smash half a dozen dead people in the five blocks to home. Once they had arrived home, Harry locked all the doors, shut the windows, closed all the curtains, and told his brothers to keep quiet. Then he ran to the gun cabinet, picked out two shotguns for Jack and himself, and a small pistol for Billy as his dad had instructed. The dead did chase them and rattle the doors and windows, and Harry thought they may have to open fire, but once they lost sight and sound of their prey, the dead seemed to lose interest and look for their next kill.

Short attention span, he thought, *just like Billy.*

"Why can't we call Dad?" Billy whined.

"You know why, Billy," Harry replied. "These Holophones are bloody expensive, so we have to use them sparingly. Dad will call us when he reaches the outskirts of Kingston."

If he doesn't, then we have to assume he is dead, he thought, as tears came to his eyes. Turning his head, he wiped at his eyes without his brothers seeing. He had to keep his little brothers occupied.

"Billy, have you checked your weapon to make sure it's safe and ready?" Harry said.

"Yes, Harry. You've asked me that twice now," he replied indignantly. "I'm not stupid, you know."

Jack gave a loud guffaw at this.

"I know you're not stupid, little mate. I'm just on edge, that's all," Harry replied, ruffling the kid's hair. "All right, who is hungry then? I'll make you up some sausage sandwiches."

"Yeah, that would be nice, Harry," Billy replied, sounding a bit more chipper than before.

"All right, just sit tight. I won't be long," said Harry. And as if in afterthought, he continued, "Can you take a peek out through the curtains and make sure none of the dead are around? Jack, you look out the backyard for trouble as well."

"Sure, Harry," said Billy as Jack lumbered out the back. "Can you put heaps of tomato sauce on the sanga for us, please?"

"Will do, kiddo," Harry replied.

Moving up to the curtains on the window, Billy looked out on the empty street. He really loved his big brother Harry. Jack could be a pain in the butt sometimes, but Harry was always looking after him. Just like the way he kicked down the door when he saved him from the principal. He could have been an action hero like the movie stars from the latest Chinese movie blockbusters. Billy had a poster of Jackie Li in his room. He kicked all the bad guys' arses and always saved the day.

Just then, he saw a small white flash of something running down the road and across to the park. Was that a puppy? Billy had always wanted a dog, ever since the last one passed away. *Dad loves dogs too,* Billy thought. *I'm sure he won't mind if we borrow this one. I mean, I would be saving it from the dead people, right? I could be across the street and back before Harry found out I was gone.* Making a quick, and in hindsight, dumb decision, Billy grabbed his pistol and sneaked out the front door. Checking to see that the street was clear, he crept across the road and into the park, making sure he was holding the pistol the way Dad had said, and also the cool way the movie stars did. *Where the hell did it go?* he thought. Suddenly, he heard a small yelp, from beyond the nearby tree and building. Moving slowly in that direction, he whispered, "Here, puppy; here, mate. I won't hurt you." He should have brought over one of their sausages. That would have brought the puppy straight to him, for sure. Rounding a corner of the park's public toilet, he froze as he almost walked into the back of a woman. *I wonder if she is alive or dead,* he thought, as he stepped slowly backwards to get away from her. Whilst thinking he was being very cool like Jackie Li, he stumbled over a tree root that protruded from the ground and fell to the ground.

"Shit," he said a bit too loudly.

Looking up, he saw the dead woman was now walking towards him. He knew that the woman was in fact dead as her guts were hanging out of her stomach, and also, to his horror, she seemed to be munching on a small hairy white creature.

She ate the puppy! he thought in horror. "You bitch!" he screamed, and staggering to his feet, he pumped three shots into her chest. *Oh, crap,* he thought as the woman continued to walk towards him. What did Harry say? Oh, yes, head shots. Carefully lining the shot up the way Dad had taught him, he fired one clean shot straight through the head. She fell down instantly.

Phew! A feeling of relief, then nausea crossed his mind as he thought about the puppy. *I better get back quick,* he thought. Hopefully Harry hadn't noticed he was gone yet, he thought as he bolted back across the park and street to his front door.

As so often happens when a youngster is running, he wasn't fully aware of his surroundings, and just when he almost made it to his front door, he was yanked off his feet by a hand reaching out from the neighbours' front porch. Dear old Mrs Holland looked down at him. Dear old, dead Mrs Holland.

"Harry!" Billy screamed as their old dead neighbour bent forward over the fence to bite him.

Billy was then aware of a shadow crossing his line of sight, and then heard a comforting voice. "Here, eat this," Harry said as he blew Mrs Holland's head off with his shotgun.

Billy was then lifted up to his feet and thrown back into the room.

"There are dozens of them at the door, Harry!" yelled Jack.

Dozens! How are there that many now? Billy thought. *I only … fired a few shots in a local park and screamed at the top of my voice twice when I was supposed to be keeping quiet. Dad is going to be so angry when he gets home.*

"Billy, get the ammo and guns out of the cabinet. Now!" Harry shouted.

Billy scrambled out of the room and grabbed as many guns and gun cartridges as he could. The noise was deafening as Jack and Harry pumped shot after shot into the ugly heads that were now bashing on the front door and smashing the windows. He hesitated as he saw two long silver metal railings that were joined together by some sort of wiring. *What the hell is that?* he thought.

"Billy. Get your little arse out here now!" screamed Jack. "You are in so much shit with Dad when he gets back."

I know, Billy thought as he laid out the weaponry on the floor. Picking up his pistol, he went to join his brothers.

"No," said Harry, "you stay there and pass the ammo, do you hear me?"

"Yes, Harry," he answered meekly.

"But first, I want you to ring Dad," Harry said as he continued to fire shots at the crazed horde at the windows.

"Ring Dad!" said Billy in a panicked voice. "No way, Harry. I'd rather fight the dead men."

"You ring him now, Billy!" Harry shouted. "You can think of this as payback for what you have done. Call him now," Harry continued, "and tell him what's happening here."

"Yes, Harry," Billy replied. Slowly, he moved over to the

Holophone and dialed his father's number.

In a few moments, his father's face appeared on the holographic image. He seemed to be on an old gravel road with a bunch of mountain bike riders. He hoped he was close by.

"Hi, Dad," Billy said.

'Billy! What's that noise in the background? Is that gunshots I hear?" His father sounded a bit anxious.

"Yes, Dad. Jack and Harry are just shooting some dead people."

"What do you mean shooting dead people?" His Father was now sounding frantic. "Are they at the door?"

"Yes, Dad. But some are now trying to get through the windows."

"What do you mean getting through the windows?" His father seemed to be grabbing his chest right now.

His dad's friend Jon now stepped into the holograph. "Billy," he said, "tell your brothers that we are just five minutes away. Tell them to hold on, and that help is on its way. Okay?"

"Yes, Mr Dayton," Billy replied, and then the connection was severed.

Running back into the room, Billy noticed that the dead people his brothers had shot were now becoming a wall of bodies in front of their house.

"Reload this," said Harry as he passed over an empty gun and continued firing with a new one. "So where is Dad? Is he coming?"

"He's five minutes away, Harry. He and Mr Dayton are riding towards us now," replied Billy.

Harry fired another shot and said, "And did you tell him why we are firing guns right now?"

"No, sorry, Harry. I must have forgotten," Billy replied as he continued reloading.

Outskirts of Kingston

"We're going in right now," shouted Ray.

Jon was trying to calm him down. For a moment there, he thought he was going to have a heart attack.

"We can't just rush right in there. We have no weapons to defeat dozens of the dead," he said.

"They are my sons. We can bloody well try," Ray insisted.

Jon paced as he thought. "So the dead are attracted to noise, so they all should be congregating or moving to your house right now."

"Yes, I know," said Ray, hands gripping at his mountain bike.

"How long do you think the ammo will last?" Jon asked.

"I have a lot stacked away. They should be able to keep firing for another half an hour or so."

"Half an hour?" said Jon, stunned. "How much ammunition do you keep in your house?"

"Enough," Ray said with gritted teeth. "It's a hobby of mine. Anyway, I don't see anyone complaining now that my boys have enough weapons to survive the apocalypse."

At this word, Reverend Rainswood's ears pricked up.

Not now! Jon thought.

At a steadying hand from Mary, the reverend decided to keep quiet. Wise girl, that Mary.

He wished he had time to think of a detailed plan, but he didn't, so now was the time to throw the dice. He knew Sarah wouldn't like it.

"All right, listen up, everybody. This is how we are going to play this," he started. "Mary, the reverend, Dog, Sarah, and Nick are going to move directly across the highway and hide in the bushlands and keep heading south to the Huon."

Sarah started to interject, but Jon held up a hand. She didn't say anything, but the look she gave him told him he was in for a good talking to. If not yelling. He had never seen Sarah angry before, but that didn't mean that she could not chuck a tantrum as good as the next person.

"Sarah and Nick have knives, so if you see any of the dead on the highway, leave them to do the killing." He looked at Sarah, who still looked angry, but he felt a moment of panic that he wouldn't be there to protect her. "I have your number on my Holophone, so get to safety in the bush and wait on my call. We will catch up." Turning to Dave, he said, "You wait here for ten minutes at least, and by that time, most of the dead should be at the Beasley house. Hopefully, you should have a clear run to get your girlfriend. You can either join us later to the south or you can hole up in your house; it's your call."

"Thanks, Jon," Dave replied. "I'll see what Christine says when I see her." He then moved off to make a Holophone call to her home.

"Me and Ray are going to ride off directly to the house in five minutes," Jon continued.

Ray nodded in approval at this, but Jon thought this was going to be the longest five minutes of Ray's life.

Turning to the biggest group, Jon said, "Well, you guys better head off now. Remember, get across the highway, head up the road, but as soon as you can, get into the trees for cover."

"You're not budging from this plan, are you, Jon Dayton?" Sarah said in a tight voice.

The reverend and Mary moved away at the tone of her voice.

Ray called Nick and Dog over to him. No doubt he was placing Dog in Nick's care and was giving him strict instructions on how to handle him.

"And what master plan do you have to get through the dead and into the house?" she continued.

"I haven't thought of that yet. The Beasleys have lots of guns, so I'm thinking we may have to shoot our way out."

Ray looked over as if about to say something, then decided the better of it and kept talking to Nick.

"Do you know how to fire a gun?"

"No, but I'm a quick learner," he replied.

"And whilst you are running into danger, you are just sending me away like a child," she replied.

"You are in danger as well," said Jon.

Looking over at the highway, he noticed there were dead people walking around between the cars, but only a few, so they should be okay.

She was starting to look really angry now.

"You know that I'm heading away from trouble," she said in a really tight voice now, "and you are heading into a swarm of dead people."

"I have to go, Sarah," Jon pleaded. "Ray is not thinking straight with his kids and all. I have to watch his back."

She just kept looking at him for a long moment with that angry face, and then suddenly strode up to him, grabbed him by the back of the head, lowered his face, and kissed him. He thought she was going to hit him at first, but instead, she was kissing him. Really kissing him. Jon was so shocked he couldn't move, but in a few moments, he was kissing her back. All his built-up feelings of the day, all the feelings he'd had for her over the years were now released as he felt her mouth on his and her body pressed against his. This was not a tentative first-date type of kiss. This was a lover's kiss.

Finally, after God knows how long, they stopped kissing and just stood there, face-to-face. Jon was breathing like he had just run a marathon, and he was pleased to see that Sarah was breathless as well. Looking into his eyes, she said, "You come back to me, Jon Dayton. Do you hear me?"

"Of course I will," he said in between breaths, looking back into those lovely green eyes.

She took a quick glance downward. "Besides, you have a lot of work to do," she said, grinning, and walked away.

What did she mean by that?

He walked over to Nick and Ray. Nick seemed to be laughing behind his hand, and Ray said, "I know we are going to Kingston, Jon, so there is no need to point to it."

And what did he mean by that? Nobody was making any sense now.

It was only when he tried to sit on his bike that he realised what they were on about.

Well, that's embarrassing.

But it had been a crazy day, he remembered, whilst making certain adjustments, and ignoring the sniggers.

Soon, all the groups had positioned themselves in the direction in which they were headed, and the seriousness of the situation settled on them all.

"Well, I guess it's time to go," Jon said, looking over at Sarah. He had this strong urge to run over and take her in his arms again.

The entire group then said goodbye and good luck to each other. Nick and Dave shook hands. Ray gave Dog a cuddle. But Sarah just smiled at him with tears in her eyes, and turned and walked away.

What am I doing? I should be protecting her, not letting her leave on her own like this.

He fretted as they crossed the highway and moved on to the road headed towards the Huon. The few dead walking aimlessly around didn't seem to notice them as they made it safely across. Dog was the only one who looked back occasionally as he walked alongside Nick.

"Well, Dave, I guess this is it," said Jon. "Remember, wait at least five minutes, and then you should have a fair chance of making it."

"I've got my knife. I'll be okay," Dave said, and then gave Jon and Ray each a big back-slapping hug.

"Take care of yourselves, my friends. It's been a real trip," Dave said as Jon and Ray slowly rode off towards Kingston.

"Do you think we'll ever see him again?" Ray said as the left him behind.

"I hope so," replied Jon. "I hope we get to see them all again."

Sarah!

It felt like he had an empty hole in his chest, as he and his mate Ray rode into Kingston.

The Battle of Kingston

The streets are empty, Jon thought, as they cycled down the main road into Kingston's town centre. He wondered where the people were. How many survived? Are they just all holed up in their houses like Dave's girl, Christine? He noticed no movement at all as they cycled past the local shopping centre and entered the suburban streets.

How are we to survive this? Is this the end of humanity?

Yesterday, he had been complaining about how humans were ruining the environment. Now Mother Earth had a good chance of cleaning itself up. Was this someone's plan? He looked into the sky and … yes, he could still see the comets, if he looked hard enough. But why couldn't the cameras detect what was obviously in the sky?

Well, if it was some sort of diabolical plan by some weird

scientists or world power, it wasn't for him to find out. All he had to do was get Ray and his kids to safety, head for Sarah, and then the Huon. He wondered if the people down there had formed some sort of resistance. Sarah's mum had probably stood at the barricade at Grove and glared at the dead until they decided this woman was too tough to eat and walked away. And how did the dead eat the living so easily? He had seen bite marks some people gave each other in the heat of a sporting battle or pub brawl, but these dead people bit into a human body like it was a piece of chocolate cake.

He suddenly heard the distant sound of gunfire, and his thoughts returned to the matter at hand.

"Ray. We better slow down now," he said.

"What! I can't slow down now. We are so close," Ray replied.

"That's why we need to slow down," Jon said. "We can't just blunder in there. We will just get killed, and what good would that do your kids?"

At the mention of his kids' safety, Ray slowed down as they neared his home street.

Slowing their bikes to a halt, Jon and Ray took a quick glance around the corner that led to his street. It was a disaster. Fifty metres in front of them, there must have been hundreds of dead packing the street, which was at least two hundred metres long.

"Shit, shit, fucking shit!" Ray growled quietly. "How the fuck are we going to get past these fuckers?"

Jon took another look at the scene. Ray's house was two hundred metres away to the east, but looking in the opposite direction, it also continued for roughly another two hundred metres to the west. It was a long, straight road, and the road to the west was dead men free. Across the road, a side street was empty as well.

"All right, Ray. I have a plan."

"Not one of your sensible ones, I hope," replied Ray.

"No. You will like this one. It involves me doing something very stupid," Jon replied with a grin.

The Holophone was a wonderful new piece of technology. Everybody loved it. But unfortunately, only the rich and powerful could afford to use it regularly. It did, however, have a number of other handy application uses, which included a noisy alarm that would go off is someone entered the wrong security pin number more than three times, and a megaphone that the user could use if they were in any sort of emergency. Well, they were in as big a trouble as anybody had been for quite a while, so Jon rode his bike out and up the middle of the street to stop ten metres behind the dead. "Hey, mother fuckers. My name is Jon; how all you dead people doing on this fine day?"

The first hundred or so of the dead slowly turned around to face him as he rolled slowly backwards. That's not what he needed, so he turned the volume up as far as it went and said, "Listen to me, you heart-dead pieces of shit. I said, how you all doing?" The volume of the noise was frightening. *These things should be illegal*, he thought. *I feel like I've burst an eardrum.* But it had the desired effect, as the mass of the dead now started walking towards him. He had sent Ray off a few minutes earlier down the side street. The plan was for him to distract as many of them as possible, and Ray, who had circled the block, was to call the kids and ask them not to shoot him as he entered their house from across the park.

"Well, I'm doing okay, if you're interested," he said as he continued rolling backwards on his push bike. "Had my first kiss with the girl of my dreams today." Yep they were all following him now. He could see Ray now in the distance; he looked to have been rejoined with his boys.

To tell the truth, Jon was feeling pretty invincible right now. He had gotten everyone safely out of Hobart. He had his first kiss with the woman he loved. *Love!* In his shock, he dropped the Holophone. "Shit," he said as he looked at the smashed disk on the ground. He then noticed that the moaning of the dead wasn't entirely coming from in front of him. Slowly turning around, he saw a large group of dead about ten metres behind him. They had appeared from around the corner, where Ray and Jon had just been and had been creeping up on him whilst he was shouting the roof down. And now he was in the middle. Trapped!

Ray smashed the last of the dead outside his house with another garden stake. *Hmm, very handy, these things,* he thought. Then he surveyed the hundreds of bodies that surrounded his house.

Well, the garden will need a bit of fixing, and is that our headless neighbor, Mrs Holland, lying at the front doorstep?

"Boys!" he shouted. "Good shooting." He had never liked that bitch.

Harry, Jack, and Billy rushed out of the house, shouting, "Dad!" as they all embraced in a big hug.

"Okay, now who is the one who didn't keep quiet like I told you?" he said, looking straight at Billy.

"I tried to find a puppy," Billy replied in a forlorn voice, his head down. "A woman ate it."

"Well," said his father, "I think I may have found a new dog for the family."

Billy's eyes lit up at that.

"Dad," said Jack, "why is your friend Jon talking about kissing some girl?"

Ray strode back out onto the street and saw that Jon was leading the dead away from them, like planned. But behind him, there was another group walking towards him.

"Quick, boys, get the weapons out. The day is not over," he said. "Harry, bring out the special gun."

Well, pride often goes before a fall, Jon thought. Kingston was a big place. It was stupid to think that there were only a thousand of these dead things. The lack of 'alive' humans suggested there may be as many as ten thousand of the dead walking around. They could have been congregating in any number of areas. Who knows what other battles were happening in this place. He just might have sent Dave to his death, he thought with guilt and pain. Grabbing his knife, he prepared to die. *Sarah, I'm so sorry,* he thought as the two groups of dead moved towards him.

It was then that he heard a high-pitched whistling sound. *What was that?* The dead had stopped as well.

"Jon," Ray called out, "lie down on the ground."

What? Why did he want him to lie down? Looking up the road, he saw Ray and his sons. They all looked to be carrying some serious weaponry, but Ray was holding something quite strange-looking on his hip. It appeared to be two long silver metal railings with a hollow centre in the shape of an old Gatling gun. They all had earmuffs on as well.

"Trust me," Ray shouted.

He did trust Ray. He was trouble, but he was his mate. So Jon lay down on the road.

"Oh, and it's going to be loud," said Ray.

Loud! How loud? Jon thought as he covered his ears. Then, suddenly, as he looked up, the air seemed to catch on fire as traces of light sped across his view. He noticed the dead were falling around him. But not just from shots in the head; their bodies were literally exploding.

Covered in gore, he was still aware that he hadn't heard any noise yet, and then, *Boom!* A massive noise assaulted his ears as he felt his body vibrate off the ground. It sounded like a chainsaw.

And just as quick as that, the noise stopped. It might have taken all of two seconds, at the most.

What the hell had just happened?

"Can I get up now?" he said. Or maybe he shouted because his ears were ringing so badly.

"Yeah, mate, you can get up," Ray replied.

Staggering to his feet, he saw the three Beasley boys were jumping up and down, laughing, in front of their father. He caught the words 'awesome' and 'cool' as his hearing started to return.

Jon looked down and noticed chunks of meat on the ground where the dead humans used to be. Turning around, he saw the same chunks of meat down the road. That thing must have shredded everything that was standing on a four-hundred-metre long road! *Amazing,* he thought. But then he noticed something odd about the street.

"Hey, Ray, didn't one of the shopping centres used to be there?" he said, pointing down the end of the road.

"Um, yeah," Ray replied. "It's one of the drawbacks of these things. The projectiles don't seem to stop."

"What do you mean, don't stop?" said Jon.

"Well, they do stop, but maybe after five kilometres, give or take a few hundred metres," said Ray.

Five kilometres!

"You didn't point that thing where Sarah and the others are riding, did you?" he said in a panic.

Ray hesitated. "Hmm, no, I think they are farther south by now."

"You *think* they are?" replied Jon in a rising voice.

"Yeah, I'm sure they moved farther south by the time we got here. Anyway, the shots seem to be going upwards a little. I didn't quite get the trajectory right," Ray said, sounding confident, or bluffing so Jon wouldn't get angry.

Jon looked at the damage and tried to figure out where Sarah would be right now. Surely she would be safe, unless she got all pig-headed, and decided to wait for him.

No, Jon was sure that she would be moving away from him, farther up the road. He hoped.

"Where did you get that thing?" he said, walking up to them whilst stepping around the chunks of meat. "And how does it work?"

"Well, I'm not really sure how it works," said Ray, shrugging. "It has something to do with magnetic energy or something like that. I got it off the Internet from a dodgy guy called McKay."

"Illegal?"

"Very illegal," Ray replied.

"You got to be careful, Ray. Tasmania has some of the strictest gun laws in the world," said Jon without thinking.

Ray just looked at him.

Yeah, I know. It doesn't matter anymore, Jon thought.

"Do we have enough projectiles for it, Dad?" said Harry.

"Should be enough to get us out of here, mate," Ray replied. "The metal it fires is small." He felt at his backpack. "It's the pace it picks up from these Railing thingamabobs that really causes the kick," he said and grinned.

"The way Big W exploded was awesome, Dad," said Billy.

"Well, with a bit of luck, mate, we might knock down K-Mart," he replied with a laugh and then mumbled that the local Taxman's Office could do with a bit of redecoration.

"Ray, I broke my Holophone," Jon said. "Can I borrow yours to call up Sarah?"

"The one you kissed?" piped up Billy.

"Yes, that's the one," Jon said, smiling at him.

"I'm sorry, Jon," Ray replied, "but I used up the last of my credit calling the boys just then. It's on automatic payments and I won't be able to recharge it till next payday."

Damn! thought Jon. Sarah might think he was in trouble now, especially after the noise.

"Dad," said Harry, "as much as I love the new gun, it was loud. And I mean *very* loud ..."

As if on cue, the sound of distant groaning could be heard coming from all directions.

There could be ten thousand of these things, Jon thought again.

"We better go. Ray, do you have any weapons for me?"

"Yes, I do, as a matter of fact," Ray replied. "Considering you have never used a gun before, you can be our close combat defence." He handed him over something in a wrapped blanket. Opening the blanket, Jon discovered a long sword. Removing it from the sheath, he noted it was curved and silver. It looked extremely sharp.

"Ray, is this what I think it is?" Jon asked.

"Yeah, mate, a samurai sword. I got it off the Internet from ..."

"a dodgy guy called McKay," they both finished together.

"Well, thanks, mate; it certainly is a beautiful thing," said Jon. And it was; dangerous, but a beautiful sword, nonetheless.

"Dad, are we going to live in the Huon now?" said Jack.

"Yeah, mate. We have a few friends we need to catch up to first, though," he said, looking at Jon.

Jon never considered that they might want to stay in Kingston. But society had collapsed for all he could see, and the best option was always to go somewhere remote and safe with good lands, so each of them could become as self-sufficient as possible. And Kingston was not like that, and maybe it would be that way for some time to come.

"Dad," Harry said again, but this time with a bit more urgency.

"Right you are, fellas; we're off to the Huon," said Ray.

"How far is it, Dad?" Jack wanted to know.

"About twenty kilometres," replied Ray.

"Can we take turns on the bike, Dad?" asked Billy.

"No, mate. I'm afraid we have to leave them behind. I can't fire this thing from the back of a bike, and riding leaves gaps in our defence. It's a tight formation we need to get out of here."

Jon had to agree with him on this. The young boys would no doubt ride on way ahead of them.

"Harry, you take the rearguard," said Ray. "Jon, you stay in the middle, and here are some earmuffs for you." He threw him a spare pair from his bag. Always prepared, was Ray. "Billy, on Jon's left. Jack, on Jon's right. And me, well, I get to take point," he said with a wolfish grin.

"I've packed some sausage sandwiches for the trip, Dad," said Harry, looking straight at Billy.

"Well, then. Guns, family, friends, and sausage sangas. What else does a man need?" said Ray.

Sarah, Jon thought as they walked down the road.

Two kilometres south of Kingston

Sarah wiped at her eyes as she cycled with her companions away from Kingston. *Stupid man,* she thought. *How dare he just kiss me like that and then leave me on my own. Well, I kissed him, but that doesn't matter,* she thought, half-crying again.

Poor Mary was struggling as she had to use the push bike not only for her own weight but her father's as well. The reverend was sitting on the seat, muttering about not having enough faith or something like that. He was acting stranger and stranger by the minute, Sarah thought. Nick had offered to take Mary's place, but she refused, saying her father was her burden to bear, but Sarah didn't think it was meant in the way that it first sounded. Nick had to constantly keep Dog interested in him so he didn't run off in search of Ray.

"Okay, everybody," said Sarah, panting, "we are coming to a clearing on the right that has some bush land we can take cover in."

That was the order Jon have given her, she thought sulkily. But he had said to keep on moving, so she was staying put.

"Thank Christ for that," said Mary breathlessly, earning a glare from her father.

"C'mon, Dog," said Nick, "we're almost there." The dog ran alongside Nick, tongue hanging out as he panted.

Slowing to a stop at the side of the road, they started to walk their bikes towards the bush.

Not one single car had they seen since the highway, thought Sarah. Not one. It's like the cars were all bottle-necked at the end of the Southern Outlet and nobody got past. She wondered what had happened to Mary's brother, Peter Rainswood. He had a very expensive-looking 4WD vehicle. Perhaps he made it through. Strangely, neither Mary nor her father had mentioned his name since he had bailed on them in such a cowardly way.

Once they found a secure spot with a good view of all surroundings, they sat down.

"I'm starved," said Mary.

"Here," said Nick, producing a Mars Bar from his pocket.

How long had he kept that? It must be pretty soft and soggy by now, Sarah thought. But Mary said thank you and flashed him that cute smile of hers. Nick said you're welcome in return and blushed.

Bloody hell! That should be me and Jon sitting there flirting, Sarah thought angrily. *Instead, he decided to play a superhero and go off to rescue someone.*

That was harsh, she thought after a moment. Ray's kids were in trouble and needed saving. *God, please keep them all safe,* she prayed.

"Aren't we meant to keep moving, Sarah?" said Mary.

"We can just rest up for a bit," she replied, lying. She needed to teach Jon that she was not one to be ordered around. But the truth was, by waiting here, she got to see him that much quicker.

"It's so peaceful here," she said, looking around. "You wouldn't think that the world had gone to pieces sitting here."

"Aye, the calm before the storm," the reverend rambled. "His wrath is just taking a rest."

"Please, be quiet, Father," said Mary.

"No, I will not be quiet, Daughter. It is you, as a woman, who should be quiet!" he snapped, as Mary's face paled.

Sarah didn't like the looks the reverend was giving them. He looked to be a broken man.

"And I will not sit here and watch as you flirt like a slut with this heathen," he continued, pointing at Nick, who looked back in shock.

"I think you have said enough, Reverend," Sarah said coldly. *I wish Ray was here to give him a mouthful, or maybe a good punch in the head. Calm, Sarah, just keep calm,* she thought.

"We should all stick together," she continued.

"Whores," the reverend muttered in reply and grabbed his bible to read.

Dog was suddenly very still and looking back towards Kingston.

"Oh, no," said Nick. "Do you think he has caught the scent of—"

He didn't finish the sentence as the small hill behind them exploded.

"What the bloody hell was that?" shouted Nick, grabbing Mary by the arm.

"I don't know, but we have to move now," Sarah replied, getting quickly to her feet.

"It was God's Angel of Death," the reverend shouted with glee, then started a bizarre sort of dance.

He is mad, she thought.

"Shit. The dog has gone. Ray is going to kill me," shouted Nick.

"It's not your fault, Nick," said Sarah. "The poor thing must have been terrified." *Just like me* "Now pick up your bikes, and let's get moving."

Okay, Jon, she thought, moving through the trees, *I will take your orders under advisement next time.*

"Sarah, you better call Jon now. I think this is an emergency," Nick said, whilst Mary and the reverend followed.

"Okay. I can call him whilst we move," Sarah replied.

But once she dialed the number, she found there was no response.

"Nick," she said, starting to get a little anxious. "It's not working."

"Hang on," said Nick, as he looked closely at the disk. "I think the response mechanism says that the disk you are calling is damaged."

"What do you mean, damaged?" she replied, feeling a chill inside her chest.

"Wait a moment. I need to do some hacking," he said as he brought out a small Internet pad from his jacket pocket. He then plugged the disk into the Internet socket.

"You see," he said as he typed rapidly on the pad, "people think that the Holographic Projection is only on when you use the Holophone to call someone." He continued typing on for a few more seconds, before he continued, "But the holographic image is always on and are always being watched."

"By whom?" said Mary.

"By the same people who monitor your emails and Holonet usage," Nick replied.

"The government," she said quietly.

"Yes, Mary. And by hacking into Jon's phone and the government surveillance department, which should be in disarray as much as the rest of the world, I should be able to bring up the last image it had before it was damaged or destroyed."

Sarah's heart was starting to race as Nick kept typing away.

"And here we are," he said as the bright holographic image of Jon appeared before them.

"Well, what is he doing?" said Mary.

"I don't know. It looks like he dropped the disk," Nick said.

Yes, Sarah thought, *he looks like he is staring down at the disk in shock. I wonder what he was thinking when he dropped it.*

"I can't see anybody around him. Shouldn't Ray or the kids be near him?" she said aloud.

"Well, a mate of mine on the Holonet showed me this trick where you can expand the field of viewing from the two-metre radius to twenty metres," said Nick as he resumed his typing.

"Your friend is a smart fellow," said Mary.

"Yeah, he is that, but McKay can be a bit—Okay, here we go," Nick said as the field of view expanded to twenty metres each way.

"Oh, no!" said Mary, grabbing onto Nick's arm.

Sarah just stood in shock as the image view showed Jon surrounded by hundreds of the dead.

"What is he doing, you asked, Mary?" cackled the reverend. "He's dying, that's what he is doing."

Sarah burst into tears.

The K-Mart store exploded as Ray shot another round into the dead, or rather, through the dead, and into the shopping centre, which was about five hundred metres away. Jon wondered whether the Taxman's Office was next.

"Ray. You have to keep the shots down," shouted Jon.

"What?" Ray shouted back.

"Keep the shots down. Otherwise, there will be nothing left of this place," Jon replied.

There was nothing much left already. It was starting to remind Jon of a village in the Middle East during one of their decade-long wars.

Ray took off his earmuffs and stopped for a breather. The dead ones were not within a kilometre as far as he could tell. But the boys had sharp eyes and would yell out if any arrived.

"I'm sorry, mate, but if I keep the shots at a steady level, I can take out more of them. But if I lower the gun, the projectiles might explode too close to us. It's a small margin of error," he said.

He was right, Jon thought, nodding. The gun had taken out hundreds, if not thousands, of the dead ones. It was just his worry that a person may be hiding in some building or house that Ray was demolishing. Plus, he didn't like seeing one of his hometowns destroyed like this.

"We need to get them in a bottleneck and finish them off as much as we can," said Jon.

"All right, may I suggest the top of Butterworth Street, which looks down on Kingston?"

"As good as any," Jon replied.

"Okay, then." Turning, he shot a volley through the nearby Taxman's Office. "It's quicker this way," Ray said with a grin.

What the hell was happening in Kingston? Nick thought. It looked like Godzilla had come to town with all the building walls crashing to the ground and that weird wailing noise.

Nick had to keep Sarah moving. After seeing the last photo of Jon, she seemed unable to stop crying. He had to urge her onwards, and only by telling her that her mother was waiting for her was he able to keep her moving forward.

"The Lord has spoken; the Lord had spoken," the reverend raved as they finally reached the road.

"Shut up, Father," Mary pleaded.

"I told you, girl. You must be silent and obey," he raved.

"I don't care what you or your stupid bible says," said Mary in despair.

"What did you say?" In a rage, the reverend slapped Mary's face hard. As she cried out, he raised his hand to strike her again until Nick stepped between them and punched the reverend square in the face.

"The Lord spoke to me, and he asked me to tell you to shut the fuck up!" Nick shouted at the reverend who was now lying flat on his back. "Not only was your son a coward," he continued, "so are you." There was nothing more disgusting in Nick's mind than a man hitting a woman.

Sarah and Mary looked at Nick in stunned silence.

That was the first time I have ever hit anybody, Nick thought. *I wish I had done that to the bullies at school. It might have saved me a lot of grief.*

The reverend crawled back up and snarled at him with his bloodied, broken nose, and he seemed to be squaring off with him.

Nick considered going for his knife, when the sounds of groans came from out of the trees.

Without Dog to warn them, the dead people were nearly on top of them before they even knew they were there.

Damn, Nick thought. *The noise of whatever is happening in Kingston is attracting all the walking nightmares from the bush.*

"They are coming for you," the reverend spat out.

It was then that Nick did something that would haunt him for the rest of his life.

"Only a true priest of God can be unharmed by the dead," he said quietly.

The reverend looked shocked at first, but in his madness, a broad smile came across his bloodied face. Turning around, he walked towards the dead with his arms open wide and began proclaiming from the bible. He only managed to recite two verses before he was bitten in the face, then they dragged down, screaming, as the dead began to rip open his stomach.

Forgive me, Mary, he thought, as he ran to his companions, shouting at them to ride on. Mary and Sarah soon took off on their mountain bikes, with Nick riding close behind. In a daze, Nick still noticed that Mary now rode a lot quicker.

For fifteen long minutes, Jon watched as Ray fired volley after volley into the mass of dead people, who, in turn, just kept on walking up towards them at the edge of Kingston. What were they doing? If their brains were still working, why didn't they realise they are walking into a meat grinder? But no, they just kept coming at them, groaning and moaning in their mind-numbing tone. And the other ones in other areas of Kingston were attracted to the noise, so they decided to join in on the fun. During this slaughter, Jon noted that none of the dead were young children. The thought filled him with grief. Where were they? Did the dead eat the young and infants first?

It was only when Ray finally stopped firing that he started to believe that all the dead people were gone. The scene below was of blood and utter destruction. It made him ill to look at it.

"Are they all gone now, Dad?" said Jack, taking off his earmuffs.

"I think so, Son," Ray replied. "Most of them, anyway. But I think now is the time to move on, as the ammo for this thing is running pretty low."

Good, Jon thought. Now he could catch up to Sarah.

"Dad," Billy shouted whilst pointing, "look, a dog!"

They all turned around as a black-and white sheepdog came running down the road towards them.

That dog looks familiar, Jon thought.

It looked very familiar, he realised, as a feeling a dread came over him. As Dog passed him, he took off up the road at a run.

"C'mon, boys, we have to follow Jon," said Ray just as Dog came bounding up to him.

They lost sight of Jon for some time, but as they crossed over a small rise in the road, they saw him in a battle with a least a dozen of the dead. He seemed to be standing over a half-eaten corpse, Ray thought with a scare.

"Harry, can you take a shot from here?" he asked his son. "Only the ones on the outside mind," he cautioned.

"Yes, Dad," said Harry as he pulled out a rifle.

Harry took head shots of the dead in a slow and careful manner. One by one, he culled the group down to a smaller size. The ones in the middle, however, seemed to be getting cut to pieces by an erratic swordsman. Limbs were falling, and heads were being decapitated, but finally, Jon stood there resting on his sword with his head down as the dead lay still.

Ray asked his kids to stay where they were and walked up to him alone.

"Mate, are you all right?" Ray said quietly.

"It was the bloody reverend," he said, panting, as he pointed to the mess on the ground. "First, I got Dave killed. Now that mad bastard of a priest. What if … what if …" He looked up at Ray with panic in his eyes.

"We don't know that yet, mate, about Dave or Sarah. Nick is a good lad; perhaps he took her to safety. That girl Mary is a smart cookie. And Sarah is probably the smartest of us all," said Ray. He then pointed out the obvious.

"Have you found the mountain bikes yet?"

"No. No, I haven't," Jon said, looking around.

"Well, who do you think took them, then, these dead fuckers?" replied Ray, pointing at the limbs and heads on the road.

A small part of Jon's mind noted that Ray only swore when his kids weren't close by. A small part of Ray's mind noted that the eyes on those severed heads were still looking at him.

"You're right," Jon said, wiping his eyes as he straightened up. "We better keep going then." As quick as that, he turned around and strode down the road.

Ray rolled his eyes. *Love does addle your brain sometimes,* he thought, and then turned and beckoned to the ones he loved as his three boys and Dog came running down the road.

He looked down at the corpse of the reverend. "So he still didn't show up, then?" he said.

The reverend didn't reply, just looked at him with dead eyes. His family then arrived at his side.

"Is everything okay, Dad?" said Billy, who was constantly hugging his new dog.

"Yes, mate. We're now on our way to the Huon," Ray replied.

"Who or what was that, Dad?" asked Jack, pointing at the jacket and bloodied carcass on the road.

His kids had not bat an eyelid at today's destruction. Once he got them settled, he needed to talk to them about what they had seen and make sure none of them suffered any long-term effects. Then he needed to sit down and have a few beers and make sure he had suffered no long-term effects either.

"A very strange man," Ray replied. "Nobody worth stressing over, Jack. Better men and women have died today."

"He looks a bit stressed, Dad," said Harry, nodding at Jon, as they all watched him decapitate a couple of more stray dead people as he marched straight down the road.

Hmm, Ray thought, *he's getting pretty good at that.*

"Women can do that to you, son," he replied. "Women can do that."

The ride to the Huon consisted of periods of flat roads, then a long slope downhill, which was followed by a long haul upwards as they moved over the mountain that separated the Kingston area from the Huon. Nick urged his companions to build up as much speed as they could on the downhill slope so they could at least get a good head start on the uphill climb. Once the momentum stopped, then began the hard slog.

I wish I had another Mars Bar, Nick thought.

Looking over at his companions, he noted they were both crying a little. *What do I say? Do I offer some sort of condolence?*

"I'm sorry, Mary," he said, starting to pant at the climb.

"That's okay, Nick," she replied, starting to sound breathless herself. "As you probably noticed, he wasn't the best of fathers. Mum ran away years ago. I just wish she had taken me with her." She sounded wistful. Looking at Nick, she said firmly, "You did what you had to do" and then faced forward and kept peddling.

Does she know what I said? I'm sure I said it quietly to the reverend, he thought. *No, it must have been about the punch, that's all.*

Turning to Sarah, he said, "I'm sorry about Jon. He was a good man."

"Thank you," said Sarah. But she was looking straight ahead with such concentration that he knew not to push the matter further. They rode in silence until they reached the plateau of the hill. There, they decided to have a rest before they continued on the descent. With no traffic, and hopefully no dead to avoid, they should be in Grove in no time at all.

Looking up at the sky, Nick noted the moon was rising. *What a day,* he thought. It had started off as just another day in the office, then turned into the utter destruction of society.

"Sarah," he said whilst looking into the sky.

"Yes," she replied, turning weary eyes toward him.

"The comets have stopped."

Jon was exhausted but kept pushing on as they finally reached the Grove barricade. They had a few skirmishes with the dead on their long walk over the mountain. But the sword was so light in his hands, and once he got used to the basic moves needed to defend and kill, he found that the dead were just a minor hindrance in his search for Sarah.

When Ray had noticed that the mountain bikes were gone, he allowed himself to hope that she was alive, but why then wasn't she waiting for him? Every corner they turned, he hoped that she would be there, but he was disappointed again and again. He had this horrible feeling that he had walked past her as she lay injured or that she was dead in the bush land somewhere and he would never see her again. But he held on to the plan that their destination was Grove, and that no matter how long it took, they would both find each other there.

"I'm tired, Dad," Billy said.

Jon felt a moment of shame that he had pushed the boy so hard. The older boys, Jack and Harry, had handled the journey fine, but young Billy was only twelve years old.

"We are almost there, Son," their father replied. Ray was handling the journey well too. He may have put on a bit of weight after he retired, but he was still physically fit. Dog was just enjoying himself as he walked with Ray and Billy, wagging his tail happily.

Coming up to the barricade, Ray put away his monster-killing gun in his carrying bag and said something to the boys about saving it for a rainy day.

"Hold up there, and don't move," a voice came from behind the barricade.

"Why? And can you turn that music down a bit? It's enough to wake the dead," said Ray.

"Ha, that's very funny, big man. Just wanted to make sure you're not dead, that's all," said the voice.

"Well, do I look like I'm dead?" said Ray. "I may look tired, but I've still got the strength to come over there and pound your head in if you don't let us through."

"All right, all right, keep your trousers on," the voice replied.

Jon just wanted to jump the barricade and keep on walking, but he had to ask.

"Have you seen a girl by the name of Sarah Butler come through? She's a slim girl with auburn hair. Should be travelling on mountain bikes with a young girl of sixteen and a young geeky kid of eighteen?"

"No, I can't say that I have," the voice replied. "A number of people have been through, but I've only been here for an hour or so."

"She related to Jane Butler?" another voice said.

"Yes, she's her daughter," Jon replied.

"Oh, bloody hell, we definitely would have let her in, then," the other voice said.

"Scary woman," the first voice said.

They all turned around as they heard a groaning noise from up the hill.

"Can you let us in now? We look to have company," Jon said.

"Hold your horses, mate; they only run at you if you start to run," the voice said.

Jon had never thought of that, but remembering what had happened in the city, it did make sense.

"And what happens if you stand still?" he said.

"I don't know, mate," the first voice said. "Why don't you stand there and find out?"

Jon now heard laughing from behind the barricades.

Okay, Jon thought, grinding his teeth, *it was a stupid question. I deserved that one.*

"Hey, are you Ray Beasley, used to play for the Kangas?" a third voice said.

"Yes, mate," Ray replied, expecting the usual adulation.

"I hate you. You knocked the Collingwood skipper right out," said the third voice.

"Oh, for fuck's sake," Jon snapped, "just let us in."

"Okay, all right, all right. No need to chuck a tanty like that," said the first voice. "Grogan, open the barricade for these people please, mate. I'm sure they're not dead, judging by the potty mouth of this bloke."

Finally, they let the group through.

"You lot just head up to the Community Hall. It's just a five-minute walk, straight ahead. They have food and shelter there. Also, the councilors and policemen are there, trying to work out what we're all to do for the next few months," said a middle-aged man with a beanie. He must have been the first voice.

"Oh, and here," said another as he passed them all a banana and an orange each. "On the house, and enjoy them, as this may be the last time we see them for a while."

Jon and his company said thank you and then pressed on the last five minutes of their journey.

In the background, he heard the noise of a rifle being fired.

"Oh, nice shot, Robbo," said the first voice.

Sarah was asked to help cook some food in the Community Hall for the stragglers who were still coming to the barricade for shelter and safety.

Her mother had embraced her on her arrival and consoled her on the loss of Jon. But she soon had her working in the kitchen, as she thought Sarah needed to be active to help distract her from her grief.

Cutting onions, she thought. Her mother had her cutting onions, which was probably a way of covering up the tears that kept coming to her eyes.

Jane Butler was ruling the roost; decisions needed to be made, and nobody was better at making decisions than her mother, and also badgering people into following her decisions. Even right now, she could hear her mother in a heated argument with somebody.

Nick and Mary had taken the offer of one sleeping bag each and were now fast asleep in the corner of the hall, where a lot of other refugees were sleeping too.

Refugees.

Tasmania was blessed with a mostly peaceful past; it was hard to think that now so many people were bereft and lost. So many people had died.

Jon, she thought, as tears ran down her cheeks again.

"Sorry, Miss, have you been crying?" a young boy said as he came into the kitchen area.

"No, of course not," Sarah lied, wiping at her eyes. "Just the onions."

"The lady at the front said to come down here and ask for some food," the boy continued.

"Yes, that was probably my mother," Sarah said.

The boy looked at her for a moment. "Oh, yeah, you can tell; you look a lot alike."

"I know, I've been told that quite a few times over the years," she said, smiling back at him.

"Dad reckons I look like him, but most people say I look a lot like Harry."

Sarah paused for a moment, looking at the boy, thinking how he looked vaguely familiar.

"How old are you?" she asked.

"Twelve."

"My goodness, you are very tall for a twelve-year-old," she said.

"Yes, we are all tall in our family. I'm not quite as tall as Dad, though. But I soon will be. He said it's in my Beasley genes."

Sarah froze. *It's the boy from Ray's Holophone.*

"Your dad is Ray Beasley?"

"Yep, that's my dad."

"And he is here now?"

"Yep," he said, nodding. "Dad and Jon are out there right now, arguing with your mother."

Dad and Jon?

Sarah started to feel faint, and her breath was now coming out in gasps.

"Jon Dayton?" she managed to say.

"Yes. We had a massive battle in Kingston. But Dad killed all the dead men and saved Jon, too," Billy replied proudly.

She struggled for breath as her mind went numb, and all she could see was a blurred image of the boy as her eyes filled with tears.

"Are you okay?" he asked.

Sarah couldn't speak, so she just shook her head.

"Dad!" the boy shouted. "I'm sorry, but I think I made this lady cry."

"What do you mean cry?" said Ray as Sarah heard his loud footsteps come closer.

Sarah saw his big frame step through the doorway.

"Oh, dear, Sarah Butler, Jon has been so worried about you," said Ray, grinning. "Your mother wouldn't tell us where you were until we apologised for losing you."

She saw Ray and the boy leave the kitchen as Ray bellowed, "Jon, she's here!"

Sarah heard fast-running footsteps, and then saw the man she thought was dead standing in the kitchen doorway.

A few seconds later, she was gently being held in the arms of that man, who was saying, "Sarah, I love you. I love you, Sarah," over and over.

Two men aged in their sixties were quietly waiting for one of the scouts to arrive. The two men had been through so much together that their friendship had grown beyond the measure of mates and into a state where they both considered themselves to be brothers.

"You still wearing that wanker's hat?" said Ray, grinning.

"Listen, Ray, this was a present from my eldest daughter, you know," Jon said, knowing Ray was trying to take the tension out of what was going to happen today.

It wasn't exactly a present as meant in the olden times. Ash, his daughter, had come across the hat whilst looking through the clothes collected and stored from before the Collapse, as they now called that fateful day twenty years ago.

"Anyway," he continued, "at least I'm not wearing a possum on my head."

"C'mon, mate, I look like Daniel Boone and Davy Crockett," said Ray.

"Those men wore a raccoon hat, which looked kind of cool. You, old mate, are wearing a dead possum on your head," he replied with a smile.

Ray laughed as he stood there in furs and wool made from various animals that most people wore nowadays, and then bent down to scratch Dog behind the ears. This was actually Dog the Third, to be exact. Whilst retaining the black-and-white colour of Dog the First, this 'grandchild' of a sheepdog stood at about a metre high and must have been bred from a small horse, Jon thought.

Jon took off his hat and scratched at his grey hair, wondering when the scouts would come back.

He loved this hat. When he was a kid, his father, Len Dayton, who was a huge fan of the old western movies of Hollywood's heyday, made his son watch as many western movies as he could, and Jon grew up to love them as much as his father did. There were so many good actors in that day, but there was one actor Jon thought was the best, and his name was Clint Eastwood. Jon loved all his films, but one of his favourites was a film called *Pale Rider*. In that film, he wore a hat that was identical to the one Jon now wore. When Ash turned up with this hat and presented it to him, along with a lovely long coat, which he also now wore, Jon smiled, kissed his daughter's cheek, and said thank you in a calm voice. But the little kid inside him, the ten-year-old boy who used to love the Eastwood films, was jumping up and down and thinking how very cool it would be to wear this hat whilst riding in the middle of Grovetown.

Placing the hat back on his head, his hands nervously ran over his sword on his hip and the bow and arrow slung across his shoulders. Since the day when gun ammunition ran out, Jon had organised all of the citizens of Grovetown to be trained in the bow and arrow to defend their livestock from predators, and to defend themselves, their family, and the community as a whole from bandits and zombies.

Zombies! A word used by the young ones to describe the dead who had ruined Jon's world. Probably a word found in school, which was now taught by Nick Fields and his wife, Mary.

Where are the scouts? he thought. He worried at what was taking them so long. Had they been caught? He worried every time he sent the scouts out to locate any of their enemies. He worried most of all because his son, Jesse, was with them.

As if on cue, one of the scouts arrived and informed them that the bandits had been found.

"They are hiding in an abandoned wooden warehouse about one kilometre west of here, sir," a tall blonde-haired girl named Rachael said, saluting.

"Do they look like they are staying put?" said Jon, as it was only midday by his reckoning.

"That's the strange thing, sir," Rachael replied. "They sound like they are drunk as skunks."

Ray's ears perked up at the mention of drunkenness. The fact that beer was no longer around was the biggest tragedy of the Collapse in Ray's book. However, what they considered to be alcohol in this day and age should put them at a distinct advantage.

"Tell Jesse we're on our way," said Jon.

"And you keep your head down, young missy," said Ray.

'Will do, Pop," replied his granddaughter, and flashing him a smile, the sixteen-year-old girl disappeared into the bush land. Whilst Ray was protective of his sons and grandsons, his protectiveness of his only granddaughter went to a whole new level.

"And watch after your brother," he shouted, hoping she would hear.

"Jack would kill me if the twins got hurt," he said to Jon in embarrassment, as he knew he had a loud voice.

"All right, let's go." He signaled to the fifty of his ragtag army who stood patiently waiting behind him.

Bows unslung, arrows nocked, the fifty-two men and women moved to join the ten scouts Jon had sent first.

How he had gone from working in a government job to leading a hometown militia was beyond him. When he suggested that people needed to learn to use new weapons to defend themselves, Jane Butler had seized upon this idea, and somehow, over the years, he had become Grovetown's de facto military general. He used to insist that people not salute him, but over time, people just ignored his request and saluted him anyway. The young people especially were very serious about his leadership position and insisted on being called soldiers. No doubt, the soldier idea came from Nick Field's teachings at school. He was adamant that the kids be taught their history, as he said knowing where you came from gave you a good idea as to where you are headed. Also, that mistakes of the past should help you avoid mistakes in the future. It never stopped mistakes in human history that Jon recalled, but it was an honourable notion anyway.

The militia was a rotational position of a hundred men and women of ages sixteen and over, initially formed to protect the community from zombies from outside and within. Two soldiers were always posted outside the hospital, and others made constant rounds of the Huon, just in case any zombie outbreak happened. The community was in a constant state of vigilance, as anybody who died from illness, accident, or just old age would immediately become one of the zombies and start attacking people. Thinking on this brought a tear to his eye.

There was some sort of light at the end of the tunnel in regards to this, though. As with all communities in whatever Age, children do die. Eighteen years ago, a one-year-old girl had died from a heart illness. The parents advised that hours after the child had passed, there was no zombie-like state. In the time since, there have been more youth deaths, and still no zombie reanimations occurred in them. It seemed that anybody born after the Collapse was free of the virus. Freeborn, some of the elders of the community were calling them.

As the zombie threat diminished, or at least was contained, the militia was called upon more and more to fight bandits. Scum of the earth, they were. Whilst everybody worked hard to rebuild and survive, these bastards just stole, killed, and raped their way through the countryside. All of the bandits who were caught by Jon's militia were killed and had their heads cut off and spiked as a warning to others. It was a brutal way of doing things, but these people needed to be stopped. It was in recent years that he heard rumours of a gang led by a man called Joe Mason. The rumours said he was an ex-soldier who had ruthlessly led a band of killers to the east for many years.

A few days ago, killings had occurred in the lands between Kingston and the Huon, and the survivors mentioned Mason's name. Jon sent scouts out to see if they could find this gang. They had, and this had led to where they were today.

Eighteen-year-old Jesse Dayton lay still on the ground as he hid behind some thick native vegetation fifty metres away from the old wooden warehouse. *What are they doing?* he thought. They were shouting at the top of their lungs and staggering around, barely able to walk. His father had told him about places called 'pubs' and how they were considered to be some sort of entertainment. But they all looked like they had just been beaten over the head with a large stick instead.

Jesse watched as one man ripped open a girl's top and started having sex out in the open. Was this rape? No, she looked like she was enjoying herself, not being assaulted. Dad said there were women in the gang, and no mercy was to be shown to any of them, as they were just as guilty as the men.

He also said they were 'as rough as guts'. He didn't know what that meant, but looking at the women here, he could make a good guess.

"You enjoying yourself, Dayton, you dirty perv?" Rachael whispered as she scrambled over to Jesse's side.

"No … I was … oh, shut up, Beasley," Jesse whispered back. Rachael just chuckled softly.

"Is the General coming?"

"Yes, sir," Rachael replied in a serious tone.

Jesse faltered over the sir comment. He was the leader of the scouts, but he worried that the others may think he was in this position purely based on being Jon Dayton's son. But the scouts didn't seem to mind, or if they did, they kept their opinions to themselves.

"Have your brother and Taylor gotten into position yet?" he asked.

"Yes, Taylor climbed the tree like a monkey, and Rob climbed the tree like the ape that he is," she said, smiling at him.

"What about Liam and Isaac?" he asked next.

"Yes, they both managed to get underneath the warehouse at the back. They put dried grass and wood layered with what kerosene we have left. It should go up like a tinderbox."

"Well, all we have to do now is wait, I guess," he said.

"They shouldn't be long," Rachael replied. "They may have to drag my grandfather half the way, but they should be here soon," she said, laughing quietly.

Jesse smiled too. Uncle Ray was a character; his sons were too. Harry, Billy, and Jack, Rachael's father, were all wonderful people, whom Jesse considered to be his extended family.

"Go back and tell Dad—sorry, the General—that all is ready and we will wait until he arrives."

"Okay, sir," Rachael said, then nodded at the couple going at it in front of them. "I'll leave you to your … contemplations," she whispered, and then she was gone.

Bloody Rachael Beasley, he thought. But a part of his mind noted that he could still feel the pressure of where she'd had her body pressed against his.

Jon and Ray stood at a safe distance, looking at the rectangular warehouse. Jon stood with his hand on his chin, in thought. Ray was just trying to get the possum tail out of his face, but he managed to say,

"Rachael says that the warehouse has only one exit at the side. They can't get out the back way or the two ends unless they smash the windows, so some of the boys have set a fire ready to burn at the back of the warehouse to flush them out."

"Any ideas as to what numbers we are looking at?" replied Jon.

"They think about thirty, all up."

That's strange, Jon thought. Surely from what he had heard there needed to be more than that to cause such carnage.

Jon nodded and looked at Ray. "So ten at the back, five at each end, and thirty at the door, then?"

"That should do it, I think," said Ray.

"Oh, and Ray," said Jon.

"Yes, mate?"

"Send in the dog," Jon said, smiling.

Jesse lay there watching the bandits staggering around, shouting and swearing. The couple that were still 'doing it' up against the side of the building were being encouraged by others standing not five metres away. This definitely was not his sort of thing. *Maybe I'm a romantic,* he thought drily.

He suddenly heard panting noises coming from behind, and on turning, noticed Ray's pony-sized dog walking up. Looking around the building, he saw shadows moving behind the tree line. Rachael moved up next to him again and said, "Showtime", with her bow at the ready.

Jesse wasn't sure what that actually meant, and probably neither did Rachael, but he presumed it meant that the ambush was about to commence and unslung his bow.

"What's Uncle Ray's dog doing here?"

"Just a diversion," said Rachael.

They heard a 'garumph' sound as Dog wandered past them. Tongue lolling out of his mouth and slobber going everywhere, he walked out into the clearing and then lay down when he reached within twenty metres of the warehouse.

Jesse then heard shouts of, "What the fuck is that?" and "Is it a small horse or a dog?" as Dog rolled over and started scratching his back in the dirt.

These shouts brought out about twenty more of the bandits. *That's nearly all of them*, he thought.

Jon watched as two dozen or so roughly dressed, filthy-smelling scum stood there looking at Dog. He wondered which one was Joe Mason. Glancing to his left, he saw his son lying low on the ground near Rachael Beasley. Both had their bows at the ready. He then gave a signal, which was repeated down the line and around the back of the warehouse.

Suddenly, he could smell smoke, and within moments, a good-sized fire was coming from the back of the building.

"Drop them!" he shouted, and as the bandits looked over at the sound of his voice, thirty arrows flew through the air, striking most of them in the chest. Some of his soldiers, however, were good enough to shoot out people's eyes, saving a second kill. He heard screams and the smashing of windows from the back and sides of the warehouse. Moving around to the side of the building, he saw a few bandits trying to escape through the windows. The orders were to wait until they had jumped from the window before taking them out, due to the fact there may have been two of them trying to get out the same window. One of the bandits was on fire as he fell to an arrow.

There was a moment's silence, and Jon was about to give the next order when a naked woman ran out of the warehouse door screaming, "For the Mason Gang, motherfuckers" and firing a loaded machine gun at nobody in particular.

"Down," Jon screamed as they all hit the floor with bullets firing over their heads.

Where the hell did they get a gun from? I haven't seen one fired in years.

"Taylor!" Jon shouted, and a few seconds later, the silence fell again.

Scrambling to his feet, he saw that the woman with the gun lay dead on the ground with an arrow protruding from her eye.

Looking up at the trees, he saw a young girl named Taylor with wild curly hair and a cheeky grin give him the thumbs-up.

Damn, that was good shooting, he thought, as he nodded to her in gratitude.

"Brains and spikes, quickly," he yelled, and everybody came forward with their own trench knives, custom made by the town blacksmith, to finish the job before the bandits had a chance to rise as zombies.

It was so brutal to do this, he thought. Some of the bandits were still alive as they lay writhing on the ground, some with two arrows in their body. But all of Grovetown soldiers believed that stabbing a bandit's brain through the eye and decapitating them was the right thing to do, even as they lay there begging for mercy. It was an us-or-them mentality. *And here I am, giving them the orders to do it.*

What a mad world, he thought as he watched pretty sixteen-year-old Rachael Beasley bend down and drive her knife through a man's eye. She hadn't hesitated for one moment, and now brought out what looked like a butcher's knife and took off the man's head. Blood spattered all over her fur clothing as she did it. He couldn't look as his son did the same thing to the next man. What would Sarah think of her son doing this?

Taylor's cousin Liam gave a yell as one of the dead bandits started to rise as a zombie, but his younger brother, Isaac, quickly jumped on the thing and stabbed him through the eye.

"Be careful, everyone. Zombie reanimation occurs within one to two minutes," he said in a commanding voice. Or what he thought was a commanding voice. Perhaps he should try that quiet, steel voice that Clint Eastwood had. After all, he did have his hat. But he doubted that would have worked when that woman started firing her gun.

Ray came running up to Jon with Dog now following closely behind, slobbering everywhere. *How calm that dog was,* thought Jon; with arrows and bullets flying around, he just rolled on the ground, unconcerned, and then started licking his balls. *A bit like his master,* he thought, smiling to himself.

"All finished at the back, Jon," said Ray, as the warehouse began to crumble with the fire.

Jon nodded and gave out another order to make sure the fire didn't spread to the trees. Last thing they wanted was to start a bushfire whilst being stranded a few kilometres inland from the road.

"Ray, follow me for a moment," said Jon as he walked up to the naked woman.

"What do you think of that?" he pointed at the body.

"Well, she's a bit skinny for my taste," Ray started.

"No, I mean the gun," said Jon, with a smile.

Ray bent down and picked up the weapon and studied it.

"Anything unusual?" asked Jon.

"Well," checking the gun, he said, "she didn't have much ammunition nor could she shoot straight, otherwise we might all be dead, but ... holy shit, Jon, this gun looks brand new."

"Well, let's hope she didn't have access to any new ammunition," Jon said.

"Indeed," replied Ray, "but why hang on to this gun for so long?"

"I'm not sure," Jon said, looking over at the warehouse. Something was not right about the events of today, but he couldn't quite put a finger on what it was. It seemed all too easy.

Final orders were given to throw the headless bodies into the warehouse fire. And as they walked away, thirty heads of evil, lazy, and selfish men and women stayed where they were, impaled on spikes. On the ground in front of them was a placard with the name *Bandits* written in blood.

Grovetown, thirty-one kilometres south of Hobart

Rachael toyed with her long braided hair as she watched Jesse talking quietly with his father. *Such a solemn boy,* she thought. Due to the closeness of the Beasley and Dayton families, she had grown up with him for as long as she could remember, and had always thought of him as one of her brothers. It was just recently that she began to think of him in a different way.

"Penny for your thoughts?" said her Grandfather Ray, who, as always during long marches, would stay by her side and impart some of his 'sage-like wisdom' as he liked to call it, but which usually involved the telling of lots of jokes.

"Nothing worth talking about, Poppy," she said as she entwined her arm through his.

She knew she was his favourite. She had three brothers, Rob, who was her twin, and Ben, who was eight, and Sean, who was four. But being the only girl in his family, he tended to be very protective of her. He even got jealous of her maternal grandfather, Tom, whom he always referred to as 'that dickhead'.

"What does that saying mean, Pop?" asked Rob.

"Well, Bobby boy," said Ray, "a penny used to be a coin, which got replaced by cents. Well, I think it did," he mused. "Anyway, it's a saying that means I will give Rachael some money for her thoughts. It's just a phrase, my boy."

At the mention of money, Jon Dayton turned to look at them.

"What was money like, Pop?" said Rachael.

"Well, it was good when you could get your hands on it," replied Ray, "but it wasn't very well spread across the people. By the time of the Collapse, one percent of the population owned about forty percent of the money."

"So there was small number of rich people and a large number of poor," said Rob.

"Yes, yes, there was," said Ray with a touch of sadness in his voice. "Different levels of poor as well. Some couldn't afford to pay their electricity bills, some couldn't afford a place to live, so they lived on the streets, and some couldn't afford proper food and they died."

"And the rich people could have whatever they wanted with this money," said Rob, "and the poor people just had to get by on their own?"

"I'm afraid so," replied Ray.

"That doesn't sound like a very good way to live," Rachael said.

"No, it wasn't, pumpkin," he replied. "It wasn't at all."

"What was electricity like, Pop?" Rob asked.

"Bright and warm, Bobby," said their grandfather, "bright and warm."

Jon Dayton turned around at the mention of the word money. He thought it was bizarre how that little piece of paper could have ruled everybody's lives like it had. He remembered reading that there was only five to seven trillion dollars of actual cash in the world and that the rest was borrowed against people's future earnings, an IOU on future generation's debt or something like that. It seemed like countries were living in a world of numbers, of which none of it actually existed.

Now he lived in a town where money did not exist. People just worked to provide food and shelter for themselves and the rest of the community. Jobs were given by the Council to people who wanted them, not just people who wanted to make heaps of money. Nick and Mary were a prime example. They wanted to teach the kids and had a passion for it. Not because they needed a job to pay the mortgage off, but because they truly wanted to do it.

He wondered what would have happened to the illegal drug industry before the Collapse if money suddenly was declared pointless. The war on drugs, which raged for decades, would have been won overnight, as why would anybody in their right mind set up a chemical laboratory to get some poor druggie hooked if they didn't receive anything in return? Sure, some people in Grovetown grew their own dope, but it was not as if they had set up their own meth lab. The illegal Arms Dealing industry that provided weapons to tyrants around the world for centuries would have stopped as well. Huge reduction in money-based crimes such as fraud, theft, drugs, and prostitution, would have freed up jail cells for longer sentences for evil such as murderers, rapists, and pedophiles. His community was not a perfect one, but he didn't miss money. He didn't miss it at all. The thought of jails brought up a subject that had been on his mind a lot lately.

"Jesse, I need to talk to you about what happened today."

"In regards to what, Dad?" Jesse replied, looking at him with the face that Jon used to have many years ago, except Jesse had a glow about him, one that all of the freeborn had. It was as if they were healthier than the older generations.

"The bandits and what we did," Jon said.

"They needed killing, Dad," Jesse replied.

"They did, I agree. But in the olden days, people like that were sent to jail for many years. It was believed that every person deserved a second chance."

"But we have no jails, Dad, just a holding cell for drunken idiots to sleep it off."

"I know, Son. I just want you to be aware of the way things were." He was struggling to articulate his words. How could he explain a world that his son had never known? "We can't put those people in jail, because we are struggling to survive ourselves, and we don't have the manpower to watch these men and women for years. But there was an old saying of 'innocent until proven guilty'. What if some of those people we killed today were innocent of any wrongdoing?"

It was the way Jesse had beheaded that man today that was bugging him, he realised. They were all cutting them like pieces of meat, not human beings. It was barbaric.

"But they were the Mason Gang; that woman screamed it out. We've had many witnesses come forward and mention that man's name. They raped and killed many people," Jesse replied.

"But do we know that all of the people we killed today did that?" Jon said. "There could have been a captive in that warehouse. There were a few freeborn in there too. Did they do the killings? We can't be sure."

Jesse looked on with that thoughtful face of his.

"I'm not saying this as a way of changing what happened today," he continued. "I'm saying this in hope of changing things in the future. Everyone deserves a fair trial, even them, and maybe one day, we can give them one."

In Grovetown's twenty-year history, there had only been three trials: one for murder, one for rape, and one for pedophilia. This was such a small number, for a community that ranged from four thousand to one thousand members over the years, due to hunger riots, illness, and zombie and bandit attacks.

It was decided pretty early on that people like that were not to be tolerated in a place where food was scarce and discipline needed to be maintained.

Fortunately, the cases were pretty clear-cut, as the evidence was so strong. The accused, once found guilty, were beheaded and had their heads placed on spikes in the town centre as a warning.

Jon himself sat in on the jury for the pedophile case and was quite happy to wield the sword that took his head.

But he wondered about the many zombie outbreaks in the community over the years. Did they just die of illness or old age, or were they murdered beforehand? How would they ever know?

"Dad," said Jesse as they walked within a few hundred metres of home.

"Yes, Son?" he replied.

"Look." Jesse pointed.

Jon looked down at the wall of Grovetown. What started off as a simple barricade had, over the years, grown into a ten-metre-high fort-like wooden wall, which now spread for kilometres to encircle the entire town.

He saw the usual soldiers patrolling the wall and the large bell that was used to sound the alarm for the arrival of zombies or bandits. But when he looked along the top of the wall, he saw a glint of auburn hair.

"Not again." He sighed.

"She always waits for us," Jesse said.

"Well, she should be at school," Jon said, exasperated. "How does she continually wag class like that?"

"She's very sneaky, I think," said Jesse.

"Stubborn too," Jon replied. *I wonder where she gets that from,* he thought, knowing all too well that a certain grandmother's personality trait may have skipped a generation.

Walking up to the wall, the soldiers on duty opened the two-sided twenty-metre-long gate.

After entering, Jon dismissed all of the soldiers—apart from Jesse, who stood staring at Rachael as she left—and looked up at the rampart.

"Lily," he said in his best I'm-not-happy father's voice.

A few seconds later, a six-year-old girl carrying her favourite dolly and in her favourite dress stood at the top of the stairs that led from the rampart down to the ground.

"Come down here, young lady," he said. And after a moment, she walked carefully down the stairs with a very somber look on her face.

Resisting the urge to pick her up and shower her with kisses, he continued in his serious voice, "You know you can't just skip classes like that. Mr Fields would be worried about you."

She nodded at that.

"And schooling makes you smart. We all need to know as much as we can about life, Lily," he continued.

"Yes, Daddy," she said quietly, looking up at him with her mother's face.

"So promise me there will be no more waiting for me and Jesse up on the rampart."

"Yes, Daddy," she lied.

I can't help myself, he thought, and picked her up and cuddled and kissed her until she was helpless with laughter.

"So as a punishment, young lady," he continued as he held her in his arms, "we are now going to visit your Nanna Butler."

"That's not a punishment, Daddy," Lily replied.

"I didn't say it was *your* punishment, Lily."

Jesse just laughed.

Jane Butler lived in one of the original houses in the community. It was fortunate that it already had a fire stove to keep the house warm and for cooking. Most houses that had electric heating had been abandoned since the electricity supply stopped.

The community houses now varied from self-made cottages to American Indian teepees. Some houses were ingenious in the creativity, the use of old beer bottles, car tyres, and timber were sometimes combined to build a house that did the job well. Jon thought it funny how survivors of the old timber industry and green movement had combined to create such an individual town.

"So you've come to visit your old Nan for a change. That's a pleasant surprise," chastised Jane Butler as she sat on her couch, cuddling her youngest granddaughter.

Lily just looked from her grandmother to her siblings. *God, I hope she's not picking up any ideas,* Jon thought.

Ash sat to her grandmother's left, wearing her furs and holding two dead rabbits in her lap, as she had just returned with her friends from hunting in the south.

"Well, I had to hunt for some food, Nan. You know I am busy most of the time," Ash replied. She was a tallish dark-haired girl of sixteen years, who had her mother's face, and thankfully, her personality. *She was a lovely girl, his eldest daughter,* Jon thought with a smile.

"Hmmph!" said her Nan. "You should be studying at University to become a doctor or studying the law. Not running around the bush hunting for rabbits and looking after the home."

They all just looked at her in silence; she was in her seventies now, and Jon was hoping that she wasn't losing the plot.

"I know those days are gone," she snapped. "No need to look at me like I need to go to the loony bin."

Phew! Thank God for that, Jon thought.

"It's just she is too smart for this. All of the advancements women have made in the last century or more, seem to have evaporated, and now we are back to being just the homebodies."

"Some of the women fought with us today," said Jon. "They are not just delicate flowers to cook us meals."

But he agreed, it was such a shame that all of the freeborn could not get an education like he had been able to. Well, if he had wanted to; *he had actually been incredibly lazy at school,* he thought ruefully.

Nick and Mary did educate the kids well with basic stuff from the town library, but they would never have the knowledge of a surgeon or a scientist. They had fallen so far behind, technology-wise. *I was no help either, I couldn't even explain to them how a TV or radio worked. I started mentioning invisible airwaves, and the kids were looking at me like I was talking some sort of voodoo magic.*

"And how did the battle go?" said Jane, turning her sharp gaze on him. "Did you kill Mason?"

"We killed all of them. But we weren't sure what he looked like," he replied. "In hindsight, we should have taken one of the witnesses with us. But they all seemed too terrified to come at the time, and we had to move fast."

"Did we take any casualties?" Jane asked.

"No, thank goodness. But one of the women came out firing a machine gun. It could have killed us all, if not for some sharp shooting from one of our scouts. A female scout," he added.

"The woman with the gun was screaming the name Mason Gang, before she died," said Jesse.

"Did you perform your duties, Grandson?" Jane asked.

"Yes, Grandmother," Jesse replied. "Well, at least I tried."

"He did well, Jane. He did us proud," Jon spoke up as Jesse looked at his feet in embarrassment.

"A gun! Where on earth did they find a loaded machine gun, after all this time?" Jane said in a thoughtful voice.

"It was a new gun as well, but not much ammunition," Jon said. "Perhaps they came across it on one of their raids. It all was a bit strange; they were roaring drunk at midday, and there were only thirty of them."

Jane sat there for a moment in thought. Bossy she may be, but she was one of the smartest people Jon knew.

"I smell a rat," Jane finally said. "A Tyrant who ruled the east for years is defeated in a day and had such small numbers. There is hardly anybody left in the Channel area, if rumours are true. Jon, be mindful. It may well be nothing, but someone may be playing a game with us. The key, if this is true, is to find who, and whether they are playing a short game or a long game," she said thoughtfully.

"We will keep our eyes and ears open," Jon replied.

"And minds?" said Jane.

"And minds," Jon agreed.

Jane then returned her attention back to her grandchildren. Well, the elder ones at least.

"I have some news today of some importance," she said. "It appears we have finally made contact with the Kingston community."

Jon felt a chill as he remembered the last time he had seen Kingston, with Ray firing that strange weapon.

"Now that Mason isn't a problem," she said, glancing at Jon, "two hundred or so of their community will be arriving in Grovetown. Arrangements need to be made, but we are hoping they will arrive within the week. They wish to discuss trade."

"Trade!" Jon said in a sharp voice "Why should we trade? Shouldn't we just share our resources? After all, they have a small community like ours, barely over a thousand. I don't see the point in the return of bartering."

"Well, the council seems very intent on making this happen," she replied.

"We will see about that," Jon grumbled.

Something else that Jane had said caught his attention.

"I'm sorry, but did you say two hundred people?"

"Yes, and that's why it's important that Jesse and Ash be aware that the Mayor of Kingston, as he titles himself, will be bringing many Freeborn with him," Jane said in a meaningful way.

What was she on about? So they were bringing lots of young people down here to—No!

"Do you mean this is like some sort of dating arrangement?" Jon spluttered.

"Of course, how do you think our species will survive? It's very hard to find a partner with our small population," she said.

"Whilst Jack Beasley was married and had four children at a young age, Harry and Billy are still on their own."

"Well, I'm not letting some Kingston boy come down here to lay his hands on my daughter," he growled.

'Dad!" Ash exclaimed in embarrassment.

"What about Jesse?" Jane replied "Is it all right for a young girl to come down and lay her hands on him?"

"Nan!" Jesse said, equally as embarrassed as his sister.

Bloody hell, he thought. *She has me there.* Jon was brought up in a time where a father would be pleased if his son met a nice girl, but the idea of a boy touching their daughter would bring thoughts of violence to the mind. Hypocritical it was, but that was just the way it is. *Or was,* he thought ruefully. *Times have changed.*

"Hmm, maybe ... we'll see," he grumbled.

"Anyway, there might be an older lady in there for you ..." Jane risked saying.

Jon was stunned. Why did she have to say that?

"No. I met my true love, and I was lucky enough that she loved me back. That's better than most men get," he replied quietly.

Jesse and Ash were looking at him with sad expressions. Lily was just looking around the room, wondering why everyone had gone silent.

"Well," said Jane after a moment, and to his surprise, she was in tears, "it's time we skinned those rabbits." Then she began ordering everyone into making a big family dinner.

The wall that protected Grovetown was very adequate at keeping the zombies out. What they called soldiers in this day and age patrolled the ramparts day and night in an attempt to stop any bandits from breaking in and causing havoc. They didn't, however, look for people wanting to escape from the inside out. In certain areas, you could simply dig a small hole at the base and scramble underneath. Carl Cooper was now doing this at near midnight, as he had a pressing engagement out in the bush land with an old ally, a real soldier, a complete bastard.
A medium-height man who was now bald on top, he still wore a suit like the one he had worn back in his heyday as a leading politician in the Tasmanian Parliament. How things had changed on that fateful day. He went from being a real high-flyer who had the ears of all the rich of the day, to dragging a dead premier's corpse out of Parliament and begging a soldier captain for his protection. It was only due to the amount of laughter he caused with the premier's corpse that Mason had allowed him to join their merry band. And it was only on the proviso that he keep the premier with him at all times that he was allowed to stay with them. Dear old Premier Pratt was his constant companion for three years, until the stench became too much even for Mason.
His unit was initially made up of nineteen innocent young lads from all over Hobart. They all looked up to Mason as their leader and protector as he led their unit in their armoured trucks safely to the Channel area in the south. But after a few months, some noticed how erratic his behavior was, as he started killing not just the zombies, but people as well. A few of the soldiers objected, and after their objections were noted, he turned a machine gun on them. This silenced the others for a while, with some deserting him, but as he travelled south, he killed some more of the unit and picked up a few recruits along the way, and these people were not the nicest of people, to put it mildly. Hence, The Mason Gang was formed. Only Craig Bradfield and

Steve Perrin were left of the originals, excluding himself, of course, he thought sarcastically.

Outside, he stood with his back against the wall and waited till the above soldier had moved on. It really was an empty gesture having a soldier patrol the wall, he thought. There was no electricity for any sort of floodlights, and any flames that the guards had would hinder their nighttime vision and not help at all. That self-righteous prick Jon Dayton had only provided guards as a measure to quell the community's fear. But Cooper was a politician, and his profession excelled in spreading fear. Quickly moving out to the trees, he waited for his escort.

"Hey, Cooper, you cunt. Over here," he heard a voice say.

"I can't see you. It's pitch-black here," he whispered.

"Just walk straight ahead, you dopey prick," the man replied.

Carl walked straight ahead and fell flat on his face. Standing up, he wiped at his nose, which was now bleeding. He thought he may have ripped his suit jacket.

"Oh, sorry about that, mate," the man said, laughing.

Carl walked gingerly forward until he could hear the whicker of a horse.

"Keep coming; you're almost there," the laughing man said.

As Cooper reached him, he noticed there was a second man waiting for him farther back. Strangely, they were both wearing some sort of glasses. *Nighttime goggles*, he thought. Well, the ammunition had run out, but at least Mason had something left of his army days.

"Your friend here has a pretty impressive set of goggles," he said to the second man.

"I have them too, and he's no friend of mine," a rough voice replied.

"Oh, I'm sorry. I couldn't see them from here," he lied.

"Yep, Mason gave it to us especially to see you safe," said the laughing man.

"So the other man here knows the way to the Mason camp just as well as you?" Cooper said to the laughing man.

"Well, of course he does, you stupid fuckwit; we both just came from there."

"Good," he replied, and quick as a snake, drove his knife straight up through the man's chin and into his brain.

Bending down to take the dead man's goggles, he said to the second man, "So there will be no more jokes at my expense tonight, then?"

"No. No, there won't be," the rough voice replied.

"Well, that's nice to hear," he said, wiping the blood off the goggles and placing them over his head. "Please, lead on." He gestured to the second man.

And after taking the dead man's horse, they both moved off into the night.

He knew the dream would come. It always did after anyone mentioned Sarah.

The first two births were difficult, but Jesse and Ash were born safely, as the medical care they had was still adequate. Then there was ten years without children, and they thought there would be no more babies. It was with a mixture of happiness and dread that they learned they were expecting a third child. Sarah was now forty-five, and there was a famine and riots in the street. All basic medical supplies were now gone. Sure, there were still midwives in the community, but if you had any complications with the childbirth, you were on your own.

After a twenty-four-hour labour, Lily was finally born, but the midwife informed him that Sarah had lost a lot of blood and was not likely to survive. On her way out, she handed him a knife. He sat by her bedside in tears as she drifted in and out of consciousness. When she woke, she would tell him that she loved him, and he would tell her he loved her. She went from moments of being totally lucid to being completely delirious. It was in her final moments that the dream always began.

"Let me hold the baby, Jon," whispered Sarah, her face so pale and the sheets of the bed covered in blood.

"Of course," he said as he passed Lily over to her hands.

She looked down at the baby with sad and tired eyes. "Where did you get the name Lily from?" she said softly. "I like it. It will suit her, I think."

"Just from an old movie," he replied quietly.

She looked over at him and said, "You will look after her, won't you, Jon? Her and Jesse and Ash?" she said quite firmly and with all of her remaining strength.

"Of course, Sarah. I would die for them if need be," he replied.

"No, my love, the only dying today will be me," she said as she sighed and left him behind.

He sat there and watched as she passed from this life into the next. He couldn't comprehend that she was gone. He wiped at his eyes and knew he had to do something, something important. But what was it? He could hear a baby crying. Lily, that's right, Lily is crying. I need to get some milk for her; she needs to be fed and kept warm. Finally coming to his senses, he looked at his child cradled on her mother's chest and saw her mother was looking at her too.

Sarah then leant forward to bite the child as Jon's hand snapped out and grabbed her by the throat. The knife in my pocket! Sarah was groaning, and her teeth were snapping only a few inches away from the baby. A newly reanimated zombie looked only a little different than the person they were when alive. It was only the older zombies who began to decay, so he felt like he was strangling the woman he loved. He pulled the knife out of his pocket with his free hand and moved it slowly towards her eye, those beautiful eyes that were now lifeless, soulless maybe. Closer and closer, he got. He had to do it, he thought, he had to, as he drifted on the edges of insanity. The knife. Her eye. Her brain. *Forgive me, Sarah,* he thought.

He thrust the knife deep and woke up screaming.

"Daddy, are you all right?" he heard Ash's voice say with concern.

Jon sat up in his bedroll and looked around the large teepee that they called home. He could see her face by the firelight, looking upset, and noticed Jesse was awake as well.

"I'm sorry, Ash. I didn't mean to wake you," he said in a voice wracked with emotion.

"Dad, it's not your fault. Please believe that," she said.

"I know, sweetheart," replied Jon. "Now go back to sleep; we have a big day tomorrow."

Ash came forward and kissed his forehead, then tucked him back into his bedroll and went back to her bed.

He lay there for a few moments, biting his lip so he wouldn't burst out crying. They would hear him and worry about him. *I'm the parent, I am meant to worry about them.* He had suffered so many panic attacks over the years as a result of Sarah's death.

Soon, he heard the padding of footsteps and felt a tiny body move into the bedding, then a small hand reached out and started brushing her fingers through his hair.

"It's okay, Daddy," Lily said.

She continued this for a few minutes until he fell asleep.

Mason's Camp, five kilometres west of Grovetown

Carl Cooper finally made his way out of the trees and onto the gently sloping grass field that was the Mason Gang's camp. Because of the vigilance of Dayton's defence force, Cooper convinced Mason to keep the camp hidden behind kilometres of dense bush land that could only be found by a tracker, blind luck, or a traitor's betrayal. Mason chafed at being kept hidden for so long, but Cooper just had to keep him calm for a bit longer, until his plans were fully realised.

Nodding goodbye to his escort, who said nothing and just pointed towards the middle of the camp, he rode his new horse through the filth-ridden camp of over a hundred bandits.

Well, we shall both find out whether Mason wants his expensive goggles back, he thought. He quelled the urge to hold his hand over his mouth and nose to stop the putrid smell entering his lungs. Jesus Christ, these people smelled like they just bathed in shit, which was probably closer to the truth than he would have liked to have known.

Finally reaching the middle of the camp, he spotted Joe Mason lounging on his makeshift chair by a roaring fire. He was wearing his usual furs, but underneath, if you looked really closely, you could see the tattered remains of his captain's uniform. *A proud tradition of ANZACS we had, and you just pissed all over it, you son of a bitch,* Cooper thought.

Mason was a big man, who, when he'd first met him, had short-cropped black hair. Twenty years later, he was still big and strong, but had long curly hair and a huge black beard. Mason reminded him of a nineteenth-century bushranger by the name of Mad Dog Morgan. Very applicable, he thought.

Standing behind him were his two favourite henchmen, Steve Perrin and Craig Bradfield. His number two and three in the pecking order of villains, you might say. To survive twenty years with this man, these two needed some huge balls. Cooper only survived fifteen years.

Perrin was a skinny man with long, greasy hair that made you itch if you looked for too long, and Bradfield was a bull of a man with a completely shaved head. Funny to think they were just scared teenagers when they first met.

"Well, well, the prodigal son has returned. Got tired of sucking your fellow councilors cocks yet?" said Mason, who then smiled, showing his brown, rotten teeth. "And why are you riding Clark's horse? And where is Turner?"

"Clark had an accident. He fell down onto my knife," he said, sliding off the horse. "Talkative Turner left me at the camp's edge."

Moving over to the fire for warmth, he continued.

"I left your crew five years ago, remember? And yes, I had to do some 'sucking', as you call it. But being a member of the council has had its benefits," said Carl, glancing at Perrin and feeling a strong need to bathe. "Besides all of this, we made a deal last week, Mason."

"Oh, yes, of course we did," Mason replied. "I was to get rid of the dregs of my gang, whom I could no longer feed nor wanted and Grovetown would think the threat of the feared Mason Gang was defeated. Did it not go as planned?"

"Not as much as I had hoped it would," Cooper replied with gritted teeth. "Apparently, they were pissed out of their heads at midday, and some mad bitch ran out of the building firing my machine gun."

"Ha!" Mason laughed out loud. "That was probably Mad Zelda. I'm surprised she had time with all the men she liked to fuck."

"I don't care about who or how many she liked to fuck," Carl replied, glancing at Perrin. "All I know is that Dayton and his sheep are now wondering where the hell that bitch got a new machine gun from, and why the dreaded Mason Gang was so sloppy."

Mason stood up slowly and moved around the fire, and only by sheer will alone did Cooper manage not to step backwards.

"I left them alcohol so they were an easy target," he said as he walked towards Cooper. "I left the mad whore Zelda with your gun and a little ammunition in the hope that she would take out a few of Dayton's force." Standing up close to Cooper, he looked down and whispered in a deadly voice, "And I want to know where the fuck you got that machine gun from?"

Cooper took a steadying breath and controlled his fear. "I told you before," looking Mason straight in the eye, he lied, "I found a nice cache of weapons in an abandoned warehouse." It was actually in the house of an apocalypse survivalist. After he had killed the father, who then set about eating his family, he moved in and had been there ever since.

It took him years of subtle questioning to find that sort of family; they were everywhere, if you looked hard enough. And even though the apocalypse had come, they still kept their supplies to themselves. In case there was another apocalypse, he thought wryly. "The weapons are kept in a safe place and will be delivered to you at the specific time. Okay?" he continued and held his breath as Mason looked down at him for a long period of time.

Deciding he wouldn't get what he wanted, Mason swung around, showing off one of his crazy mood swings.

"Oh, why the fuck can't we just attack them now?" he complained, sounding like a sulky teenager.

"Because, old friend," he said in his best politician's voice, "at the moment, they have one thousand citizens, who are all trained with the bow. At the core are Dayton's men and women, who number one hundred and are very well trained." Not to mention very loyal to Dayton, from what he had observed. "But I have a plan that will whittle down his numbers quite a bit; in fact, it may most likely wipe them out. So if you charge in now, you will all likely die. But if you are patient and play the fear game, you will rule over Grovetown."

I *will rule*, thought Cooper.

"The fear game?" said Mason.

"Yes, once Dayton is dead, we will begin more raids and killings." Mason's eyes lit up at that.

"Then," he said, glancing at Perrin, "once the people are in uproar, your gang, and I hope you will change your name by then, Joe, will come into Grovetown a few men at a time and slowly become the protector of the people. And if the people do not like that, well, they will be dealt with by our new guns."

"*My* guns," Mason said.

"Your guns," Cooper replied.

"Are you sure this will work?" Mason looked dubious.

"The best way to take control over a people and keep control of them utterly is to take a little of their freedom at a time, to erode rights by a thousand tiny and almost imperceptible reductions. In this way, the people will not see those rights and freedoms being removed until past the point at which these changes cannot be reversed," said Cooper.

"You're quoting Adolf Hitler to me."

"Why, yes!" Cooper replied in shock. It was well to remember that Mason was a psychopath, but he was a very intelligent one at that.

"We cannot do what we did to the East," he continued as he looked at Perrin and started to itch. "If you wish to live as a king in this world of today, then you need subjects. Living subjects, Joe," he emphasised.

"All right then, Cooper," Mason said with a mighty sigh. "We will stay here for the moment." Cooper began to relax, but then Mason growled out, "But for only two weeks."

"Only two weeks." Cooper nodded in agreement.

Now it was time for the next phase of his plan.

"One thing I need to ask before I go."

"What do you want now, Cooper?" Mason said in a tone that suggested his mood was changing again.

"I need to keep these goggles for the return ride, and I need to take your preacher with me."

Grovetown, thirty-one kilometres south of Hobart

Jon Dayton rode his horse through the main thoroughfare of

Grovetown. Or more correctly, what used to be a bitumen road. Given the rain and the lack of repair work done, it was still a pretty good road to use. Probably as the only vehicles used on it for the last nineteen years were of the natural kind, and the wear and tear usually came down to horseshoes and horseshit.

Wearing his hat, he tried not to hum the movie tune from *The Good, the Bad, and the Ugly*. He could hum it, he thought, but if the little girl sitting sidesaddle in front of him was to learn it and hum it back to her Uncle Ray, he would never hear the end of it.

"Now, Lily," he said, looking to the huge row of crops to his left, "why do we grow all of our vegetables in a common garden area here as well as at home?"

"Because if our veggies are ruined at home, we can come here for more," said Lily in a tiny voice.

"Yes," he replied, "and what's the most important reason?"

"To look after each other," she replied.

"That's my girl," he said and gave her a one-armed hug as he looked at all the people rostered on to attend the gardens. Hunting for meat came down to the individual families, and it was good for everybody to know how to hunt anyway. Given the massive population crash of the Collapse, nature's animals had made a steady increase in numbers. Plus, the old farmers to the south with their massive lands had cows and chickens to supply the community with whatever meat, milk, and eggs that was needed. For free. And he hoped to keep it that way.

Nodding in greeting to a middle-aged lady who said hello as she passed by, he resisted the urge to tip his hat and say, 'G'day, ma'am'. But then thought, *Perhaps I should have?* It was a pleasant greeting, after all. *Those western movies still have an effect on me*, he thought with a grin.

Grovetown was certainly a big place now. You didn't have to live here, as there were other small communities to the south, but people did like the company of other humans, and there was safety in numbers, and … well, he had to admit it now, the young people could meet other young people and start families. God help him if some young Kingston boy took a fancy to his Ash, he thought with a grimace.

"You are still my little girl, aren't you, Lily?"

"Of course, Daddy," she said, turning to look up at him.

Jon smiled with pleasure in return. An answer a father always wanted to hear.

Moving past the crops of food and resisting the urge to stop and help himself to some lovely snow peas, corn, and tomatoes, they came up to the open field, where horses and soldiers went through their training.

"Look, Daddy, there's Jesse," Lily said, pointing.

Jon looked on as Jesse rode his horse across the field at a fast pace towards the straw man target. *What's he doing?* As he watched, he saw Jesse unsling his bow and ... fire an arrow from his saddle!

Did I just see that? Jesse just nailed a target whilst riding on the back of a horse!

"Hold on, Lily. We are just going to see your brother for a moment," he said as he turned his horse onto the field.

Jesse's friend McCrae was first to see him, and soon all his friends came forward on their horses with Jesse. All of the scouts, he thought. They were all freeborn because they were very good riders, not because of their age.

It was time to put on his general's face. A bit hard with a little girl sitting on his lap, but he would try.

"Okay, what is going on?"

"It's an idea Taylor came up with, General," said Rachael Beasley. "She was listening to Mr Fields talk about Genghis Khan and the Mongol Empire and how they used to shoot arrows from horseback. And well, we thought we would give it a try," she finished as she fiddled with her braided hair.

"We've been practicing all morning, General," Jesse added, sounding all official.

"I don't mind that you are trying new things," said Jon, "but please let me know in future, and please be careful. It's a very dangerous thing you are trying. Those men of the Khan's army were very skillful and as tough as nails."

"Yes, sir," they all replied and turned to leave.

"Bye, Jesse," said Lily.

"Bye, little munchkin," Jesse replied with a grin. A term from the *Wizard of Oz* books he read as a kid. *I wish I could have shown him the film,* Jon thought with sadness.

He stayed and watched them for a while. They really were very good. Not surprisingly, Taylor was the best of them, hitting the target every time, and judging by the straw man target, she seemed to always make head shots. But her cousins Liam and Isaac were not far behind, Jon noted. Jesse seemed to spend most of his time talking to Rachael between practices.

They really got along well, those two. A thought from his mother-in-law sprang to mind. *No, Jon, don't get involved with your children's love lives, even Ash's,* he thought with a sigh.

"Well, okay, young lady," he said to Lily. "It's time to take you to school." He moved his horse back onto the road.

Jon soon noticed the smell of smoke but didn't remark on it due to the fact that nearly all of the houses in the community had open fires. But as they approached the library, which was used as the community school, Jon saw a hive of activity, and the smell of smoke became very strong, too strong in fact.

Making his way through the crowd, he came upon a very distraught Nick and Mary Fields with their four children.

"The place is gone, Jon. The library is burnt to the ground."

"We will find you another place to teach, Nick," he said gently.

"You don't understand, Jon," he said in despair. "The books, the books are all gone."

The preacher lay on the floor in front of the warm fire, looking at his nighttime goggles that Mason had given him for the journey into Grovetown. He tried to sleep, but there was a constant knocking sound coming from beneath the floor, and it sounded to him like there was the noise of the wind coming through the floorboards. He wasn't entirely sure what it was.

It was nice to sleep inside after decades of sleeping outside in the rough whilst travelling with Mason. *So many killings and such devastation,* he thought. He only managed to stay alive by continuing his persona as the preacher. Mason thought he was funny, he supposed, and as they had no other entertainment, he was occasionally brought out to give sermons and tell stories from the bible. They were some good stories, he thought, crazy some of them, bullshit the rest, but entertaining, nonetheless.

The other thugs of the gang thought he was just an idiot, so they left him alone for the most part.

He sniffed at his furs and could still smell the stink of smoke and fire. He loved burning things. He loved it with a passion. When Cooper told him what he wanted him for, he almost wet his pants with joy. His father had been mad, he remembered suddenly. *Perhaps I'm just mad in a different way*, he thought.

Anyway, there was nothing wrong with burning a little building down. *Nobody was hurt*, he convinced himself.

Again came that sound from below the floorboards. What was down there?

"If you're going to try to catch some sleep, you need to move away from this area," said Cooper as entered the room. "She can smell you, and she won't sleep until you have moved away." Who was she? He had a wife, he recalled. Perhaps she was downstairs?

The preacher had learned to do as he was told without asking questions, so he stood up and moved over to the couch.

"Um, no, not the couch, please; you smell like shit. Smokey shit," he said with a smile that didn't reach his eyes.

He was a cold bastard, this Carl Cooper. Whilst the gang was filled with violent thugs, this man never indulged in any violence or rape that he saw, but he seemed just as dangerous in his own way and was one of the highest members of the gang before he disappeared. *That's right*, the preacher thought, *his wife was called Daisy, I think;* such a sweet name for such a fucking bitch.

"I have found a place for you to reside nearby," Cooper continued as he put on his suit jacket. "You will be staying there for a while." Then he gave him directions as to where it was.

"But you must wait until dark before leaving my house. Do you understand?"

The preacher nodded in the affirmative. "You want me to stay close by?" he said. "Most people do not want to associate themselves with a religious nutter."

"Why, that is where you are wrong," Cooper replied. "I have plans for the town, and your religious fervor is part of it."

"So I'm not just here to burn down a library, then?"

"No, of course not. I could have done that myself if need be," he said as he ran his hands over his mostly bald head. "Your 'expertise' as such was required for the library, but it is your religious zeal that I need."

The preacher thought about all the buildings he had burnt through the Channel area. What had started out as an accident had turned out to become his addiction. He had started with just small outbuildings, but as of last year, he burnt down a whole shopping complex. He watched with tears in his eyes for hours as the whole centre collapsed into a pile of charred debris. But as for religion, well …

"There is something you need to know, Councillor Cooper," he replied in a formal tone. Best to be honest from the start, he thought, especially with this man. A politician could see a lie from a mile away because they were so good at it themselves. "I don't actually believe in what I preach. In fact, I have never been a strong believer in God. The past twenty years has reaffirmed my belief that God, if he exists, doesn't give a fuck what humans do."

Cooper just looked at him for a moment and then burst into laughter, genuine laughter that actually reached his eyes.

"Oh my, do you mean to tell me that there are TV evangelists who don't actually believe what they preach and are actually just in it for the money?" Cooper said whilst wiping the tears from his eyes. "Unheard of," he said sarcastically and continued to laugh.

The preacher just sat there until his laughter abated. He didn't bristle at Cooper's laughter because he knew it was true. History was filled with so-called holy men who promised you eternal salvation but all they really wanted was your money, obedience, or sexual favours, or all three combined. The catholic priests took a vow of poverty, but the Vatican was one of the richest institutions on the planet. Or had been.

"How can I help you, Councillor?" he said once Cooper's laughter had finally stopped.

"Did you know that since the library was burnt down so tragically last night, that books in this area are scarce?" Cooper said as a serious look came over his face. "In fact, the only major source of reading comes from you, with the stash of bibles you have brought with you."

The preacher, in his escape from the zombies, had made a mad dash to safety in his 4WD vehicle. Because of the power of the vehicle, he was able to get through the blockade of the Southern Outlet. It was unfortunate that in his hiding in the Channel area, he became caught up with Mason. It was, however, fortunate that, due to his level of bullshit skills, he managed to stay alive for so long. In the vehicle he had escaped in had been at least a hundred bibles. It seemed that his father had so many of the things that he boxed them up in all of the vehicles that they owned. Why did he keep them? He wasn't sure. They were sure heavy sometimes as he lugged them around for twenty years. Perhaps it was some tie to the old world, maybe.

"So, you wish me to go out in the community and preach the Word of God?"

"Yes," replied Cooper, "but in a kindly way."

"So, no hellfire and brimstone?" said the preacher.

"No. We have been through that. I think now we need the peaceful part of religion. But with just a touch of hell retribution to keep people in line," Cooper said, rubbing his chin with a thoughtful expression.

"You want a cherry picker, not a fundamentalist priest, then?"

"Yes, that would be ideal. But I want you to specifically include historical inaccuracies, and the disturbing ones, such as slavery, rape of virgins, genocides, incest, that sort of thing."

Why did he want him to do that? But the preacher was a coward, and he would do as he was told, regardless of what he thought about it.

"Also, you need a cleaner image," he said as he looked at his scruffy clothes. "You need to say that you walked the wilderness for the last twenty years and repented your sins of greed and whatnot, and found your true calling as God's servant. That will cover where you have been and what you have been doing, I should hope." Turning a sharp eye towards him, he said, "You do realise if word gets out about your connection to the Mason Gang, you are fucked, don't you?"

"Yes, I do," replied the preacher. *And so are you,* he thought, but kept that to himself.

"So that is why I need you to burn those clothes," Cooper said, ignoring the glint in the preacher's eyes when he mentioned burning, "and become a clean-cut, respectable man again. Nobody must recognize you from what you are today," he finished.

The preacher looked down at his furs and the huge flea-infested beard he had. *This beard kept me warm for years,* he thought sadly. "I can do that, but please, Councillor, I need to know what your plan is, or how my part is of any worth."

Cooper looked at him for a long moment, obviously deciding whether to tell him the plan, or at least a part of it. He then began to pace the room.

"My plan will take at least a few years. We cannot ride roughshod over these people; they must be treated with kid gloves. Even though the basic population is stupid and will follow us blindly, there are a few members of our community who are very smart. Dayton in particular is a threat to my plans and should be taken care of quite shortly, thanks to your burning skills."

He then stopped pacing and looked at the preacher.

"You see, there have always been four elements that have kept people in line for millennia. I am the first element, and you are the second. The third element is nearly under my control. And the fourth has disappeared entirely, but will soon come back to rule us all." He paused. "Do you understand?"

"I have no idea what you just said," the preacher said honestly.

Cooper just smiled at him. "I like your honesty, Preacher Man," he said. "If you just do as I say, then, in a few years, you will be back to the luxury that you once had. And remember," looking at him straight in the eye, he finished in a threatening tone, "we do not know each other.

"Now go and shave and bathe. I have left some new clothes for you that I hope will fit." He left the house then, obviously on his way to some council meeting.

The preacher soon cleaned and shaved himself. Back to the luxury he once had, that was a lie, he thought. But just having the power over people was intoxicating, and the women, oh, yes, the women; he hadn't been laid in years, but he remembered the good old days. Perhaps he could even invoke a new ritual in mass where people burnt things in offering to God. Perhaps the women could do it naked. No, that was sounding very pagan, he thought. I am a Christian man; that sort of thing is confined to the bedroom, he thought, half laughing to himself.

Once shaved and dressed, he looked at himself in the mirror. Perhaps he was a lot greyer than what he once was, but he still had a bit of charm, as he practiced his facial expressions. A kind smile, yes, there it is. Compassionate, yep, he still had it. Anger, no, he can't do that anymore. Benevolent, gracious, good-humoured, he went through them all.

By the time he was finished, the preacher was dead, and Peter Rainswood, by the grace of God, had miraculously returned from Heaven.

Fifty children sat in the Community Hall, listening to their teachers. It was decided long ago that kids would be educated from the age of six to thirteen. The education was basic and consisted of mathematics, science, history, reading, and writing. Self-defence classes included karate, basically because one of the teachers actually was a real-life black belt, and of course, archery, which would be used later to hunt and protect.

Jon thought about his scouts and their archery training. He remembered teenagers before the Collapse who would be gossiping on their phones, texting, or staring at the Holonet. Now they just practiced at making good kill shots, he thought with some sadness.

He looked over at Lily, who was saying out loud a word that the teacher had written on the blackboard with chalk. Thank the maker some people had kept these things. Kids twenty years ago were learning from Internet pads. Now, those things were useless.

Her teacher said that Lily was very bright for her age, he thought proudly. Maybe she would make a good community leader in the future. But he worried about things like immunisations, which were no longer available. All his kids had been through the measles, mumps, and chicken pox, and had all gotten over them fine. But what about other diseases? he worried.

"We're only teaching by memory, Jon," Nick said.

"We need more books," Mary stated firmly.

Nick and Mary had been together for almost twenty years, had four good kids, and were very much still in love. He was always envious when he saw them together, as they had first met on that fateful day. The day that he first told Sarah he loved her.

"The mayor of Kingston is due to arrive today. I will ask him if the Kingston Library is still there," Jon replied. He had this worrying feeling that Ray may have blown it up.

"Jon, you have to understand. Without history books, the past can be rewritten," said Nick. "I could sit here and say the world is flat and was ruled by an alien called Zod from the planet Krypton, and nobody would know any different."

Jon just looked at Nick.

"Well, all right. I'm exaggerating a bit," said Nick, blushing, "but you know what I mean. We run the risk of going back to the dark ages."

"I agree with you totally, Nick. I do know where some books may be, but I'm just afraid of going there."

Nick and Jon just looked at each other. Yes, that was a big risk. But surely it should be safe by now.

"Do you remember when I told you about the hieroglyphics in the Egyptian pyramids, Jon?" said Nick quietly.

Jon nodded.

"There were some pictures of what looked like helicopters and planes, and it looked like the men were carrying electrical torches," he continued. "I worry that a thousand years from now, some people will see pictures we left behind of TVs, computers, and radios and wonder why such primitive people had these."

"I'll do what I can, Nick. I promise," Jon replied after a moment, not realising what this promise would end up costing him.

Just then, Jesse and Rachael came running up.

"The mayor of Kingston has arrived, Dad," said Jesse.

"I better go, Nick. I'll talk to you soon. Keep an eye on Lily for me, please. She just may skip out of school again to see what was happening," he said as he saw her looking over at him and her brother.

"Mary," he said as he tipped his hat to her. Holy crap, he thought, I almost said ma'am.

Jon, Jesse, and Rachael arrived at the northern gates of Grovetown to find a procession of over two hundred people being greeted by the community's head councillors, Jim Allenby, Mark Brady, and Carl Cooper.

The mayor of Kingston was a big man by the name of Michael Nash, with a huge grey beard. He appeared even larger by the fur clothing he was wearing, and the wicked-looking axe he wore on his hip. He had brought his wife with him, a short-statured lady by the name of Maria, and three daughters named Jessica, Zoe, and Phoebe.

"Dad, look at the soldiers," Jesse said.

"They're wearing a green sort of uniform," said Rachael. "Where did they get the dye for that?"

"No doubt we will be trading things for that dye soon enough, Rachael," Jon said as he looked at Carl Cooper in his suit, talking animatedly to the mayor.

But the hundred or so soldiers did look impressive. They wore weapons similar to his people, and the age range was from freeborn to middle-aged, just like theirs, excluding himself and Ray. Perhaps their own militia deserved to look as smart.

"Look at that bloody axe."

Jon gave a start, as he hadn't heard Ray approach. He noticed that he seemed to be dragging his equal-sized son, Billy, by the collar.

"Um, Ray, is there any reason you seem to be choking your youngest born?" questioned Jon.

"Oh, this little bugger, he wouldn't come when I asked him to. I mean, how am I to find this boy a woman if he doesn't make any effort?"

"Dad, most of the women I see are freeborn," said Billy. "Isn't it a bit creepy for a thirty-two-year-old to be checking out teenagers?"

"Well … yes, maybe you're right," Ray said, releasing his collar. "Is that why your brother Harry did a runner? No doubt he wasn't meant to be hunting today, hmmm?"

Billy just looked at his dad and simply said, "Yes."

"Well, all right then," Ray said, sounding petulant. "But don't say your old man is not interested in your well-being."

"Sure, Dad," said Billy, patting his father on the shoulder. "We're both pleased for your concern."

"What about you two?" Ray said to Jesse and Rachael. "Seen anybody who takes your fancy?"

Jesse and Rachael just blushed, looked at the ground, and mumbled what Jon thought was a negative answer. He also noted that they didn't look at each other when they responded. Ray looked at Jon with a questioning expression, but Jon just said quietly to him, "I'll tell you later."

Soon, Jim Allenby came forward and introduced the mayor. "And this here is my brother Jon Dayton, who is in charge of our defence forces," Allenby said, who, apart from being a councillor, was an aboriginal elder and liked to call all his friends brothers and sisters, which Jon felt was quite heartwarming.

"Very pleased to meet you, Mayor," Jon replied formally. "I hope your journey here was safe."

"Yes, it was very safe," the big man replied. "We didn't have any trouble at all. And I did send my scouts far and wide."

"Well, we believe the bandit threat has been reduced significantly in a recent skirmish we had with them," Jon said, noticing Cooper and Brady had now joined the group.

"The Mason Gang," the mayor replied. "I hope it's true that they are finished. I have heard dark stories about them, very dark," he finished quietly.

"I would like to discuss the Mason matter with you further during your stay, Mayor," said Jon, hoping to gain some more insight as to their numbers.

"Of course we can discuss this issue later, General," interjected Cooper with that false smile of his. "But tonight, we are going to have a feast and celebrate the first contact between the Huon and Kingston in twenty years."

"As you wish, Councillor Cooper," Jon responded formally. "I do need to ask some questions now, though, if I may." Not awaiting his response and ignoring his glare, he continued.

"Recently, we had a fire that burnt down our only library; would, by any chance, the Kingston Library still be there?"

"No, I'm sorry it is not" replied the mayor, "We have so few books now. A lot of buildings were destroyed on the day of the Collapse. It was believed the town was fired upon by some sort of aircraft."

Billy and Ray just looked at each other, but fortunately, said nothing. Jon just nodded in disappointment. It looked like he may have to take that risk now.

"One last question, Mayor: do you by chance know of a man called Dave Lawson? He would be in his forties now, but was a stocky man with a large beard, much like yourself."

"Again, I am sorry, General" said the mayor, "but I have led my community for some years and haven't heard of that man."

Jon's head just dropped. *He's dead, then,* he thought. Ray placed a hand on his shoulder and said, "I'm sorry, mate."

"I hope tonight we may feast and drink to our fallen; we have lost so many over the years," the mayor said quietly as he noted Jon's grief. "I have brought many from my community down to meet your people, including my family." He gestured for his daughters to come forward. "I know this must seem very rude of me to suggest our young people meet like this, but we are a small community such as yours, and as such, I worry that the human population may become extinct in the south if we do not do something to rectify this. One dose of the flu or another illness could wipe us out entirely."

"I agree, Mayor," Jon replied. "I did not like the idea at first, but these are different times." Sighing, he continued, "As much as I don't like my daughter having any sort of boyfriend, it is a good idea." *But please don't tell my mother-in-law I said that,* Jon silently begged.

"I understand the fatherly concern with your daughter," the mayor said with a grimace. "Believe me, I understand."

Well, Jon thought, *I'm not the only father who can be a bit possessive. And he has three daughters.*

The first two girls came forward and were obviously freeborn from the youthful smiles and gestures. Jon saw Rachael was glancing sideways at Jesse to see if he showed any interest. Jesse was polite in greeting them but had no particular show of emotion, and Rachael looked quite pleased.

Then the eldest daughter, Jessica, came forward, and it was obvious that she was not freeborn. In fact, she was a fully grown woman in her late twenties. And she was gorgeous.

Jon looked over at Billy and Ray and tried not to laugh.

Billy stood there with eyes wide and jaw hanging open, and Ray had now placed his hand back onto Billy's collar.

"*Let* me introduce you to my youngest son, Billy," announced Ray as he barged past Jon with his son in tow.

"Pleased to meet you, Jessica," Billy said after his father had released his collar.

"Very pleased to meet you, Billy," said Jessica and gave him a shy smile.

Holy smokes! Jon thought. *Now that girl is a stunner.*

Ray obviously thought so too, as he started talking about how they used to live in Kingston as a way of getting the conversation going.

"So you were in Kingston on the day of the Collapse?" said Jessica.

"Yes," Billy replied. "We had to fight our way out through thousands of zombies to make our way down to Grovetown, or Grove, as it used to be called."

Jon hoped Jessica didn't think Billy was exaggerating, because they had literally had to get past thousands of zombies.

"I never saw many zombies," said Jessica. "Something was thought to have killed most of them on that very day. It was said there was a dragon that destroyed them and most of the buildings," she finished with a laugh.

The mayor and Ray seemed quite pleased with the way the conversation was going. Billy was a nice lad, and standing at two hundred centimetres tall, with large shoulders and a strong physique, the mayor may have been hoping for some healthy and strong grandchildren. This might increase their chances of survival due to the lack of hospital care in the society they now lived in.

It felt so strange for Jon that he had gone from a world of overpopulation to one that encouraged marriage and big families so the community could survive. A place where people talked about feasting instead of buying takeaways and wore knives, axes, and bows without looking over their shoulder and wondering when the police would arrest them. It was a crazy world, where he wondered whether he had stepped back in time four hundred years, as if he were on a *Dr Who* episode.

Electricity was the key, he thought. Someone needed to find a way of getting that source of energy back again.

As Jessica and Billy's conversation continued, Jon motioned Ray over to him.

"C'mon, you old dragon, let's take the mayor to the camping grounds."

"Indeed," said Ray, grinning.

"We have some rat bags in our community," Jon said, gesturing to the mayor, "but Billy is not one of them."

"That's nice to know," said the mayor with a smile.

So the Kingston procession continued as they made their way to the open pasture that was normally used for horse training and archery and set up their camp.

The Community Hall that had stood for decades now had never seen this many people before. Or not for as long as Jesse Dayton could remember. At least four hundred people mingled in the hall, and the rest of the community ate and drank outside.

His father, Uncle Ray, and the mayor stood nearby with his grandmother and sisters. Everybody was here. *Except Rachael,* he thought as looked around the hall.

"So, Mayor Nash," said Jane Butler, who was standing nearby, holding the hand of her granddaughter Lily, "how did you manage to survive? It was said that Kingston was nearly destroyed on that evil day."

"The town centre was pretty much destroyed," the mayor replied. "But the outer suburbs were left intact." With a grimace, he continued, "Truth be told, I was sheltering inside my home, petrified, with my wife and daughter. I didn't know what to do. Then came this high-pitched noise, followed by loud explosions. The zombies just left our street, transfixed with the sound. I don't know what happened. But I would like to thank whoever did it. They are a hero in my book," he finished.

"You're welcome," said Ray.

"I'm sorry, Ray?" the mayor replied.

"You're … most welcome to our humble abode," said Ray, gesturing to the surrounding area.

"I apologise for Ray," said Jon, who gave Ray a meaningful look. People must not know about that weapon, Jon thought. If it became common knowledge, Ray would become a target. He wasn't sure whether it had any ammunition left anyway. "He seems to get a bit upset at gatherings like this, because we have no proper beer, like in the old days."

"Ah, yes, of course," replied the mayor. "I miss the old taste of Boags or Cascade," he said, sounding wistful.

Bloody hell, thought Jesse, *Uncle Ray looks like he is about to cry. What is it with this beer?* The mere mention of it seemed to make most men act like kids who had lost their favourite toy.

"We have had people try to make alcohol in our community," Jane Butler said with disgust. "The result was one death and one house blown up. We have to concern ourselves with growing food first."

"Some people in my community," replied the mayor, "tried a poor version of fruit fermentation." He screwed up his face to show how well that tasted.

"Mayor Nash," Jesse's father said, bringing the seriousness back to the conversation, "do you know how many men the Mason Gang had, at all?"

"I'm not sure, General," said the mayor. "The numbers I heard were from thirty to over a hundred. But this was over nearly twenty years of rumours. The reason I have so many armed men is because of the horrific tales I heard. I'm glad you did what you did." Looking directly at Jon, he continued, "The world is better off without them."

His father just nodded in agreement.

"Mayor," he continued after a moment, "have any of your people been into the Hobart City area?"

Everybody stopped to listen on his answer.

"Well, a few of my rangers have looked upon the city from the outlaying hills," the mayor replied. "They reported bodies lying on the ground. They stayed there for a few hours and reported no movements from the zombies." He then let out a small laugh. "One of the mad scouts rode straight down the main thoroughfare and back. Still, there was no movement from the dead. I think their evil is finally gone," he concluded.

Jon just looked into the distance with a thoughtful expression. *All right,* Jesse thought, *I have had enough of this. The zombies are finally gone, that is good, but where is Rachael?*

"Uncle Ray," said Jesse, "is your family going to show up? I mean, I have seen Harry and Billy …" Billy seemed enamored with the mayor's daughter Jessica and hadn't been seen for a while. "Is Jack going to show up?"

"Jack and …?" said Ray with a grin.

"Ray," Jesse's father said with a pointed look.

Jesse now noticed that everybody was looking at him. *Why are they looking at me with slight smiles on their faces?*

"Oh, speak of the devil," said Ray, pointing. "There is … Jack right now."

Jesse looked quickly at where Ray was pointing and saw Jack and his wife, Janine, walk in with their little boys, Sean and Ben.

They were followed by Rob, who was quickly reaching his father in height. Then came a beautiful tall girl with long blonde hair, wearing a lovely dress. She looked a lot like Rachael.

Rachael! I've never seen her wear a dress before. Well, not since she was a little girl. And is she wearing makeup? Somehow that stuff women put on their faces made them look good. Not sure how, but it did.

"Jack. Come over here," yelled Ray from across the room.

The Beasley family heard their grandfather's call and walked across the room to greet him.

Ray immediately gave Sean and Ben a big bear hug.

"How are my boys?" he said as he cuddled them.

"I'm fine, Dad," Jack said. "Thanks for asking."

"Aw, here, my boy," Ray said as he gave his son a backslapping hug.

Jesse hardly listened as he looked across at Rachael. She did not look at him at all. Somehow, that hurt him a little.

For the next ten minutes, the conversation went from family to

Mason, to the food crisis, and eventually, led to the freeborn of both communities. And Rachael still did not look at him.

It was then that the Mayor of Kingston decided to introduce some young men from his community to Ash and Rachael.

So Jesse just stood there, ignored, as Rachael smiled and talked to half a dozen of the young men from Kingston.

During this time, Jesse fought his first battle against the green monster. He couldn't understand what was happening to him. His face seemed like it was about to explode, and he had this pain in his chest. Violent thoughts were just around the corner, when he saw her smile at some guy. No, not just smile, she was flirting. Wasn't she?

"I've had enough," he said a bit too loudly and stormed out of the room as everybody turned to look at him.

Finally making his way outside, he leant against the wall and took some deep breaths. *I've never felt like this before,* he thought. It was horrible, and as he dwelt on Rachael smiling at that guy, the pain came back again.

He looked around and saw the people in front of him were yelling and laughing, which just made his mood sourer.

"Jesse." He gave a small jump at the sound of her voice.

"What do you want?" he replied, not looking at her. He knew he sounded like a real brat just then, but he didn't care.

"Why did you run out like that?" Rachael asked.

"I'm surprised you noticed," he said sulkily.

"Of course I noticed. Everybody did."

Hmm, well, that was embarrassing, but the brat inside him still didn't care. "I thought you were too busy smiling at that guy to notice," he said.

"Is that what this was all about?" she said in an incredulous voice.

"Yes, it is," he said honestly. "And the way you ignored me like that. It hurt me." It really did, he thought, as he was still trying to come to terms with that terrible emotion.

"I'm sorry," he heard her say. Sighing, she moved up in front of him, and as he was leaning against the wall, he couldn't help but look at her, especially since she was almost as tall as him.

"You see all this?" she said, gesturing to her clothes and makeup.

Yes, he could see it; she looked beautiful.

"I did all of this for you," she said, to his shock, "and when I walked into the room and saw you, I panicked."

He just looked back at her, and all of the battles with the green monster disappeared.

"I guess I'm just no good at this sort of thing," she finished, looking down at her feet.

Jesse suddenly felt ashamed.

"You look lovely, and I was just being a jealous idiot. Forgive me, Rachael. I was being a fool," he rambled as he kicked the inner brat way back into history.

Rachael looked up and smiled at him, then both of them moved closer and kissed for the first time. She *was* good at 'this sort of thing', he thought. And they only pulled apart when the nearby crowd started making wolf whistles at them.

I'm not a member of the Mason Gang, and maybe I am a romantic, he thought, as he asked Rachael to come back inside the hall with him.

Jon stood there looking at some young man talking to Ash. *Perhaps I should go over there and introduce myself,* he thought, but then he looked over at Ash's grandmother and saw her glaring back at him. 'Leave her alone', the look seemed to say. Fair enough; he sighed.

He wondered where Jesse and Rachael were.

Watching Jesse's face turn from his usual expression of self-control to looking so angry and storming off like that was a bit of a shock to his father. But jealousy could do that to any man or woman, let alone a teenager. Rachael stood staring at Jesse as he left, until Jack, her father, whispered a few words to her and she followed him out.

He hoped they had made up by now.

Turning away from Ash and back to Ray, he said, "Have they returned yet?"

"Well, old mate, I sent the young boys out to have a look. They should be reporting back very soon," replied Ray.

True to his word, his youngest grandsons returned giggling and said that their big sister was outside 'pashing' Jesse.

Smiling, Jon and Ray asked that nobody mention anything when they returned. And when Jesse and Rachael finally did return, nobody did say anything, but they all just looked at them with big smiles on their faces, until they both blushed a deep shade of red, which in turn, made everyone break out into laughter. It was a good night.

It was a good night, thought Carl Cooper, as he moved stealthily towards Peter Rainswood's tepee. The nighttime goggles allowed him to avoid a number of people as he made the five-minute walk between their lodgings. He wore a huge robe as well to help hide his identity. *You can never be too careful in the game of politics,* he thought with a grin.

Moving into the tepee, he saw that Rainswood was fast asleep in his newly acquired sleeping bag, which Carl had given him. *I wish I'd had one of those in my travels with Mason,* he thought. But no doubt some bandit would have killed him over it.

"Rainswood," he said as he kicked him awake.

"Wha-what?" Rainswood mumbled as he woke from his comfortable sleep.

"Just letting you know that tomorrow is the first day of your new job."

"Tomorrow?" Rainswood mumbled, still half asleep.

"Yes, and you better put on a good show. So get a good night's sleep," he said, half smiling to himself.

"Sure … Councillor, sure," the religious conman replied.

"Just one thing," Cooper said as he thought of Jon Dayton's face once he learned Kingston had no books. "Do you know what Jon Dayton looks like?"

"Yes," mumbled Rainswood. "I saw him tonight. I think I met him years ago as well, on the day of the Collapse. He was rude to my father, if I remember correctly."

Really! Well, that's interesting, thought Cooper.

"Well, if you see Jon Dayton at your sermon tomorrow, make sure he sees your books. Make sure he realises that you are now the town library."

"Will do, Councillor. I will make sure he does," Rainswood replied, and as quick as that, he fell back to sleep and started snoring.

I wish I could get to sleep as quickly as that, Cooper thought. But it was good to know that if he had to kill him, he would definitely be doing it at night.

"So, Ash, I saw you talking to that Kingston boy last night," Rob Beasley said with a big grin, which all of his family seemed to have.

"Yes, he seems a nice boy," Ash replied, trying not to blush as she tied her newly caught rabbits to her belt. Tim was his name, and she must admit it was nice to meet him. "He seemed a bit adventurous, though. He told me a story of riding a horse through the main street of Hobart." *It can't be true,* she thought. *Perhaps he was saying this just to impress me,* a small part of her mind hoped.

"Has he met your father yet?"

"God, no," Ash replied quickly. She could feel her father's eyes watching them all night.

"Your father is so protective of you," said Rob.

"I know." She sighed. It was so infuriating that he was always looking out for her. But, on the other hand, she found it so endearing that he loved her so much.

She worried about him, though. Sometimes he would look at her with panic in his eyes if he thought she was in danger, real or imaginary. She also secretly thought that he really didn't like the idea of her meeting a boy from Kingston because he was worried that she would marry and move away from Grovetown and leave him behind.

"Perhaps he is so protective of me and Lily because he feels that since my mother died, he has to make up for her absence," she said. "Or maybe he is worried about losing another person he loves."

She could see the sadness in his eyes when he talked about her mother. And sometimes it led to the most horrible of nightmares for him, she thought sadly. She shivered when she thought about what he'd had to do when she died.

"Uncle Ray is definitely protective of you," she continued.

"Yeah, I know. But I think Rachael is his favourite." Rob

hooked three rabbits to his own belt.

God bless the breeding habits of rabbits, thought Ash. Her father said they never had a real problem with rabbits in this neck of the woods in the old days, but since the Collapse, there were fewer humans, and so there was now an abundance of rabbits to eat.

"Did you see Rachael and Jesse's faces when we started laughing at them?" she said with a smile.

Rob started laughing. "Yes, that was awesome." He chuckled for the next few minutes as they made their way home.

"Rob?" she said after they had walked for another five minutes.

"Yes, Ash?" he replied.

"Do you ever wonder what the Huon was like before the Collapse?"

He paused for a moment. "Yeah, I do," he said. "Pop said it was very crowded compared to today. But Tasmania was nothing compared to the big countries, where people would live in big buildings, and the places they stayed in would be stacked on top of each other. There were nine billion people on the planet! Nine! Can you believe that?" He shook his head.

"Father said the air was polluted by tiny metal boxes called cars," said Ash as she breathed in the fresh air. She had seen these abandoned cars over the years and didn't think much of them compared to the freedom of a horse. "He said most people rode to work in those tiny metal boxes and stayed at a place where they didn't want to be for eight hours so they could afford the money to live in a house that they didn't fully own."

"Sounds mad," said Rob, scratching his head.

"I know!" said Ash. "I mean, nobody tells us we cannot stay where we live, and if they did, we would just pack up the tepee and move to some other land. So long as the food supply was there, we would be as happy as Larry."

"Who's Larry?" said Rob after a moment.

"I'm not sure," Ash replied, brushing her dark hair from her eyes. "Just a saying Dad says sometimes."

"Oh, like Bob's your uncle?" said Rob with a smile.

"Exactly," Ash said, grinning back at him.

They looked at each other for a moment.

"Okay, you go first, Rob," said Ash.

"All right," Rob agreed, half laughing. "Flat out like a lizard drinking."

"She's apples."

"Your blood's worth bottling."

"In like Flynn."

"Buckley's and none."

"Mad as a cut snake."

"Fit as a Mallee bull."

"Like a stunned mullet."

"Straight to the poolroom."

"A stubby short of a sixpack."

"Trackie daks."

"Done like a dinner."

"Um … oh, bugger, I can't think of any more." Rob laughed. "I'll have to listen to Pop for a few more."

Ash smiled at him as she said, "And I'll listen to Dad."

They soon arrived at the southern end of Grovetown, and on entering they saw Rob's Uncle Harry talking with Councillor Allenby. They both seemed to be watching a man standing on a box talking about the Kingdom of Heaven, or something like that, in front of a small gathering of people. Harry didn't look impressed.

Harry was in the process of doing his duty in the job he hated the most as he walked along the main thoroughfare wearing a very old pair of overalls. In fact, most people hated this particular job, unless they had no sense of smell.

As part of the community effort in keeping their society running, all people except mothers with children under the age of six, health-trained people, teachers, and soldiers were assigned a four-day work week detail in the various areas that needed to be done. The roster was handled by only six people, as everybody insisted that bureaucracy must be kept to a minimum. He could understand that as when he did that particular job, he fell asleep most of the time.

The other three days of the week could be spent doing whatever you wanted. Looking after the home, hunting, which he loved, looking after the vegetable garden and chooks that he and Billy had, or just generally relaxing, which he found quite boring. The areas he enjoyed working was the communal vegetable garden, helping the local blacksmiths, repairing stuff, as he loved fixing things, looking after the animals, water irrigation, and travelling south to the farmlands. These were all kind of fun for him, and the diversity kept his mind occupied.

But the job he hated was fixing, installing, or removing people's septic tanks. Even with people's improved diets and the removal of all chemicals from daily use, those bloody things still got blocked, and as he stood here, he could really smell the pong coming from his clothes. So if he could smell it, then other people …

"Holy Mother of Crap, you smell bad, Harry," said the sixty-year-old Jim Allenby as he strode up to Harry.

"Yeah, just doing some shit work," Harry replied with a sigh.

"Ah, got to be done, my friend," Jim said with a laugh. "Hope you got to the bottom of the problem."

"Yeah, it took a while, but I fixed it up in the end." Harry smiled.

Harry liked Jim Allenby; everybody did, really. Since the days of the Collapse there had always been three Councillors who have made the final decisions on how things were to be done. It was initially Jane Butler, a police commissioner, and the mayor. But over the years, it changed to people voting every year for someone they thought was smart. No political parties in this town. Well, except for Carl Cooper, who was the only Councillor Harry had seen 'door knocking' for the job as they used to say. Dad said he used to be a politician in the old days. He looked like a smug bastard, Harry thought, and he much preferred good blokes like Jim Allenby.

There was something about aboriginal elders. They were ordinary folk just like the rest of them, but an elder seemed to have a look of wisdom. They could say 'stick sharp knives down your underpants, Harry; it's good for the circulation' and you would just nod and think how that was such sage advice.

"How are the discussions going with the Mayor of Kingston?" said Harry.

"Yeah, good, my brother," replied Jim with a frown.

"What's the problem? You look worried."

"It's this trading discussion that Carl Cooper is determined to put through. It has me concerned."

"I know Jon is upset about it," said Harry. "I think he wants to debate it at this afternoon's council meeting."

"Really!" said Jim. "Well, that's good." He had a small smile on his face now. "Always good to have someone else's opinion." Harry thought Cooper was maybe being a bit too forceful with his trading opinions.

They soon arrived at the southern end of Grovetown, where Harry had his next 'shit' job to complete, when they came across a well-presented man in a suit, standing on a box and preaching something about God.

"Oh, no, not one of these guys," said Harry. He remembered them coming to his home when he was a kid to talk about Jesus and the word of God and watching his father tell them politely to leave them alone. He figured his father would have said more blunt words, but he tended to keep a civil mouth when his sons were within earshot.

The man was a very clean-cut middle-aged man and was talking about his wanderings through the bushlands for the last twenty years as a hermit who was seeking the meaning of life. He said he had been a corrupt man of God, but after the Collapse, he repented his sins and wanted to preach the true message of Jesus and seek redemption.

He was very good, Harry thought, but sometimes, his eyes would linger a bit too long on the young girls who were watching him. What is he up to? He wasn't preaching the hellfire of the fundamentalist, probably because the people have been through hell already, but he seemed to be preaching the nicer side of the bible, with just a hint of a threat. There were some good words to be found in the bible, Harry thought. But to suggest it was the word of God was just plain ridiculous. Unless God was a complete schizophrenic, that is.

Just then, his nephew Rob and Jon's daughter Ash walked up to them. They must have been hunting, judging by the amount of rabbits they were carrying. *Ah, now hunting,* thought Harry wistfully, *wouldn't that be nice right now.*

"Hi, Uncle Harry, how are—Holy shit, you smell bad," said Rob, smacking a hand up to cover his nose.

"Be careful, Rob. I might give you a family hug," he said with a smile, making a big hugging gesture.

"Hi, Ash," he said as he turned to the tall dark-haired girl who reminded him so much of her mother.

Sarah Dayton had been a lovely lady. Ash was lucky to have had a mother like her. It was so sad when she passed away.

Harry could barely remember his own mother. He often wondered if she was still alive. She had gone to the mainland last time he heard. So many years ago now, he thought sadly.

"Hi, Harry," Ash said, smiling back at him. "What's that man preaching about?"

"Funny you should say preaching," Harry replied. "He is talking about the creator of the universe."

"Does he know him, then?" said Rob.

"He says he does," said Harry.

"Can he prove it?" said Ash.

"No, apparently, you don't need proof, just belief," and as soon as he said that, Harry felt an incredible case of déjà vu. Where had he heard that saying before? And why did that man suddenly look so familiar to him?

"God could be a woman," Ash said primly.

"No, apparently, God is a man," said Harry.

"What, he has a penis?" said Rob, now laughing.

Harry laughed too. Rob, it seemed, took after his grandfather.

"So are you saying that the creator of the universe can only relate to half of the human species?" said Ash. "Well, that's not very all-knowing."

"Help me out here, Jim," said Harry.

"No, mate, you're on your own here," Jim said with a smile. "My people never wrote that book."

"Mine didn't either, and we are your people now," Harry replied.

"That's very true, Harry," Jim replied quietly. "We are one tribe now."

"Why is he saying God wrote that book?" said Ash.

"Well, Ash, the bible is stories written by forty authors over a sixteen hundred-year period," said Harry.

"Well, why is he saying God wrote that book?" Rob repeated.

"Well, they believe that God beamed the message into their … brains, I think," Harry explained.

"What?" said Ash and Rob at the same time.

Just then, Jesse and Rachael showed up. They were holding hands, but as soon as they saw their family, they broke apart. Still a bit shy.

I'd like a woman to hold hands with, amongst other things, Harry thought wistfully, and then gave a mental start at his melancholy. *What is wrong with me? Must be all the shit I have on me,* he laughed to himself. But he knew in his heart that he had gone to the community hall last night with the faint hope of meeting someone nice.

"Why does that man believe we cannot be good people without the bible?" said Jesse, sounding offended.

"I'm not sure," Ash answered after a moment of listening to him. "He says that evil people are punished by God."

"Well, that's good," Jesse replied. "But I like to be a good person because it's the right thing to do, not because anybody would punish me for being bad."

"Eternal punishment!" exclaimed Rob. "Well, that seems a bit cruel. Forever is a very long time, if it's time at all?" he finished with a frown.

"But he loves us!" said Ash in a shocked voice. "That's not a normal way of behaving. I mean, if I said, 'I love you, Rob' but if you didn't do as I say I would send you to eternal punishment, wouldn't you think that was a strange sort of love?"

"Yes. Creepy love," replied Rob, who was still frowning at the man in a suit, then he smiled at Ash and said. "But isn't it, I love you, Tim?"

"Shut up," Ash said.

"If people believe that God is cruel, then maybe that gives us humans an excuse to be cruel as well," Jesse said with that thoughtful look he sometimes got. "Dad said some people definitely used that excuse for centuries as a way of doing horrific things in the name of religion."

"But again, where is the proof?" said Ash. "And why do we have to follow somebody's beliefs from thousands of years ago?"

"Because if you don't, you go to hell," said Harry.

"And who says that?" Ash asked.

"The people who want you … to believe in their stuff," Harry lamely replied. *Why am I bothering with this?* he thought. *Perhaps I should be doing important stuff, like unblocking shit.*

"You don't need any proof with religion, Ash," said Jesse.

"Well, that's just plain stupid," Ash replied in a huff.

"Dad said that religion was broken into two parts," said Jesse. "The first part was spiritual sayings like, 'treat other people the way you want to be treated' which was quite good, and I think has an eternal sound to it. But the second part was social teachings." Jesse was looking much like his father now with that frown of concentration on his face. "The people thousands of years ago thought that men or women who committed adultery should be stoned to death. Even kids who were disobedient to their parents," he said, looking at all of them and now showing a small smile.

"We'd all be dead by now," said Rob. "In fact, the human species would be extinct," he finished with a laugh.

"Exactly," said Jesse. "But social teachings change all the time. And what was thought to be normal in that day is not normal in this day. And that is where religion fails badly, I think," Jesse concluded.

Rachael, Ash, and Rob just looked at him and nodded. He was a deep thinker, young Jesse, Harry thought. Perhaps one day he would make a good councillor.

Jim Allenby was maybe thinking the same thing as he looked at Jesse with a big smile on his face.

These freeborn think so differently, Harry thought. *It's like they are clean slates of free thinking and can view things from a different perspective. Was our generation so brainwashed that we just accepted things without questioning them?*

"He just said God hates something, Uncle Harry," said Rob.

"Hate is the lowest form of human emotion," said Ash thoughtfully as she stood with her hand on her chin. A gesture which again reminded Harry of her father. "By saying the word hate', that man is basically saying God is just like one of us. Hmm, that doesn't seem right."

"I don't like the idea that religion was involved in politics," said Rob. "Pop thought that the old politicians were arrogant enough as it was, without having the belief that God was on their side."

"What's that man talking about, Uncle Harry?" said Rachael. "I just heard something about a talking snake."

Harry sighed. *All right, I'll try to tell them and join the debate.* "Apparently, God created man and then a woman from the man's rib, but told them not to eat an apple from a tree. But a talking snake convinced the woman to eat the apple, and God never forgave them. Then, thousands of years later, he impregnated a virgin and had his own son, who was also himself, and wanted that man tortured and killed so—Oh, fuck this. I'm going to clean some shit." Harry walked off, parting the crowd like the Red Sea with his stinky overalls.

The four freeborn just watched their big friend and Uncle Harry walk off to go and … clean some shit?

Jim Allenby roared with laughter, and after saying goodbye, moved off into the crowd, wiping tears from his eyes as he went.

"Does anyone know what Harry was talking about?" asked Ash.

"I don't know," said Jesse. "I was told at school that there are more planets in the universe than there are grains of sand on the entire planet. The creator must be something way beyond our comprehension. This apple-eating story sounds a bit weird," he finished with a concerned look.

Jesse was a deep thinker, just like their father, Ash thought. It was a shame new ideas were shunned by organised religion.

"Mother said she believed in God," Ash remembered, as her brother turned sharply to look at her. "But she said belief was not evidence. And to force your belief onto other people was both arrogant and ignorant."

"I think I recall that," Jesse said quietly. "Why did she tell us that at such a young age?"

"Perhaps she knew that men like that would always be around," Ash suggested, nodding towards the man in a suit. "She said God was the 'Unknowable' and death was a mystery journey that we must all eventually take." Looking at Jesse, she said, "Dad wrote all her sayings and beliefs down in a small notebook. I think it was his way of keeping her with him." With a sad smile and a guilty expression, she continued, "I came across the book one day and read it."

"Oh," Jesse said as he looked at the ground and nudged some rocks with his boots.

Rachael moved closer and held his hand, which Ash found a very moving gesture.

"You!"

They all turned at the loud voice that came from across the crowd. Ash was surprised that it came from one of their school teachers, Mary Fields of all people, and she looked angry, very angry.

Mary Fields was doing her rounds at the communal vegetable garden with her children. So healthy, she thought, as she looked at what her family would be having for dinner that night. Beef was being brought in from the south as well today, which was good, as they were getting tired of eating rabbit and wallaby every night. Perhaps they might have some lamb, although she was always careful not to tell her children what the meat actually was. Once they found out it came from killing those cute little creatures, she may not get them to eat it again.

I do miss gravy, though, and pasta sauce and chocolate, she thought. But cooked tomatoes do make for a great camouflage of the brussel sprouts she was going to have to force feed her kids that night.

"Did you hear that man preaching about God?" said Louise, a longtime friend of hers, as she walked up next to her.

Mary felt a chill as her past came back to haunt her. The last time she'd heard anybody mention God in any religious way was on that day that her crazy father hit her. The day she met Nick; the day the world ended.

She really should walk back to the Community Hall, where they taught the children four days a week, and where her family now resided. But instead, she asked where the man who was preaching was and what he looked like.

On learning it was right at the southern end of the town and that he was a well-dressed, good-looking man of middle age, she asked her friend Louise if she would take her kids back to her home and ask Nick to mind them for a while. Then she began the long walk to the south.

She had this horrible feeling in her stomach. It couldn't be him, could it? There must be other religious types out there. But after what they had all seen and still no arrival of any saviour, religion had taken a backseat for almost two decades, and Tasmanians were not very religious on the whole. If it was him, was he as mad as her father turned out to be?

She had only grieved for her father for a few days. He had been her father, but he wasn't a nice man. She never told Nick that she had heard what he said to him that led to his death. She had said to him 'you did what you had to do' on that day, and she meant it. Besides, she could tell that Nick felt enormous guilt over what he had said, and she would not add to this guilt by letting him know she knew the truth.

Arriving at the southern gate, she looked at a well-presented man standing on a box that held some bibles. The man was handsome, with a charming smile, a lot greyer and wrinkly than she remembered, but yes, it was him. A feeling of anger swelled in her chest as she looked upon her long-lost brother.

"You!" she yelled across the crowd.

Her brother stopped preaching and looked in her direction. He stared at her for a few moments, then the blood drained from his face as he recognised his little sister.

"I remember you, Peter Rainswood; you don't have a spiritual bone in your body!" she spat out. "You left Father and me to die, you miserable, lying coward."

"I-I have repented … and changed," Peter said, now stuttering and floundering. Gone was his smooth charisma, and now he looked at his sister in fear.

"All you want is those young girls at the front," she shouted, and very quickly, those young girls left the area.

"Our community gets along well, Peter Rainswood. We don't need any divisions caused by your dogma. We don't need any more power structures here; we are all equal!" she shouted.

"Humanity is sick and tired of your narrow-minded belief that only you know all the secrets of the universe. Humanity is sick and tired of your arrogance that only you can provide the keys to

Heaven's gate. Now get out of here, coward," she said, pointing to the surrounding mountains. "And don't come back."

Peter Rainswood, former pin-up boy for the Christian Brotherhood of Tasmania, righteous Preacher of God himself, when confronted by his little sister, picked up his books and left at a run.

Jesse, Ash, Rachael, and Rob just looked at Mrs Fields in absolute shock. Their teacher was such a lovely lady. Sure, Jesse had seen her get angry with her students sometimes, but the students usually deserved it for mucking around so much. But this was pure hatred.

"Are you going to ask?" said Ash.

"Why me?" Jesse protested.

"You're the closest," she said.

"No, I'm not …" Looking around, he realised he *was* the closest to her, as everybody else had left the area pretty quickly. Town gossip was going to fly with this one.

"Go on," Rob said with a grin.

Sighing, Jesse took a few steps towards Mrs Fields, who was still looking at where the preacher had stood. Peter Rainswood? Was that his name?

"Excuse me, Mrs Fields," he said quietly.

She turned slowly towards him but had a glazed look in her eyes. "I'm sorry, Jesse," she finally said. "My past just caught up with me. I think I may have just made a bit of a scene."

"I think you did, Mrs Fields," Jesse agreed. "The town gossips are going to talk about this. Your ears will be burning for some time."

"Oh, dear." She sighed. "Nick will be upset with me."

"Mrs Fields, I have to ask. Who was that man?"

"Why, Jesse," she said softly with a sad smile, "that was my brother." He looked at her with shock. "I had to put up with the lies, power, sexual gratification, and money grabbing for so many years," she continued in a firm voice. "I will not stand for that anymore, and nor should we as a new society, Jesse Dayton."

She walked off on her way back home, and Jesse stood still for a moment. Her brother! How could they hate each other like that?

Looking back towards his friends, he saw that Rachael had entwined her arm through Rob's. They must have heard. Walking up to Ash, he placed an arm around her shoulder. "I love you, sister," he said.

"I love you, brother," she replied.

"We better tell Father what happened here," said Jesse, feeling uneasy. His instinct told him something major had just occurred.

Running through the crowds, Peter's mind was in a haze, and as he entered his home, he threw the books on the floor.

Things had been going so well. Those young girls at the front were lapping up every word that he said, and he was starting to remember the power that he once had. Until *she* turned up. Fucking bitch! That fucking bitch! How the fuck did she survive? On that mountain bike, maybe? Dayton had had a mountain bike on that fateful day as well, he remembered. What were the odds of that? Perhaps they should have advertised those bikes in the old days as 'guaranteed to get you out of a zombie apocalypse'.

There were no rumours of any preacher in town, so his dumb arse father must be dead. At least that was good news. But that little bitch of a sister was still alive.

He had failed in his first test. Cooper was probably going to kill him. Would he? He would definitely kill him if he did a runner back to Mason. *No, he won't kill me,* he thought. *I'm the second element of his master plan for society's domination.* Whatever the fuck that meant.

He felt the need for some anger release as one of his blinding headaches returned. He needed a goal, something to burn down perhaps? He suddenly began to smile. He hoped Mary's home was flammable. Be a shame if it caught fire, especially if she was in it.

Jon Dayton sat nervously as he awaited the beginning of the council meeting. What was Peter Rainswood up to? The last time he had seen that man was the day he almost ran him and his friends over in his flashy 4WD vehicle. Perhaps he was a genuine religious man. But from what Jesse had told him about what his sister, Mary, had said, he sounded like just another con artist. Their father had been a genuine nutcase from what Sarah had told him, that was for sure.

Anyway, he had to focus on what he had come here to say today. He had to express his concerns on the trade discussion.

Looking around, he noticed that the Community Hall was now packed, just like the earlier feast they'd had; there must have been at least four hundred people crammed in the room. *I didn't know we had that many chairs,* Jon thought with an inner smile.

He hoped Nick and Mary didn't mind this many people being in their school, and in fact, where they were residing nowadays. But the area in which they lived was at the back of the Hall, and all their belongings would have been kept away from the public. Jon's own home was an old tepee-style of tent; they had no lock and key for their belongings, as they had the same items that everybody else had. There was nothing of any value to steal, and that was part of why Jon had come here to voice his objections to trading in any way.

The council meetings were genuinely quiet affairs, with people coming in to ask for help or to vent their anger at whatever problem they had. The three councillors would sit in judgment of their grievances, and the decision they made was final.

Today, however, all of the people from Kingston were here, and the rest of the seats were taken by Grovetown residents.

Jon sat off to the side, where the petitioners would wait for the councilors' arrival. He was the only one waiting.

Suddenly, there was a buzz amongst the crowd as the councillors arrived. They would sit in front of the audience on a semi-raised platform so everybody could see them. First to enter was Jim Allenby, whom Jon considered a friend, second was Mark Brady, a bookish type of man who usually looked to Jim for guidance in making his decision. He thought this was the key to whether he won today's discussion.

The third man to enter was the one who had proposed the idea of trade in the first place. Carl Cooper was his name, thought Jon, with a hint of distaste, a man who had been a high-flying politician in the old days; some said he was even destined to become the next Premier of Tasmania. It must chafe at him to be relegated to a simple councillor, but proposing trade between the two communities suggested he was still stuck in the old ways.

Jon was here to convince him otherwise. Well, to convince Brady and Allenby at least.

"Welcome, one and all," announced Allenby as he took the middle seat.

Jon wondered if even sitting on the right-hand side of Allenby bothered Cooper and his pride.

"My, there are a lot of people here today," Allenby said with a laugh.

"I'd like to thank the Fields family for allowing us to meet in their school," he finished with a smile.

Jon looked over the crowd and saw Mary and Nick with their children, sitting in the far corner of the room. Mary did not look her usual switched-on self but gave a small smile and nod to the bench. Nick saw Jon and smiled at him.

"We have only two items of discussion today," Allenby continued. "The first is the idea of trade opening up between the Kingston and Huon communities, which has been proposed by our very own Councillor Cooper, here to my right."

Cooper gave a nod and one of those politician smiles that never reached his eyes.

"Due to the fact that we have not been using money or trading in any way since the Collapse," Allenby said, "I believe this is a serious matter that we all need to discuss. That is why I am glad Mayor Nash and some leading members of his community are here with us today."

The big, burly man who sat in the front row nodded to Allenby in respect. And … was that Billy Beasley sitting in the front row as well? He was looking pretty happy sitting next to the mayor's daughter Jessica. *Most people would be,* thought Jon drily. The poor people sitting behind his massive frame, though, had to lean to the left and right so they could get a decent view of the front.

"As you can see to the side of the hall, Jon Dayton sits waiting to address us all on the matter of trading. Debates are usually rare at Grovetown, as we are usually of one mind," said Allenby with a smile. "Food, shelter, education, and health are our main concerns, and we work at jobs purely on the basis of maintaining these four things. But today, we are here to address what we are to do with trading, and no doubt, from this will be the eventual return of money."

Jon noted that Cooper's normally impassive face twitched at the mention of money.

This wasn't about trade, Jon now realised with a shock. This was about the reintroduction of the money system into their lives. Allenby must have known this, Jon thought, as he began to frantically rethink his speech and strategy.

"As the debate is primarily between Councillor Cooper and General Dayton, we ask that they put forward their views in a civil manner," Allenby continued. "So to start off, will Jon Dayton step forward, please."

Jon slowly stood and moved to the centre of the room in front of the councillors. His mind raced as he searched for a way to get his views across. The debate had changed from simply trading with each other, which was an issue for today only, to the reintroduction of money, which would affect everybody's lives for years to come. And he was debating a seasoned, professional politician. Could he win this?

He looked at his family sitting near the front row. His eldest daughter, Ash, was looking worried for him. No doubt concerned that he would lose this debate. His other daughter, Lily, was sitting on her grandmother's lap as per usual, and even the hard face of Jane Butler was looking concerned for him. He looked at his son, Jesse, who was sitting next to his girlfriend, Rachael Beasley. He looked to the left of Rachael and saw the Beasley clan, who were all looking at him in expectation. Finally, he looked at his best friend, Ray. The man who made him laugh for all these years and was a pillar of inspiration for him through all the dark years that they had been through. He looked at Ray and decided to 'throw the dice'. He could only try his best.

"I came here to talk against the idea of trading with our neighbours. But it turns out this will be a debate on money as well," he said. "This is a natural turn of events, as one would obviously lead to the other." He took a deep breath.

"If we are to go back into the world of money, I wish everybody to reflect on what those days were like, and what it will mean for our community to return to them. I want you all to remember the wealthy and the banking system. The way money was distributed was always designed to make the rich wealthier and to keep the poor struggling.

"Did you know that the day before the Collapse, one percent of the world's population owned forty percent of the world's wealth? The richest ten percent owned eight-three percent of the wealth, and fifty percent of the world's population owned only two percent of the wealth." He began to pace across the front of the room as he talked. "I want you to look around at all the people in this room. Does anyone here feel less equal than anybody else?" Nobody said anything. "Back in my day, when money was around, we were not equal at all. We were financial slaves." A few people looked around at each other when he said this, but a surprisingly high number of people were nodding in agreement.

"This is perhaps a bit dramatic a terminology, but it is no less than the truth," he said as he continued to pace back and forth. "We lived in supposed democracies, but really, if the truth was to be told, we lived in plutocracies. But the truth could not be told because the wealthy owned the media, and it was said they owned the politicians."

"I object to that, Dayton," Cooper, who had decided to stay where he was, said in a cold voice. Obviously so he could look down on Jon.

"I take that comment back," said Jon with a sigh. It was the truth, and everybody knew it. But to insult Cooper was not a good way to start a debate.

"But it wasn't just the way the wealthy ruled us all; it was the way money affected our lives in other areas. Take, for example, the cigarette industry, which led to people getting lung cancer." He paused for a moment. "A horrible way to die," he said in reflection. "But the government did little to stop this, as they made a lot of taxes out of the smoking industry, but nobody here today," gesturing to the hall, "would think of growing tobacco because there is no money to be made out of it."

He looked over at Cooper, who said nothing.

"One in three people in my day were obese. When was the last time any of you saw a fat person?" he asked the crowd. They were all slim. They all had been for years, he realised. Even he and Ray were healthier than they had been for decades.

"People's diets were of their own free will," said Cooper.

"But couldn't the government have ruled that we had too much sugar in all of our food?"

"Again, this is free will of the public."

"Or maybe a healthy sugar industry was good for the economy?"

"That's just your opinion," Cooper replied.

"True, but in the old days, there was something known as a Global Market," Jon continued. "You know, all the vegetables and fruit that we eat every day from our own gardens or the communal garden just down the road, well, in the old times, we used to import them from other countries because they were cheaper." The young people were looking at each other in bewilderment now. Why would you import something from far away in another country that you could grow yourself? "To stop the fruit from going off, or seeding, for the long journey across the globe and then to your local supermarket, pesticides were sprayed on the food, and then the public ate them.

"We walked the streets and breathed in the fumes from the vehicles because the government could not break away from the oil and coal industry, due to the taxes they made.

"And then we wondered why we got so sick." He shrugged.

"But that was fine, because the pharmaceutical industry made billions of dollars a year with their medications, a part of which went to the government in taxes."

He looked at Cooper, who said nothing.

"So why do we need the money system?" He turned to look at Allenby. "Your people survived for tens of thousands of years without money, did they not?"

"Ah, yes, but we did trade and barter," Allenby replied.

"But you didn't have any banks," Jon said with a grin.

"Um, no, that we didn't."

"But with respect, your people did not invent many things," interjected Cooper.

"We invented things that we needed to survive," replied Allenby in a placid manner.

"But that is what I mean about money," Cooper said. "It drives people to create new things."

"Things that will make them rich," Jon protested.

"Yes, if need be," replied Cooper.

"Are you saying that the people who made medical and scientific breakthroughs throughout history for the benefit of all mankind were only doing it so they could earn a few bucks?" Jon asked.

"No, of course not."

"So would they have made these breakthroughs without the monetary system?"

"No, they needed money to buy the equipment for their research and to have a medical research facility."

"Why?" Jon said.

"Because …" Cooper was now stumped.

"Because the monetary system said so," Jon finished for him.

"Well … yes. It was the way things worked," Cooper said angrily.

"I am starting to believe we were living in a world of control," Jon said quietly, looking over at Nick. "For argument's sake," he continued, "say today, in this town, a scientific man or woman wanted to research into a new field of clean energy."

"We have no electricity," Cooper replied.

"Agreed, but for argument's sake, say we did have electricity right now," he replied. "That person would have all the resources they needed to complete their studies for free."

"They would have had resources in the old days, Dayton."

"But who would have supplied the money for this research?" Jon asked.

"Money would have been provided by the government, or they would have been privately funded," Cooper said.

"So are you saying the people who invested money in this scientist would not have any influence over the research? No vested interests, perhaps?" said Jon.

"The government concern was always for the people, not in making big profits," said Cooper.

"Bahahaha!" came a huge laugh from the crowd.

"Um, Ray Beasley, if you could keep it down, please," said Allenby, who wore a small grin.

"Sorry, Jim," said Ray, wiping tears from his eyes.

"You see, this is my point, and this is what I agree with Cooper about," Jon said, to Cooper's surprise. "Money was the driving factor of our society. But we only made constant advancements in areas where huge profits were to be made. The money lenders would not have it any other way." The story of Nikola Tesla's free energy and the Banking Clans sprang immediately to his mind. "Money held human advancement back in so many areas and in so many ways. And it ruled all of us, whether you were aware of this or not," he said as he looked across the crowd. *Was he getting through to the people?* he wondered. Or would they go back to the old ways?

"Political changes and ideologies also came and went," he continued. "And they all failed because there were always people involved who hungered for that money because money was power."

"Without the money-driven economy, people will become lazy and expect others to do the work for them," said Cooper.

Jon turned to Cooper. "And there weren't lazy people before? I seem to recall lots of people who would sit idly by and receive handouts from the taxpayer."

Cooper couldn't argue with that, for anybody with a long memory would remember him complaining about the 'entitled' population who were a burden on the taxpayer's wallet.

Jon turned back to the audience. "People will never change. There will always be good and bad people in our lives. Lazy people, smart people, kind people, and evil ones. But what I am asking is for a change in the society we live in and what drives that society. A society where a man or woman would work hard in a factory for a whole year and earn $50,000, whilst someone famous would earn over a million dollars for making a TV episode in just one week was just so morally bankrupt I ..." He began shaking his head at the injustice of that. "I am not saying our society will be perfect, because there is no such thing. But one day, when we get electricity back—and we will one day—I would like to see our children get a free education, to expand their minds as much as possible; they would study for a career in which they had a passion for, not because it paid the most money; a scientific community not hindered by big business so free energy can finally have its day; a society where people in authority cannot be bribed by money; a place where we can be free of the stress of financial debt in whatever form it took."

Not just mortgages and credit cards, as he remembered a few addicted gamblers in his time. "And most importantly, a place where we could all finally be treated as equal. Thank you for your attention," he said and sat back down.

Well, I tried, he thought, as the crowd began to quietly discuss what he had said.

He noticed Mayor Nash was in deep discussion with his entourage. Ray looked over at him and gave him the thumbs-up, and to his private joy, he saw Ash and Jesse smiling at him with what looked to be pride. Well, at least that made it worthwhile. Even Jane Butler was smiling at him!

"Councillor Cooper, do you have any reply?" said Allenby.

"Yes, I do," Cooper said as he stood up. "The money system was in place for thousands of years," he said with a tight smile. "It worked in driving the world to where it was. We would all be living in caves if it wasn't for money. The money system created jobs, in which people worked. A moneyless society may see people working in fewer areas and maybe only a few days a week. Laziness will ensue, believe me. I vote that the bartering system commence now, with the plan in a few years to introduce a monetary currency of some sort, and then we can get back to the way things were. An ordered society, where employment and prosperity will grow for all."

Oh, man! Jon thought. He sounds like he is running for an election. It's a wonder he didn't say that 'we had to make cutbacks to balance the budget'. Hopefully people would realise that was just political spin. The older people would at least. Laziness! Well, maybe, but not for a very long time.

"Well, that leaves me and—" Allenby was interrupted as Mayor Nash stood up.

"I apologise for the interruption, Councillor Allenby. But what I have to say may be of some importance to today's meeting."

"Please, by all means, proceed," said Allenby.

"Well, to put it simply," the big man said, "I and members of our community," nodding to his companions, "have decided that we wish to take no part in any bartering system."

Everybody looked at him in shock.

"We made a deal, Nash," said Cooper in disbelief.

"Well, some deals are meant to be broken," replied the mayor. "Listening to Jon, I began to remember those days," he said. "I remember working in a low-paid job, getting retrenched, having to struggle to pay the mortgage and the bills and to put food on my family's plate. And there were people much worse off than me." He looked around the hall, and his voice began to rise with venom. "I remember the rich one percent who ruled us across the globe and lived in utter decadence, whilst we all struggled to make ends meet. Now I serve no one, and I work for nobody but my people. Us!" He punched his chest and shouted, "I won't turn back. I am a free man!"

Suddenly, applause broke out from the crowd, and this soon was joined by more and more people, and then Jon heard Ray cry out in a triumphant voice, "Yes, fuck the rich!" which was then joined by a loud cheering from the rest of the audience as they all stood up.

Jon could now see why the mayor had led his community for so long. Free man! Freeborn, he thought. Perhaps that term could take on a new meaning from this day on.

This wasn't retaliation against rich people as such; this was a reaction against a system that made people too rich and the gap between the have and have-nots so huge. This was a rage against inequality and injustice.

He looked over at his family and saw them all cheering and smiling at him. Jane allowed Lily to run over to him, and he picked her up and gave his little girl a big hug. This was the best day he'd had in a very long time.

If only Sarah could be here to see it. Maybe she was watching from somewhere, he wondered briefly, but again, he remembered her saying, 'You can't prove that.' He wasn't arrogant like Peter Rainswood or his like, and he definitely wasn't like Carl Cooper, as he saw him looking at him with barely concealed hatred.

You can't win them all, Cooper, he thought with a grin.

It took a long time for Jim Allenby to calm the audience, but when he did, he simply said, "Well, I take it that's a no vote, then?" and everybody laughed.

Nodding to the other councillor, Mark Brady, he stated, "Please let the records show that Grovetown and Kingston have voted against any sort of bartering or monetary system. And we shall remain two communities connected by a common bond of sharing. Not a common bond of money."

And people again broke out into cheering once more.

"Well, I don't wish to put a damper on proceedings, but we still have another issue to address," Allenby said once everybody had settled. "And this involves books, or the lack thereof."

After talking about education of the children being so important to him, the promises he made to Nick, and thinking that Peter Rainswood may have had the only books in the Huon, Jon had no choice but to offer to lead an expedition into the city centre of Hobart in the search for educational material. It needed to be done, and he wouldn't have worried except for the fact that Carl Cooper was now looking at him with a small smile on his face.

Two days later, preparations were almost complete for the journey into old Hobart town. Jesse and Rachael decided to go hunting together in the mid morning, but as teenagers in love do, they spent most of the day making out.

"I'm still getting over the council meeting," said Rachael breathlessly as she was held in Jesse's arms.

"Oh, I thought it may have been me that was on your mind," Jesse replied with a grin.

"Of course you are, Jesse," she said, smiling back, "but the way the people shouted and applauded like that. It was so uplifting."

"People Power, I think they call it," said Jesse thoughtfully.

"Your father was brilliant," Rachael said, looking for his reaction.

"Yes, he was," he replied, looking at the ground. He was so proud of his dad, but as a typical teenager, he couldn't express his feelings to his father properly.

Rachael burst out laughing.

"What!" Jesse said, looking up.

"You Daytons are so funny," Rachael said, grinning. "I give your family a compliment, and you look at the ground in shyness. If that was my father, or let's say, if that was my Pop who made that speech, he would be strutting around like a peacock and retelling the tale to everybody who would have listened."

Jesse laughed. "Yes, he would at that. I have no doubt."

They both then turned at the sound of a loud voice coming from the distance.

"Well, speak of the devil," said Rachael with a smile.

"Who is he talking to?" said Jesse.

And as Ray Beasley came closer, they noticed Dog was strolling alongside him, with his big tongue hanging out of his mouth and tail wagging.

"Man's best friend, of course," said Rachael as she reluctantly moved out of his arms.

"Poppy, over here," she shouted, waving her arms and walking towards him.

"Ah, there you are, sweetheart," he said as he walked up to them wearing his usual fur clothing and that funny possum hat of his.

"And young Jesse is here, I see; now there's a surprise," he said with a grin.

Dog just looked at them as he slobbered all over the ground.

"We were just hunting," Jesse said.

"Of course you were," replied Ray, who looked at their belts and noticed they hadn't caught anything. "Wildlife a bit rare today, then?" he said, half laughing.

"Um, yeah," Jesse replied, trying not to blush and failing.

"I'm only stirring you both," Ray replied with a kind smile.

"Why, young love is a wonderful thing. I remember being madly in love with this beautiful young girl. We spent many a happy time wandering off on our own, just like you two," he said wistfully. "Loveliest girl I have ever met; my god, she was a stunner," he said with a reminiscent look.

"You must have loved my grandmother very much," said Rachael sweetly.

"What! Oh, her, yes, I loved her too, I suppose," he replied with a grimace.

"Now I didn't come out all this way to check up on you, Rachael. That's your father's job," he continued. "I just came out here to tell you Jon wants to see you and Jesse about the trip to Hobart. He asked for you and others to meet him at Jesse's grandmother's house. He looked in one of his serious moods." Jesse just nodded and went to pick up his bow and Rachael's belongings.

What did his father want to talk about? Everything was in readiness for the trip. It could be dangerous, but everything was when you left the safety of Grovetown. He hoped he wasn't going to stop him from going. Ash and Lily would be by themselves, but they had managed fine in the past.

"Lead on," he said and gestured to Dog as they all headed back to home.

Jon sat on the couch at Jane Butler's house with his daughter Lily fast asleep on his lap.

"I hear that a farmer to the south has successfully grown a crop of Hemp," said Jane. "That should be good in the coming years as that stuff was used to make all sort of things."

"Yes, that's good. It was a shame commercial Hemp was suppressed so much in the past because it was so cheap … " He trailed off as his mother-in-law was looking at him with an arched eyebrow.

"I bang on a bit too much about money, don't I?"

"Yes, just a little," replied Jane with her usual sarcasm. "You won your battle with that, Jon. Now let's concentrate on the one at hand."

She was right, as usual, he realised as he sat there looking down at his youngest child. Lily was so precious to him, he thought. She looked so much like her mother, even more than Ash did. It was heartbreaking that Lily had never known her. Perhaps that's why she frets when I'm away, and perhaps that's why I fret when I'm away from her, he thought ruefully as his breathing pattern began to increase.

"You will look after Lily while I'm gone?" he said in a half-panicked voice.

"Of course I will," said Jane, sounding offended. "We get along just fine. And you're not the only one who loves that child, you know. I am her grandmother, after all. Anyway," she continued, "you will only be gone for two or three days."

"I'm aiming for two," Jon replied, still looking down at Lily. "The quicker we get out of there, the better."

There was a quick knock on the door, and then three huge men entered the house.

"Knock, knock," said Jack with a smile as he walked in, followed by his son Rob.

"Well, come in, you three," said Jane. "Don't stand there letting the cold air in."

Jon was surprised that Harry had come as well.

"Harry, what brings you here?" he said.

"Well, I thought I might tag along for the journey," Harry answered. "Be good to see Kingston and Hobart again after all these years."

"He's missing Billy; that's the real reason," Jack said with a grin. The Mayor of Kingston and his tribe, as Jim Allenby would like to say, had left early yesterday, and Billy had gone to Kingston purely on the fact that Jessica had gone back home with her family. I guess after living with his brother for decades, it was hard for Harry to now be on his own.

"I would appreciate the company," Jon said with a smile. And he meant it as, like all the Beasleys, Harry was strong and had a good head on his shoulders. "In fact, I would like you to take Rob's place."

"What! But, General—" Rob stopped as Jon raised a hand.

"I'm sorry, Rob, but I need you to watch my family while I'm gone."

"But, sir—" Rob started to protest.

"Rob," said Jack in a firm voice, "looking after Jon's family is more important than a journey to the library."

"Yes, Dad. Yes, General," Rob replied in a typical sulky teenage voice.

Just then, Ash knocked on the door and entered the room.

Hmm, I wonder if she will sulk like Rob at being left behind, thought

Jon, as he gave a big sigh.

"Hello all," she said, smiling, and everybody smiled at her and said hello back.

She was well liked, his eldest daughter.

"Ash, I was just telling Rob that he is staying behind to watch over my family."

"And by family, do you mean me as well?" The smile had now gone, and she glared at him and said in a tight voice, "I bet you are letting Jesse go! Is this about Tim and me meeting him in Kingston?"

My God, she gets angry in the same way her mother did. And yes, he was taking Jesse with him. Did this mean he was more protective of his daughters than his son? Yes. Was it because his daughters looked so much like their mother that he felt a strong sense of panic at the thought of losing them? Yes, he thought in all honesty. And as he was contemplating this, he wasn't fully aware that his breathing was getting faster again and his hand was reaching for his chest.

He was then saved from more of her teenage tantrum by Ray, Jesse, and Rachael, as they also entered the house.

"All right," said Jane. "I'm putting this young one in bed for an afternoon nap." She lifted Lily from her father's lap and added, "I expect that some voices will be raised, but I hope you will all act like adults," she said, giving direct looks to Rob, then Ash and … then Jon! *Why are you looking at me?* Jon thought. That bloody woman!

But still, he waited until she returned as he did want her counsel on what they were about to do.

They all took seats, and some sat on the floor as there were nine of them all up, and the Beasleys tended to take up a lot of space.

"What I am about to say is based on a hunch only," he started as they all watched him intently. "It goes back to the day we fought the Mason Gang."

"We think it was too easy," Jane chipped in.

"Too easy?" said Ray with a frown.

"Yes," said Jon. "That feeling is based on all of what we heard about that gang. It seemed so odd that they ruled a whole area to the east for two decades, but were just a drunken rabble when

154

we wiped them out."

"Perhaps nobody was organised enough in the east to fight back," said Jack.

"Maybe," said Jon. "And maybe I am being paranoid, because I know I do worry too much about losing lives of our people. Especially the ones I love the most," he said looking at Ash and Jesse.

"So you think there are some of Mason's gang still out there?" said Harry. "Why? What are they waiting for?"

"For Jon to leave," said Jane.

"Do you mean they will attack you on your way to Hobart or attack Grovetown?" said Jack, shocked. "And how would they know that you would leave?"

"I don't know. It's a puzzle I haven't worked out yet," replied Jon. "All that I know is they raped, murdered and pillaged their way through the whole Channel area, and from all reports, there is hardly anybody left living there. Then they were seen on our territory, and we wiped them out in ten minutes."

"Then there was the gun," said Ray, and everybody froze as they knew that was a weapon that could change everything.

"Rachael told me about that," said Jack finally. "It was brand new you said, Dad?"

"Never been used, Son," he replied. "In this day and age and with that gang, it seems a bit odd."

"But they could have gotten that from one of their raids, or found it in an abandoned house," said Jesse.

"Yes, that is true, Jesse." Jon sighed. "And maybe I am over thinking everything. But my gut says something isn't right about the Mason Gang. So that is why I am taking precautions. It's always better to be safe than sorry."

"What do you mean?" said Ray.

"I've decided to take only sixty people with me. Thirty on horseback for the journey on the road and to carry the books back, and thirty on foot, led by Harry, to scout and screen the outlying areas in case we are ambushed." Harry was a very good tracker. If there was anybody out there, he would find them. "If we have to leave Hobart in a hurry," he continued, "we can take everybody out riding double." Turning to Jack, he said, "I want you to keep the other forty here in Grovetown; in fact, I want you to recruit past soldiers and fill the walls with as many people as possible until we get back."

"Okay, will do, Jon," said Jack, sounding determined.

"Rangers," said Rachael.

"Rangers?" questioned Jon.

"Yes, it's the same term the Kingston people use. I think it has a better sound, more protective than aggressive. If that's all right?" she said pleadingly.

"That's fine, Rachael. In fact, it's a good idea," he said with a smile. "Perhaps we could dye a uniform green in the future." She smiled back, and Jon thought he would be quite pleased to have her as a daughter-in-law.

"So, can we get rid of the term General, then?" asked Ray.

"Yes, please. I always hated being called that," said Jon with relief.

"How about just being a captain then? Just like we had in the footy teams," Ray said with a grin.

"Captain of the Rangers," said Harry. "I like that."

"Grovetown Rangers," said Rachael.

"Hmm, sounds like a soccer team," said Jack.

"Footy team, please," interjected Ray.

Jon was starting to feel more at peace, and his heart rate was slowing down, until he heard Rob say,

"So why am I to stay here and watch over your daughters?" which earned a glare from his father, Jack.

Jon felt his breath catch at the question, "Because I need my wits about me for this journey, Rob, and … and … I can't … do … that if I'm … so damned worried about my girls." As Jon said this, his body began to shake, his breathing became rapid, and tears fell from his eyes. *Somebody please help me,* he thought. *I'm so embarrassed; what is happening to me?* But his tears still fell, and he could only control his breathing and stop shaking when Ash rushed over to hold him and whisper comforting words.

The whole room was silent as they watched their friend and family member trying to control his distress.

"Rob, you have to understand," his grandfather said gently, "we were lucky enough to live in a peaceful society; we never saw much violence, but on the day of the Collapse, we saw thousands of people killed in horrific ways. It shook us to the core, and it affects individuals in all different ways. Just watch after his family. Please," he finished as he looked over at his friend.

Rob nodded, probably feeling ashamed that he had caused Jon to break down like this.

Jesse just looked at his father in shock as he heard him say, "I'm sorry" to Ash, over and over, who was almost rocking him like a baby and telling him everything was all right.

Jesse thought back to his schooling and remembered his teacher talking about something called post stress trauma or something like that, and how many of the older community were never the same people after their society fell.

That day of the Collapse must have been a nightmare for anybody, let alone a peaceful man like his father, and he knew his mother's death was a major part of this as well, if not all of it. Jesse had grown up in a world of violence, so maybe he was just used to it. He wasn't sure if that was a good thing or not.

"I think we have discussed enough for today," said Jane Butler, looking up from Jon as she wiped at her eyes. "Make your preparations with the … rangers, Jesse, Harry, and Jack. Choose your people wisely. Ray, you go and inform the councillors, for I think we all need a night's rests," she said, looking back at Jon. "Then the expedition to Hobart will start first thing in the morning."

That night, Carl Cooper opened the floor door and walked down the stairs into his secret cellar. Or the secret cellar of the previous owner, he reminded himself. He was still shaken by what had happened two days ago when all of his plans had gone to shit.

The council meeting had been a complete disaster. Who would have thought that people resented the rich like that! He had been sure the peasants were well under control, but one stirring speech from that fucking mayor and they all went crazy. Dayton had also beaten him in a debate with his caring words about equality and justice. Don't those dumb fucks know there are people meant to rule and there are people who are meant to obey? It's the natural order of things. Always was and always will be. *Read your history books, if we had any,* he thought with irony.

It was the disappearance of television and other media outlets that was the problem Cooper faced today. They had no media entertainment and control to keep the sheep from thinking for themselves. Twenty years of freedom from the idiot box had actually increased people's intelligence. They were now aware of their surroundings.

This moneyless society was doomed to fail. One thing he knew about human nature was greed. Sooner or later, someone would bring money back into their lives, and Cooper was determined that it would be him, by one means or another.

Order, Control, and Obedience; those were the three pillars of a fruitful society.

Then he heard that the idiot of a preacher had run away from his own sister. The religious zeal that was just one manner of controlling people was dead. He guessed humanity had faced one too many catastrophes of which no saviour had come to rescue them, and they all gave the collective 'middle finger' to the invisible sky god above the clouds. And just this afternoon, that big idiot Beasley had informed the council that Dayton was not leaving until tomorrow morning, and he was only taking sixty of his so-called rangers. Carl had been hoping that he would take the lot of them, and they would all be killed in one fell swoop.

He sat down on a bench and started the timer on his old solar stopwatch; built to last these things were, which was why they didn't sell well in the old market system. Didn't those manufacturers realise that items that lasted for years were no good for their business and the economy?

He looked over at the two locked cells that the survivalists had in the cellar. So weird that family was, so paranoid, and so fortunate for Cooper. It had taken him a while to find the keys to the cells when he first moved in, but now they were hanging up on the wall close by.

The second element had failed him, he thought, and the fourth had been shunned by the people. But he was still the first element, and looking at all the ammunition and guns in one of the cells, he thought he still had a chance of controlling the third element.

He looked down at his stopwatch as it just passed the five minute mark. *Hmm, I wonder how long it will take this time,* he thought as he glanced over to the rectangular wooden box in the second cell.

He tapped his fingers impatiently on his legs. He still hadn't decided what to do next. It all depended on what happened in the next meeting with Mason. Would his plan work? It was risky.

Suddenly, he heard a low moan coming from the wooden box. Daisy was her name. He had married her, or what you call getting married in this day and age, ten years ago. She was one crazy bitch, he remembered with fondness. She used to ride him like a horse so he couldn't walk properly for a week, shoot and kill as many people as the most savage of the bandits, and still cook him up a meal fit for a king. God, he loved her, or lusted after her.

Truth be told, he was a little scared of her. But she was the one who came up with the idea of moving down the Huon and getting away from the pointless destruction of Mason. She was the one who told him to murder the survivalist, and she was the one who gave him the idea for taking over this town.

And then, one winter four years ago, she came down with a fever that could not be treated by any natural remedies that they all had to use nowadays and died within a week.

For some reason, maybe fate, he couldn't do what he had to do and kill her properly, so he gagged her, threw her over his shoulder, and took her down to the cellar cells.

After watching her moaning and groaning in her cell for half a day, he got bored and left her there.

It was only a day later that he noticed the groaning had stopped. So he walked down the cellar stairs and stood there in shock as she was lying on the ground, looking like she was asleep.

He stood there for about five minutes, too stunned to approach and wondering what he should do, when he noticed her nose starting to twitch, then her arm moved, and then her legs. A few minutes later, her eyes opened, and she stood up and started groaning at him against the cell bars and making biting sounds with her teeth.

He continued this experiment for over a year and found out that she would consistently groan for a day when he left her alone, and then stop. He would go back to the cell after a longer and longer duration and find her asleep on the ground, and then the same reaction would occur. Five to ten minutes in his presence, and she would come back to life, or death as it may be.

He also noticed that due to the amount of time she had been sleeping, her body had deteriorated at a far lesser pace than good old Premier Pratt, but recently, she had begun to stink badly. Because of this smell, he had decided to keep her in a box. This was kind of risky, but each time she would fall 'asleep', he would quickly come downstairs, enter the cell, pick her up, and place her in a wooden box he had made for her.

So long as he was quick about it, and he was, she would not show any reaction that she was aware of him in that brief time. The last time she had been awake was when that dumb bastard Rainswood had decided to sleep on the floor just above her. The zombies must be very good at smelling human flesh. He was surprised the preacher hadn't noticed the smell coming through the floorboards, but then again, Rainswood smelt just as bad.

Suddenly, the top of the wooden box was pushed open, and his lovely wife rose from her sleep. She still looked half-decent, he thought with a grin.

"Hello, Daisy. My dear wife," he said as she started moaning at him, craving to eat his flesh.

He looked down at the stopwatch. Ten minutes exactly.

"And that is why," he said to himself, "Dayton, my old friend, you are totally fucked."

Jon and his family stood outside of Jane Butler's house, all ready to leave for Kingston.

"Is everything prepared?" Jane Butler said as she brushed dust from the shoulders of Jon's long jacket.

Jesse was waiting for his father on his horse a few metres away. He had already said his goodbyes.

"I think so." Jon sighed, looking down at her. "You look

troubled … are you … are you worried for me?" he said, startled at the thought.

"Of course not," Jane said sharply and smacked his arm. Hard. Ash stood to her grandmother's left, grinning at them as she held Lily by the hand.

"I want to apologise for the way I acted, Ash," her father said, now facing her. "It wasn't the way a father should behave," he said in embarrassment.

"Dad, I understand, about everything." She came forward and also started fussing with his jacket. "Here, I have brought you a present for your journey."

And Ash brought out a small brass telescope from one of her numerous pockets in her fur clothing.

"It's good for seeing long distances and for clocking people over the head if they disagree with you," she finished with a grin.

"Where did you get this from?" It was truly a great present, he thought, grinning from ear to ear.

"Oh, you know, we women have a talent for finding a bargain." Jon burst out into laughter. No doubt that was a saying she picked up from her grandmother.

"Thank you, Ash," he said, giving her a big hug.

Rob then arrived, walking Jon's horse from the stable. He seemed to wearing every weapon he had available, perhaps just to show him that he was serious about protecting his family.

"Thank you, Rob," Jon said as he handed the reins over to him. "I'm sorry I made you stay."

"That's okay, Captain. I understand," he replied as he stood next to his family, towering over them.

Everybody seemed to be saying, 'I understand' to him today.

"Is your grandfather ready?"

"Yes. Harry, Pop, and Rachael are waiting for you down at the gate."

He just realised that he had separated Rob from his twin sister. "Rachael will be safe. We will all look after her."

"Yes, I know." He smiled back. "If my uncle and grandfather can't look after her, then nobody can. Well, except maybe Jesse." Jesse grinned at him.

Now came the time that he was dreading.

"I guess this is goodbye then," he said as he faced his daughters. Lily looked like she was about to cry, so he adjusted his katana sword on his hip and crouched down on his haunches, looking at her at eye level.

"I will be back by tomorrow night, sweetheart."

"Yes, Daddy," she replied in that small voice of hers.

"I was thinking that maybe you could look after my hat for me whilst I'm gone," he told her, as he handed his precious Eastwood hat over to someone far more precious. "It would make me happy to know you were keeping it safe for me for when I get back."

"Okay, Daddy." She smiled as he passed her his hat, which was normally a largish hat, but now seemed huge in Lily's tiny hands.

"We will look after it," said Ash as she picked Lily up and held her in her arms.

Standing up, he looked at his two daughters and felt tears come to his eyes. This wasn't a panic attack like he'd had before. This was tears because he loved them.

"Never forget that I love you," he said as he embraced both of his daughters.

"We know," said Ash as they broke apart. Lily put her head down on her sister's shoulder. "We love you too."

He nodded goodbye to Jane and Rob, and then turned and mounted his horse.

He looked down at his daughters one last time and said, "Never forget."

"Never forget," Ash replied with tears in her eyes.

Harry leaned against the corner of the gate, looking over the thirty men and women he had under his command. They were all fit and healthy, he observed, which was good because they had a lot of bushwalking to do.

As the thirty horsemen and women rode down the main road, his people were to roam the nearby bushlands to look for any planned ambush by Mason or any other bandit. They couldn't do it on the high passes of the road, but for most of the journey, they would be providing good protection for the riders.

He wasn't sure about Jon's hunch that Mason and his gang may be still about, but he wasn't about to take any chances.

"Why are your people carrying shields on their backs?" said Jack as he walked over to his older brother.

"Just an idea I had from reading the history books." *When we had them,* he thought grimly. "We all have bows, trench knives, and short swords, but the riders have more protection with the maneuverability of their horses. We are just stuck out in the open. Be good to have some extra protection," he finished.

"Where did you get them from?" replied Jack.

"Well, that's the funny thing," said Harry. "They are from the old police station." He took his shield off his back to show him.

Jack held up the round grey shield and examined it.

"They're very light," he said.

"Yes, but very strong, and if you crouch down, you can cover yourself from any arrow attack."

"What, even us?" Jack said, laughing.

"Well, maybe not us," Harry answered with an impish grin.

Both Jack and Harry were of the same height, but Jack seemed heavier in width. Billy seemed to be the slim one. Well, slim compared to his brothers.

"How did you do with the recruitment?" he continued.

"Good," replied Jack. "There are so many people here who have had soldier—sorry, ranger—experience that I now have over a hundred people at my disposal. They know Jon is going to Hobart for the books, so nobody is suspicious as to why they were really needed."

"Do you believe Mason is out there?" asked Harry.

"I'm not sure," replied Jack, "but you know it's better to be …"

"Safe than sorry," they both finished up together.

"Oh, look out, here's trouble," said Jack, laughing.

"Well, well," came a booming voice. "My, aren't you a couple of handsome lads. Must have had a good-looking father," Ray finished with that big grin of his. In fact, it was a big grin that they all shared, even Rachael.

He walked his horse up to them and was followed by that mountain of a dog of his. I wonder if Dog and the horse are related, Jack thought with a smile.

"Still wearing that possum on your head." Harry laughed as he patted Dog and was rewarded with a big amount of slobber on his arm.

"It's my good luck possum," he replied with a smile. "The bastard was a bugger to kill, just like me, I hope."

Jack suddenly felt a chill that his brother, daughter, and father were walking into possible danger.

"You will be careful, I hope, both of you. You will look after Rachael?" Jack said with a touch of concern. He was starting to realise how Jon felt with his daughters.

"We will be okay," his father said, patting his arm. "Takes a lot to stop a Beasley, and nobody lays a hand on my granddaughter," he finished with steel in his voice.

"We'll be all right, mate," Harry said with a nod.

Just then, they heard the sound of horses as Jon and Jesse rode up with twenty-seven other riders following behind.

"Time to mount up, Ray," said Jon. "You taking Dog with you?"

"Yes, mate, the poor beastie pines when I'm away."

He did, actually, thought Harry. Dog may look like a brute, but he was a big softy whenever Ray left him. Harry knew this because he was the one who generally had to look after him.

"Jack, do you have enough people to protect the town?" continued Jon, who had now taken on his serious face.

"More than enough, Captain; over a hundred."

"Good, good," Jon replied, breathing a sigh of relief and looking up at the large bell that was only rung when Grovetown was in desperate danger. "Well, it's time to leave."

"Just a moment, Captain," said Jack, and he walked over to his father and brother and gave them each a backslapping hug. Then he walked over to Rachael, who was on her horse next to Jesse. He reached up and took her hand.

"You be careful, little one," he said with a frog in his throat.

"Of course, Dad," Rachael replied. "We will all be back by tomorrow night," she assured him, gently squeezing his hand.

"Jesse, you look after her," he said, releasing her hand and turning towards him.

"I promise," Jesse replied in a solemn tone.

"Okay, then," he said, still with that damned frog in his throat as he stood back to let them pass.

"Tomorrow night," said Jon with a nod as he rode forward.

"Look after our people," said Harry as he began to run.

"We will bring back some good books for the grandkiddies," said his father.

"I love you, Dad," Rachael said, smiling as she rode out, followed by her friends Isaac, Liam, Taylor, and McCrae.

Jack stood at the gate for a few minutes as he watched the thirty riders walk their horses up the main road towards Kingston. He could pick out his father due to that large animal called Dog walking alongside of him, and of course, his stupid hat.

He saw his brother direct two groups of runners to move to the bush land on each side. Shields, bows, and food packs bounced on their backs as they began to run.

He saw his daughter smiling and talking to Jesse and their friends as they rode on their favourite horses. Thick ropes and metre-long camping shovels hung from their saddles, and bows and arrows were slung across their shoulders. Some even had small containers of the precious kerosene. Jon had them all prepared for any situation.

They will be fine, he convinced himself as he watched them all pass into the distance like ghosts.

"Close the gate, and man the ramparts," he said to the forty rangers who were left behind. They would take shifts, but he would make sure there were always at least forty rangers at the ready should any attack happen.

And as the gates closed, he said quietly, "They will be fine."

But as we all know, life is not always fine, and tragedies will occur. And if Jack's mind could have foreseen just two days into the future, he would know that not many of them would be returning, and he would have been running up the road right now screaming for all of them to come back.

Kingston Beach, twelve kilometres south of Hobart

Billy should have been feeling as content as he had ever been, as he walked along the sandy beach of Kingston. He had experienced in the last two days something wonderful that he had never had before, but his thoughts kept drifting to his family in the south. *Where are they?* he kept thinking over and over.

"Are you all right, Billy?" Jessica said as the sea breeze blew back her long brown hair.

"Yes, fine, Jess—No, that's not true; I'm not fine. Where the bloody hell are they?" he said in exasperation.

"Perhaps they got held up and delayed the trip," Jessica suggested.

"That's what I'm worried about," Billy replied with a sigh.

"I'm sure there is a good reason," she said with that lovely smile of hers. "Do you remember the old days? We could have just called them up on the phone."

"Yes, I remember," he said with a sad smile. He had strong memories of talking to his father on the Holophone when the zombies were either trying to eat him at school or at home. Harry had saved him both times. He wondered where his older brother was. It seemed strange not having him around. For over thirty years, they had lived together, and now he could feel his absence even after only two days.

He wasn't even sure who in his family was coming to Kingston, except for his dad, who had been Jon's constant friend and companion for so long.

All he knew was, on that brilliant day at the council meeting, Jon had promised to send his soldiers into Hobart to retrieve some books, and they were meant to arrive here last night.

It was only a twenty kilometre journey between Grovetown and Kingston after all. But knowing Jon as he did, he knew that the twenty kilometres would take as many hours as was necessary, as Jon would do all that it would take to make sure they didn't walk into any bandit trap. But it wouldn't take overnight.

"The jacket looks good on you, I think," Jessica said.

"Thanks," he said, feeling embarrassed.

This morning, Mayor Nash had presented him with a green wool jacket, which all the rangers in this area wore. He must admit he did like it. Mayor Nash said it took the makers an extra bale of wool to make the jacket fit across his shoulders.

Jessica smiled up at him with her blue eyes, and he bent down and kissed her again. He was constantly kissing her, as she was so damned beautiful and so likable. His father said that some beautiful women only cared about their looks and never worked on being a good human being. Superficial, he called them. The universe seemed to have blessed him to let him meet a lovely girl like Jessica.

He must keep an eye out for a nice woman for Harry, he thought.

"I was wondering if you would like to come with me and see my old house," said Billy. He wondered if it was still there; it wasn't the sturdiest of houses to begin with. It might not be still standing.

"I'd like that," replied Jessica, smiling at him with pleasure. Billy wished they still had some guns and ammunition in that house. But he did remember that Dad and Harry had cleaned all of the weapons out of the cabinet, because he'd had to carry most of them to Grove and complained the whole way.

"Billy, Jess," a loud voice shouted from back on the road. They turned and saw Jessica's father on his horse, beckoning them towards him. Behind him were about fifty riders, all wearing the green uniform that Billy now wore.

Walking quickly towards him, they noticed he had a serious look on his face.

"We've had scout reports of thirty horsemen moving towards us from the south road," the mayor said.

"Thirty!" said Billy. "That doesn't sound right. Jon would have taken at least a hundred with him."

The mayor frowned as he looked into the distance.

"The bandits that Jon's soldiers killed recently numbered only thirty," Billy continued.

The mayor gave him a sharp look.

"Right, that settles it," said the Mayor in a firm voice. "We are going out to confront them," and his hand reached down to stroke the massive axe he carried.

"Please, Mayor," Billy said. "The fact that they are riding down the main thoroughfare suggests they are either arrogant, stupid, or this is some sort of trap. Please let me take some scouts to the surrounding bush land. If they are planning a trap and have men there," he continued, "we will find them and kill them; at the very least, we can outflank the riders."

The mayor looked down at him with a smile. Then he looked at his daughter and said, "You've done well here, my girl."

Jessica blushed, and so did Billy.

The mayor turned around and said to his second-in-command, "Get twenty of the scouts now." Then, after a pause, as if in afterthought, "Oh, and they are following Billy's orders."

Harry and his fourteen rangers on this side of the road stepped stealthily through the bush land on Jon's left flank. It had been an exhausting day; it rained heavily for most of the journey, but at last, they were coming within sight of Kingston.

To Harry's relief, they had not come across a single sight or any piece of evidence that there was any enemy waiting for them, but Jon, as cautious as always, would insist on a slow and steady progress.

So his people would move through the bush where they could, and when they came to a part in the road where they had to join the riders, Jon would ask him to scout ahead for any possible danger.

The only danger Harry had come across were two massive holes in the road that they had to cautiously navigate themselves and the horses around the edges to get across. One of the holes angled downwards off the road towards a cliff that would have led to a five hundred-metre fall into the rocks and trees below if anybody fell into it. The years of rain had taken a heavy toll on some parts of the old highway. It almost looked like a waterfall when the rain was heavy.

Jon was sure that if there was a trap, this is where it would be laid, so he sent a few scouts ahead, and then they waited half an hour. All up, it took over an hour to get by each one of them.

He was looking forward to a rest, food, and shelter, Harry thought with a sigh. The mayor owed them a good feed, and he was itching to see his little brother Billy.

Harry then froze as a scout to his left held up his hand in a fist as a sign of contact; he then pointed one finger in the air to relay that this was only a noise contact, not a visual. These signals were repeated up and down the line, and the person who was closest to the road would report this to Jon.

It could just be wildlife roaming through the bush, but Harry still crouched down behind a nearby tree and lifted his bow and pointed an arrow into the trees ahead. His ears and eyes strained for any sound and sight of any animal or enemy as he scanned the area.

Suddenly, he saw a tuft of blond hair from behind a fallen tree, maybe fifty metres in front of them.

He raised two fingers for the sign of visual contact as his scouts readied themselves for battle.

What was he to do? They could just play the waiting game like Jon always did. But, no, he was a Beasley; his type were not patient. What would his father do?

"You need a haircut, mate. I can see your ugly blond noggin from way over here," he called out.

He saw the blond hair twitch and heard him say,

"Well, at least I'm not going grey yet, Harry."

Harry let out a sigh of relief, lowered the bow, and stood up. He smiled as he saw Billy do the same and walked over to him and gave him one of the famous Beasley backslapping hugs.

"What's with the green jacket, you wanker?"

"Ah, you know, I think it suits my eyes."

And they looked at each other and laughed.

All of the scouts now stood up and greeted each other, Grovetown wearing their furs, and Kingston with their green jackets. *Hmm, I hope they weren't offended by the 'wanker' comment,* thought Harry.

But for nine months a year, and due to the heavy rain, Tassie forests were mostly dark green, and he had to admit their clothing blended into the background better than his.

Rachael would be very keen for our mob to start wearing these jackets, he thought, especially after changing our name to rangers.

So they all moved down onto the main road, and Harry saw that Jon and his father were talking amicably to Mayor Nash, and a large congregation of people on horses or standing on foot surrounded them with smiles of relief on their faces.

"Big feast tonight, my boy. Compliments of the mayor," said

Ray, smiling at him as the mayor nodded to him in approval. "You bloody beauty," replied Harry with a laugh as his stomach rumbled loudly.

Grovetown, thirty-one kilometres south of Hobart

Carl Cooper walked through the trees on his way to the Mason Camp. He could have rode, but riding a horse out at this time of night would have led to some questions being asked, which he didn't want, especially since the security in Grovetown had been ramped up by the son of an idiot Jack Beasley, who was probably right this minute walking around the walls, glaring into the distance.

That man looked like he could break bricks with his bare hands, he was so huge.

Anyway, he needed time to think as he made the five-kilometre journey west of Grovetown, plus the moaning sound from Daisy was starting to drive him mad.

He must have looked like something from an old science fiction film as he wore his huge robe and had his nighttime vision goggles on, but he would rather look like a freak than fall flat on his face in the dark.

What was he to do? he wondered, as he reached the outskirts of the Mason encampment. He had the guns, but he would not give them to the gang until he was sure of his position. None of the gang knew where he lived, and he always gave the impression that the guns were kept in a secret location, so he was sure that the guns were his to keep and give as he willed; so long as they didn't torture him for the information, he thought with a shiver.

He had to make sure that it was him who led Grovetown, not Mason, otherwise everybody was as good as dead. At least with him as a leader, people would be killed only if they disagreed with him.

He wondered at how much he had changed. The Collapse must have changed everybody in various ways. Had this man always been inside of him, just waiting for a chance to get out? Or had the day when ninety plus percent of the population were brutally killed changed him forever?

He didn't know, and he didn't care. *It is what it is,* he thought, as he entered the camp.

"Oh, look, it's a Jawa," said one of the guards as he walked past.

"Shut up," whispered another. "That's Cooper from Grovetown. He killed Clark for being a smart prick."

"But Clark was a smart prick."

"I know, but he killed him, right?"

"So what?"

"Well, that Jawa comment—Oh, doesn't matter."

Cooper smiled to himself. Stupid dumb fucks.

Walking up to the middle of the encampment, he saw Mason sitting in front of the fire, eating a well-cooked rabbit on a spit. Bald-headed Craig Bradfield was standing behind him, and was that talkative Turner next to him? Interesting, Cooper thought.

"Good evening, Joe," Cooper said, taking off his goggles. "How are you this fine evening?"

Captain Joe Mason just looked at him with that mass of facial hair that he had and kept on eating the rabbit.

This isn't looking good, Cooper thought with a grimace.

"Are you ready for the next stage in our plan?" Cooper hadn't worked out what the next stage was just at this moment, but judging from Mason's stares, it shouldn't be too long until it started.

"And where is our loyal friend Steve Perrin?"

Mason froze, put down the rabbit, and walked over to his tent. He soon came back out holding a long clump of greasy hair. On the end of the hair was the head of Steve Perrin.

"Ah, so Steve must have upset you in some way, I guess."

"You could say that," Mason agreed with gritted teeth as he started walking over towards him.

He suddenly noticed that a large number of men were moving up behind Bradfield and Turner and were watching the proceedings with great interest. He wondered if Mason noticed the amount of men that were now gathering. Maybe or maybe not; psychopaths were so hard to judge, and twenty years of rule brought with it complacency.

As Mason moved closer, he saw that Perrin's head was snapping its teeth. So he didn't brain-kill this man, then. This will test his nerve and reflexes.

"I'm tired of waiting for you, Cooper," Mason said in a tight voice, as he came closer. "Your so-called fucking plan is a bunch of fucking crap. I'm calling the shots now."

Cooper remained where he was, with his hands in his robe pockets. *No, you're not, Mason,* he thought. *One way or another, you're not in charge now.*

Mason now stood within a few feet of Cooper and thrust Perrin's head inches in front of his face and started shouting. "I saw you looking at Perrin when you were here last," he screamed, as spittle from his mouth flew into Cooper's face. "I know you were conspiring with him."

Conspiring? Such a big word, Joe, Cooper thought.

"No, actually, Perrin was very loyal to you," he replied.

"What do you mean loyal, you smug cunt?" he demanded, as another spray of spittle went across Cooper's face.

I'm dying to wipe my face, Cooper thought with exasperation, but he kept his hands where they were.

"He was loyal, Joe. See, look at him now; even in death, he is trying to bite my face and defend you," he said, trying not to lean back from Perrin's gaping mouth.

"You always were a smartarse, Carl. I should have killed you years ago." He stepped even closer, and Perrin's teeth were now centimetres from Cooper's face. "Now, where are my guns?" he screamed.

"Right here," Cooper said in a calm voice and lifted his hand in his robe, which was holding a pistol, and blew a large hole in Mason's stomach. He looked over at Bradfield's men and saw them disappear into the darkness.

Cooper then walked over to Mason, who was now rolling on the ground, screaming and trying to stop the bleeding from his guts. No, he wasn't screaming, he was actually crying, Carl thought with a laugh. The scourge of the East, the great tyrant Joe Mason was crying like a little baby. Sure, it must hurt, Cooper thought, but even in death, you did have a reputation to consider.

"You ruined my best Jawa robe," Cooper said as he put a finger through the bullet hole in his pocket. "Oh, and say it, don't spray it," he scoffed, as he finally got to wipe his face.

He looked over at Perrin's head lying next to Mason.

"He was actually loyal to you," he said again, as he fired a shot straight into Zombie Perrin's brain. "It was Bradfield who wasn't."

Cooper had many talks with Bradfield over the years, and a few private conversations in recent times gave him some hope of what would happen today.

Big Bald Bullheaded Craig Bradfield walked over with his new second-in-command, Talkative Turner.

"You stupid bastard, Mason," said Bradfield as he looked down on his old leader and planted a boot in his ribs. "For twenty years I followed you, and look what we have for it." He gestured to the bog hole of a camp. "We are all sick of wandering around in the bush. I want a home," he shouted and planted another well-placed kick to the ribs, which earned more squealing and crying from the dying Mason.

"All Cooper had to do was glance a few times at Perrin and you then killed him in your paranoia," Bradfield continued with another kick. "And you didn't even realise that the people you left with Mad Zelda were all loyal to you."

Then Cooper heard screams come from the darkness.

Obviously, Bradfield's men were killing the rest of those loyal to Mason.

"So what are your plans?" Cooper said to Bradfield in hope.

"We will follow you," said Bradfield. "I see the way you work." Looking down at Mason and giving another well-placed kick, he seemed to delight in making him cry out some more. "You get things done. We should have followed you years ago."

Cooper felt a warmth building up in his cold heart.

"So you are the Bradfield Gang then, from miles to the north. Mercenaries for hire, travelling all of Tasmania, men who are always willing to defend the defenceless in their hometown," Cooper said.

Bradfield laughed. "Yes, I guess we are, especially after the Hobart disaster. But the only problem is, we liked to get paid in money."

Sweet Jesus, all of my Christmases have come up at once, Cooper thought with a laugh.

"The only two hindrances I see are that some of Dayton's ranger's may survive the trap in Hobart. However unlikely it is that anybody would."

"Turner will lead some of our men and women tomorrow morning to stop that. I know a perfect place for a trap, four kilometres out of Grovetown," said Bradfield, nodding at his companion, who just grunted his assent.

"Be sure to make sure they know that this is Mason doing the attacking, in case any survive. Dayton is still suspicious that you are still around." Suffering from paranoia though Dayton was, in this case, he was completely correct. "Also, if Dayton should send a rider back to Grovetown early tomorrow to warn them or ask for reinforcements, let them pass through, but give them a scare, will you? I want all the people in Grovetown too frightened to come out of the fortress."

"Mason will be doing the attacking tomorrow," Bradfield agreed with a nod. "Won't they, Turner?" Turner just grunted.

"But the Bradfield Militia," he continued, "will take care of them when they arrive, in say a week's time?"

Cooper looked out into the darkness. "So you are keeping some of Mason's loyalists alive then?"

"Yes." Bradfield said. "If we come into Grovetown with the Mason Gang's freshly killed heads, we will be hailed as heroes."

"Brilliant," Cooper said, nodding. "My dear boy, Bradfield, you should have been leading this merry band for years. We could have run all Southern Tasmania by now."

"Thank you, Councillor," he replied with a grin.

Similar to the classic military and political strategy, Cooper thought with approval. Create an enemy to keep your own people in line, make the changes that you always wanted, then kill your own creation and be hailed as saviours.

"The other problem is Jack Beasley and his surviving forty rangers."

"Well, they won't be able to stop seventy mercenaries with guns, now, will they?" Bradfield said with a pointed look at Cooper. *Seventy!* So Mason had at least thirty loyal people out there. "No, they won't," Cooper replied as he pulled out two shotguns that were tied under his robe and handed one each to Turner and

Bradfield.

"Meet me outside the northwest side of Grovetown at midnight tomorrow," he said. This was very close to his house. "Bring twenty men with night vision goggles with you. There are a lot of guns and ammunition to carry."

The cell at his home was chock-a-block full of weapons. Bradfield breathed a sigh of relief and smiled as he handled the shotgun. Cooper thought he just might trust Bradfield. Well, a little anyway. Turner looked at the shotgun, and the big man with light skin and curly red hair actually laughed with pleasure and said 'thank you" in that rough voice of his.

Well, what do you know, Cooper thought with surprise. *Is there nothing that a loaded shotgun can't fix?*

Cooper then put on his goggles and began to walk away. Bradfield gave a small cough and nodded at the ground.

"Oh, yes, of course. How forgetful of me." Cooper walked over to the still-crying mess that was Joe Mason. "Goodbye, Mad Dog," he said and put a bullet in his head.

Peter Rainswood had another fit of the giggles and had to place his gloved hand over his mouth to stop the family above him from hearing.

This is so much fun, he thought, as he placed another collection of dry wood under the community hall.

Nobody had caught him, or even seen him as he scurried around the nearby area. Any sort of protection this community had was all on the fortress walls, looking outwards.

The only trouble he found was the occasional spider web or rat that he came across as he crawled his way under the building.

For the third night running, Peter had come down from the home where he slept most of the day, and with his night goggles and wearing his decent-sized hooded robe, had placed enough flammable material under the hall that when it was time to light a match, it should go up in a matter of minutes.

And it was all so easy.

Work details were always travelling south to fell trees and bring back freshly chopped wood. And then they just left this wood in a covered area for anybody to take. Fucking madness, he thought as he stifled another giggle.

He could hear his sister talking to one of her kids, who was obviously having trouble sleeping. *I hope you burn, bitch*, he thought, as he listened to her kind words for one of her shitty little ankle biters. Never for a second did it cross his mind that these children were of his blood, his own nephews and nieces.

All was prepared, he thought. He had obtained a little kerosene can so he could burn the building down easier. So he could burn the hall down right this minute, if he wanted to.

But nobody was around at this time of night to watch, and a part of him required an audience for this sort of event.

So he decided to wait until the right time before lighting the match. It needed to be some momentous event, where everybody would stare and marvel at his creation.

Peter scuttled out from under the floorboards and crept back to his home, giggling under his breath.

Kingston, twelve kilometres south of Hobart

Riders and scouts lined up for the journey into Hobart. While the southbound lane was still full of twenty-year-old burned-out and rusted vehicles, the northbound lane was virtually clear for their ride into town. Nobody had driven *into* the city on that fateful day.

Jon noted that some of the vehicles had human skeletons still in them. They must have burned in the cars' inferno. Too dead, even for the dead. One day, he hoped this highway would be cleaned up and the horror of that day would only be remembered only in the history books.

Whilst the night spent at Kingston Beach had been one of food and laughter, this morning, a nervous mood had come over his people at the journey they were about to undertake.

Jon, in his keenness to get this day over and done with, had asked everybody to be up and moving at the crack of dawn. With a bit of luck, they should all be home a lot earlier than expected. The idea of arriving back early and surprising Ash and Lily brought a smile to his face.

"You sure you don't want us to come with you?" said Mayor

Nash as he sat upon his horse with a number of rangers behind him.

"No, we will be fine," Jon assured him. "Three hours to get there, thirty minutes in the city, three hours to return. I'm sure no bandits would be mad enough to live there with all the corpses on the streets." In fact, the corpses still being there meant there were no bandits there at all, he thought. "Just have a nice lunch waiting for us when we get back," he said, smiling. Jon thought Mayor Nash was a fine fellow. He and Ray got on like a house on fire. He had even given Ray a gift, he thought with a sigh.

"Look at it," Ray had said last night in excitement as he showed Jon his new axe. "It's a bit hard to use from a horse," Jon had said, but Ray just grinned like an idiot, pointed at it, and kept saying "just look at it" as his sons Harry and Billy were also grinning in the background.

"Right you are then," said the mayor, smiling back. "We'll have nice warm broths of stew ready for your return," and then he nodded to Jon and Ray and rode back to his community.

"Are you coming with us, Uncle Billy?" Rachael asked with a grin, knowing all too well that Billy was spending the morning with Jessica.

Rachael was also wearing a new green jacket. *Bloody hell, that didn't take her long,* thought Jon.

"No. I think I'll hang out here for a bit," mumbled Billy in reply, looking over at Jessica. This earned him a few sniggers from the nearby riders, as they both rode off together.

"All right, then, I see no need for any more delay," said Jon.

"A mountain bike right now would be handy," Ray said suddenly as he looked at the long, empty highway.

"You hated those things," Jon replied. "I seem to recall they put any chance of you having any more kids in jeopardy. Anyway, you definitely can't swing an axe from a mountain bike."

Ray laughed. "I've got enough kids and grandkids to be going on with, I think," he said as he looked over fondly at Harry, who was standing by his side and Rachael over to his right, who was sitting on her favourite horse, smiling at Jesse.

"And I can certainly give it a try," he continued.

"Kids?"

"No, the axe," he replied, laughing again.

"Shall I say 'Forward Ho' like in the western movies?" Jon asked, trying to alleviate some of his tension.

"Wasn't it Tally Ho?" replied Ray.

"I thought that was used for a Fox Hunt?" said Harry.

"Oh, yeah, that's right, my boy, but I think if you said 'Forward Ho', the young ones wouldn't know what you were talking about."

"Indeed," said Jon.

"How about, let's get this show on the road."

"What are they talking about?" said Rachael, fiddling with her reins on her horse.

"Not sure," replied Jesse.

"Something about a fox hunt?" chipped in McCrae.

"What's a fox?" said Taylor.

"A sexy woman," her sixteen-year-old cousin Isaac said.

"It's an animal, idiot," said his older brother, Liam.

"How do you know that?" replied Isaac.

"Read it in a book once," Liam said with a pointed look at their Captain, Ray, and Harry.

"Aaahh, yes. Books," said Jesse in a loud voice.

Jon looked over at his young rangers when he heard the word 'books' said a bit too loudly.

Jesse, his eldest child and only son, who looked just like he himself had at that age, Rachael, with her long blonde hair in a braid, pretty as a picture, who would hopefully one day be Jesse's wife, Jesse's lifelong best friend, McCrae, who liked to be called by his last name because he hated his first name, and nobody could really remember what it was. Eighteen-year-old Taylor with her wild curly hair and cheeky grin, who was also the best archer he had ever seen. Taylor's cousins Liam, with dark curly hair, and Isaac with straight blond hair, both of whom Taylor liked to boss around all the time. Beyond them was tall red-haired Jason, a small blonde-haired girl called Sally, fiery Fiona, who was the toughest of them all, including the boys, and whom Ray referred to as their own 'qualified scrag fighter', whatever that meant.

He looked at all of them and hoped that he could bring everyone home safely.

Taking a deep breath and deciding not to give any orders, Jon lifted his right hand and made a pointing direction northwards, and they all began to move, with Ray's dog racing down the highway first.

Feeling safe now and out of any perceived Mason attack, his rangers moved along the highway in a double file of horse and foot.

"I have a spare possum hat if you want one?" said Ray suddenly.

"No, I'm fine," Jon told him with a smile. "The vitamin D will do me good."

And as the sun came up, Jon and Ray were returning to the capital city for the first time in twenty years.

"Do you think they will be all right?" said Jessica as they sat down together on an open grassy field near the highway.

"Yes, I'm sure they'll be fine. Your scouts reported no life in Hobart when they were there before." He started eating the cold meat and vegetables that they had gathered from the leftovers of last night's meal. "In fact, that young brash fellow named Tim said he had ridden through the middle of the city."

"Yes, he is a bit of a lad," replied Jessica with a grin. "He seemed quite disappointed that Ash wasn't part of the group who came."

Yes, he did, Billy thought, nodding his head, and he had been amazed to see that Jon had a long conversation with him. He even ended up shaking hands with him!

"Well, if Hobart is a ghost town, then they should all be safe and back by lunch."

But his eyes kept drifting to the highway, and he watched them march all the way down the road until they were gone.

Southern Outlet, one kilometre outside of Hobart

Jon was glad of Ash's present as he took another long look through the small telescope at the main road of Hobart City. The highway out of Hobart began with a steep climb up and over the hills, and the visitors from the south all stood at the top of that hill, waiting for Jon to give the command to commence the descent.

It's so green, thought Jon. Cities were always thought to be concrete jungles, but when people left, it was soon overtaken by Mother Nature.

"What do you think, Ray?" he asked his friend, who was leaning down from his horse to pat Dog.

"Dead as a dodo," replied Ray.

"Not the terminology I was looking for," Jon said with a grimace. Thinking of all the corpses he could see lying on the ground, he cringed.

"Oh, you know what I mean," Ray said. "The place is dead, as in zombie-free sort of dead."

Jon sighed and looked down once more on the city. The side of the highway they were using was all clear, and it looked like it was clear all the way into the city heart. The other side of the highway, the southbound lanes was jammed up with cars. Once in the city centre, they then had to take a left turn for only three blocks, but these three blocks would be full of burnt-out vehicles. Jon knew this because, twenty years ago, they'd had to ride out of that mess. *Perhaps Ray's idea of mountain bikes was a good one,* he thought with another sigh. But they had books to carry, and all the riders were carrying special bags that could be slung over the horses for the journey back home.

"Right," said Jon, trying to still his nervous heart. "Thirty horses should do it."

"You don't want us to come?" said Harry.

"No, I think you may slow us down if we had to make a run for it," Jon replied. "Stay up here, and provide some cover if any bandits show up."

"Okay, no worries, Captain," Harry agreed, nodding.

"Oh, and Ray, no dogs please."

"Yes, mate."

"Babysitting duties it is, then." Harry groaned as he bent down and placed an arm around Dog's shoulder to keep him from following his father.

Hobart City Centre

Jesse rode alongside of Rachael as they made their way down the main street of Hobart.

"So this is what the capital looks like," he said, as he looked at all the long-abandoned buildings. He wasn't impressed at all. Give him the forests and open spaces any day. This place looked too grey and drab.

"It's eerie," Rachael said softly, starting to look nervous. "I can't wait to get home." Her voice seemed too loud because there was no life at all in this town. The only other sound heard was their horses' hooves.

"We will be okay, Rachael," he assured her, looking at her with love in his eyes.

"I know," she said, smiling back at him.

Jesse looked down at some of the corpses they passed lying on the road. "Rachel, the corpses, they still have loose skin on their bodies, but it's pale white, and reminds me of a prune."

"They look like big white blobs," Rachael replied with a shiver. Some of their eyes were hanging out of their heads.

"It was the type of skin you have when you spent too much time in the bath," said Isaac behind them.

"Well, you don't have to worry about that, then," Liam said with a wrinkle of his nose.

Behind them rode their cousin Taylor, who smiled at the exchange.

Jesse looked up at the dark clouds gathering in the sky. Years and years of being rained on, but why haven't their bodies decayed?

He then asked his father, who was riding in front of him, the same question and was surprised and a touch scared as he and Uncle Ray both turned to look at him with concerned looks on their faces.

"I think we need to move faster," said his father, and the horses broke into a trot.

McCrae rode alongside Taylor as usual, trying to chat her up … as usual.

"Why do you think we are riding so fast?"

Taylor looked across at him in surprise. "Um, maybe because we are so far away from home and are surrounded by hundreds, if not thousands, of corpses," she said with those rosy cheeks that he so admired.

"Yeah, well, they are dead, right?" replied McCrae, trying to impress her with his untroubled attitude.

But Taylor was now looking into a nearby building with a long front window. Inside were lots of those shiny car things that people once used instead of horses.

"Taylor? Are you all right?"

"No … I-I thought I could see some bodies inside that building … and they didn't look like the others on the ground."

"What do you mean?" said McCrae, losing his carefree attitude and now sounding a bit nervous.

"Well, they looked … "

"What?"

She looked over at him with a face a lot paler than before. "Preserved."

Jon turned his horse at a fast trot into Harrington Street, which was where the town library resided. He felt the hairs on his neck stir and felt as if a thousand eyes were watching him.

Three blocks they had left to ride, which they had to do in two single files, due to the burned-out cars jamming the street.

As he passed another burned car, he again saw a human skeleton. So why on earth did the other bodies look like they did?

"Ray, is it just me or have you got a bad feeling about this?"

"I'm shitting bricks, to be honest, Jon. I don't mind admitting it."

Jon looked at his friend in shock. Ray was always so cocksure about, well, everything really, but now his friend's sudden uncertainty added to his own anxiety.

Must remain calm, Jon told himself. One thing he knew about great leaders of history was that they always remained calm in a crisis, at least on the outside. He wasn't a great leader, he knew that, but he did try his best.

"Jason, Sally," he called out in his most commanding voice, "you stay here and guard this corner." On the second corner, he ordered Taylor and Fiona to stand guard. Eight other riders were sent to mind the outlying street corners, and Liam and Isaac were sent to the block ahead as they finally reached their destination.

He then nominated seven riders, including Jesse and Rachael, to stay and mind two horses each so the other seven rangers could go inside the library. Ray and Jon stayed on their horses, trying their very best not to look too anxious.

"It's a walk in the park, isn't it, Ray?" said Jon.

"Piece of piss," replied Ray, but he was looking at all the buildings surrounding them like he was getting claustrophobia.

"McCrae, take your people inside the library. Grab all the books that we discussed, and move fast. I want to be gone from here in ten minutes," Jon commanded.

McCrae saluted and ran up the library steps quickly with his people holding those large hessian bags that, when draped across the horse, would carry a large number of books.

Jon looked at one of those pale white corpses on the ground, a complete mess of a human body. He kept thinking of a peeled and boiled potato that had been stepped on when he looked at it.

"Why do they look like that?" he said again.

"I'm not sure," Ray answered, then dismounted, and after giving his horse to Rachael, smashed his axe into its head.

Great, thought Jon, *now I'm thinking of mashed potatoes with tomato sauce on top.*

Ray removed his axe and froze as he looked into the takeaway shop across the road.

"What's the matter?" asked Jon.

"It's that corpse slumped against the wall there."

Jon dismounted, gave his mount to Jesse, who grumbled about now holding three horses, and followed Ray into the shop. They moved slowly over to one of the zombies, whose legs were on the floor with its back up against the counter. Its head was slumped forward, so thankfully, they didn't have to look at its face, but the smell made them gag.

"Twenty years," said Ray, holding a hand over his nose, "and it still looks like it has half its meat on its body." Looking over at Jon, he continued, "But the ones outside, the ones who have no protection from the elements, end up looking like a peeled Mr Potato Head."

Jon looked at the prone zombie. Its clothes were in tatters, the skin was flaky and falling apart, and beneath, you could see the muscle fibres, and ... was that a rat living inside of its body?

"And the people who were burned alive on the day of the Collapse without being infected are now complete skeletons," Jon finished, trying not to throw up.

"Let's get the fuck out of here as soon as possible," said Ray.

"Agreed."

And as they walked quickly back to their horses, they were unaware that the nose of the dead body against the counter had begun to twitch, and the rat inside had darted away.

Jason sat on his horse for the longest ten minutes of his life as he looked at the dead city.

Well, at least being stationed here meant they would be the first ones out, Jason thought with relief, as he gazed down one of the streets.

Sally was no good for company or protection, he thought as he tried to steady his nerves; she just kept on peering into one of the building windows.

"What are you looking at, Sal?" he said, trying not to sound annoyed. "You're meant to be looking down the street watching for bandits, not gazing into that window."

"Look!" She suddenly pointed.

Jason ripped out his sword and looked in the direction she was pointing, but saw nothing.

"What?" he almost shouted. "Why did you scare me like that?"

"Oh, I'm sorry, Jason." She giggled. "I was looking into this building, and, well, look at all of those dresses." She pointed again.

Oh, bloody hell, thought Jason. Take a woman into the most dangerous place they had ever been, and she still takes time to think about clothes. This must be one of the places that the old people called shops, he supposed.

"I need to get one," she said as she dismounted from her horse.

"We have orders, Sal," Jason protested.

"I won't be a second, Jason," she insisted, and he didn't even have time to reply as she darted into the building.

I'm going to kill her when she gets back, he thought in frustration. Now I have to look in both directions. The captain will kill me if we are attacked and I didn't give a warning.

Then he heard a loud scream come from inside of the building. Ignoring his previous thought about giving warnings, Jason jumped from his horse and ran headlong into the building.

His last sight of this world was of Sally being held down, with blood pouring from her neck and her stomach being ripped open, as dozens of zombies then descended upon him.

"So, you and McCrae, hey?" said Fiona as she made practice swings with her large mace.

Taylor thought that somehow the blacksmith in Grovetown enjoyed making vicious weapons a little bit too much.

"What do you mean me and McCrae?" replied Taylor, adjusting the bow on her shoulder and scanning the streets around her.

"Oh, you know, Taylor and McCrae sitting in a tree … " She then started to make kissing sounds with her lips.

Taylor gave a loud guffaw at that. "McCrae is just a friend."

"Oh, yeah, sure," Fiona scoffed.

"Anyway, what about you and Jason?"

"Piss off!" Fiona said, sounding offended. "Boys are just for punching in the head."

Taylor raised an eyebrow at her.

"Well, okay," she said as she blushed, "maybe I would like to punch him a few more times than some of the others."

Taylor was about to smile, when she heard a scream come from the street corner ahead.

Tennis balls, thought Isaac. What the hell was tennis? But he enjoyed the green fluffy bouncing things as he banged them against the ground and caught them on the way up.

Tojo, his horse who was named after his Grandmother's cat,

didn't mind them either, as he kept flicking his head towards the green ball. Trying to eat it probably, Isaac thought with a smile.

"Isaac, you dipstick," Liam said with gritted teeth. "You're meant to be watching the street ahead for trouble."

"What's a dipstick?"

Liam seemed stumped for a moment. "I don't know. Something I heard Dad say once. Now just keep an eye out, will you?"

"All right, keep your hair on," said Isaac, earning a confused look from his brother.

He moved his horse over to one of the white zombies lying on the ground and proceeded to bounce his tennis ball again.

For the next few minutes, he made a game of bouncing the ball between his or her arms and legs, trying not to hit any part of the body. Or what was left of it.

He stopped when he caught a flash of movement from the corner of his eye. He looked for a few moments at the street ahead and saw nothing of any particular note, then bounced the ball once more.

It took him a few seconds to realise the ball had not bounced back up to his hand as expected. He looked slowly down to the ground and saw that the ball was stuck in the zombie's hand and the thing that he had thought was long-dead was looking back up at him with cold, dead eyes.

Liam was frustrated with his brother, again. Why did he have to be such a pain in the arse all the time? He told him to stop bouncing that bloody ball and he did, for about thirty seconds.

He made up his mind that when he got back home, he was going to move out. He was eighteen now, a man grown. Sure, his mum would probably worry about him, but you know, that was just the way of the world, he thought, knowing deep down he was going to miss her and that his bossy cousin had told him on numerous occasions that he was a mummy's boy.

Suddenly, Isaac had stopped bouncing that bloody ball. Praise the Maker of the Universe, Liam thought.

Looking over at him, though, Liam's face went pale, as he saw his brother transfixed at what was thought to be a dead zombie lying on the ground, except this zombie had decided to play catch.

He now saw that the pale white slime of fleshy skin, which was supposed to be long-dead from this world, was slowly lifting itself off the ground.

This was making a big slurping noise as it detached itself from the road tarmac, which had been its constant friend for the last two decades.

Still, his little brother wasn't moving.

"Isaac!" he screamed, and riding towards the slimy thing, Liam took out his sword and beheaded it in one flowing stroke.

The body fell, but the head bounced down the street and landed with its neck facing the sky. Liam took a few seconds to realise that the eyes, albeit they were upside down, were looking back at him.

"What, what was that?" said Isaac, sounding terrified.

"I'm not sure, but we need to tell the others."

As he said this, he began to hear a low moaning sound. Looking up the long street that led away from the library, he was horror-struck by what he saw.

He remembered, as a child, his grandfather telling him a story about people who were looking to set some sort of world record. They would line all of these dominoes up against each other in a massive room or arena, and after setting up thousands of the things in some fancy design, the first domino was knocked over. This set in place a chain reaction, which would lead to all of the dominoes being knocked over one at a time. That was the exact opposite of what he saw today.

As he looked up the long street, he froze as he saw bodies rise, one by one, as far as the eye could see, and they all seemed to be looking directly at him.

All pale and rotting, they slowly made their way to a standing position, and just like a baby learning to walk, they began to stumble towards him, all the while making that awful moaning sound.

He suddenly realised he was being shaken. What, what was happening, he thought. He looked over at his brother, who was the one shaking him. Why was he doing that? he thought in a stupor. He heard his brother screaming at him. He heard the words 'red ones'.

His brother leaned across his horse and slapped his face hard. Awakened from the trance, he now heard the words.

"They are pouring out of the buildings. The red ones are walking fast. Let's go."

Jon and Ray had just remounted their horses. He was about to ask Jesse to go and check up on what was keeping McCrae's team when he heard a distant scream from near the main road. That was where Jason and Sally were, but all he could see were two riderless horses. He saw Taylor and Fiona look in that direction as well, but suddenly, Taylor looked to her left and began firing off arrows. Fiona turned to the main group and screamed as she brought out that lethal weapon she used.

Jon then heard horses being ridden at a fast pace, and he looked northwards and saw Liam and Isaac screaming words out. He picked out the words, "There are thousands of red ones!"

Ray then shouted out, "Jon, the takeaway shop!"

He looked over at the shop and saw that the zombie that had previously been lying down against the shop counter was now standing up and staring at them.

He then looked down at the smashed white zombie on the ground, looked back at the zombie in the shop, and knew what the phrase 'red ones' meant.

Jesse then yelled about zombies coming out of the buildings.

"Rangers, we are leaving!" Jon shouted at the top of his lungs.

But it was too late. It had been too late from the moment they set foot in this town.

Harry was getting bored as he and his thirty men and women sat on the ground, waiting for Jon to return. However, he did have the job of watching Dog very carefully to make sure he didn't run off in search of his master.

"He'll be back soon, mate," he said as he patted the dog.

Dog just looked at him, gave him a big slobbering kiss, then went back to pining for Ray.

"I'm sure they will be back soon, people," Harry said as he stood up and wiped the saliva from the side of his face.

"Would have been nice to see Hobart," said one of his

companions, a middle-aged man named Alan.

"Could have caught a flick," said Phil, who was also old enough to remember the old days and the great movies they were privileged to have seen.

"I think we might be seeing the best part of it," Harry replied, looking down on the grey concrete slab that was starting to look presentable with all the green plant life growing.

"Be nice to get back to Kingston," said another of his scouts. "I mean, they can sure cook up a storm."

"We can do a feast as good as them," replied Leanne proudly. She was one of the few female scouts he had with him.

"Stand up, people," Harry said, "and start doing some stretches; we have …" he trailed off as he looked down at Dog.

Despite being a monster-sized dog, he was always very friendly to everybody. Always happy to be patted and played with, and everybody knew he was a safe dog to have around the little children.

But now, Harry looked down at the black-and-white beast, and a feeling of trepidation overcame him. For the first time since he had known him, Dog was growling. He was looking at the city and growling.

Liam and Isaac rode straight towards Jon with a horde of zombies on their tails. The horses were running, so the zombies were running; he had learned that lesson years ago.

Jon brought out his sword and wheeled his horse around; he knew they had only one way out.

He then saw a rider from the outlying streets make it to the library road, but she was being swamped by countless zombies, who brought her and her horse down to the ground, screaming.

He saw McCrae and Brennemo, who was nicknamed The Viking, running out of the library to their horses, but the five people behind them were swamped by oncoming zombies. The poor horses, he thought numbly, as he looked upon one being torn apart. The poor riders, he thought in complete terror.

"Jon, we have to go now!" shouted Ray.

Jon felt helpless, but there was nothing he could do but run. Swinging his sword and decapitating one of the zombies, he pushed his horse forward. "Jesse, lets go, now!" he shouted as he looked upon his son's terrified young face. *I have to get him out,* Jon thought. That's all that mattered. Jon had lived a long life, but Jesse's was just beginning.

He heard Ray pleading the same to Rachael. He knew Ray was thinking exactly the same thing.

The streets were now packed with zombies, and they all had to push their horses hard to make their way through. The zombies were many, but their bodies were frail. If the horses could keep their feet, they should be able to get out of here.

He could see Fiona up the front swinging that mace of hers; *bloody hell she was good,* he thought as zombies were smashed one by one to kingdom come. Taylor was also firing the last of her arrows as she rode, nailing head shot after head shot.

Three blocks, Jon thought, and then they could race their horses at speed to the highway and perhaps get past the line of sight of the zombies. Three blocks, he kept saying in his mind, as he swung his sword time and time again.

Isaac was caught last in the line of horses. Typical, he thought, as he saw Liam and Taylor riding ahead of him. He looked to his left and saw big Ray Beasley swinging that mighty axe of his. He counted the horses as they rode in two lines between the cars and found that there were only ten. Ten! That was all, out of thirty.

I suppose it's not too bad being at the back, he thought. At least all Tojo had to do was jump the decapitated zombies. As soon as he thought this, Tojo stumbled and fell, dropping him down fair on his arse. Murphy's Law, he thought, another saying from his grandfather that he didn't understand.

"Wait up, Tojo," he cried as he saw his horse stand up and continue after the others. *Bloody horse,* he thought.

He was suddenly aware of all the zombies surrounding him. Standing up quickly, he drove his sword straight through the head of the closest zombie and climbed up on one of the car roofs.

He stood there in the middle of Hobart town, surrounded by hundreds of zombies, all wanting his flesh. He stood there with his heart racing, hands shaking, and nearly catatonic with terror. He stood there alone.

Liam watched as Taylor and Fiona's horses rode through the last of the zombies in this nightmare of a street and onto the main road. He felt a burst of relief as he too made his way to the main road. Now all they had to do was get past the white zombies and a few red ones on the road, get to the highway, then they could all leave this evil town.

This turned out to be easy, as riding through those pale white bastards was like punching a hole in a wet paper bag. With a quick glance behind, he saw Isaac's grey mare, Tojo, was running behind him. *We're almost there*, he thought with elation. In his elation, he didn't notice that the horse was riderless.

Isaac watched the pasty white zombies who could barely walk, and the half-decayed red ones who were able to run, from the top of the car. But they didn't seem to be able to jump or climb; all they could do was reach out to him, groaning.

"Think, Isaac," he said aloud as he looked around the street. "Okay, it's easy; all I have to do is make it one more block to the main road," he said, looking up towards the empty road.

"Once I am there, I can use my superior swordsmanship," he said with a crazy laugh, "and that combined with the fact that my adrenaline is going mental, I should be able to get myself to the highway." *But how do I get past all these bloody smelly bastards?*

Isaac took a long look at the road ahead. The zombies were all around the cars but couldn't climb them. The cars were all jammed bumper to bumper. What would a hero do?

Tasmania has only ever had one hero, his grandfather had told him, and then he came up with a hero's idea, a crazy idea, but an idea nonetheless.

He took a deep breath, then moved forward saying, "Bonnet, boot, roof," as he took three leaps to the other car. He then took another breath and leapt forward again, 'bonnet, boot, roof'. He lifted up his sword and took another three leaps. The main road was getting closer and closer as he continued jumping from car to car. Nearing the end of the blockade, he raised his sword to the crowd of red zombies who were moving along with him and stepping all over the white ones, who were almost literally breaking apart.

"And Captain Blood bids you a fond farewell!" he shouted as he leaped from the last car and hit the road, running flat chat up the main street. He hoped Errol Flynn was a fast runner as well.

Harry looked down the highway in shock as he saw the riders coming out of Hobart.

One, two, three ...nine, ten; only nine riders and ten horses! Harry's heart was racing as his eyes strained to see who was riding out of Hobart. *Where is my family?* he thought in panic, and gave a sigh of relief when he saw his father riding alongside of Rachael. They were all riding at a fast gallop. Even from here, Harry could see the fear in the riders and horses.

"What happened?" he said as they finally reached him.

"The zombies are alive," his father said with grief in his voice. "They're all a-fucking-live."

"How is that possible?" said Harry. "After all this time?"

"I don't know," his father said miserably as he reached out and touched his granddaughter's shoulder. No doubt, if he was off his horse, he would be hugging her right now. Rachael looked absolutely devastated.

Jesse was on the other side of Rachael. His hand reached out to hold hers, but he was watching his father intently.

"And the rest?" Harry said with a forlorn hope they would be arriving soon. He knew the answer before he even asked.

His father just shook his head in sorrow. Tears were swelling in his eyes as he said, "They were just kids."

Harry looked over at Jon. He seemed in a daze as he gazed back at the city.

"Captain, what are your orders?" Harry said, trying to sound official. He didn't like the haunted look in Jon's eyes.

"Orders?" he said absently. "Sorry, Harry. I'm not ... sure what to do next," he almost mumbled and went back to gazing at the city.

"Where is he?" Taylor suddenly screamed, looking around at the nine riders.

Liam looked around in horror. "He was just behind me!" *I saw him. Didn't I?*
"You should have watched him!" she shouted, almost bursting into tears.
Liam looked at the riders and counted nine. He then saw one horse missing a rider.
Bloody Tojo, he thought, as tears began to build in his eyes.
"Here he comes," said Jon quietly.
Everybody turned and saw a youthful blond-haired kid running as fast as he could up the hill with his sword in the air. It should have been a joyful reunion for his family, if not for that fact that four hundred metres behind him, lots of other people were running after him.
Lots and lots of dead, red people.

"Line up now," Harry roared to his scouts as they began to follow his orders. "Get your shields and trench knives out. We have to stop these fuckers" said the huge man as he walked along the two lines of men and women.
"We could make a run for it," one of the scouts called out.
"If we turn and run, they will cut us down, piece by piece," Harry replied. "The dead will not stop. They will run and run until they catch you. But if we stop them here to a walk, we have a chance."
There were only ten horses and ten riders as an exhausted Isaac finally made their line and was embraced by his brother and cousin.
"Thanks for waiting," Isaac said to his horse.
They couldn't get everybody out together on horseback. They were all stuck in a battle that would take all day, if they survived that long, Harry thought grimly.
He looked at Jon for some sort of reaction, but he just sat on his horse, staring down at the city.
"Jesse, you have to help. You need to speak to your father," Harry said in a pleading voice. "I think he is the only one who can get us out of here. I've fought so many skirmishes with bandits over the years," he glanced over at his captain, "but your father always won the battles for us. Always."

Jesse nodded and walked his horse over to his father's side. He knew his father suffered from panic attacks; he had seen the last one himself. He had to think of a quick way of getting him back to being a leader again, something that would shock some sense into him.

Jon looked at the city in complete despair. His hands were shaking badly. All those zombies! Grotesque, sick, evil-looking things. All of them clambering for their blood and succeeding with so many of his people.

Twenty kids now dead. Twenty! And he had led them to their deaths. Just like with Dave and then Sarah, he had let them down.

He watched as the red-coloured zombies approached. That smart kid Isaac had somehow survived, but he had brought their deaths with him. Thousands of zombies were now pouring out of Hobart, as far as the eye could see, maybe tens of thousands, all following each other in some sort of hive mentality.

They were three hundred metres away now.

He couldn't think straight. He knew a way out, or a way of destroying most of the zombies, but the ideas would not form properly in his mind.

Perhaps his death would be a relief. Would Sarah be waiting for him? He missed her so much.

"Dad, I don't want to die here."

Jon turned his head slowly in the direction of the voice he had just heard. His son, Jesse, had walked his horse over to him. "What, what did you say?"

"I don't want to die here," Jesse repeated, "and I don't think Ash or Lily would be happy if we died here either."

Ash and Lily, his beautiful girls, and his son, his precious boy, who was now right in front of him.

The zombies were now two hundred metres away.

He struggled for the words.

"Jesse, the southbound …lane … is full of old cars."

"Yes, Dad," Jesse said in an encouraging voice.

Ray, Rachael, and Harry had now come over within hearing distance of him and Jesse. They looked at him in desperation

"There … there is a small part of the highway … where you … I mean we … can cross from the northbound … to the southbound road," he said.

His son nodded at him.

"It's about two … kilometres from Kingston."

"Yes, Dad. I know the clearing that you mean."

The zombies were within a hundred metres; he could hear them groaning. The scouts and riders were all looking at him now. His breathing was calming, and his voice grew with authority.

"Ray, take Jesse … and the riders, and find Billy; get as many Kingston men as you can … use your ropes, push the cars to the sides of the road, and turn them over." He was back to himself now. "Break holes in the petrol tanks when we get there, and cover the highway with fuel; you have only three to four hours to get this done before we arrive. We're going to burn them all."

"Yes!" Ray roared as he and Dog and the other riders took off towards Kingston at a gallop.

Jesse stayed for a few moments. "Thanks, Dad." He then smiled, a sight that warmed his father's heart, and galloped off after the others.

Jon looked at the sky and hoped the rain would stay away for some time to come. It would rain, though. It rained nearly every day.

He turned his attention to the horde of red meat on skeletons as they lumbered their way to the lines. They were fifty metres away now.

Unsheathing his katana sword, he called out, "Harry!" and pointed it towards the mass of zombies. "Stop them."

Harry remembered playing the game of rugby when he was at school. A lot of it involved smashing your bodies against the opposition with the occasional punches being thrown. He felt like he was about to set up a scrum now.

"Get your shields together, people," he yelled as he walked behind the first line of men and women. The outlet was only a two-lane highway. A bit backwards for the Twenty-first Century, but old Hobart Town could be a bit like that sometimes. Today, he was very grateful for the small highway, as he could break his team up into two groups.

"You people," he called to the nervous fifteen who were at the front, "I want you to bend low and lean your shields and bodies into the zombies when they hit." He gestured to the other fourteen, which would be fifteen when he joined them. "The second row will come over your shoulders with their shields to protect you from any hands and biting."

Timing was everything. If they leant in too early, or if the second row moved in too late, the whole scrum could fall to pieces.

Jesse, Rachael, and Dad would be waiting for nobody. A part of him thought this may be for the best, but the twenty-nine people that he had chosen for this expedition were his friends, his mob, his community, and his tribe. He would get them out of here, no matter what.

Harry suddenly thought of his job at cleaning the septic tanks as the zombies came closer and closer.

He looked over at Jon and nodded.

Jon walked his horse back and forth behind the line of men and women whose job it was to stop the zombies from running. He took out his telescope and looked down on the city. Hobart was emptying; even without the telescope, he could see swarms of red walking along the main road of Hobart, passing or walking over their crippled cousins, the dead ones with pale white skin. With the telescope, he could see red coming from over the Tasman Bridge. Thirty versus maybe a hundred thousand, that's good odds, he thought, trying to quell a mad laugh from coming out of his mouth.

Forty metres; Jon suddenly smelt a wave of rancid air, which nearly overcame him. The sight of flesh-eating zombies soon brought everything back to focus.

Twenty metres; he could see the muscle fibres of the human body move as they kept lumbering forward; they had little hair, and he couldn't tell whether they used to be male or female.

Ten metres; he saw their wide eyes. They were wider because they had no eyelids. This just gave them more of an insane look, if that was even possible.

Five metres.

Were they running faster?

Three metres.

Yes, they were. Jon felt his body fill with terror.

One metre.

Crash.

He saw the zombies run flat out into the shields of the front row. Two of the front row leant too far forward and hit the zombies too hard with their shields. They were not aware how light and flimsy the dead people were, and both of them lost balance and fell forward. Jon saw them screaming as they were dragged into the following zombie horde.

"Harry, fill the gap," Jon shouted.

Alan and Phil, two aged campaigners, soon filled the gap as Jon quickly shouted another command.

"Second row, forward."

The second row of rangers moved behind their friends and leant their weight and shields to the wall.

The zombies, whilst light in weight, made up for this in sheer numbers.

"Push, hold the devils," Jon shouted as his people heaved against the oncoming storm. "Don't let the bastards through, not a step, not an inch!" he continued as he rode his horse back and forth along the line.

He looked down at the rangers' feet and saw them sliding backwards, inch by inch. He saw Harry with his broad back, straining against the tide of death. Men and women were crying out, pleading with their friends to hold on.

This battle of strength went on for another minute as Jon shouted out whatever encouragement he could.

This wall had to hold, or they were all dead.

Jon saw one zombie reaching his hand over one of the shields. He took out his bow and shot an arrow into its head. The zombie stopped and stood there as a buffer, between his people and the dead.

A buffer!

"Harry," he called out, "I want your people in the second row to bring out their trench knives."

"What! Are you sure, Captain?" Harry yelled back.

"We need a buffer."

Harry looked at him for a moment then nodded.

Reaching into his pocket, he brought out one of those wicked World War I knives, lowered his shield a little, and slammed the knife into the nearest zombie's eye. This zombie stopped dead, truly dead, but with the mass behind him, he didn't fall. Then the pressure on the line in front of Harry eased a little.

The people around him saw what had happened, and the action was repeated down the line.

The shield wall was now beginning to hold.

Jon, on his horse, looked over at the zombies behind the dead ones and saw they had stopped moving forward and now just stood there looking at them. They were still groaning for their flesh, but the running and pushing had stopped.

Hive mentality indeed, Jon thought.

The shield wall was just that, a wall. But they couldn't stand here all day.

"Ladies and gentlemen," Jon called out, "we have stopped them to a walk." An exhausted group of twenty-eight looked over at him. "Now begins the twelve-kilometre journey to Kingston."

They looked at him with weariness, but there was an underlying determination to them all.

"We cannot just lead these zombies to Kingston," he continued. "We have a duty to kill as many of them as we can before we get there."

His people nodded their heads at this.

After a few minutes rest, he asked the second row to step back ten metres. The first row would walk backwards at a steady pace, and when the zombies would come too close, they would kill them with swords or trench knives. This would continue for fifteen minutes, and then the second row would take over, and the first group would have a break.

"If we are methodical," Jon continued, "we should kill thousands of these bastards before we reach Kingston."

And by then, he hoped Ray and Jesse would have the trap prepared.

"Heave!" Billy shouted as he and one of the Kingston men lifted another car on its side. This one had no skeleton in it, he noticed with relief.

He felt so ashamed, though, shaking his head in dismay, just so ashamed of himself.

Whilst he and Jessica were enjoying a romantic morning by themselves, twenty young kids had been killed in horrific fashion.

He almost wept when he heard the names of the kids fallen. And his own kin had almost died; he didn't even know whether his big brother, the best friend he ever had, was still alive!

He thought back to when he had seen only nine riders return from town. They were riding fast, and he felt a moment of alarm until he could make out Rachael and his father, with Dog running at his heel, riding down the road. Danger, the riding seemed to convey. Disaster, the pace seemed to mean. Death, the number of riders said.

He looked over at young Isaac, who was helping lift one of the final cars, and thought about his tale of survival. What a story he would have to tell his kids about, if he lived that long.

Mayor Nash had half of Kingston out moving all the cars. A pathway of upended vehicles went from the clearing to the northbound lanes, across to the southbound lanes, then all the way to Kingston. Everybody moved quickly, as they knew what disaster waited for them if this trap failed.

Mayor Nash had also sent fifty rangers on foot to help Jon out. Jesse had ridden back and forth this morning, giving updates on how far away they were and how many zombies were left.

Jesse had reported that only four of the Grovetown Rangers had fallen, two in the initial attack and two later, from weariness. Carrying a shield and fighting with a sword for three hours could exhaust anybody, no matter how fit. The mayor's men should help with fatigue.

He also said, to everybody's shock, that the number of zombies was close to a hundred thousand, half of Hobart's initial population before the Collapse. Billy didn't know if this trap they were making was large enough.

He didn't even know if fire would stop them, looking at the dark clouds gathering over head.

But he kept this concern to himself.

He hoped Jon had another plan up his sleeve, just in case.

Knowing Jon as he did, he thought he just might.

Mayor Nash rode up to Billy. "Any news from Jesse?"

"No, but he should be back soon," Billy replied.

"Any reason you are up here at this end of the trap?" the mayor said, looking at Billy with that sharp look he sometimes had.

"I'm going to be the one who punctures the first tank," Billy said in a determined manner, as his hand clenched onto his sheathed trench knife on his hip. He was taking five men with him to start the trap.

"With the zombies just ten feet away from you?"

"Yes."

"It wasn't your fault you weren't there," the mayor said with a concerned look. "Nobody knew that the dead … were in a sort of coma."

A coma! He never thought of it that way.

"I know, but my brother is out there fighting. And this, to me, feels like my duty to perform," he said firmly.

The mayor gave a strong nod of his head at that.

"Just be careful," he said, "you will be in the front line you and your men."

"We have bows," Billy said. "We will create a safe gap."

"Well good luck, my boy." He reached down and clasped his shoulder. "My daughter is very fond of you," he said with an affectionate smile. "Oh, and keep your feet; fuel is very slippery." With that said, he rode back to Kingston.

"Sir," one of his men called out, "all the cars are in place."

"Thank you," Billy replied.

"Isaac," he called out, "get your people onto the northbound lane, and stay out of sight. If the zombies catch a sight of any of you, all of this will be for nothing."

Isaac nodded and grinned. If anybody could get out of a tricky situation, this boy could.

Jesse watched as seventy-five men and women took turns in cutting down zombie after zombie after zombie.

In the hours since the Kingston rangers had arrived, people could take longer breaks to recuperate. This led to fewer deaths. At the moment, twenty-five Rangers from Grovetown were left, one had just fallen when she dropped her sword from fatigue; a second of lost concentration could be your last in this fight. Kingston had not seen one ranger fall.

They fought so well. Maybe it was because their hometown was closer. But everybody knew this was a do-or-die event. The zombies would not stop, they would not parley; they would relentlessly hunt every man and woman down.

The numbers were staggering. His father thought that maybe over the last four hours, they had killed twenty to thirty thousand of the things, but they just kept on coming and coming.

"We are almost at the crossing, Dad," Jesse called out.

His father looked around with tired eyes. It was sometimes hard to remember that he was not a young man anymore, but a man in his sixties. He looked down what was left of the empty northbound highway.

"Are Isaac and his people in place?"

"Yes, Dad," Jesse replied.

His father took another long look down the highway to Kingston. If Isaac was there, he couldn't see him, which was good.

"Go to Billy," his father said in a tired voice. "Tell him to get ready for the crossover and handover."

Jesse took off at a gallop.

Billy and his five men were standing tall and had their bows trained on the oncoming zombies. All the seventy-five rangers had filed past them in the clearing between the highways in lines of five. So it didn't take long for Billy to be in the last line of defence.

Harry had given him a pat on the shoulder as he walked past and said he would meet him at the end of the highway. He looked exhausted.

Jesse and Jon had stayed behind, as they were both on horse and could get away from the zombies fast if need be. Jon also stayed because it was his plan, after all.

They both had their bows out and targeted the zombies as well. "Drop them," Jon ordered, and eight arrows were released and killed the first row of the zombies with head shots. "Reload," he called, as they put another arrow to their bows.

"Again," Jon ordered, and another eight zombies fell down. They had a bit of space now.

"In a normal walking pace, in files of three, sling your bows, turn, take out your trench knives, and stab the fuel tanks as you walk towards Kingston," he said in a calm voice.

Billy took a deep, calming breath. It was hard to remain calm when you had your backs turned to these hungry monsters, but he did as he was ordered.

They walked in files of three for two reasons.

One, three holes would release the petrol quicker. And two, some of these cars had petrol tanks in different areas.

Billy would be mortified if he was putting holes in the wrong area.

"Remember to puncture the lowest part of the fuel tank," Jon said, still sounding calm as he looked back at them from his horse. Or maybe because he looked so tired, Billy thought.

His first puncture struck the right area as petrol poured out of the tank. Such a bad smell, that stuff, no wonder it poisoned the environment.

"Keep your steps regular," Jon continued in that composed voice. "It doesn't matter if you miss, just keep walking at a normal pace. We cannot give them cause to start running again."

Even though Jon was sounding relaxed and confident, it was very hard for Billy to remain so with all that moaning and groaning going on twenty paces behind him. The urge to look over his shoulder was almost overwhelming. But, step by step, they walked past each car and gave one swift stab with their knives.

Billy, in his bravado, had decided to be the last of the three on his side of the road, but as he remembered the mayor's words about not losing his feet, he kept taking short little steps.

He was glad nobody was watching him, apart from the dead, as he was pretty sure he was stepping like a ballerina as he walked down the highway.

Isaac put a hand over his mouth to stop from laughing. Why was Billy walking like that?

As per earlier orders, Isaac and four other riders had, as quietly as they could, ridden up the northbound highway for the two-kilometre stretch. There was a thick tree growth between the north and southbound highways, but since Isaac had put his hand up for being the closest rider to the crossing, he had to make sure he wasn't seen by the zombies.

He wondered why he volunteered for this mission.

Perhaps it was because Taylor had been browbeating him about falling off his horse in the city, then fussing about him and telling him how worried she had been. Even Liam was getting a bit clingy. They were strange, his family, he decided.

He watched as all the zombies walked after Billy and his men. When would the zombies stop? Were they going to keep following them forever?

One of the requests from the captain was, when the order came for the fire arrows, he was to note if the zombie numbers were still as bunched up as they were now and had been in town.

They needed to know how many more of them there were.

Pushing Tojo back a few steps into further bush land, he watched for the high-flying flame arrow that would mean the trap had been sprung.

Thirty-three survivors of the Grovetown Rangers and over a hundred of the Kingston Rangers gathered at the end of the highway and watched as Jon and Jesse and their six companions led the zombies down the highway like the Pied Piper.

Mayor Nash looked over at Ray. "Um, why is your son walking like that?"

"I'm not sure," Ray replied with a bemused look. "Perhaps he is worried he will slip over?"

"Ah, that would be my fault," replied the mayor with a laugh.

"They're getting close now," said Harry. "Do we have a plan B if the fire doesn't work?"

"I don't," replied his father, "but I'm sure he does," he added as he looked at Jon.

Reaching the end of the highway, Jon waited for Billy and his men to move past him, then gave the order for the flame arrows.

"Light them up," the mayor commanded to two of his archers. The two archers wet the cloth tied to their arrows with kerosene, and turning to a nearby campfire that had been burning for some time, lit the arrows.

They moved up closer to the highway and sent two burning arrows high into the air.

"Burn, you motherfuckers," Harry said quietly as he saw two more arrows fly from the higher ground of the northbound highway.

Isaac stood there patiently with Tojo, keeping one eye on the zombies, whose depth had not changed one bit by his reckoning, and one eye on the sky, waiting for his time to send an arrow. He saw a flame arrow two hundred metres down the road fly high into the air. Taking out his tiny can of kerosene and a box of something called redheads, which everybody said was rare and precious, Isaac lit his arrow and sent it over the tree line.

He walked Tojo out of the trees and saw that the road was now on fire. *Perhaps, I should have a closer look.*

"Isaac," he heard said in a loud, clear voice. He turned and saw Taylor beckoning him to come to her.

Bloody hell, she's just as bad as my mother, he thought grumpily. But he mounted his horse and road straight to her. He didn't want another ear-bashing from his cousin.

Harry watched as the southern outlet blew up into flames. The zombies were burning, but only some were falling quickly. It was a bizarre scene to watch. Firstly, their tattered trousers would catch on fire, but they would still be looking at the rangers in front of them, moaning for their blood.

Then, when the fire took a strong hold, it consumed their whole bodies, but the only recognition they showed that they were on fire was the way their hands were moving, like they were trying to swat a fly or something similar.

Harry noticed that the zombies with the holes in them seemed to be falling first. It looked like they were burning from the inside out. The ones without holes were just turning a burned dark colour and continuing to walk. They looked more frightening, if that was possible.

The horde of zombies had been reduced by maybe as much as four in five—the plan had failed.

The plan had failed, Jon thought with anguish. He had known it was a futile hope that all of the zombies would be killed, but he still wished that only a few would survive rather than the thousands of burned devils that kept on marching towards them. Mayor Nash had sent a few rangers forward to kill the ones that approached from the highway, but Jon knew that this would not be enough.

He saw Isaac and the riders return. He gestured for the youngster to come over to him.

"Captain." He saluted.

"Were there still many zombies left when you last saw them?"

"Yes, sir," Isaac responded. "Just as many, I think. At least the road was jam-packed full of them."

Jon sighed, then brought out his spyglass, as Ray liked to call it, and looked down the highway.

They were still coming.

The burned ones were sparse, though they still numbered maybe two thousand, but behind them came a horde of red ones. It looked like they were the reserve army, coming in to save the day on a battlefield that once looked to be lost.

"Mayor, I would like you to withdraw your people."

The mayor looked back in shock. "What do you mean, Jon? We have to face them here."

Jon looked behind them at the houses and streets that made up the community of Kingston; he then looked down the road, the one that led them back to the Huon.

"There are too many of them, Mayor, and bringing them into Kingston would lead to skirmishes that would last for days. In fact, it is a battle that I believe we would eventually lose."

"But we have to fight," the mayor said, stroking his axe.

Billy, Jessica, Ray, Jesse, Rachael, and Harry had all now moved closer. And behind them, more and more people were listening in to the conversation.

"We will fight, but at two ends of the battle," Jon replied. "My people will stay here and draw the hordes away from Kingston and down the road to the south. I have a couple of plans that I hope will kill most of them."

Jesse wondered what plans his father had in store. He thought he knew one of them as he looked upwards to the clouds.

"Are you sure about this, Jon?" the mayor said.

"Yes, Mayor. Once the last of the zombies have gone, I want you and your men to follow them and take them down from behind," Jon replied. "However, you must only draw the attention of a small number of them at any one engagement. You can't afford to have the whole lot of them turn around and attack you at one time."

"How do we do that?" said Billy, who had obviously decided to stay with the Kingston rangers.

Harry and Ray looked at him in surprise. The mayor and Jessica just smiled.

Jon remembered a long time ago when his Holophone made a noise loud enough to attract at least a hundred of them. They had no such technology anymore.

"Noise," he said. "A limited amount of noise will attract them, piece by piece. You have to practice at this, Billy. You'll soon get the hang of it," he finished with a smile.

"Well," the mayor said and sighed, "I guess we better move off then."

"Just one thing, Mayor," Jon said. "I need to send a message to Grovetown about what has happened today and what is coming towards them. I need your fastest rider, as my riders and horses are exhausted, and they have a lot of digging yet to do."

He looked towards Jesse and Rachael.

Behind them, he heard the whispers from Isaac and Liam about digging. They sounded perplexed. Jesse just nodded his head; he knew what his father had planned, Jon thought proudly.

"Well, one of our fastest riders is sitting right next to me on our fastest horse," said the mayor.

Everybody turned and looked at Jessica.

"What! No," said Billy in a panic.

"It's okay, Billy," she said gently. "You will all be needed for the coming battles. I have to play my part."

"But what about the Mason Gang?" Billy asked Jon.

Jon paused for a moment in thought. "They never attacked us on our way into Kingston. If they were around, I'm sure they would have tried something. Harry found no traces of them either." Jon sighed at his own paranoia. "Now I don't believe that they even exist anymore. She will be safe"

"With tens of thousands of zombies on our trail," Jessica said to Billy, "I think we have more urgent things to worry about."

"I'll send two other fast riders with her, Billy," said the mayor, who placed a hand on her shoulder. "She will be protected."

Billy gave out a long sigh and nodded his head.

Seems like love was growing quite quickly between these two, Jon thought with a smile.

"Ray would make a great name for a grandson," he whispered to his old friend.

"Indeed," Ray replied with a big grin.

"Well, we will all meet again once this horrible day is done," said the mayor, as he leaned over to kiss his daughter's cheek.

"Not one person is to be seen, Mayor," said Jon.

"Not one person," the mayor replied, nodding; then, with a loud whistle, led his rangers back to Kingston.

Jon ordered a few of his own men to replace the ones at the end of the highway in killing the burned ones. But they all had to move soon, as the horde of red ones were fast approaching.

Billy gave Jessica a long kiss goodbye before she rode off with two of her father's escorts to Grovetown. She looked a natural horse rider as she took off down the road.

"Where's my kiss?" said Harry.

"You're not pretty enough," Billy replied.

"So you've decided to stay in Kingston, then?" said his father.

"Yes, Dad, if that's all right."

"Ha, my boy, you are thirty-two years of age. You don't need your old man's permission."

"But I would like it nonetheless, Dad."

"You have it, my boy," his father said with a proud smile. "She's a lovely girl."

Billy smiled at his father.

"We better get this plan underway," Jon said quietly.

"Yes, I better leave now," said Billy.

"Remember the noise level," Jon advised.

"Yes, sir." Then, looking one last time at his father and brother, Billy rode off after the mayor and his men.

"Harry," said Jon, "get your people lined up here."

"Will we be fighting again?" Harry asked. "We are all pretty tired."

"No, Harry," Jon reassured him. "No engaging the enemy, just leading them away from Kingston and into a big hole."

"A big hole?"

"Yes." Jon looked over at Jesse. "The hole in the road at Leslie Vale. Make it wider. Make it deeper. And make it hot."

Jesse nodded, patted his shovel and kerosene can tied on the saddle of his horse, then he and Ray and the other seven riders took off at a fast trot.

Four kilometres outside of Grovetown

Turner sat on a recently felled log, relaxing, as he took a big bite into a recently cooked snake.

A bit chewy, he thought. But it filled the gap in his stomach, and it was much better looking at a dead snake than a live one. He looked down the sloping grass that led to the main road from Kingston.

It was a good place for a trap.

Bradfield was always a smart bloke. If Dayton's people decided to attack his men, they would have to ride up the hill towards him on their right, and they couldn't retreat away from them, as there was a sharp hill behind them on the left of the road. Their only choice was to run the gauntlet and head straight down the road.

But he had a little trap prepared for them, if and when they arrived. The surprise of the ambush should take out at least most of them, he thought with confidence.

Dillon, his second-in-command, and third overall now, he guessed, came over and informed him that some of the men had been sent much farther on to warn of any arrival of Dayton's men.

"Good," Turner grunted his reply and waved his shotgun in Dillon's general direction.

It was funny watching Dillon twitch whenever the gun was pointed at him. Such power these weapons had. He couldn't wait for Cooper to release all of the other weapons. They would rule all of Grovetown with an iron fist. No more wandering around the bushlands. They would have a home after all these years.

Standing up, after choking down the last of the snake, he was about to order the twenty men and women he had with him back to chopping down another tree, but stopped as one of his riders from the north came racing towards them.

"Three riders coming fast," the scout said as he brought his horse to a halt.

These must be people coming to warn Grovetown of what had happened in the city if they were riding so fast. So some of Dayton's men had survived after all!

"Beanies, hoods, and balaclavas on now," he grunted to the men and women around him. "We are not to kill them, do you understand?" He waved his shotgun in the air to show that he was the boss. "They need to believe we are the Mason Gang. Understood?" He took a deep breath. This leadership thing required a lot more talking than he was used to.

His people nodded and grinned maliciously. Most of them thought terrorising people was fun, as did Turner.

Placing a balaclava over his recognisable curly flaming-red hair, he mounted his horse and rode out of the tree line.

Jessica and her two escorts were closing in on Grovetown fast. What was she to say when she got there? She realised she was about to tell a town that twenty-five members of their community had been killed horribly and an army of tens of thousands of zombies were about to descend on them.

Her father had offered her as one of the fastest riders, and she had to admit she had felt a moment of trepidation, but Billy had been so brave in his battles with the dead, that she didn't want to let him down in any way.

What a surprise meeting him had been!

She had never really met any man in Kingston who made her heart skip a beat, and she had gone with her father and family to Grovetown with little hope of meeting anybody.

Then she watched as Ray Beasley dragged his youngest son in front of her, and then ... yes, her heart had begun to race. And over the following days, she realised that this man who was giant-sized compared to all others, well, except for the other Beasleys, was so humble and kind.

It had only been a few days, but she was starting to think that she could easily fall in love with him. The fact that she was worried about him right now suggested she was well on her way.

"Jessica. To the right!" one of her escorts shouted out.

She looked over to her right and saw dozens of hooded men riding out quickly from beyond the tree line.

"Faster!" she called out to her men and horse.

She looked again to her right and saw one of the men lifting a ... gun, she thought with shock. That man had a gun, and this was confirmed by a loud boom that rang out above their heads.

The bandits were trying to cut off their access to the road ahead.

"Mason wants your cunt for dinner," one of the bandits yelled.

"Fuck Mason," another called out. "I want this bitch for myself."

They were maybe a hundred paces to her right and closing in on her fast.

Jessica had never been more terrified in her life, and the horse seemed to sense her fear and began to run even faster

Another gunshot went over their heads as they headed down the last few kilometres to Grovetown.

"C'mon, girl," Jessica shouted to her horse, and maybe to herself. "We are almost there."

She looked behind and saw that her two escorts were still with her, but the bandits, having failed in cutting them off, were now riding behind them. She urged her horse for even more speed and looked behind once more to see that their pursuers had slowed down a little. She wondered why until she saw the fortress that was Grovetown.

"Back again," she said, elated and petrified at the same time. Her body was shaking uncontrollably.

Guards were looking down at her as she reached the gate.

"Quick, get in," said one of them as others opened the gate. She gratefully entered the safety of the town.

Dismounting, she and her escorts quickly ran up the stairs to the rampart.

She looked up the hill towards the two dozen or so hooded bandits who were just sitting on their horses, watching the town. She watched as their leader with the balaclava raised his weapon.

"Get down," Jessica shouted to her escorts and the guards.

They all hid beneath the wooden wall and heard a gunshot ring out overhead.

It took a minute for her to get the courage to stand up again, but when she did, she saw that the bandits were all gone.

She turned to one of the guards. "I need to speak to Jack Beasley straightaway."

Leslie Vale, twelve kilometres from Grovetown

It had already been a massive hole before they arrived, but it was a third of a size bigger now. It was maybe eight metres deep and twenty metres across, and five metres wide.

The last of Harry's people had now moved around the pit via a tied rope that they used from tree to tree. They all stood, waiting for the zombies to arrive.

"It won't stop them all, Captain," Jesse said to his father, who was standing next to his horse.

"I know, Son," he replied, looking at the dark clouds in the sky.

They had spent the last hour digging, but also finding dry wood and leaves from the nearby bush land. It was difficult with all the rain they had, but there were always covered areas, and they had all found a decent amount of fuel for the fire. With the added real fuel of kerosene, it was now starting to build up to a hot heat. Red-hot coals filled the bottom of the pit.

"Get ready to cover your noses and mouths," Jon called out.
The zombies would burn, which was good, but they had to remember that this was human flesh that was about to be burnt, no matter how corrupted.
"Bang your shields," he said and nodded to Harry.
Harry's people, who stood two metres away from the pit, brought out their swords and knives and started rhythmically banging their shields.
The zombies knew where they were; they could see them from a hundred metres away, but it was always good to add some encouragement.
"Here, kitty kitty," Phil called out.
"Come to Papa," said Alan.
Jesse smiled, but he noticed his father was still looking at the sky.
"It's going to rain heavy, I think, Dad."
"Yes, it is," his father replied, now looking at him. "When the zombies start getting across this pit, and they will eventually, what do you think our next trap will be?"
Jesse felt the pressure of pleasing his father, but he thought he knew what the answer was.
"The hole at Lower Longley seven kilometres from here, it has a downward slope that leads off a five hundred-metre cliff. That height will destroy even these dead things."
His father smiled at him, and Jesse felt warmed by that smile.
"And what would make it easier for the zombies to fall off that cliff?"
"A smooth surface and lots of rain," Jesse replied immediately.
His father reached out and clasped him by the shoulder.
"You make me so proud."
Jesse looked at the ground in embarrassment.
"Here they come," Harry called out.
And everybody covered their mouths and noses as they watched them fall face first into the pit. They could immediately hear a sizzling sound above the moaning.
They weren't even looking at their feet to see if there was a hole in front of them, Jesse realised, amazed; they just focused on the humans straight ahead and fell.
"Add more fuel," his father called out.

And the rangers began throwing wood, leaves, and kerosene on top of the first zombies.

The flames built up, but soon it became apparent that the rate of zombies falling in the pit was smothering any chance of a major fire getting a strong hold.

Jon turned to his son. "Take your people to the next trap. The rain is coming soon. I want that surface as smooth as an ice-skating rink."

"A what?"

"Never mind." His father smiled. "Just set the trap; if it rains as hard as I expect, we could win this battle without raising another sword."

Grovetown, Community Hall

Carl Cooper took a steadying breath as he walked into the hall behind Brady and Allenby. He had to keep Jack Beasley in town. It was crucial that Dayton, if he was still alive, not receive any aid or warning whatsoever and that he walk blindly into the ambush.

Turner must be a competent thug, as the whole town was in an uproar about the attack on the Mayor of Kingston's daughter by the dreaded Mason Gang.

The hall was starting to get packed again, as people were arriving from everywhere, just like in that bloody money debate with Dayton. Fear was building, which was good.

This time, Cooper was going to win.

As soon as the crowd was settled, Allenby asked Jessica Nash to come forward.

"Miss Nash," Allenby began, "please accept our apologies for today's attack by the Mason Gang."

"That was not your fault, Councillor," Jessica replied.

"Nevertheless, that attack took place in our territory, and we take pride in the protection of our citizens."

Good reply, Cooper thought. We just need to take some 'extra' care of our citizens today.

"Ladies and gentlemen," Allenby announced to the hall, "we have some bad news to convey on the matter of Captain

Dayton's expedition to Hobart."

A loud humming noise went around the room as people began to whisper in anxious voices.

Build the fear, people, build the fear, Cooper thought with an inward grin.

Just then, Ash Dayton and Jane Butler rushed into the hall. They had caught the last sentence of Allenby and stood against the wall with fearful faces.

"If you could explain, please, Miss Nash."

Jessica took a deep breath, and in a loud, clear voice so everybody heard, said, "The zombies of Hobart have awakened."

The room broke out into a cacophony of sound as all the people either cried out in shock or called out asking for the fate of their loved ones.

"Can you explain a bit more, Miss Nash?" said Allenby in his calm voice.

For all that Cooper chafed at being second in charge; he had to admit, albeit grudgingly, that Allenby was a good leader. It was a shame he had to die in the coming months.

"At the break of dawn, Jon Dayton and his people left for Hobart in the search for new books for all of us. The zombies, who we thought would be truly dead by now, awakened," she said, half turning to the people behind her. "There were sixty in all when they left, and when they arrived back, there were only thirty-five."

The crowd broke into shouts as to who was dead and who was alive, but Cooper hardly heard them.

Thirty-five! How on earth did that many survive? Hobart must have been full of zombies, so how could any of them get out? Dayton! Please tell me that bastard is dead.

"Please, listen; there is more," said Jessica, trying to calm the crowd. "I will give you the names of those alive and dead as soon as I can, but you all need to be aware that the zombies followed them."

That quieted everybody, including Cooper. There must be a hundred thousand of them at least.

"Dayton's rangers fought hard and fought well. Half of the

southern outlet was set on fire in efforts to burn these things, and it was successful up to a point, but at this moment, tens of thousands of the dead are following them."

"Here?" Cooper cried out, almost rising out of his seat.

Bloody hell, I need to control myself a bit better if I am to lead these people. Be calm like Allenby, he thought with gritted teeth.

"Yes," Jessica replied. "But I believe Jon Dayton has some plans in culling their numbers some more."

So the bastard was still alive. Turner had better finish them off. That man had more lives than a cat.

Ash Dayton reached out to hold her grandmother's hand when she heard her father was still alive.

"So we need to prepare our defences," Cooper said more calmly.

"Jack Beasley, do you have any thoughts on this?" said Allenby. The big man rose from his seat; he seemed a bit hesitant, which was a good sign in Cooper's mind.

"I wish to lead some men out there to help Dayton's people, Councillor."

"You seem a bit conflicted there, Captain," said Cooper.

Jack looked over at Cooper. "I'm no captain, Councillor. Jon Dayton is our captain," he insisted in a show of the loyalty that gave Cooper bouts of jealousy. "It's just …" He hesitated for a moment. "My father, brother, and daughter are out there," he finally said quietly.

Be compassionate, Cooper; come on, you must remember how?

"But you know that with the bandit attack today, that your men and women must stay here," he said in his best empathetic voice.

"Yes." He sighed with a sad look on his broad face. Cooper almost felt sorry for him. Almost.

"I worry that Jon may be attacked by these animals," he continued.

"He has many animals following him now," Cooper replied with an equally sad face. "Miss Nash says that tens of thousands of zombies are on his trail."

Tens of thousands of the fucking things! Why didn't Dayton just die in Hobart as planned? He could have had the whole town to himself for an eternity.

"I'm sure once the bandits see these zombies, if, of course, the bandits are still around, they will disappear like the cowards they are," Cooper continued. "Fighting zombies is only for brave men and women." *Or idiots,* he finished in his mind.

"My father's people are fighting the zombies from the rear," said Jessica. "He's not alone. Billy leads them."

Good girl, Cooper thought, reassure this big oaf that everything will turn out just fine. Your brother leads the cavalry, all will be well.

"Jack," said Allenby, "I know this is a tough decision, but I see this as follows: Jon Dayton has, by some miracle, managed to get over half the rangers out of a terrifying situation. He is now in front of the zombies, and knowing him, has a few more plans in reducing their numbers." Allenby was looking at Jack in an almost pleading way. "The Mason Gang is still at large, and we now have two reports that they have guns. We all know about what they have done to innocent people in the past. If you leave us, we could be defenceless from a raid. Sure, everybody here knows how to use a weapon, but Dayton had trained his people well. You are the backbone of our defence."

Cooper was overjoyed. Allenby had just put forward the very argument he was intending to make.

"All right, Councillor." The big man sighed. "If it is the wish of the council, we will stay."

Allenby looked over at his fellow councillors, who nodded their heads in agreement.

Jack Beasley sat back down and placed his hands over his face.

"Jessica, I'm sorry, but if you could now give the names of those who died," continued Allenby.

And as Jessica Nash gave out the names of the ones who were lost, wails of grief came from around the hall. Grief and fear. *Turner, it is now all up to you,* Cooper thought. *Don't let me down.*

Leslie Vale, twelve kilometres from Grovetown

Mayor Nash started to notice his people tiring as they hacked their way through another horde of zombies.

He had them organised into four groups of twenty-five, two groups on foot and two on horse, as they made the twenty-kilometre journey south. The killing would be done on foot by one group with the other as a reserve, and the ones on horses rested in between shifts. They all would take fifteen-minute alternating shifts.

But killing was a tiring business for anybody, even the fit young men and women he had at his disposal.

His expected son-in-law-to-be was turning out to be an expert in attracting a small number of zombies for each engagement. After making too much noise and attracting thousands of zombies the first time, then not making enough and getting only a hundred to turn back the second, Billy had quickly learned the right level of noise, and each time, approximately three to five hundred of those bloody things would turn around at one time.

Very simply, he had each team sing out in a one-note tune. Mayor Nash thought it reminded him of the sound the old Tibetan monks used to make, but perhaps not quite as deep, and the result was definitely a lot more violent, he thought with a wry smile.

"Mayor, you need to see this," one of the rangers said as he ran towards him.

"Trouble?" he asked.

"No, Mayor, just very disturbing," the ranger replied.

The mayor wondered how something could be considered disturbing after all they had seen that day. A part of him didn't want to know what was ahead, but it was his duty as mayor to lead these men and women, and lead them he would.

As he rode his horse after the ranger, he became aware of a strange smell. Riding closer, he thought he could smell a barbecue, like in the old days. Finding what was making this smell almost made him sick.

In a pit of about twenty metres across, he thought he saw a pool of black eels wriggling in the dirt.

Looking closer, he realised that these were not eels but burned body parts of hundreds of zombies. All of them were jammed in the pit like sardines.

God only knew what the condition of the zombies at the bottom of the pit were, but at the top, blackened hands, arms, and faces were moving in a desperate attempt to get out.

The other zombies must have stepped on top of them to get across.

Some of the blackened faces were now looking up at him, and he thought he was going to vomit, but to save face in front of his people, he cried out angrily,

"Put some fuel on these bastards. Let's finish the job!"

A few rangers with cans of fuel came forward as commanded. "Burn them," the mayor said. One of his men threw a burning branch on the pit, and it burst into flames once more.

"Where's Billy?" he said, trying to ignore the smell of burning meat.

"He's gone on with a group of twenty-five already, Mayor," one of the rangers replied, looking at the tied rope that went around the pit.

The mayor looked down at the blazing pit. The eels had now stopped wriggling.

"We better catch up, then."

Thunder was then heard above in the clouds. The rain began to pour down.

Lower Longley, five kilometres from Grovetown

Jesse and his friends hauled Liam up and out of the last trap they had to use. Due to the heavy rain over the years, the road from Grovetown to Kingston was full of potholes, but there were two holes that were massive.

The first hole had now been filled with zombies, who were, hopefully, burnt to a crisp by now.

The second hole was high in the mountain range and led to a cliff, which provided a very scenic waterfall off the edge and down to five hundred metres below.

Jesse's people had been carefully digging and removing all rocks and branches to make sure this hole was very smooth at the bottom. They were lucky to find that the bottom was full of clay instead of dirt. Once the rain started, it became very slippery indeed.

Liam and Isaac had insisted on being the ones lowered into the hole as per usual, and all the others held on to them tightly by rope.

Isaac, in his usual bravado, had gone with one metres of the edge, until Jesse gave a strong order for him to step back. It was as much a shock for Jesse as it was for Isaac that he sounded so forceful in giving an order. Perhaps he was learning more from his father than he thought.

The last of the rangers were now moving around the pit via the usual tied ropes, which went from tree to tree. Jesse's people were lucky that they managed to get their horses past before the storm hit, because now, with the rain, he saw the rangers struggle against the rainwater that was coming down from the above heights.

The water was now moving in a torrent off the mountain, down the angled hole, and straight off the cliff. All was now in readiness, as everybody had made it to the other side.

"Do you think this will work, Dad?" Jesse asked.

"I think it will," his father replied quietly. "But always prepare for the worst in this job, Son."

"I won't forget that after today."

"No, you won't." His father gave him a sad smile.

"No more fighting for us, pumpkin," said Ray as he wrapped his big arm around Rachael's shoulder. "We're heading home now. If these buggers want to follow us now, well, we will just have to have some target practice from the town walls."

"That's good, Poppy," replied Rachael, placing her head on his shoulder. "It's been a bad day. I want it to end now."

Ray looked at his granddaughter. Sixteen she was, and for her to go through all that they had today filled him with grief. He wondered whether she would come to terms with the friends she had lost today. Probably not, he thought sadly.

Dog, who had been sitting at Ray's side, suddenly began growling.

"Here they come, sweetheart," he said to his granddaughter. "One last time."

"Bang your shields!" Jon shouted out.

And the zombies walked straight at them, eyes focused on their prey, mouths groaning, a hunger that could not be abated, and an evil that would never stop, unless their brains were destroyed.

As had happened with the first hole, the zombies just walked straight off the edge of the road into the beginnings of a waterfall. The rainfall was strong, the angled hole was slippery, and the result was perfect.

The zombies just fell and were swept off the cliff in a matter of seconds. Sometimes Jon worried that one of them would get snagged on something and jam up the flow, but it didn't happen. Isaac and Liam had done a perfect job.

The rangers, who had started out standing in a downpour of rain with worried faces, which they had worn all day, began to smile; the smiles led to laughter, and the laughter led to cheering. Even Dog had stopped growling.

"And goodbye to you, sir," said Phil as he watched another zombie go off the cliff.

"Have a pleasant trip," Alan added.

Jesse looked over at his friends, who were a few metres behind him, carefully looking over the cliff's edge.

"Smash! Did you see that one's head explode?" exclaimed Liam gleefully.

"Yeah, it was like one of those watermelons," said Isaac.

"What's that?" replied Liam.

"Not sure." Isaac frowned.

"Idiots," Taylor grumbled good-naturedly.

Ray came over and gave Jesse's father a big hug.

"Pure genius, old man," said Ray.

"Indeed," his father replied.

Rachael moved over to Jesse and planted a big kiss on his lips, which made everybody call out and whistle. She said the three little words quietly to him, and he said it back to her.

For about thirty minutes, they smiled and cheered as zombie after zombie was swept off the cliff, until finally, they were all gone and a silence descended on the hill.

Harry walked over to his father and raised his shield. "For the captain," he shouted, and everybody raised their weapons and cheered once more.

It was a day Jesse would never forget for so many reasons, a day in which he would look back and cry, but his father's smile in that single moment, he would always remember with joy.

"Let's go home," his father said.

"Home sweet home," Ray added.

"Billy is going to get a surprise when he catches up with us," said Harry.

Four kilometres outside of Grovetown

Turner looked to his left as two fast-approaching riders came straight towards him.

"Are they coming?" he grunted out.

"Yes, Turner," one of the riders replied.

"But we watched them destroy the zombies," said the other.

"What do you mean destroy the zombies?" Turner replied, aghast.

"Washed them off the cliff," the first rider said. "It took about half an hour, but all the zombies are gone."

"Dayton is a genius," said the second.

"He's a dead genius," Turner replied, brandishing his gun, but he was just as relieved that the zombies were all gone. "How far away are they?" he continued.

"Only five minutes now."

"Numbers?"

"Ten riders, twenty-five walking."

"That many!" Turner said in shock. Cooper and Bradfield had promised there would be far less than that.

Turner gave a quick appraisal of the trap. He hoped Dayton wouldn't notice the angled trees on the road. The storm should reduce his visibility a little. Turner wouldn't give him much of a chance to notice anyway. They had the high ground, and Turner had a gun. They had to hit them hard, and Dayton was the key.

"Get your masks on," he shouted to his thirty gang members. "Remember, we are the feared Mason Gang, should any of them escape."

Turner and his gang stood behind trees for cover and waited for Dayton's people to come in sight.

Here they are, Turner thought with a grin. At the front were eight riders who looked like teenagers, the way there were animatedly talking to each other. Only one of them noticed the trees lying by the sides of the road.

Behind them were the twenty-five scouts, who were all mingling around two elderly riders. One of them must be Dayton, he thought with certainty.

"Wait for the teenagers to get past the logs," he commanded. This would mean the scouts and the two horsemen would be more bunched up together.

"Step out from the trees," he commanded as they all walked out from the tree line.

"Aim for the two riders," he commanded as he heard thirty bowstrings being drawn back and a few laughs from some of his people at the expected carnage they were about to bring.

"Loose."

Jesse was smiling at Rachael as they made their way home. They had lost so many friends, but for just this moment, they intended to be happy for the few minutes that they could.

A relaxed mood had overtaken the rangers, all of them believing they had passed all the dangers that they would face that day.

"Nearly there," said Rachael, smiling at him.

"Yes, we—" Jesse stopped talking and looked down at the fallen logs on the road. With the near-blinding rain, he barely noticed them.

"What's wrong?" Rachael said, suddenly concerned.

"It's the fallen trees," he said as they walked their horses past them. "They look … cut." As he turned sharply towards his father, he heard his father scream, "Shields!"

Harry was looking up at his father on his horse and talking amiably as they always had for so many years.

He looked ahead at Jon when he heard him scream something. Suddenly, Harry felt a punch on his back where his shield was held. Turning around, confused, he saw that an arrow was now lying on the ground. He looked upwards to the nearby trees just in time to see an arrow fly through the air and enter his chest. It went straight through his heart.

"Harry!" Ray screamed out in terror, but before he could dismount, three arrows lodged into his body, two in the chest and one in the neck. He fell down dead next to his eldest son.

Jon Dayton was watching his son talk to Rachael and marveled at how beautiful young love could be. *Perhaps I will be a grandfather in a few years. Perhaps Jane Butler would be a great-grandmother,* he thought with a grin.

He watched his son look down at the logs on the road. *They weren't there yesterday,* he thought, He then noted the angle of the logs, and the blood drained from his face. "Shields!" he cried out as two arrows entered the side of his chest.

Jesse saw as many as half the scouts fall with arrows in their bodies. He watched with terror filling his heart as his father and his horse fell after being hit with numerous arrows.

"Jesse!" Rachael screamed, pointing towards a small hill on their right.

Jesse looked up and saw, at the least, thirty masked bandits who were preparing to send another volley of arrows. One man in the front appeared to have a gun.

"Shields up, Rangers!" he shouted out to those who were still alive. But his father had no shield, and picking one up from one of the fallen scouts, he ran over to protect him.

When he got to him, he saw his father was bleeding badly from his wounds. Quickly, he dragged him behind his now-dead horse and covered them both with his shield.

"Son," his father spoke weakly. "Remember … your duty."

My duty! What was my duty? Jesse thought. *I am completely lost.*

"Tell me what to do, Dad," he pleaded.

"You have practiced …for this …" His father's chest heaved as he gasped for the air needed to speak. "Remember …"

What did he mean practiced? And then he knew what his friends had been practicing at.

"I understand, Dad." He nodded at his ashen-faced father.

"I … knew … you would." He smiled one last time and reached his hand up to his son's cheek. "Never … forget" were the last words he said as his hand fell to the ground.

Jesse looked at his father in complete disbelief. The rock in his life, the foundation on which all his actions were based upon, was dead.

He felt a swirl of emotions fighting a war with each other for dominance. Grief, denial, tears, and just behind those was the emotion he needed right now: rage.

Waiting for the next volley of arrows to stop falling, he sprinted over to his friends.

"Line up," he ordered his eight riders. "We're going to do this just the way we have been practicing." His voice sounded cold to his own ears.

"Phil. Alan," he called out to the men who were close by, huddled behind their shields, waiting for another volley of arrows. "The fallen," Jesse continued. "You have a minute to do what is right."

Phil and Alan looked at him in confusion for a moment, and then the realisation of what Jesse was asking dawned upon them. Phil just nodded and said, "It will be done."

"Taylor," Jesse called out, "the man with the gun, he is yours." Taylor gave a sharp nod.

Jesse looked at the distance between them and Mason's Gang. How many shots could they fire in that time? He would soon find out.

"Rangers, it's us or them," he called out, and all eight riders charged forward, screaming.

Dillon was laughing his head off as Dayton's men and women fell. First of all, it was the two riders who took the brunt of most of the arrows, and now they had the rest hiding behind their shields. Only the teenager riders were left untouched as they saw their comrades fall, one by one. Dayton was dead, and they were in complete disarray.

Then something completely hilarious in Dillon's mind happened. The teenagers were riding in a suicidal attack towards them.

"Look out, fellas," Turner shouted in a laugh. "We've got some pubeless wonders about to descend upon us."

Dillon laughed along with the others, and they began to unsheathe all their weapons.

This should be fun, Dillon thought. There was a pretty girl with long braided blonde hair riding second from the left. She looked a bit of an all right, in his mind. Make sure we keep her alive … for a while anyway. The one on the far right looks like she could eat bricks for a living; in fact, she could probably break bricks with her bare hands.

All of the bandits were chuckling and preparing for the short battle when they saw Turner fall backwards with an arrow protruding from his eye. Dillon looked around and saw other bandits fall to the ground with arrows.

What was going on? There weren't any archers around. He looked down to the road and saw people were now moving around, but nobody was firing arrows at them.

He looked back at the riders and saw something he didn't think was possible. A girl with wild curly hair was riding her horse with her knees only as she was firing arrow after arrow from her bow. The bandits who had been laughing a minute ago were now less than half their number and running for their horses in terror.

Dillon thought he better join them, but as he began to run, he screamed out in pain as an arrow entered his back, and he fell to the ground.

He turned his head from facing the grass and saw the brick-eater standing over him.

"For Jon Dayton" she said and smashed her mace into his skull.

Phil and Alan watched as Jesse Dayton and his seven companions rode back down towards them. Jesse was carrying a shotgun on his shoulder and had a face like death. They were all covered in blood, from the second killing they'd had to perform. So were Alan and Phil.

"I don't like the look of this," said Alan quietly.

"Denial is a strong thing, my friend," said Phil, looking at Jon's son. "Grief will come to him eventually."

"How many are left?" Jesse said in a hard voice.

"Eight can walk, which includes me and Alan," said Phil. "Four need to be carried." He nodded at their horses.

"Did you do what you had to?"

"Yes, Jesse, we did," Alan said quietly.

Jesse just nodded his head at this.

He's going to pop if he doesn't release his emotions soon, thought Phil.

"What about my grandfather and uncle?" asked Rachael.

"I'm sorry, Rachael. I'm very sorry," Phil said softly.

Rachael began to cry, and Jesse wanted to put his arms around her, but a wall inside of him wouldn't let that happen.

"We better get moving," he said in that dead voice instead. "We don't know if there are any more out there."

"We will stay and wait for the Kingston mob," replied Phil. "Billy Beasley is with them, and he needs to know from us first."

"Thank you," Jesse replied.

The four who needed to be carried were helped to mount the horses, with the owners walking at their sides, and so eighteen of the twenty survivors made their way back home.

Rachael stayed for a few moments and looked back at the battle site with tears in her eyes.

"I think I need to stay near Jesse," she said to them, almost seeking their approval.

"We understand," replied Phil.

"We will lay the fifteen in a row and cover them the best we can," said Alan.

"Thank you," she said and rode after her friends.

Billy and his twenty-five people finally made it past the hole in the road, which led to the waterfall off the cliff. His group was last now in the shifts taken in fighting the dead.

"Sir," one of the rangers said to him.

He wasn't sure why they had taken to calling him that; he was a newcomer to their community, but he was too tired to question them.

"Yes, what is it?" he replied.

"One of the men looked over the cliff whilst we were waiting for everybody to cross."

"And?"

"You better have a look, sir," he replied with a big smile.

Billy followed the ranger and found a large group of his men smiling and pointing as they looked over the edge of the road. Walking up to them, he was finally able to see what they were staring at, and soon, a big smile came over his face as well.

"Jon, bloody, Dayton," he said with a laugh. "You've done it again." He looked down on thousands upon thousands of smashed corpses lying in the valley below.

"Looks like we can rest easy, lads," he said with a grin.

They all turned around as they heard a horse approach.

"No doubt it's the mayor, wondering where all the zombies have gone," Billy said with a laugh.

And to his surprise, it was the mayor who was riding towards them, leading an extra horse; he also looked very serious.

"Mayor, do you see where the zombies went?" Billy said, pointing to the valley below.

"I know now, lad," the mayor replied. "Friends of yours a kilometre down the road told me."

Billy was starting to think that the mayor was sounding too serious for a battle that had just been won.

"What's the matter, Mayor?" he asked.

"You better come with me, Billy," he replied with sadness in his voice.

"Jessica, is she all right?"

"I'm not sure," the mayor said, now sounding distraught. "But what I am about to show you has nothing to do with Jessica."

Billy felt his heart pounding as he mounted the spare horse. The ride south seemed like a dream for him, as all he could feel was his fear, and all he could hear was the horses' hooves on the road.

It didn't take long to reach a clearing that had clearly been the site of a recent battle. He looked over at the hill to the right and saw dozens of bodies lying at various angles, obviously left where they fell.

This was a sharp contrast to the fifteen bodies all lined up neatly in a row on a gently sloping area of grass.

His heart began to race when he saw Dog lying next to the last corpse and howling towards the sky.

"I'm sorry, Billy," said the mayor. "It was the Masons."

Billy dismounted and walked to the line of the corpses. He didn't want to start with the one next to Dog because he wanted just another moment of not believing his father was dead.

He saw Phil and Alan standing nearby with their heads bowed in respect.

He walked along the line and recognised all of the faces. He noted some of the eyes had been stabbed, as was the case with all deaths that were not freeborn. One day, his eyes would be stabbed as well.

He stopped as he reached the middle of the line, taking deep breaths. He didn't want to go any farther, he really didn't, and perhaps if he turned around and walked away, he could pretend all this never happened.

Another howl from Dog brought him back to his senses.

Say goodbye to your father. He deserves that at least. Billy thought. *No man could have asked for a better father.*

A part of him wondered where Harry was. Surely, he would have waited for him, and they could have mourned together. Then the thought that Harry was in this line, almost brought him to his knees. *No, no, no!* he thought as he walked to the last three.

He saw the face of Jon Dayton. Oh no, poor Jesse, he thought. He must be devastated, but where was he? He wasn't in the previous line. Who would lead the fight against Mason now?

He stopped and closed his eyes when he reached the last two. I don't have to look, he told himself again. *But you do, Billy,* a voice said in his head; *you know you do.*

Opening his eyes like a child who was scared of the dark, Billy began to focus on the last two corpses.

The silence of the clearing was broken by a grown man screaming.

Grovetown, Fortress Walls

Everybody who could use a bow was up on the Walls. No work was going to get done for the next few days, that was for sure, thought Ash.

Ash herself had insisted on guarding the ramparts as well, specifically the north gates so she would be the first one to greet her brother and father when they arrived.

"I'm not sure if I'm disobeying your father by being here?" Rob said.

"I'm sure my grandmother and sister are fine," replied Ash. "And I know you are as anxious to see your family, as I am mine."

Rob grunted, but she knew that this was true.

Ash looked along the lines of people anxiously awaiting the arrival of their loved ones.

Zombies, bandits, and surviving members of the Hobart expedition, this was a day that would be remembered for years to come, Ash thought as she gazed along the lines of people on the defensive walls.

She stopped as she noticed one pair of feet was standing on a box. She moved away from the wall and noticed those feet were connected to very short legs.

I don't believe it, she thought angrily.

"Lily Dayton!" she yelled out. "You are in so much trouble when I get my hands on you."

She saw those little legs give a twitch, and as she was walking towards those legs, she saw her little sister's face poke out between the other bodies. She was carrying her father's hat.

"How on earth did you get here?" Ash said in a firm voice.

"Nan fell asleep," she answered in that tiny voice and looked up at her with innocent eyes.

"Oh, no, Lily, that face may work on Dad, but not your big sister," she said as she grabbed Lily's hand. "I am taking you straight back to your grandmother, and believe me, she will not be happy with you, young lady."

And Ash was about to take her home when she heard the cry of 'Riders' yelled out.

She went straight back to where Rob was standing and lifted Lily into her arms instead.

"Are they ours?" she asked anxiously. If they were bandits, she would have to take Lily back home straightaway.

"Yes, I think so," replied Rob, squinting up the hill. "They are moving slow, anyway," he continued.

It took another few minutes before they realised it was their own people.

Ash counted eight riders, some of whom looked injured and ten people walking.

"Only eighteen!" someone cried out.

"Rob, there was meant to be thirty-five survivors," she said, holding Lily tighter.

"I know," Rob said, sounding anxious. "I can see my sister, but my uncle and Pop aren't there." He ran down the stairs to the front gate to where his father and family were now standing. Ash looked up the road until she could see Jesse riding at the front. His face! Oh no, his face looks like death.

Lily began to cling to Ash tighter.

"I don't see Daddy," she whimpered.

"I know," Ash replied, brushing her sister's hair with a shaky hand as she watched the guards open the gate.

Rachael dismounted and ran straight into her father's arms, crying. She said a few words to him, and the big man cried out and would have fallen down in tears, if not for Rob and the rest of his family holding him up.

Murmurs grew, and Ash heard the words Mason and ambush. She kept watching Jesse, looking for a reaction, but he was just sitting on his horse, staring into the distance.

"Jesse!" she yelled out. "Jesse!" she yelled again when he didn't respond. Her hands were shaking terribly, and Lily was already crying.

Slowly, he turned and looked up at his sisters.

"He's gone," was all he said.

Ash burst into tears.

Nick Fields sat down on his chair as Mary told him the news about Jon and Ray. *I'm the last,* he thought. Twenty years ago, five of them had fled Hobart in fear, and now he was the only one left. Jon had asked him to come to the south with him. His own family was from the north, and he didn't know whether they were alive or dead, but Nick would not have met Mary if not for Jon.

Nick heard a scratching noise from below the floorboards. No doubt more of those rats he had been hearing lately. Perhaps they should get a cat, he thought, a very large cat.

"The town is a mess," Mary said. "Everybody is walking around worried at what will happen next. Losing Jon has been a huge blow for our community," she continued. "He had beaten the bandits time and time again."

"Perhaps his son could take his place?"

Mary paused in thought. "Yes, he could in time, but eighteen years is too young to take on such a responsibility."

"Some eighteen-year-olds have children nowadays," Nick replied, "especially since we have no methods of contraception."

"Agreed," Mary replied. "But cleaning a baby's bottom is a bit different from leading an army to war."

He thought again about what had happened with Jon and Ray.

"Mary," he said with a sigh. "The books … the trip to Hobart."

Mary came over and looked him square in the eye.

"It's not your fault, Nick," she said firmly. "We all thought those devils were gone for good. Nobody knew that they would lie dormant like that."

Nick nodded his head. Mary was right again, as always. But this was another death he would feel guilty about till the day he died.

Mary suddenly gave a twitch of her nose. "What's that smell?"

Nick got up and walked over to the door that led to the community hall. He opened it and saw that the whole place was on fire.

"Fire!" he screamed as he slammed the door.

Nick and Mary looked down at the floorboards and saw smoke coming through the gaps.

"Grab the babies, Mary!" Nick shouted as they headed into their bedrooms.

"It's everywhere," Mary screamed as she picked up her youngest baby and held the second youngest by the hand.

Nick came back into the room with his two other children, picked up a chair, and smashed it through the window, and then he threw the two eldest through the gap; rather cuts and bruises than burning to death.

He then lifted Mary through the window whilst she was carrying the youngest baby. Nick now held the second youngest child and decided to do a commando roll out the window, preferring to hurt his back than land on his child.

Gathering his family, he checked to see if they were all safe, and he breathed a sigh of relief that they were.

"That was no rat," Nick said.

"What?" Mary replied.

"Someone was under our house," Nick replied. "Look at the hall, Mary," he said, gesturing to the now-flaming ruin. "It went up in a matter of seconds. A normal fire doesn't start like that."

"Just like the library," Mary said quietly.

Nick felt a chill. What were the chances of two fires happening in a matter of days?

He looked around the crowd that was now gathering. This community had no firemen, and when a fire as strong as this took a hold, all you could do was watch.

All you could do was watch, thought Nick as he scanned the crowd and stopped on a man in a big robe.

There were still a few hours of daylight left, and he could see everybody clearly as they ran to the hall, so why was that man wearing that hood and standing still? In fact, looking closely, he could see that he was rocking back and forth on the balls of his feet as he stared at the fire. He was enjoying this, Nick thought with disbelief.

"Mary, mind the children. I need to speak to that man in the hood."

"Please be careful, Nick," Mary said in a pleading voice.

"I will," he replied with a gentle smile.

Turning to face the hooded man, his smile became anything but gentle.

What to do? he thought. *Should I just sneak up on him or just try the direct approach?* The man looked so enthralled with the fire, he didn't think it mattered either way, so he walked directly towards him.

The hood he wore was big, but as he got closer, he could see that tears were falling down the man's cheeks.

This nutjob needed to be interrogated at the very least, Nick thought.

"Hey, you!" he called out as he reached the man.

He was surprised that the man looked at him in terror and began to turn away, but thinking that this man may have killed his children filled him with such anger that Nick reached out and grabbed his robe, pulled him back towards him, and punched him square in the face.

The man fell to the ground, screaming like a child.

"I'm making a citizen's arrest," he called out to the watching crowd as he lifted the man to his feet. "Someone please get Jack Beasley and Jim Allenby."

Mary came running over with the children. "Take that man's hood off," she commanded, and a nearby person from the crowd lifted his hood. He looked like a ranger, judging by the weapons he was carrying.

Mary's face went pale.

"Who is this, Mary?" said Nick.

"That's my brother," she replied with a snarl.

Well, how about that, thought Nick. *I've only ever punched two people in my life, and both have been my in-laws.*

Billy rode at the front of one hundred and two rangers as he made his way down to Grovetown. He collected all his father's and brother's belongings, along with Jon Dayton's sword and spyglass, which he was sure Jesse or Ash would want, maybe even Lily in the years to come, and placed them in one of the hessian bags he had found. The ones that were initially meant to carry the books from Hobart, he thought with despair.

He took another deep breath and tried to rid his mind of his brother's and father's faces as he laid them to rest.

He had screamed when he first saw them lying dead, and for how long he knelt there, weeping, he couldn't say. Then the mayor had asked him gently whether they could bury them all and lay them to rest. He said, yes, this would be a good place for them to lie, but now he was worried that Jack and the rest of the family would object to their family being buried in a place of such violence. Let alone what the Daytons and other family members would say.

Dog was still lying next to his father's grave. No amount of coaxing would get him to move. He thought the dog might starve to death if they couldn't get him to stand.

Billy wanted to lie down there as well, but he had to know if Jessica was safe.

I'm so selfish, Billy thought; whilst I was crying, I didn't give any thought as to how the mayor would be feeling about his daughter. If Jessica was killed, Billy didn't know what he would do. Perhaps he could take his grief out on the Mason Gang. This war was surely about to start.

As he rode up to the gates, Billy saw dozens of guards looking out from beyond the wall. All of them gave a nod to the rangers from Kingston. These two communities would have a strong bond for years to come because of this day.

As the doors opened, Billy saw Jessica standing there with her two escorts, and he slumped in his saddle in relief.

The mayor jumped off his mount and ran to his daughter and hugged her. Billy slowly dismounted and joined them.

Jessica looked up at him. "I'm so sorry, Billy," she said softly and wrapped her arms around him.

"We thought you may have been hurt or worse," Billy said softly.

"They chased us, but we got past them," she replied and looked up at him with a serious face. "Your brother was ordered to stay behind the walls; he's suffering so much, Billy."

Billy nodded as tears began to swell in his eyes again.

"We will go and see him now."

The mayor gave his daughter another hug, nodded goodbye to Billy, then took his men to the open pasture, where they had been staying only a few days before, which now seemed a lifetime ago.

As Billy and Jessica made their way to the front of Jack's house, Rachael ran out of the front door to embrace him.

"Thank goodness you are here, Uncle," she said. She looked like she had been crying for hours. She had been very close to her grandfather, and he'd literally adored her.

"I came as soon as I could," replied Billy, but too late for some, as a vision of Harry and his father's bodies flashed through his mind's eye.

Billy then noticed Jesse was standing nearby in the shadows; he hadn't seen him come out of Jack's house.

"I have your father's belongings, Jesse," he said softly.

"Please give them to my sisters," he replied in a flat voice.

"I'm so sorry about your father," Billy told him gently.

"Excuse me, I need to check on the gates." Jesse walked away without another word.

Billy gave Rachael a questioning look.

Rachael just sighed, and tears began to fall again from her eyes.

"Where is your father?" he asked gently.

"I'll take you to him."

Billy walked inside their house and was immediately embraced by Rob and Janine, Jack's wife.

Both looked like they had been crying for some time as well.

"He's out the back," Janine said with relief that he was here, and then welcomed Jessica into her home.

As he walked out to the backyard, he saw his brother standing, waiting for him.

Billy was shocked by the tears on his brother's face.

"I should have rode out to help them," he said in a ragged voice.

"It wasn't your fault," Billy replied. "Jon believed that the Mason Gang was no longer around. I heard him say this at Kingston. That's why Jessica was sent with so little protection."

And they attacked her; just more reason to kill these bastards.

"But we knew they were a threat when Jessica arrived," Jack said in desperation.

"And your duty was to protect the community, which you did," Billy replied. "They could have come for the town if you left. You did the right thing."

Jack began to slump with relief at Billy's words.

"What's wrong?" Billy said.

"I was so worried that you wouldn't forgive me," Jack replied with tears in his eyes.

"There's nothing to forgive," Billy insisted, shocked at his brother's admission. "In fact, I need your forgiveness for what I did with Dad's .and Harry's bodies." Billy thought he was about to start crying again.

"What do you mean?" said Jack in confusion.

"I buried them near where the battle occurred," he said, looking for his brother's reaction.

"Does it have a beautiful view?"

"It will one day."

"Then we will make it more beautiful," Jack said as he embraced his brother.

After a moment, they stepped back and began wiping their eyes.

"What are we going to do now?" said Jack.

"We hunt the Masons down," Billy answered in a harsh voice. "That's what we do. We find them and kill them for our family's honour."

Jack nodded. "But how do we do that without Jon to help us?"

Billy was saved from finding an answer when Jack turned around and began sniffing at the air.

"Bushfire?" Billy said.

"No, I think it's coming from close by," replied Jack.

Rob then ran outside and told them the community hall had been burnt down and that Nick had made a citizen's arrest of his wife's brother.

"What!" Billy and Jack said together.

"Well, that was what I have just been told," Rob replied, "and they asked for you, Dad."

"I'll come too. I feel like interrogating somebody," Billy offered.

Jack just clenched his huge fists.

Jim Allenby stood in an empty barn and watched as Jack and Billy Beasley tied Peter Rainswood tightly to a chair in the middle of the room.

Peter Rainswood, with his freshly broken nose, had been seen by numerous people standing outside the community hall, crying, as he watched the place burn down. Some people said he seemed to be crying with joy, not sorrow. The tears you see when a parent watched their child get married, or when a mother and father welcome their newborn child into the world.

The rate at which the hall was destroyed and evidence gathered from the rubble suggested the fire had been deliberately lit. Besides, Rainswood stank of kerosene and appeared to be half crazy, so he was the prime suspect.

But why, was the question that needed to be answered.

Maybe the answer was the accused's own sister, who stood nearby, glaring at her brother. It was very clear that these two siblings despised each other.

"Why did you do it, Peter?" she spat at him. "My children were in that building."

"I didn't do it, Sister," Peter replied in a panicked tone, his eyes flicking around the room.

Not the bravest of men was this Peter Rainswood. This could be of some use, Allenby mused. But whilst he looked scared of the Beasley brother, he seemed more terrified of his sister.

"You did it, you bastard," Mary shouted, "just like you burned down the library."

Peter gave a start at the mention of the library. "I did not," he replied weakly. "I am a holy man."

"You're a fake," his sister replied.

"Never," Peter replied shakily. "I am the second element."

Billy and Jack shared a glance. What the hell did that mean?

"When did he arrive in Grovetown, Mary?" Allenby asked.

"I first saw him the day after the library burnt down," she replied.

Could be a coincidence, thought Allenby, but he doubted that.

"And where had you been before this, Peter? Twenty years is a long time to be surviving on your own," asked Allenby.

"I wandered the wastelands in penance for my sins," he replied, gaining some confidence in a forced repentant tone that he had used for years.

"Twenty years wasn't enough for your sins, you slimebag," his sister raged at him.

"God requires sacrifices of his children, and—" He stopped when Allenby raised his hand.

"Please don't give us that religious spiel," Allenby said calmly. "We are not sheep here, understand?" Moving closer to Rainswood, he asked in a firm voice, "Where have you really been?"

This coward was not smart or violent enough to survive on his own, and clearly, that wandering hermit routine was a lie.

"I was roaming the bush … as I said," he lied as his eyes were back to his nervous best, now that he knew he could not bluff them with religious talk.

Allenby turned to Jack and Billy. "Boys, I give you the council's permission to beat the truth out of him."

"You can't do that," Peter screamed. "Cooper wouldn't allow it."

Allenby froze. What did he mean Cooper wouldn't allow it?

How did he know Carl Cooper?

But clearly, the mere threat of violence was having the effect he was after, so he continued on with his plan.

"Jack, hit him," he commanded, and as the big man moved closer, Rainswood threw himself to the side, and he and the chair fell to the floor.

"I am the second element, Cooper is the first, and the fourth rules us all," he said, panting, as he huddled on the floor.

Mary gave him a puzzled look.

"What is all this element shit he's talking about?" said Billy as he lifted Peter and his chair back into an upright position.

"I don't know. I think he is just a tad mental," replied Jack. "But when he fell over, he spilled this from his robe." He held up a pair of night vision goggles.

Bloody hell, Billy thought, *why didn't we think to check that massive robe of his?*

"What is that?" asked Mary.

"It's military issue night vision goggles," replied Jack quietly. "Dad," his voiced hitched a bit before he continued, "Dad showed me a pair when I was a kid."

"So now we know how he moved all the flammable material at night and wasn't seen," said Mary. "But what soldier did he get it from?"

All of the people in the room knew of only one soldier, the name that had been on everybody's lips the past week, the name that had everybody living in fear.

Billy shared a meaningful glance with all the others in the room. *It's time to toss the dice,* he thought.

"Mason," he said sharply, and Rainswood's head in his nervousness snapped towards him in complete fear and panic; everybody saw it.

Allenby looked at Rainswood, and his mind swam. Was this idiot involved with Mason? And where did Cooper fit in with all this? Allenby walked right up to Peter and looked him straight in the eye. It was time to finish this.

"I don't like violence, Peter. I really don't," he said in a cold voice. "But if you don't tell me the truth right now, I am going to allow these two big men here, who have just lost their brother and father to Mason and his gang, to beat you within an inch of your life."

Peter looked back at Jim Allenby in terror. He looked over at Billy and Jack and saw death and grief in their eyes. He looked at his sister and saw her smiling.

"I ... can't ... tell you," Peter replied in panic.

"Last chance," Allenby said.

"They will kill me," he replied.

"You will have my protection."

"I ... I ..."

"Jack," Allenby said firmly and stood back a few paces. And as Peter watched the huge man come forward, grab his robe, and raise a huge fist to hit him, he screamed out:

"Cooper recruited me from Mason's to burn down the library and start a religious order."

Everybody was silent for a moment as they took in the ramifications of what Peter had just said.

Allenby walked back into view and said calmly, "And how does Cooper know Mason?"

Peter was panting raggedly now. He was a dead man, he thought, but he clung to one hope.

"You promise me, that if I confess, you will protect me from Cooper?"

"I promise," Allenby replied

"And these two?" he said, indicating Billy and Jack, who still held him by his robe.

"Them as well," Allenby replied calmly.

Peter took a deep breath; he had no choice now.

"After I fled my father's house, I had nowhere to go. I ended up joining Mason and his gang. I was with him for nearly twenty years. Cooper was with him for fifteen."

Everybody stood in stunned silence. Councillor Cooper was a member of Mason's gang, the very ones who had attacked and killed so many of their friends?

"This can't be true," said Jack. "He was a leading politician."

"Dad said the politicians could be just as bad as anybody else," replied Billy. "Worse, in some cases, as they had so much power."

Allenby just watched Peter in silence.

"Why did he want you to burn down the library?" said Billy.

"I don't know," Peter replied, still trying to control his breathing. "I really don't, honestly."

"And why burn down the community hall?" said Jack.

Peter glanced at his sister.

The bastard, Billy thought.

Mary walked over to him and slapped his face, hard.

Peter squealed like a child. "You whore," he cried out in pain.

"Protection or not," Jack said calmly, "if you say that word again to my friend, I will knock you out."

Peter shrank back in his chair.

"Jack," said Allenby, "round up as many rangers as you can. We are all going to visit Cooper right now."

Jack untied Peter, then Billy came over and lifted him to his feet. "You're coming too, holy man," he said.

"Are you sure Peter is telling the truth?" asked Jack.

"We will soon find out," replied Allenby.

"He is," said Mary in a confident voice.

"Are you sure?" replied Jack.

"I've seen him lie for so many years," she replied. "Preying on people's fears, insecurities, and bank balances. Making them feel like they were part of something special. God's chosen people, he would say, as if God was some kind of bigot." She shook her head and looked at Jack with sadness. "I got to learn when he told the truth."

Peter looked at his sister in shock.

"Let's go," said Allenby.

"Very nice, good cop/bad cop routine, by the way," Billy said as he dragged Peter towards the door.

"Thanks," Allenby and Jack said together.

"Cooper was a politician," Mary said suddenly, and everybody stopped and looked at her.

"What do you mean?" replied Allenby.

"The first element is politics," Mary replied thoughtfully. "The second is religion," she pointed at her brother, "and I think the third is soldiers, such as Mason."

"Then what is the fourth element that will rule us all?" said Billy.

"It must be very powerful to control the first three," Jack added.

Cooper counted the money that he had stashed in one of his spare bedrooms. It really didn't matter that the money was not hidden, as he had made it quite clear that he wanted the monetary system to be brought back into the community.
The survivalists had hoarded their money as well as food and weapons, in anticipation of the apocalypse. Cooper had counted over fifty thousand in cash and coin that they had previously stashed in the cellar.
The local bank would have been pleased to have had this in their accounts, Cooper thought. Especially with the hundreds of thousands of dollars they had already had.
One of the weapons in the cellar would be big enough to make a hole in the bank vault after Bradfield had arrived.
He remembered his days in the Tasmanian Parliament. For hours, they had argued about balancing the budget and cutbacks they had to make to government services and employment so they could pay back some of the interest they owed to the international banking groups.
Now, all the three councillors had to do was organise things. There were no political parties with ideologies about how things should be run. No kissing up to the public with promises you knew you couldn't keep. Just as long as you organised things well, the community was quite happy to vote you in again for another term. They actually voted for people they thought were intelligent. Cooper laughed when he thought of all the dumb arses that used to be nominated to run for election by the anonymous backroom dealers that ran the party agenda.
Cooper remembered when big business owners used to wine and dine him, and private donations were made to the political party. All in good faith, of course; there was never any expectation that the money donators would receive any favourable political decisions in return, he thought drily.
It wasn't the best system, he knew that deep down inside, but he was convinced that money was what drove the human society to reach higher levels of technology. And if they were to get back to the standard of living they'd had before, money would be the

driving factor. It would take a while, he knew, but get there they would, under his leadership, of course.

If, as a consequence of this, there would be poor people again, well, that was just their plain bad luck. Intelligent people made lots of money, and if you were just too dumb to make it in the money world, well, that was just stiff shit, as far as he was concerned.

He wondered if he could control the money when it began being circulated again. Perhaps he could charge interest on loans? He deserved this after all the hard work he was doing in bringing the society back from its knees.

Moving out of the bedroom, he walked to the window that looked across at most of the community. What a day it had been. He was overjoyed when he learned of Dayton's death, and this came with the added bonus that he had miraculously succeeded in destroying the zombies of Hobart. Maybe one day they could eventually return to the old town. The pale white zombies that were left behind would surely be no problem.

But he couldn't believe that Turner and his people were all killed. Thirty, they numbered, and yet, even though they had the advantage of surprise, they still could only kill half the numbers that they lost.

Bradfield Mercenaries only numbered forty now, plus the Mason prisoners they kept. Still, with the weaponry they would have after tonight, they would be unstoppable.

The survivalists had enough ammunition and guns in the cellar to last for years. Forty of Bradfield's people should have enough ammunition to last for a year, if they were frugal.

Bring in Mason's heads as proof that you are the heroes, was the plan. Stay for a while, until they get used to you. Then slowly usurp Jack Beasley's rangers as the muscle of this town.

Inch by inch, the takeover should be, just as the masters in the past had done.

He looked again over the small town in which they lived.

All was finally going to plan, he thought; after all his scheming over the last five years, he was finally within reach of his goal.

And then he froze as he saw that there was a massive hole where the community hall used to be. *It must have burned down whilst I was counting that bloody money,* he thought with shock.

But how did it burn so quickly?

His face began to drain of its blood. The question was not how, but who burned it down.

No, he couldn't have. Could he?

Yes, he did.

He began to pace the room as he thought of all the consequences of the preacher's action.

He loved fire, that was plain as day. His sister lived in the hall, and he hated her, that was also as plain as day.

He had to find Rainswood and kill him. He was a loose cannon who could ruin everything.

He stopped pacing as he saw a group of armed men move up the slope in his direction. He looked more closely and saw Jack Beasley standing high above the crowd and directing a number of his people to his left and right. This gave him a clear view of the people in Beasley's immediate vicinity.

The first person he saw on Jack's right was Jim Allenby, and his normally calm face seemed to be covered in worry. The second person he saw was on Jack's left was his brother, Billy. His face looked angry, very angry. The third person he saw was being dragged by the collar of his huge robe.

And when he saw the face in that robe look up towards his house …

"I'm a dead man," Cooper whispered.

All his plans had gone to dust. He had to flee now if he was to survive. He grabbed a shotgun he kept hidden in his bedroom, put on his large robe with the hole in the pocket, and ran out the door.

Jack sent four of his rangers to the left and another four to the right. The nearby citizens began to move away once the rangers brought out their bows and arrows. They soon surrounded Cooper's house and waited for Jack's orders.

"Dayton would advise caution," whispered Allenby.

Jack thought for a moment and looked over at his brother. They both took a step back, lifted their legs, and proceeded to kick the door down. They were their father's sons.

Jesse stood in front of the open northern gates and looked up the road that went to Kingston. What was wrong with him? He didn't seem able to show any real emotions.

Never forget your duty were the last words his father spoke. Wasn't it? Jesse thought it was. Well, he intended to live up to his father's last request.

'He's gone,' was all he had said in a cold voice to his sister, and he then just watched as Ash broke down into tears. He half-carried her back to their grandmother's home as she was crying so uncontrollably, and then she wouldn't release her hold on her little sister until her grandmother talked to her in soothing words. All the while, Jesse watched this happen as if he weren't really there.

He left the house as his sisters were being consoled by their grandmother, walked to Jack Beasley's home, and the same thing happened. Rachael was crying, and he couldn't provide any comfort whatsoever to the girl he loved.

"Excuse me, young Jesse," he heard a voice say behind him. Jesse turned around and saw Councillor Cooper standing with a well-worn robe covering most of his face.

"Councillor," Jesse said in a flat voice, "what brings you to the north gate?"

"I'm just passing through, Jesse, that's all," he replied with that smile that never reached his eyes.

"I'm sorry, Councillor," Jesse replied in confusion, "but after today's attack, do you think it is wise to walk out like this?" He didn't even have his horse with him.

"It's council business, my young friend," he replied. "Nothing to concern yourself with," and patting his shoulder, he walked out of Grovetown.

"Look at all this money," said Billy in shock.

Money had disappeared from their lives nearly twenty years ago, and Billy was surprised when they came across such an amount hidden in a box in one of Cooper's bedrooms.

"I wonder where he got all this from," said Jack, who was still angry that Cooper wasn't there. He had other rangers on the lookout for him, but so far, nobody could find him.

"Do you think he carried this around with him for twenty years?" asked Billy.

"I doubt it," replied Jack. "What would he use it for?"

Allenby looked at the brothers. They both looked so tired. This morning, their brother, Harry, and their father, Ray, both of whom Allenby was very fond, had been alive and well, and now, they not only had to deal with their deaths, but Mason and Cooper as well.

"I don't think he would have carried that around for twenty years," he offered, indicating the heavy box. "Maybe he found it from the previous owners of this house. They were survivalists, from what I recall."

"What's a survivalist?" said Rob, who was standing in the doorway to the bedroom.

"Oh, just people who prepare for the apocalypse," replied Allenby. "They store things, such as money, food, and weapons."

All four of them looked at each other in silence.

Weapons!

"Where would they store things?" asked Billy quietly.

"Usually in what was called a panic room, or maybe down in a cellar," Allenby said.

They all now looked at the floor.

Jack spun around to his son. "Rob, get everybody to rip up the carpets; look to see if there is anything unusual on the floorboards. Tear this place apart, if need be."

Ash wiped at her eyes and kissed her grandmother goodbye.

"Be tactful," said her grandmother, who was also upset at their father's death.

"I will," Ash assured her, shifting her bow on her shoulder. Everybody carried weapons now, and probably would for some time to come.

"He will break soon enough," Jane Butler said, "but don't rush it so he shatters entirely."

She had to make him grieve or show some sort of emotion. It wasn't normal the way he was reacting. She thought he may injure himself or someone else if this continued.

"Yes, Nan," Ash replied with a teary smile and walked towards the northern gate to see her brother.

Jesse walked up the ramparts and watched as Councillor Cooper walked up the main road, away from Grovetown.
What is he doing? Doesn't he know there are bandits out there with guns?
Dad never trusted him, Jesse remembered, and as his father's face came to his mind, he shut it away behind the wall he had created. Never forget your duty, Jesse thought, and watched with curiosity as the councillor took a sharp turn to the left and disappeared into the bush land.
Where is he going?

"Bring Rainswood down here," ordered Jack as he stood in amazement at the amount of weapons in Cooper's cellar.
"So many weapons," Billy said in awe.
"This is most likely where Mason got that new gun from," said Allenby. "I feel so ashamed that my fellow councillor was betraying us like this."
"Don't, Jim. That smarmy bastard fooled us all," said Billy.
"But why didn't he just give these guns to Mason?" Allenby said with a confused look. "They could have just took us over with this amount of weaponry."
"Control maybe," mused Jack. "Perhaps he needed to be sure of his position in the new world."
"And why does the second cell have only an old box in it?" asked his son Rob.
"Who knows, Son," replied his father.
"Maybe he might help us," said Billy as Peter was dragged down the stairs.
"Right, time for some straight answers, Rainswood." Jack said as he stood over him.
"Of course," the nervous man replied.
"How many are in Mason's gang?"
"After the battle last week, a little over a hundred."
"So maybe seventy now," said Billy.
"And where are they camped?" Jack continued.
"As of a week ago, five kilometres west of here," Peter replied,

trying to give Jack his best smile.

"Can you find this place for us?" Jack said.

"I only travelled at night, I'm sorry," Peter replied. "I had those night vision goggles on. The bush was very thick in some parts." Again, he tried that sickly smile of his.

Jack looked at him and grunted. "I'm getting sick of looking at you, Rainswood." Peter's ingratiating smile became a nervous one again.

Turning to one of his rangers, Jack said, "Glyn, put this prick in the other cell. We will work out what to do with him later."

"Yes, Jack," Glyn replied and scruffed him by the nape of the neck and threw him in the other cell with the wooden box.

"You smell like shit," Glyn said as he locked the cell door.

"Seventy" said Rob nervously. "But we can fight them now with these guns."

"We could," Billy replied, "but the other cell is nearly empty."

"Are you thinking he gave them half of his weapons already?" Allenby asked.

"Well, why is this cell full and the other one empty?" Billy replied, gesturing to the second cell.

"Perhaps it is a rainy day," Jack said to Billy quietly. Billy looked back at his brother for a moment and nodded, saying, "It is slightly drizzly indeed."

Allenby was not sure what they were talking about, but knowing them as he did, whatever it was would have a big impact.

"I'm not sure why this cell is almost empty," Rainswood said uneasily as he stood by the wooden box, "but I would like to let your guard here know," gesturing towards Glyn, "that the smell is not coming from me but from this coffin here."

"Coffin!" exclaimed Billy.

"Yes, and when I was here before," replied Peter in rising panic as he heard a moaning noise come from the coffin, "I seem to recall Cooper mentioned he had a woman down here."

"Glyn, get the cell keys quickly," said Jack.

But it was too late, as a zombie quickly rose from the coffin and bit deeply into Peter's arm.

Peter screamed in agony as he hit the floor and looked up and saw Cooper's wife.

"Daisy," he screamed out, and as she was about to attack him again, he saw her head explode.

Was that a bullet? He wasn't sure anymore as his heart raced and his vision began to blur. He tried to stand, but he couldn't move his legs. He was vaguely aware of people entering the cell, and then he heard someone say, "I'm sorry, Peter."

Sorry about what? he wondered, as his vision dimmed. That was the last thought he ever had as his head exploded.

Allenby slumped against the cell door. He hadn't seen a zombie in quite a few years as up close as this, but that was not what had shocked him.

"That was Daisy," he said, "Cooper's wife."

He looked at the others in the room, who stood there in disbelief.

"She's been dead for four years," he said finally.

"Bastard!" roared Jack, who looked like he wanted to blow someone else's head off. "He knew!" he stormed. "He knew about what awaited Jon, Harry, and Dad in Hobart. He sent them there to die."

"Round everybody up," Billy said to Glyn. "We need to let everybody know what Cooper has done."

"I'll get Jesse," said Rob, who then climbed the stairs quickly. Little did they know that telling Jesse right now was not the very best of ideas.

Ash walked the last distance to the northern gate, wondering how she was going to approach this. Slap his face and tell him to grieve for his father would be the way their grandmother would handle this. Or have a conversation about something else such as the Mason Gang, which would lead on to their father's death. Maybe she could bring up arranging some flowers for his gravesite.

Dad!

Ash felt another strong sob come out of her mouth. What am I doing? I need to grieve some more, not worry about Jesse. And poor Lily was still shaking with tears, and had been ever since she learned her father would not be returning.

Ash stopped and focused on her breathing, trying to bring it back to a normal level. She had given up on making her eyes look normal; she looked a wreck, and she knew it.

Finally, she saw Jesse standing on the rampart, looking northward.

"Jesse," she called out and saw him turn to her with a frown on his face.

"Ash, what are you doing here?" he said in that dead voice of his. "You should be looking after Lily."

"*You* should be looking after Lily!" she yelled back at him. "Our father died today, and we should be grieving and paying our respects." So it looked like she was taking her grandmother's way of handling this.

"I know our father died. I was with him," he shouted back angrily, and just at the end, she heard a crack in his voice.

Perhaps I am getting somewhere, she thought, but she was interrupted as Rob Beasley came running down the street.

"Jesse, Ash, you have to come to Councillor Cooper's house straightaway."

"Why?" Jesse replied as he walked down the rampart.

"Cooper was behind the whole thing," Rob said excitedly. "He recruited Peter Rainswood from the Mason Gang to burn down the library. Rainswood confessed to it. Both of them travelled with Mason for years and years. When we went to Cooper's house, we found he wasn't there, and eventually, we found a cellar with two cells." Taking a deep breath, he continued, "In one cell was enough guns and ammunition to kill everybody in Grovetown a hundred times over. In the second cell was his wife."

"His wife?" Ash said in confusion.

"Yes, his wife, Daisy," Rob said. "But she had been dead for four years."

"What?" Jesse said in that dead voice that made Ash very uneasy.

"When Rainswood was placed in the cell with what we thought was just a single box of guns, Cooper's wife, Daisy, awakened from that box and attacked him."

"Are they both dead now?" said Jesse with a face like stone.

"Yes," replied Rob, now feeling at bit uneasy himself. "Cooper sent us to Hobart knowing what would happen. He sent the rangers to find new books, because he burned all the others. He sent them all to die."

Ash thought Jesse's face could not possibly get any harder, but she had been wrong. Very wrong.

A dark red colour took over her brother's face, and his mouth became an angry, tight scowl; he held his knife on his hip hard enough that she thought it might break. She even took a step backwards, thinking he was going to attack them, but suddenly, he turned and ran up the road, screaming Cooper's name.

Rob looked at Ash in shock.

"Have they found Cooper yet?" said Ash.

"No," replied Rob.

"Well, I think we have now," she replied and ran after her brother.

"But he might have a gun," Rob yelled out in warning, but the Daytons were already gone.

Cooper is most likely running to Mason, thought Rob, as he saw Jesse turn left into the bush land. The war was about to begin. He ran quickly back to Cooper's former house.

He killed my father; he killed my father. These words raged through his mind as Jesse ran through the bush.

He saw where Cooper turned westwards, and he knew he was headed to Mason, but he had to get to him first. He had to kill him, he had to kill him, and the more that thought went through his mind, the faster he ran.

Ash struggled to keep up with her brother. He was running so fast. Ash heard what Rob had called out, but she knew that even if Jesse was aware that Cooper had a gun, he wouldn't stop chasing him. He had lost all control. He wanted revenge; so did Ash, and she began to run faster.

Rob rushed into Cooper's house. He saw his father glance towards him with a grim face.

"Um, Dad," he said.

"Yes, Son?" he replied. "You look like you've done something that you're regretting."

"Yes, I have, Dad," he replied, looking a bit pale. "I told Jesse about Cooper."

"Well, that's all right," his father replied, confused. "We told you to let people know. So where is Jesse now?"

"He's chasing Cooper."

Jack looked at his son for a moment in silence.

"Was he going westward?" he finally said.

"Yes, Dad, he ran straight up the road, then to a sharp left through the trees. He looked very angry," Rob replied.

"He's not the only one," Jack said as he walked outside and looked around at the people who had gathered. Guns from the cellar had been handed out to all the rangers.

"Jesse Dayton is running after Cooper," he said to Mayor Nash. The mayor looked over to his hundred rangers, who were handling their new guns.

"It could be risky," said the mayor thoughtfully, "most of my people don't know how to use these weapons."

"They will learn quickly enough. Get those who know how, to explain the procedures and precautions to the others," replied Jack. "Besides, we may just have enough firepower to end this quickly."

The mayor looked at Jack, waiting for more information, but Jack began to walk northwards.

As they made their way out of the northern gate, Billy came running up the road to him with their father's carrying bag.

"Ready, Billy?" said Jack.

"Ready," he said, nodding to his brother.

Cooper stumbled on yet another branch as he made his way west through the dense bush land.

What was he going to do when he got to Bradfield? In his panic to leave Grovetown, he never considered that his failure may lead to Bradfield killing him.

He had no bargaining chip. He was just as expendable as any of the other bandits. Perhaps he could convince Bradfield that moving north would be a good idea.

In fact, he thought with his usual brilliance, old Hobart town was now a safe place to go. Well, apart from those pale zombies that he heard about. Maybe if he mentioned the title of King of Hobart to Bradfield, they could head south straightaway.

Bradfield said he wanted a home. Well, Hobart had thousands of empty houses waiting to be claimed.

He started to feel more relaxed, until he heard an oncoming noise from behind him. Some animal was crashing through the native vegetation and heading in his direction.

Pulling out his shotgun, he was surprised when Jesse Dayton came running through the bush like a madman.

"Hold it there," Cooper said coldly and pointed the gun straight at Jesse, who stopped about twenty metres away from him.

"You killed my father," he said, panting, as he looked at Cooper with pure hatred.

Jesse was holding a knife in his hand, but had no other weapon that he could see.

"Yes, I did," Cooper replied in all honesty. "He was in my way and had to be removed. Are the rangers looking for me now?"

"Yes, we found the guns and your wife."

"Ah, dear Daisy," Cooper replied with a smile. "Did she bite anyone?"

"Rainswood," Jesse replied.

Cooper burst into laughter.

Jesse considered throwing his knife at him, but although Cooper was laughing, he still had his eyes trained on him.

"You're really not as smart as your father," Cooper said sarcastically when his laughter abated. "He would not have run after me without any sort of backup plan."

Jesse stared at him for a moment, then a look of dejection came across his face.

"I'm sorry, boy," he said as he aimed his shotgun at Jesse's body. "You're a freeborn, so only one bullet will do."

But before he could pull the trigger, he saw a flash of movement from way behind Jesse.

Cooper then screamed in agony as an arrow entered his right shoulder. He looked beyond Jesse and saw, in the distance, Ash Dayton with a bow in her hand.

"Jesse, get him," she called out.

Jesse growled and ran at him. His knife was raised in the killing position.

Cooper tried to raise his shotgun in defence, but he couldn't get his right arm to move properly. Left arm, left arm, he thought frantically, but it was too late as Jesse Dayton slammed him into a nearby tree and drove his knife into his chest.

Cooper looked up in disbelief at Jesse's face, which was glaring at him with pure venom.

"But you're not a freeborn, are you?" Jesse said as he pulled the knife from his chest.

What was he going to do?

He knew what he was going to do when he felt the tip of the knife touch the skin from under his chin.

"No, you can't," he babbled as he felt the knife move through the bottom of his mouth.

"I did what I did for us—" He couldn't speak anymore as the knife sliced through his tongue.

His eyes looked at Jesse in terror as he saw him shift his body weight into a position where he could get the most power behind the knife.

He tried to scream when the knife slammed upwards through his skull and into his brain.

Ash approached her brother with caution as he stood above the fallen body of Cooper.

"Jesse," she said gently as she moved closer towards him.

She flinched when he turned around, but was relieved to see her brother's normal face had returned. The one she had loved for so many years.

"What have I become?" he said in a soft voice.

Tears were now glistening in his eyes.

"Grief does crazy things to us," she replied as she walked closer to him.

"But Dad, Dad wouldn't have wanted me to do this." He gestured to the corpse lying against the base of the tree.

"He needed killing, Jesse," Ash replied firmly. "This man murdered so many of our friends."

"I know, but …"

"He murdered our father, no matter how indirect. He sent all of the people who went to Hobart to their deaths," replied Ash.

Jesse sagged against the tree. "It's just that when Dad …when Dad died, he told me to remember my duty. I don't think he liked me killing in the way that I do." He sighed and looked at his feet. "His last words were 'Never Forget'."

Ash stood in silence for a moment and wiped the tears from her eyes.

"He was a peaceful man from a peaceful time, Jesse," she replied. "I don't think he liked any of us killing anybody."

She then walked up close to him, placed a hand on his cheek, and told him what their father meant by saying 'never forget'.

Jesse finally cried.

Jack and the mayor approached slowly as they saw the Dayton kids lying against the base of the tree. Jesse's head was resting on his sister's shoulder.

Cooper's lifeless body was lying against the side of the tree, with what looked to be a knife rammed inside his skull.

Good riddance, thought Jack.

"You completed part of our revenge, Jesse," said Jack. "Will you come with us for the rest?"

Jesse wiped at his eyes and stood up. "It's my duty," he said simply as Rachael ran forward and embraced him. Jack was pleased that Jesse's regular expression had returned, and that he looked at his daughter with love in his eyes.

Billy walked forward and removed a sword from his father's carrying bag.

"Here, I'm sure he would like you to have this."

Jesse nodded and tied the sword belt around his waist.

"Thank you," he said with a smile that reached his eyes.

"Should we take Cooper's head?" asked Rob.

"No," Jesse said firmly. "We will never do that again. Removing people's heads is for barbarians."

"Then what should we do with the body?" said the mayor.

"Let the animals have him," Jesse replied. "We are no longer barbaric, but this man deserved no such respect as a decent burial."

Perhaps a step back towards more peaceful times was taken today, Ash thought.

Jesse walked over and slowly retrieved his knife from Cooper's head and wiped the blood on Cooper's fancy suit.

"Let's finish this," he said in a commanding tone.

Ash watched as leaders like Jack and the mayor nodded in agreement. His father's son, she thought with a proud smile.

One hundred fifty rangers now moved stealthily westwards through the thick bushlands towards Mason; there was still a little bit of daylight left on this horrible day.

Bradfield Camp, five kilometres west of Grovetown

Bradfield paced in his tent, still waiting for some word from Turner. "He should be back by now," he growled to himself. The ambush should have been a success.

Cooper said that Dayton's men, if they survived, should be ripe for the picking as they made their way home.

Bradfield had sent two men out to where Turner was in the hope of an answer. They were due back any minute.

He looked again at the shotgun Cooper had given him. Such a beautiful thing, he thought. The former army reserve soldier had gone without a rifle for protection for so many years, that he thought he would never see one again.

Then Cooper had provided him with one and promised there would be many more for his gang. Such power and such destruction, these things had. Nobody would stand in their way once they had the weaponry that they needed. Nobody could stop the Bradfield Mercenaries.

He heard voices raised and the sound of horses riding in their direction.

"Finally," he growled and stormed out of his tent.

He was expecting more than two riders to return and was surprised and a touch anxious to see the same riders as he had sent out.

"Well?" he demanded.

The two men just looked at each other, until one of them

mumbled, "They are dead."

"What do you mean dead?" replied Bradfield. "Of course Dayton's men are dead. I sent you to find Turner and his people."

"That's what we mean, Bradfield," the first man replied. "Turner is dead."

Bradfield's face went pale. "Is this some sort of sick joke?" he replied and lifted his gun towards them.

"No," the second rider said quickly. "We found Turner and his thirty lying dead on the rise where you sent them."

"Fifteen freshly dug graves were made closer to the road," the first man said. "So he did kill some of them."

"Fuck!" Bradfield shouted at the top of his lungs. "How the fuck could Dayton's men kill all of ours when we had the element of surprise?"

Bradfield began to pace again. Turner was not a stupid man, that's why had picked him as his second-in-command. He had heard Dayton was a good leader, but surely he couldn't be *that* good.

He looked around at his forty men and women that he had left. In the middle of the camp were fifteen survivors of Mason's men, all tied up and waiting to be beheaded for when they made their triumphant arrival in Grovetown. The camp was so much smaller than the one hundred thirty they used to have.

His thoughts were interrupted as two of his supposed guards to the east were seen walking towards him. Behind them walked three men. The one to the left was a big bearded man, carrying a huge axe, the one on the right was an even bigger man, who also carried an axe, and strangely, the one in the middle was a young kid of maybe eighteen. He was wearing a sword and carrying a white flag, but the strangeness was that he seemed to be the one in charge.

Bradfield walked up to them as bravely as he could. It was time to do some heavy bullshitting. He wished Cooper was here; he was the politician after all.

"Are you sure about this, Jesse?" said Jack.

"My father said that every man deserves a second chance,"

replied Jesse.

"But these people are not your everyday people, Jesse," said the mayor. "Some of these men and women have been killing and raping for decades."

Jesse looked thoughtfully at the mayor. Perhaps he was right. Perhaps a second chance was deserved by men who made mistakes. Not by people who were inherently evil.

"Well, we do have the advantage now," he said as he watched his people surround the camp in a major arc.

"Are you packing a pistol too?" the mayor said quietly to Jack.

"Yep," Jack replied just as quietly.

Jesse heard them, no matter how quietly they whispered, and smiled. He was carrying a pistol in his fur clothing as well.

"Go to your friends," he said to the inept guards in front of him. And as they ran forward, a big baldheaded man came forward to meet them.

"Any reason you have upset my guards like this?" the bald man said.

Bradfield considered using his shotgun on these three, but something about the boy's demeanor suggested that would be a bad idea. A very bad idea.

"Cut the bullshit, Mason, we know who you are," said Jack.

"Mason?" Bradfield said in surprise as an idea formed in his mind. "My name is Bradfield, and these are my mercenaries. We recently came across a gang," he said, gesturing to the men tied up, "and we dealt with them accordingly."

Everybody in the camp had gone silent and was watching the exchange with wary faces. Jesse looked over at the men tied up. They looked no different from Bradfield's mercenaries, except Mason's men had clearly been recently beat up.

"Where is Mason?" asked Jesse.

"I believe him to be dead," Bradfield replied.

"How do you know?"

"I have seen his dead body."

"You know what he looks like, then?" asked the mayor.

"No," Bradfield answered calmly, "but some of his men identified him for us."

He is good, thought Jesse, and the changing of gang names was genius. Nobody really knows who was who, as nobody knew what Mason actually looked like. He wondered whether this was truly Bradfield or Mason.

"You say you are mercenaries," said Jesse. "How do you get paid for your services?"

Go on, Jesse thought. *Say you get paid in money.*

An angry look came across Bradfield's face. "Look, why am I being interrogated here?" he snapped. "You're only three, and we are forty. You attacked my guards. We should be asking the questions."

Jesse said nothing, and looking Bradfield straight in the eye, he raised his hand and one hundred fifty rangers came out from the tree line, all carrying guns and pointing them towards the camp. Bradfield's face went pale as he looked around at the ambush. His people began to mutter nervously.

"A man called Cooper had all these guns in a cellar," Jesse said as Bradfield's head snapped towards him. "I just put a knife in his head maybe two kilometres from here." He looked at Bradfield intently. "He seemed to be walking in this direction." Bradfield's face seemed to melt under Jesse's stare.

"What are your demands?" he said in defeat.

"Your gun, for starters." Jack stepped forward to claim his shotgun.

"Gather all your people here, including Mason's men, and leave the Huon forever," said Jesse.

"What, and that's it?" replied Bradfield in disbelief.

"No. I want you to leave your horses behind."

"Why?" Bradfield said suspiciously.

"Because I want you to walk out of here, so we can watch you go all the way to Hobart," replied Jesse. "If you ride, then what is to say you would not turn around and come back?"

"This is a bad deal," snapped Bradfield.

"Perhaps you think you're being treated unfairly?" Jesse said in a steady and clear voice.

Bradfield almost took a step backwards at this young man's calm demeanor. "So you're just going to let us go?" he said nervously.

"I give you my word, that no weapons of our age or from

Cooper's cellar will be used against you," Jesse replied as the mayor looked at him with amazement. Jack, however, was watching Jesse with a thoughtful expression.

"Now go," Jesse continued. "You have five minutes to gather your people."

Bradfield still looked at Jesse in disbelief.

"What is your name?" he asked.

"Jesse Dayton, if it's any of your business."

Bradfield looked at him for a moment, then nodded his head and began ordering his people to gather their belongings.

"One last question," Jesse called out to the mercenary as he walked to his gang. "Are you Bradfield or Mason?"

The bald man stopped and turned. "Bradfield. Cooper killed Mason," he answered, then walked off.

The only decent thing he did, thought Jesse.

"What are you doing?" asked the mayor as they walked back to their men. "These people are killers."

Jesse ignored the question and turned to Jack.

"Do you have enough ammunition?"

"Yes, I think so, and then that will be our last. How did you know?" asked Jack with a smile.

"My dad told me about the battle of Kingston when I was younger," said Jesse. "He said he believed the weapon was still kept hidden by your father."

"Yes. I kept it hidden," replied Jack, nodding at Billy, who brought out the silver railing gun that had been used so long ago. "My father said to save it for a rainy day."

Jesse gave a sad smile and nodded his head.

"Will someone please tell me what is going on?" said the mayor.

"I'm taking your advice, Mayor," Jesse said gently. "The hero of Kingston has one last miracle to perform."

"The dragon of Kingston," said Billy.

"Fire it up, Billy," said Jack as the high-pitched noise began to ring out over the clearing "Aim at their feet"

Jesse watched as Bradfield gathered his mercenaries into one spot. They all turned and looked towards Jesse when they heard the noise.

I said I wouldn't use any of Cooper's or our weapons, Bradfield. I didn't say

I wouldn't use Uncle Ray's gun from a bygone age.

He felt guilty for a moment, then thought that the mayor was right about inherently evil people.

"For Dad, Harry, Jon, and all those we lost in the battle of Hobart," Billy said solemnly.

"Kill them," Jesse commanded. "Kill them all."

The Bradfield camp exploded.

Four kilometres outside of Grovetown

Three days later, Jesse rode his horse to the gravesite with Lily sitting in front of him. She still hadn't spoken a word since her father died. Not even her grandmother could get her to talk. Ash, riding her horse next to him, was looking at Lily, concerned.

Since both their parents were now dead, Jesse and Ash took it upon themselves to care for their little sister. They had all decided to move in with their Nan for a while. This would be hard for Ash and Jesse, as their grandmother could be very bossy, but it gave the family unit another dimension, and Lily did love her Nan.

Three days had passed since the horrible day that Father died, and Jesse had spent much of that time asleep.

It seemed that all the fighting and emotion being spent had exhausted everybody so much that the Butler house was a place of sleeping, not living.

Allenby had many decisions to make for the community's future in the coming days, but today, he declared, was a day when people could come out and pay their respect to those who had died.

Three days since the betrayal of Cooper.

No doubt Jim Allenby was hoping that this day could be a day of grieving, but also rebuilding of trust and community bonding.

Jesse took a big, steadying breath as they reached the clearing where the fifteen fallen were now buried.

He looked over at the gravesite and saw that Billy, Jack, and Rachael was standing next to Ray's and Harry's graves, with Jessica and Mayor Nash standing respectfully behind them. The hundred rangers from Kingston were waiting a distance up the road. They would be leaving today with Billy.

Jesse gave a start when he saw Dog was still lying by his master's grave.

"We should have brought some meat for Dog," he said guiltily to his sister.

"Don't worry," their grandmother said, who was riding behind Ash and holding on to her waist for dear life. "I brought some cut-up meat, just in case. Perhaps you could feed him, Lily?" she said to her granddaughter.

Lily looked at her Nan, then over to the dog, but still didn't say anything. Jesse bent forward and gave her a hug. The more upset Lily was, the more Jesse wanted to hold her.

Finally reaching the gravesite, Jack came forward to lift Lily from the horse, and then Jesse dismounted.

"He still hasn't moved?" asked Jesse.

"No," Jack replied with a sigh. "If he doesn't move soon, he will die, I think."

Lily walked forward in tiny steps and sat down next to Dog and patted him on the head. Jesse saw his Nan move slowly over and place the meat scraps in Lily's hand.

"Do you think many people will come today?" asked Jesse as he looked up into the sky. The sun was shining for a change, and there wasn't a cloud in sight.

"I'm not sure," Jack replied. "Three days might not be enough time for some people to recover."

But soon, Jesse saw a number of people on horses coming towards them from the nearby road. At the front was Jim Allenby, carrying a bunch of flowers.

"I wish I had fifteen bunches," Jim said when he arrived. "But I only have three, for my brothers." He placed one bunch each on Jon, Harry and Ray's graves.

"Thank you," Jesse said with a lump in his throat.

"Thank you, Jim," Jack said also, as he wiped his eyes.

"I was wondering if you would like to give the speech today, Jesse?" said Allenby.

"Me?" Jesse said in shock. "But you are our leader, Councillor."

"I am a councillor, yes," replied Allenby. "But you are Jon

Dayton's son, and that man kept us safe for so many years."

"I … I don't know what I would say, Councillor."

"Today is a day for emotions. Just speak from the heart, Jesse," replied Allenby. "That usually works."

Many people had brought some sort of offerings for the graves, and it wasn't long till all of them were covered in flowers or teddy bears or anything with bright colours.

Walking over to Rachael, Jesse placed an arm around her waist. "Your grandfather loved you so much, you know."

"I know," she said, dabbing at her eyes with a handkerchief. "I just wish I could tell him how much I loved him."

"Tell him," Billy said as he stood beside her.

"What, Uncle?" replied Rachael. "I don't understand."

"Tell him now that you love him," Billy said again.

"But we don't know if he will hear," said Jesse, "or even that he exists now."

"No, we don't," replied Billy as he looked down at the graves. "And it would be incredibly arrogant to suggest with a certainty that he does exist. But just in case he does, tell him now."

Rachael looked at her uncle, still uncertain whether to say anything.

Billy kept looking at the graves and sighed. "I love you, Harry," he said tearfully. "You were the best friend I ever had."

After a moment, Rachael looked down. "I love you, Poppy. I will never ever forget you."

Jesse looked down at his father's grave. "I love you, Dad," he said quietly. "I will make you proud of me. I promise."

Whether the departed heard them, they would never know until it was their time to die. But it did make them feel somewhat better that they had a chance to express their feelings.

"And don't think this is the last time that you can talk to them," said Jack as he placed a hand on his daughter's shoulder. "I intend to make this site into one of beauty and peace over the coming years." He looked down at the graves. "I love you both, my brother and father," he said and wiped again at the corner of his eyes.

Soon, hundreds and hundreds of people had come to the clearing where his father had died.

This must be everybody from Grovetown, Jesse thought as he observed them silently facing the graves.

Jesse then watched as Councillor Allenby walked up to the higher ground, the ground that led to where Bradfield's men had attacked them.

"Citizens of Grovetown," he called out, "I am glad you all have come to pay your respects to our fallen brothers and sisters." Taking a deep breath, he continued, "To speak on our behalf today, I have asked young Jesse Dayton to say a few words." He gestured for Jesse to come forward.

Jesse looked at his family and Rachael in panic.

"What do I say?"

"Speak from the heart," his grandmother said.

That's what Allenby had said too, Jesse thought, as he was feeling the growing nervousness of speaking in front of such a large crowd. Rachael and Ash nodded in agreement and gave him encouraging smiles as he walked towards the gesturing Allenby.

Speak from the heart.

He thought about what he had gone through in the last few days and what his father had taught him over the years.

He was unaware that Allenby had stood aside and, turning to face the crowd, he felt another moment of fear at their vast numbers. He was used to speaking to his friends, but this was something else entirely.

Speak from the heart.

The thought enveloped his mind as he began to speak in a loud, clear voice.

"My father and others referred to the people born after the Collapse as Freeborn. I always thought it merely referred to us being able to die without coming back as zombies." A lot of the older people shuffled their feet at this statement of fact.

Not a good way to start, thought Jesse, but he soldiered on, nonetheless.

"But my father believed we were born free in other areas as well. It was only in the last three days that I have begun to understand what he meant."

How do I explain this? he wondered as he took another breath.

"Cooper betrayed us. He betrayed us all."

And I killed him for it. Should I feel bad for the satisfaction it gave me? A question for another time, perhaps.

"He betrayed us because he wanted to go back to the way things used to be. He did not realise that things have changed. We are not the people we once were"

He looked at the crowd and saw they were listening to every word he had to say, so he continued on.

"He recruited Rainswood because he thought religious fear was a good way of controlling people." He shook his head in wonder about the way people acted because of their religion. "My father told me of the olden days when people of many different religions used to kill each other for their beliefs, all the while knowing that their belief in God had no evidence behind it whatsoever, just words written by people in the ancient past who had just about as much an idea about God as we do, which is no idea at all."

A belief was one thing, and that was fine in Jesse's mind, for he had a few of his own. But to thrust that belief on others, as if it were a fact, was a disgrace.

"Some of these religious leaders twisted the words of their prophets so they could pursue their own agenda. They did this so they could deceive people into thinking that they were not speaking just for themselves, but they were speaking for the creator of the universe itself. The evil of these men led my father to anger, the stupidity and complicity of the people who followed these men, led my father to despair. Such was the power of fear of our inevitable death. And the belief of an eternal punishment of an angry God, that people could not break away from this trap."

I want you to be free, Jesse thought with passion. *I don't want you to be a zombie of the mind.*

He looked over at his family and saw his Nan smile at him encouragingly.

"He recruited Mason,"—and Bradfield, but that was another story—"so he could use that man's violence as a way of intimidating all of us into doing what he commanded. He had to get rid of my father's rangers first, so he sent them to a trap in

Hobart." Anger built up again, but he kept it under control this time. He would never lose himself again like he had on that horrible day.

"Rainswood confessed that Cooper's plan was based on the four elements of fear and control. The first was himself as a politician, the second was Rainswood as a religious leader, and the third was Mason as a mercenary soldier. But the fourth was a puzzle to me, until I recalled his desperate attempt at the council meeting." He paused for a moment.

"It was money," he said in a strong, clear voice.

Everybody was nodding their head in agreement at this. They had all been there or heard about it when his father had beaten Cooper in the bartering debate. Jesse hoped he could do his father proud with his speech today.

"My father told me an interesting story about money from the old days. It involved a rich and famous sportsman travelling to a distant jungle, where he met one of the natives, who had no money and were considered to be the primitive people of this world. And in their conversation, he asked the native what he did for a living. The native man, who was wearing next to nothing and had an animal's bone through his nose, said he hunted food for his family, built a home for his family, taught his kids how to survive, and protected his family. The native asked the famous sportsman from the so-called civilized world what he did for a living, and the sportsman said, 'I run around on a green field and kick a leather ball between two sticks'."

People laughed at this, but he had a serious message to this story.

"But the crazy part of this story was that the famous sportsman, when he returned home, would get paid a hundred thousand dollars for playing this game for two hours, and the people in the stands watching the game would earn a fraction of that for working for a whole year. But instead of being upset at this injustice, the people in the crowd would just accept this as just part of an everyday occurrence."

The crowd had gone silent, and he looked over the people. His people. His society.

"When I look at all of you, I feel that everybody is equal. There is no us and them; there is just us. And excuse the pun, there is justice."

He looked over at his family, which included the Beasleys in his mind, and thought of all the losses they had suffered because of Cooper and his plans.

Turning back to the crowd, he made a decision.

"I ask that you all give consideration towards attending the next council meeting. My father said the young were freeborn, but I consider us all to be free thinkers. I know that is what my father meant now." Taking a deep breath, he told the crowd his decision. "I intend to put forward a few rulings so that we will never become slaves again to the four elements."

A loud cheer came from the crowd, just like it had at his father's speech, and Jesse sagged with relief. Maybe his decision today would have ramifications for years to come. But he felt it was the right thing to do.

Walking towards his family, he felt all of their embraces; he felt their love.

"Well done, Jesse," said his grandmother. "Your father and mother would be so proud." She wiped the tears from her eyes.

Ash hugged him with tears in her eyes.

Rachael grinned and said, "Free thinkers, huh?"

"Yes," Jesse replied with a blush.

"A man of many layers," she murmured.

"Great words, my boy, great words," said Jack, who gave him a rib-breaking hug.

"Indeed," said Billy, who probably broke the rib that Jack had just fractured.

"Let us know of your changes, and we will consider them too," said the mayor as he shook his hand.

He saw Allenby smiling at him.

"We have much to discuss, young Jesse."

"Yes, Councillor," Jesse replied with a nod.

He thought he just may have done an audition for a future spot on the council.

Finally, Jesse looked for the youngest and the most fragile person in his family. He found her still sitting with Dog at Uncle Ray's grave.

"Good doggy," she said as she fed him another scrap of meat. And slowly, the big dog made his way to his feet.

"He needs some water too, Lily."

"Yes, Jesse," his little sister said, and the Butler household added another family member to its list.

The Four Horsemen and the Zombies of Tasmania

The voters complacent the politician now leads
He's just a cog in the business of greed
He does not protect; he exploits and devours
He serves not the people, but money and power

The religious turn the message of love to hate
Their arrogance that only they can see Heaven's gate
They oppress women and those they deem strange
But the abuse of the children shows just how deranged

The general orders a soldier's fate
To kill his brother and sister, he must not hesitate
For the politician and the religious, he must always serve
From blind obedience, he must not swerve

The Power of Money is king over all it surveys
You are a slave of debt till the end of your days
It's a way of control; you would wake up if you knew
That the sweat of your labour benefits only the few

Be free, young ones; show us a bright new way
Let not the four horsemen bring your life to decay
But be careful, young ones, for they are easy to find
They are waiting there, lurking in the back of your mind

Lily Dayton, Hobart Mayor, year 2090

CPSIA information can be obtained
at www.ICGtesting.com
Printed in the USA
FSOW01n0944110217
30711FS